Making Mari

JOAN CROMBIE

FIRST EDITION

ISBN: 978-1-953576-27-9

Library of Congress Control Number: 2023900870

Published by

Certa
PUBLISHING

3741 Linden Avenue SE | Grand Rapids, MI 49548

Printed in the United States

Dedication

This book is dedicated to my brothers, Jerry and Colin, my first rivals and longest friends. I'm thankful we are family forever.

Prologue

Bam, bam, bam!
Mari Coleman's hand jerked, smudging her mascara. Dang! She scowled at the door. *"Hello*—I'm *in* here! Go away!"

"I need the bathroom!" came her sister's muffled protest from the hall.

"Go downstairs, Shannon!" Sheesh, wasn't that why they had another one? She leaned toward the mirror to fix the greasy smear.

In a few seconds, lighter taps sounded, followed by her mother's voice. "Mari—hey, the rest of us need to get ready too."

"I *know*! Just a minute!" Man, would they stop rushing her?

Nose to the glass, Mari artfully repaired her mascara, then lightly dabbed the blemish on her chin with concealer. Shoot. It still showed. Of all days to get a zit! Carefully she gave it a tiny tap of powder.

There. Tossing her makeup in the drawer, she backed a step and wiggled the beaded bodice of her fitted gown farther up, praying that everything stayed put for the evening. Wearing a strapless for the first time was a little unnerving, but she loved the satiny red fabric, and it was her school's color too. Plus finding it at a thrift shop was a bonus, for her dad wasn't eager to spend a wad on a fancy dress for one night. With a surge of butterflies, she squared her shoulders, giving herself the final critical eye. Dress, jewelry, makeup—check. But her hair! She tweaked a few rogue curls near her ear and sighed. It was no use. Her hair was going to do what it wanted.

She met her eyes in the mirror, still amazed that of all the students in the junior class, *she* had been chosen to assist in the Senior Recognition Ceremony, a position of honor bestowed by the high school faculty to an underclassman candidate exhibiting superior academic achievement and promising leadership qualities. She would have thought her cunning classmate JoyAnne Strang would have finagled herself into that role, but for once Mari had won out. She gave herself a proud, albeit nervous smile, hoping things would go smoothly.

Certainly the responsibilities weren't taxing, being somewhat of a Vanna White role. She simply had to physically hand out trophies and certificates to the respective recipients once they were awarded and then read the Senior Superlatives & Destinies piece at the end, a short and hopefully funny segment of the program. She was looking forward to it.

Held every spring, Ford Brentwood Academy's Senior Recognition Banquet and Ball was the upscale private high school's alternative to a traditional senior prom, which had been permanently nixed some eight or so years back after a tragic drunk driving accident had claimed the lives of two of their seniors. Parents and faculty alike determined they still liked the idea of a formal banquet and dance, but the outrageous party tone needed to be squashed. Thus, they paired it with an awards dinner to which only faculty and senior students were invited—and their respective dates, of course, regardless of ages, which naturally brought in some underclassmen. In addition, each senior student was allowed four tickets for parents or guests allowed to view the festivities from the school bleachers. Then closer to graduation, a formal awards ceremony open to the public was held in which the same honors—and more—were acknowledged again, including awards for underclassmen.

Mari's family would use none of their tickets this evening, however, as her mother was on the Ford Brentwood Academy faculty and would be attending the banquet with Mari's dad as her date. For as long as Mari could remember, her mother had held the position of vice principal; thus, Mari and Shannon's tuition-free shoo-in to the prestigious school.

Bam, bam, bam!

Shannon again, annoying as ever. But Mari was ready now. She pointed to her reflection. *You got this, Coleman!*

Her dad was topping their creaking wooden stairs as she came out. He stopped short with his hand on the balustrade to let out a whistle. "Wowzah! Look at you, Marissa Coleman! You look fantastic!"

She smiled, turning side to side to display her gown. "Thanks, Dad."

"So lovely!" her mother chimed breathlessly behind her. "That color looks so rich with your dark hair! It's the perfect dress!" Mrs. Coleman herself was already spiffed up and ready to go.

Shannon appeared beside her mother, her face puckered. "Mari, how are you suddenly as tall as me? It's like you grew six inches!"

"Duh. Ever hear of heels?" Mari lifted her hem to reveal her glitzy stilettos. It so grated her when her sister rubbed it in that she was taller!

Shannon snorted, folding her arms. "And you're going to *walk* in those? Oh, I'd love to see you fall on your face! Why can't *I* come?"

"Shannon!" their mother warned. She turned back to Mari. "What time is Weber coming, honey? We'll want some photos of you two."

Mari made a sound. "I don't want pictures with Weber! It's not like he's my boyfriend or anything!"

"He's your date! Of course we're taking photos!"

"He's late, isn't he?" Shannon cut in. "See? You shoulda asked Dougie Gordon instead!"

"Shannon!" her mother repeated.

Mari checked the time. "I told him around now, so technically he's not late yet. And Dougie's a senior, Shannon. I wouldn't ask a senior to be my date. Plus, *you're* the one drooling over him. Give it up—he's four years older than you!"

"Three. And it *could* happen." She smiled, her teeth studded with braces.

"Dougie Gordon doesn't know you exist!"

"Does too! He says hi to me every day!"

"That's 'cause he lives next door! Believe me—he's not interested in an acne-faced whippersnapper like you!"

"*Mari!*" Their mother dug her hand in her hip. "Honestly! You two are acting like eight-year-olds!"

"Yes, both of you, quit the squabbling!" Mr. Coleman agreed. "You're not coming tonight, Shannon?"

Shannon heaved a dramatic sigh. "Wish I could! *I'd* like to watch Dougie rake in all his awards too."

"I'm sure the Gordons appreciate you babysitting," Mrs. Coleman said. "It's nice that Samantha can go watch her little brother. She used to babysit you girls when you were little, if you remember. You're returning the favor."

"Yes, but it was just the two of us. She's got *four*. Plus Mrs. Gordon says she's pregnant again!"

"That's wonderful! More grandkids for Susan and her husband! Now quit your complaining, Shannon. At least she's bringing them next door. You won't have to wait for a ride home."

Mari gestured impatiently downstairs. "Look, I have to leave soon. Can we get the photos over with before Weber comes?"

Her dad snickered. "Who is this Weber guy? Sounds like a real winner!"

"Scotty Weber from my chem class. I asked him 'cause I knew he wouldn't get any weird ideas about us."

His brow shot up. "Is he blind? All right, pictures by the fireplace!" He waved her to the stairs. "Hold the railing, kiddo. I don't want you tumbling in those shoes."

But at the close of their photo shoot, Mari's date still hadn't arrived.

"I'll wait with you out there," her father offered, setting down his camera and motioning to their three-season front porch.

Mari shook her head. "You still need to shower."

"I can get ready quickly." He held the door, waving to one of the padded chairs. "Save your feet."

She smiled. "Thanks."

"And slide over—I'm squeezing in with you," he said, lowering himself to fit tightly beside her.

"We have other chairs, Dad. *Dad*—you're wrinkling my dress!"

"I want to sit by you!"

She got up and reseated herself beside him, smoothing out the shiny fabric.

"Nervous?" he asked when she was settled.

Mari shrugged. "A little. It's just reading, but I could still mess it up."

"You won't."

She let out a long breath, looking out the porch screens. Where was Weber? What if he forgot? "You don't have to wait here," she told her dad. "I'm fine."

He nodded. "I know."

His tone. Her eyes flicked up, suddenly realizing what was coming. She shook her head. "Dad—no. I already know you love me. If you make me cry it'll wreck my makeup!"

"You're going to do great, Mari! You're beautiful and poised and talented. Just be yourself!"

"Yep. Thanks. You can stop."

"There's no reason to be afraid. I've told you before—don't compare yourself to others."

"I'm *not*!"

"And don't worry about not having a boyfriend. In the right time the right guy will notice you. You're worth the wait."

"Dad, *stop*! That's why I asked Weber—who was supposed to be here twenty minutes ago. The boyfriend thing isn't *my* problem. It's Shannon who needs *that* talk if you haven't noticed! My dilemma is dealing with catty girls, and you're far from the expert on that!"

He frowned. "Have you talked to your mother about that?"

"I don't want to talk to *anyone* about it. Especially tonight. Ah—here's Scotty! Finally!" Mari wiggled herself out of the chair as her date pulled to the curb. "I'll introduce you, but we're already running late, okay?"

"I'll keep the chitchat brief. But Mari—" He caught her arm.

She observed him pulling out his wallet. "Dad, I don't need money tonight."

"Right, but listen—remember your value." He removed a large bill and held it up. "I can call it names and spit on it, but it's still worth fifty dollars." As Mari reached for the bill, he snatched it away with a grin, returning it to his wallet. "Come on—let's get you and Mr. Weber on your way!" He pushed the screen door open and guided her down the porch steps.

Scotty Weber halted on the grassy boulevard when he saw Mari in her gown. "Er—was this a dress-up thing?"

Mari gave a squeak at his jeans and T-shirt.

Her dad extended his hand. "Scotty Weber? Nice to meet you! Nick Coleman, Mari's father. Come with me, young man. You get to pick a shirt from my closet!"

The transformation of Ford Brentwood Academy's gymnasium was magical. Even Scotty Weber in his borrowed dress shirt and suit jacket felt it, offering Mari his arm as they entered the banquet side of the garden-of-lights-themed wonderland via the grand vine-and-light wrapped arbor inside the gym doors. Vertical strings of white lights alternating with shiny swaths of satiny cloth formed a boundary around the entire perimeter of the gym and down the middle, creating two large rooms, a banquet room and a ballroom. The fabric and string lights rose together in tent fashion to form a ceiling peak in each half of the gym, and another elegant vine-and-light wrapped arbor became the passage between the two areas.

They were late, though not by much. Mari gazed around in awe at the light-adorned potted trees and elaborate patio containers bursting with flowers that graced every nook of the dining room as she and Scotty waited to be seated. Eventually they were led across vinyl stick-on patio stones past a lovely punch fountain to join a table of eight on the far side of the banquet room. Mari greeted her friends and placed her little purse on the white tablecloth, taking her seat while Weber—looking snazzy in her dad's clothes—left to get them punch. She was glad she knew what a geek he was; otherwise, she might have been tempted to like him.

Next to them under a fancy vine-and-light draped pergola, another eight lucky students enjoyed VIP seating, one of whom was her least favorite person in the world—JoyAnne Strang—in a super-short, tight minidress, its neckline scandalously low with plenty to fill it. Mari rolled her eyes. That was JoyAnne, all right. Mari assumed she would be present since she was dating a senior, but why was she seated at the honors table? She had probably found a way to put herself in charge of seating arrangements, she mused. Regardless, that girl always got the breaks. Mari gazed in envy at the cozy area, admiring the hanging baskets of blooming fuchsias and string lights all around them.

She made herself turn away. Hearing water trickling, she twisted to discover an indoor waterfall in the corner nearby, the card on the limestone indicating it had been donated for the night from the local Watkins Nursery. Nice. It was a classy touch. She gazed admiringly at the plants tucked around it.

"All ready to go tonight?"

JoyAnne. Mari could already smell her perfume. With an internal cringe, she turned to face the classmate who had approached her table—JoAnne, who only weeks ago had fabricated a "hint" to several of Mari's friends that Mari had been secretly hoping for a new hairbrush for her birthday, resulting in her receiving a humiliating six of them on her special day. And although JoyAnne adamantly denied responsibility, she did confess that she thought the instigator clever. Her skin shimmered with a not-so-subtle layer of body glitter.

"Uh—hi, JoyAnne." It was a party. She had to be polite.

"Got your sheets?"

"Yep." Mari patted her clutch where she had stashed the assigned reading.

"I'll put them on the podium for you."

Mari shook her head. "Nope, I got it. I'll bring them up with me."

JoyAnne's brow shot up. "You sure? What if you drop them? There's no ladylike way to pick up scattered papers." Her eyes dropped to Mari's chest—er, lack of chest.

Mari blinked. First of all, why was she asking? JoyAnne had nothing to do with the program. Second, since when had acting ladylike ever been a concern of JoyAnne's? And yet she had a point.

"I'm not worried about that, but fine—here." Mari slid the stapled papers from her purse, unfolding them as she handed them up.

JoyAnne nodded. "Be sure to speak into the mic. Enunciate. You practiced, I hope—?"

Patronizing as ever. JoyAnne was undoubtedly jealous that *she* hadn't been chosen to read the Senior Class Destinies. "I'm ready," Mari said simply. "What's my cue? Who am I after?"

"The awards are first—which I heard you're helping with. Then is Mr. Pauly with special recognitions, but you don't need to go up for that. Then *you*—right before the class president dismisses us for the ball." She smiled. "You look nice tonight, Mari. That dress is pretty."

"Oh—thank you. So do you," Mari returned, her compliment just as hollow.

JoyAnne's brow suddenly crinkled as she studied Mari's gown. "That style—it's very classic. You know, I think Carissa Evans had a dress like that last year. Very similar. Anyway, it looks nice on you. Well, time to go join my hot date." She turned, motioning proudly to her table under the pergola—in case Mari hadn't already noticed her prized seat. "Good luck to you!"

"Thanks." Mari's cheeks were flaming as she left. Crud. Was this Carissa Evans' old dress? It was possible! If so, no doubt she and all her friends would recognize it. Her eyes darted to locate Carissa, hoping she was seated at the far opposite side of the room.

Scotty appeared with two cups of punch. "They're starting to dismiss tables on the other side. We're probably last."

"That's fine. I'm not really hungry." She stretched to see the buffet line—noticing then that most of the girls were dolled up in fancy *short* dresses. *Oh, great.* Apparently long was out this spring.

Her gaze dropped to JoyAnne laughing and leaning in toward her senior boyfriend under the pergola. Blake Stevens, Ford Brentwood's tall, handsome basketball center, seemed to be oozing with manhood by merely sitting next to her. Their fawning over each other was irksome.

Guiltily, Mari bit her lip, knowing it was wrong to wish someone off the face of the planet, but she couldn't help it. There were a million things about that girl that grated her, one being how she flaunted her perfect body. Not that having a nice shape was bad—no, Mari wasn't a prude. But the way JoyAnne threw herself at boys was embarrassing to everybody—or *should* be. She was a notorious flirt and so very naughty—yet all the while maintaining a perfectly benign façade to friends and faculty. On the surface she was polite, harmless, and flattering, but underneath she was devious, shrewd, and cruel—mostly to Mari.

A case in point was something that happened about a year ago, in their sophomore grade. During the busiest of passing times between her classes, Mari had innocently opened her locker to have what seemed like a million little condom packages burst forth to fan an array of neon colors across the crowded hallway. Everyone had stopped to gawk. She knew exactly who had done it—they had been inserted one by one through her locker vent—but JoyAnne put on quite a show in the principal's office.

"Why would you think I'd *do* that to you?" she blubbered to Mari through obviously manufactured tears.

As fate would have it, Mari's locker stood directly underneath the hallway security camera, so determining the actual culprit was impossible, and no students had witnessed anyone in that hallway outside of class. And yet somehow a video of the entire event found its way onto social media via one of JoyAnne's closest friends. And thus followed many other crude and mysteriously planted locker surprises.

But it wasn't only that. JoyAnne was smart—super smart—and yet so dang condescending to Mari in her smooth, slippery, nice way. She had the ability to consistently one-up her in every class they ever had together. Oh, Mari hated that! Whenever she got an *A*, JoyAnne would be found to have an *A plus*. If Mari scored a 98 percent, JoyAnne had a 98.5. If there was a contest, JoyAnne inevitably won it, with Mari coming in a close second. Always. *Always!* And worse, some teachers even took advantage of them by pitting the two against each other with class teams, knowing their fierce competition would make them motivate their whole group to do their best.

"I think it's a classic case of jealousy," the high school counselor told her parents in a concerned phone call one evening, which horrified Mari upon arriving home from her soccer scrimmage.

"What? They *called* you about this? Dad, you don't know her! She's so slimy! She *acts* nice, only she's dirty and mean!"

"Hey, now! Come on, Mari. Cut her slack," her father urged. "She's had a hard life. She's being raised by her grandma."

Right—like that caused a person to be like *that*! So Mari simply gravitated away from school activities that gave JoyAnne the spotlight—music, theater, and debate—choosing art classes and sports instead.

"So, Mari, maybe we should go out sometime."

Mari gave a startled blink, jerking her attention back to Weber, who didn't quite know where to focus his eyes. So he *wasn't* blind! She leaned away, responding, "Aww, thanks, Weber, but I think we should just stay friends. But thanks for being my date tonight."

He spread his hands. "That's what I mean. Let's go out as *friends*."

"Huh. Okay. Maybe. We'll see." That, of course, was simply code for "I'll tell you *no* later."

She sighed, wishing she had her Class Destinies sheets with her. The little exchange with JoyAnne had made her worried. Now would be a good time to look over her reading: *Most likely to be a millionaire by the age of thirty—Wally Marcos! Most likely to travel to space—Curt Manzie!* That, of course, was a joke, since Curt was the biggest dopehead in school, and everybody knew it. So followed the two pages of mixed senior class descriptions—serious, sarcastic, or funny—which she could now be reviewing again so she didn't botch their delivery. But before long, their table was dismissed to the buffet, and they were enjoying their dinner.

Afterward the awards program began, starting with the school awards for sports, music, and debate, student lettering, and the like. Dutifully Mari stood beside the presenter, handing out cards and certificates and trophies. As expected, Douglas Gordon did earn his share of merits, but he was only one of many students to do so.

Then it was announced that next on the program, the winner of their state's regional vocal competition would perform a solo—and who would rise to do so but JoyAnne Strang herself! Mari pursed her lips as she took her seat. Of course. *Of course!* So *that's* why JoyAnne wasn't the junior class representative! She was already in the program! Mari looked away, refusing to watch her sing. Once again, Mari had come in second. Her eyes drifted to her parents sitting at the head table, but the brightness of all the hanging string lights between them made weird spots in her vision.

"That Joy Strang girl has pipes," her dad once said after a Christmas concert. "She could really go somewhere with that voice!"

Her dad was clueless to what JoyAnne was really like.

The song ended, and Mr. Pauly came forward to present the scholarship awards. Knowing she was next after these, Mari discreetly adjusted the top of her dress, then swiped her curls behind her ear. Her hands were sweaty. She took a drink and let out a long breath, reminding herself not to rush.

Applause broke out as the New Hampton Rotary Club Scholarship recipients stood to be recognized. Then came the sports scholarships, awarded from area colleges and universities. Then the local veterans association scholarships were announced. Mari shifted restlessly as the presentations droned on. How many were there?

"And last but not least—"

Finally! She straightened at Mr. Pauly's cliché, reaching for her water again.

"—this little lady has accomplished an impressive feat. In addition to excelling in her studies at Ford Brentwood, this student has taken advantage of Taiton College's post-secondary educational opportunities, maintaining a 4.0 grade average. She becomes only the second student in Taiton history to be awarded the Taiton Achievement Scholarship in her *junior* year of high school—although she insists we haven't gotten rid of her yet, as she intends to delay the scholarship until after her senior year here at FBA. Miss JoyAnne Strang, would you please stand to be recognized!"

Mari gaped in surprise as the room erupted in applause. In her junior year? JoyAnne won a Taiton scholarship in her *junior* year? Well, now, that was one prospective college Mari could cross off her list. She would not be going to Taiton!

Weber bumped her arm. "Mari—it's you! Mr. Pauly's waving you up! Knock 'em dead!"

Don't trip, she warned herself on the way to the podium. Why had she worn these stupid shoes? As she passed the pergola, JoyAnne bared her a toothy smile, to which Mari offered a curt congratulatory nod in return. Unbelievable! But there was no time to think about it. Taking her place behind the podium, she adjusted the microphone and tweaked her papers before looking up to survey her audience. *Breathe.*

"I know you're all looking forward to this, so let's get to it! The senior class has voted, and the results tallied, so sit back and enjoy the Senior Superlatives & Destinies of this year's Ford Brentwood Academy senior class! Leading us off with the nicest smile is—Sue Shutee!" A smattering of applause. "Most promising athlete—Blake Stevens. Most epic athletic injury—Mason Henry." Laughs broke out as Mason raised one of his crutches in the air.

"The tallest senior class student is William O'Malley at six foot six. Senior class shorties are Sharon Smith and Jesús Hernández, both at four eleven. Our friendliest seniors are Ted Banks and Tyra Smith. Debate queen and voted 'most articulate' is Jackie Green. Most outgoing—Adam Wainwright. Listed as our 'most gullible student' is—Mari Coleman!"

Mari's eyes popped in horror as she realized what had just happened—but there it was—*her name,* clearly printed on the page before her. Instantly she flashed the room a face-saving grin. "Just making sure you're all awake!

It's been a long night!" Her playful self-deprecation worked, producing a second round of laughter as they got her joke.

Heart pounding, Mari anxiously scanned the remainder of the page, which she now observed had no folds in it from her purse! Someone had switched out the reading, and oh, she could make a good guess at who did it, but what did that help now? She had the room's rapt attention.

"Voted 'most artistic seniors'—Francine James and Kip Lee! Most likely to become a doctor—Terry Shields! Most likely to become a politician—Mary Cooper. Shiest senior student is Tabatha Mills, and the class loudmouth is none other than Billy Blaze!"

"Woot-woot!" Billy howled from across the room, rising to give a little dance.

"Most likely to travel the world—Denae Smith. Most likely to *never* travel—Taylor Astoni. Most likely to never move from his parents' basement—yes—Taylor Astoni!" Mari looked up to smile at the chuckles breaking out around the room. Nearby, friends were punching Taylor Astoni teasingly on the arm.

"Most likely to be CEO of a national corporation—Megan Zach. Most likely to open a restaurant—Sam Schopt. Most likely to have a McDonald's career—Mark Matthies." Laughs and applause. "Best and worst dancers—Liza Casey and Buck Adams. I'll let you determine which is which!" Laughs.

"Sexiest walk—Judy Ruder." Whistles and cat calls. "Best gym body—Barbie VanRubin." More whistles and applause. "Coolest hair—Ruby Kaste. Best biceps—Craig Barker. Most likely to remain in a training bra—" Mari's face grew red as she spied her own name again. Mind racing, she looked up to blurt, "—er—Gary Vaughn!" At his name, the room exploded in laughter, and every head turned to look at Gary—the nicest, most clean-cut, and nerdiest kid—who looked around in utter bewilderment.

"Just keeping you on your toes," Mari remarked. Now her cheeks were burning.

"Most musical—Ellen Jeffries and Toby Hill." Her eyes dropped to the next line: *Most likely a virgin at 50—Mari Coleman.* Her jaw tightened. Oh, brother. She wouldn't be surprised if one of JoyAnne's little minions was posting all this on social media again. "Goofiest laugh—Curt Brisson. Strangest hiccups—Irene West."

Then with her pulse hammering, she suddenly veered off script. "Largest bust, whether real or fake—JoyAnne Strang! Biggest flirt—JoyAnne Strang! Holds the school record for dating the most guys—

JoyAnne Strang! Most likely to have a child in her junior year—JoyAnne Strang! Oh, wait—sorry, these are supposed to be *senior* class destinies!" She paused briefly at the mixture of gasps, snickers, and murmuring. "Okay, moving on—our class mechanic: Michael Wells. Senior class comedian is—"

Mari felt a firm hand on her arm. It was Mr. Pauly, shooting her a stern look as he reached for the mic. "This concludes our Senior Superlatives & Destinies. Thank you, Miss Coleman! Please take your seat. I would now like to call on our senior class president—"

Mari didn't hear the rest of Mr. Pauly's statement, for she was making a beeline down the faux stone walk to the grand trellis where she had previously entered the gym. She had to get out of there. Bursting through the gymnasium doors, she turned at the first hallway and hurried for the exterior doors at the end, stopping halfway to kick off her heels and bolt barefoot the rest of the distance.

"Mari!" someone called from behind her. "Mari—stop!"

She hit the latch bar of the doors, gulping the cool air as she rushed outside. Oh, she hated that girl! She was livid—so angry with JoyAnne—but even more furious with herself, for now she was in trouble. Big trouble. She couldn't believe she had done that. No doubt a nice little chat with the principal was coming. Plus her parents—oh, man, her parents had had a front row seat to it all! They must have been mortified! She dropped her head in her hands.

The school doors clicked open behind her.

"Mari Coleman, what the *heck* were you doing?"

It was Dougie Gordon. Crud. Of all people. She wished she could disappear into the ground.

"What on earth was that about?"

All Mari could do was shake her head. He offered her his handkerchief, and for the first time she realized she was crying.

"Come on, I'm parked over here," he said. "I'll take you home."

Mari sniffed. "What about your date?"

"I told her I'd be back." He motioned toward the parking lot.

"My parents are going to wonder where I'm at. And Weber."

He paused. "Do you want me to get them? I will if you want."

She shook her head. "No, just take me home." She couldn't face Weber right now, and she would prefer her dad's impending scolding to occur in the privacy of her bedroom. Thank God Shannon hadn't been there!

They drove in silence, weaving through the New Hampton streets to their secluded neighborhood on Frost Street. A squad car without lights on was parked at the Sinclairs' house next door.

"What's going on there?" Dougie asked, pulling into Mari's driveway. Her house was dark.

"Who knows? There's always something going on over there." She turned to him. "Thanks for the ride, Dougie. Wish me luck with my dad."

Douglas Gordon made a sound. "You could use a good lecture, Mari! You'd be smart to listen to him."

She threw him a look. "What do *you* know, Dougie? You don't know the full story!"

"You made her cry! You should have seen JoyAnne's face! I don't care what the story is—there was no excuse for that! I'd expect a lot more from you."

Once again, *no one* understood. Mari simply got out of the car. "Good night."

Chapter One

Five Years Later

Mari Coleman winced. The Advil that the nice knitting lady had graciously supplied her had worn off, and her knee was throbbing again with gusto. Dang. If only she hadn't packed her pain meds in her suitcase! Yet how was she to know the freak storm across the Northeast would keep her sitting in the Boston airport for half a day? That wicked sleet had kept the flight monitors blinking with six long hours of delays. She shifted her elevated leg, ignoring the ugly stares of weary fellow travelers in the crowded waiting area. She *needed* two seats.

But it appeared a change was occurring behind the counter. The airline employees were now bustling about with purpose, Mari observed. With hope she watched as one of them lifted a corded mic.

"Ladies and gentlemen, thank you for your patience. We are now ready to start our boarding process for Flight 283, departing at Gate G19 with service to New Hampton. At this time, we're calling for our military personnel, families with young children, and those with special needs to board . . ."

Finally, Mari thought, feeling the room stir in collective relief. Fatigued beyond self-restraint, she gave a wide, unstifled yawn as she retrieved her cell phone from her bulging backpack. She glanced for the flight particulars on the screen behind the counter.

"Finally boarding. See you around eight," she texted, tagging on three emoji hearts and a flame. She sent a second text right after: "Can't wait to see you!"

Without waiting for her boyfriend's reply, Mari switched her phone to airplane mode and stuffed it into the front of her backpack. Will would have to wait. Her battery was already in the red, and if she used it another minute, it would be dead and useless when she arrived in New Hampton. She could kick herself for packing her charger with the load of stuff she had dumped on her aunt in her whirlwind departure.

There was undoubted merit in the old haste-makes-waste adage. Booking the first available flight home had been a thoughtless reaction to her unfortunate demise of having to leave school. Had she been thinking clearly, she would have factored in the amount of time it would take to pack up her entire dorm room, but instead she got to pull an all-nighter to do it—which, granted, had its place in the life of a college student, yes, but let there be a noble reason for it, like championing a paper or a night out with the girls. Certainly not boxing up one's possessions mid-semester because of a stupid knee injury! And had she been thinking clearly, she would have left on better terms with her roommate, who stomped out in annoyance at 3:00 a.m. to crash on the floor of the room next door.

Her Aunt Clara had been kind to take her to the airport—and brave, given the weather—and even more generous to let her store her dorm belongings in her garage, assuring her that they would somehow make room for them until Mari returned to school in the fall.

"But we'll see you before then at Missy's wedding," Aunt Clara said, white-knuckling the steering wheel as their car inched along the slick highway. Without loosening her grip, she spritzed the wiper fluid again, ducking her head to see through the bottom of the windshield as the wipers smeared a glaze of ice across the glass.

Mari nervously gripped the armrest herself, as though the action would aid them if they started to slide. "Yeah. I'll be back for that," she assured.

Oh, yes, she'd be back for Missy's wedding—aka "The Pageant." Her cousin's wedding hype outdid the Oscars, and it almost killed Mari to be her maid of honor. But what else did one expect when her overachiever cousin was engaged to a surgeon? Missy had luck and everything else.

Born a day apart, the two girls had grown up best friends—Marissa and Melissa. However, since college, things had gotten a little weird between them. It was hard when Missy had gotten engaged before Mari even had a boyfriend. Plus Missy had finished her four-year degree in three years, landing a fantastic job before receiving her diploma, whereas Mari was crossing her fingers to finish in five. It stung to be outdone at every turn, but what could she do? She hadn't asked for a knee injury.

She reached down to rub the culprit through her jeans, musing that her spring semester was not meant to be. Blowing out her knee for the second time had sealed the deal, as it left her physically unable to complete her courses. Going home was the right thing to do, but it was disappointing nonetheless. So here she was, having one of those miserable hurry-up-and-wait days. She could only hope that her sudden job possibility in New Hampton would be the silver lining on her bleak demise. Getting that would soothe a lot of angst.

Now at the prospect of finally boarding, thick lines of passengers had quickly formed at the gate, crowding out into the concourse already surging with people from a flight arrival across from them. Slipping her hand into the familiar backpack slot behind her phone, Mari carefully extracted her boarding pass. *Coleman, Marissa Jules. Seat 14B. Boarding Zone 5.* She slid it in her back pocket and, favoring her knee, cautiously stood to don her heavy backpack, centering it between her shoulders. Her group was set to board last, and judging by the throng in front of her, she would have time for one last jaunt to the restroom if she made it snappy.

Deliberately bypassing the line snaking out of the women's room, Mari limped with an air of confidence into an Executive Members Only washroom, a little discovery she had made in her many hours to kill. They weren't carding people in there or anything. Why not act like she owned the place?

As she washed her hands, another woman in a stylish outfit and shiny cobalt heels came out of a stall to use the sink next to her. A long curl of hair swung out as she leaned forward. When she looked up, their eyes met in the mirror, and with a jolt Mari recognized her. Here was only one of the most popular female movie stars in the last ten years, and they were alone in an airport restroom!

"I know who you are!" she blurted without thinking. "You're Marilee Montayne!"

The woman turned. "Guilty as charged."

Mari's hand popped to her chest. "I *love* all your movies! *Lilliana*— oh, that one's the absolute *best*!"

"That's so kind of you!" She pulled a paper towel from the decorative dispenser.

"Oh, my goodness! May I please have a picture with you?" Who cared whether it was appropriate or not to ask? "And your autograph— would you sign my journal?"

Another gorgeous smile of perfect teeth. "Why, of course, darling. But let's be quick about it. I have a plane to catch!"

"Me too!" Hastily Mari slid off her backpack and yanked it open for her phone. Quickly she snapped a photo of the two of them. Then discarding her makeup bag and a baggie of snack mix to the bathroom counter, she wiggled up her journal from beside her laptop to hand it to the woman, all the while gushing on about what a great actress she was and how all her movies were her absolute favorites.

"And what's your name, love?" the actress asked, reaching into her pricey handbag for a pen.

"Marissa Coleman. But all my friends call me Mari. M-a-r-i."

"Ah, very good!" Ms. Montayne tipped her head, her long dark hair falling to the side as she scrawled some words in the journal. Then with a smile, she closed the book, nodding to the door. "Here you go! And thanks in advance for honoring my privacy out there. Safe travels to you, Mari Coleman!"

"Absolutely! And you too!"

On her way out, Mari observed that the beautiful woman was unmistakably pregnant.

The door fell shut. When she could breathe again, Mari rustled through the journal pages to the woman's signature: *Mari, Sometimes surrender is the only way to win. God bless. —Marilee Montayne.* She eyed the words with interest, finding them somewhat strange. She would have to think about that, but hey—she had met someone famous! With a congratulatory cheer, she slapped herself a high five on the polished glass.

Promptly her grin disappeared. Ugh! What a train wreck! Skin pale beyond belief, parched lips, puffy, dark rings under her eyes—all courtesy of her sleepless night and long, restless hours at the airport. And her hair— yikes! Wetting her hands, she ran her fingers through the tangles to tame some of the wild coils. Then rummaging through her makeup bag, she found her lip gloss. That at least kept her from looking dead. She powdered her nose, then snapped the compact shut. Ms. Montayne had been super sweet, but goodness, what she must have thought of her travel-worn fan!

Travel. The thought jarred her back to reality. Her flight was boarding!

Stuffing her belongings haphazardly into her backpack, Mari zipped it shut and hurried out to take the end of the scant line of the five or so people remaining to board her plane. As she moved forward in the line, she was alarmed to find her boarding pass wasn't in her back pocket. As the final couple in front of her left for the jet bridge, Mari stepped up to the kiosk, scrambling through all her pockets, trying not to panic. She slid off her backpack.

"I just had it!" she told the airline employee, fumbling to unzip her bag. "Seriously—I put it in my pocket *one* second ago!" The attendant looked tiredly on as Mari shuffled frantically through her belongings.

After an exceptionally long thirty seconds of near panic, a cheerful airport employee in a dark blue jacket suddenly appeared beside her, waving a paper. "You must be Marissa Coleman! Looking for this?" With a gap-toothed smile she deposited Mari's boarding pass onto her outstretched palm. "God must be watching out for you! A custodian just turned it in across the way, and that doesn't happen!"

"No way!"

The waiting attendant tapped her finger on the scanner. "Right here. Let's go, ladies!"

"I can't thank you enough!" Mari said, extending her boarding pass for the resulting beep. Quickly she restuffed her bag and hobbled down the diesel-tinged jet bridge alone.

The moment she boarded, the door behind her was sealed, and every eye followed her down the aisle to her seat. Nevertheless, she had the satisfaction of verifying that Marilee Montayne was indeed on the flight—right up front in first class, drink in hand, and perusing her tablet as Mari passed by. The space next to her had been empty.

Mari's seat was over the wing in an emergency exit row between a middle-aged man on the aisle and a thirty-something already fast asleep with his head against the wall. The man on the aisle courteously moved his legs for her to get situated.

An airline attendant strode up from behind. "Ma'am, you're seated in an exit row—"

Mari looked up. "*Yes*, I'm physically able to open that door, and *yes*, I will do it if necessary!"

The attendant thanked her and continued to the front of the plane.

The aisle-seat gentleman glanced over. "Sounds like you know the drill around here."

Mari shrugged, tightening her seat belt. "Everyone's waiting on me to get out of here."

He raised his eyebrows. "Indeed. How's a young lady like you tardy after being stuck at the gate for six hours?"

She shot him a look.

"No offense. Just curious." He was trim with dark, wiry hair beginning to gray at the temples.

"I lost my boarding pass."

"You *lost* your boarding pass," he echoed, his tone laced with condescension.

But she was too adrenalized to care. "It must have dropped out of my pocket in the ladies' room, but someone found it—thank God. I know I'm late, but it was *totally* worth it!"

He eyed her curiously. "Yeah? Why's that?"

Mari turned to him with a smile. "Did you see who's on this flight?"

"Someone I should be aware of?"

"Marilee Montayne."

He looked at her without reply, so she repeated herself. "Marilee Montayne—you know, the actress! She's up there in first class!"

"Who's Marilee Montayne?"

She laughed. "You're kidding, right? She's quite famous."

He leaned out to glance toward the front of the plane. "Is that so? And you're sure it's her?"

"Completely!"

"Ah, okay, okay." He nodded. "And how was this related to losing your boarding pass?"

Mari smiled smugly. "Don't tell anyone, but I was in the Executive Members' restroom and ran into her there—just the two of us. We took a photo, and she gave me her autograph! Seriously!" She gestured to the plump bag under the seat ahead. "It's in my backpack."

"No way!"

"For real! She was super sweet." She sighed happily. "Anyway, I think that's when I lost my boarding pass—but like I said, it was totally worth it."

"I see."

"And guess what else? She's pregnant!"

He leaned away. "Really? She *told* you that?"

"No, of course not! But I could tell. I could definitely tell."

"Huh. Well, isn't this your lucky day?" He settled back in his seat as the plane began taxiing to the runway.

Mari felt a thump on the back of her seat. Glancing behind her, she spotted two young boys, the older of which she guessed was about a first-grader, judging by his new oversized front teeth. Twisting further, Mari spied their mother and groaned. She had an infant.

"Great," she muttered under her breath.

Her seatmate eyed her. "Is something wrong?"

Mari shook her head, speaking quietly, "Not yet, but there's *kids* behind us. I'm telling you, they better not kick the back of my seat! That has to be the most irritating thing! That and screaming babies. I've been on some miserable flights before!"

"You don't care for children?"

"I don't care for bratty kids whose parents don't watch them."

"Ah, I see. Yes, yes, that can be a pain." He studied her for a moment. "Do you mind if I ask your name?"

"It's Mari."

He shook her hand. "Thanks, Mari. I'm David. Nice to meet you." Then unbuckling his seatbelt, he swung around on the aisle to the seats behind him. "Boys, listen up. You'll need to be very careful not to bump the back of this lady's seat. Her name is Mari, and she doesn't care for it. Do you understand? Hank, look at my eyes and say, 'Yes.' Good boy. You guys doing okay?"

Oh, brother. His wife and kids. Mari cringed with embarrassment as the boys murmured their responses behind her.

"I know. Hang in there. It's our last flight, and we're almost ready to take off. That's the fun part, remember? We go up real fast and then we level out. Daddy's right here in front of you. And how are *you* two doing?"

"So far so good," the woman replied, patting the baby in her front pack.

The man uttered a few more words, then turned to re-fasten his seatbelt. "There—that should help some. The baby now—he's a gamble! We'll both keep our fingers crossed on that one."

"I'm—very sorry," Mari said simply.

"No, no, it's all right. We call those teachable moments. It's good for parents to teach their kids manners, don't you think?" He shot her a look.

Touché. She slunk back into her seat for takeoff.

Once they were in the air, Mari's fatigue caught up to her. Within minutes she was solidly out, dozing soundly through the beverage and snack service, stirring only for a second when her neighbor got up and told his boys he was going forward to stretch his legs, but promptly she fell back asleep.

Later when Mari awoke, his seat was still empty. Over the intercom, the pilot was announcing that their descent would soon begin and that flight attendants would be coming through the cabin to collect trash or unwanted items. Mari yawned and stretched, peeking back at the family behind her, who were all fast asleep. Next to the window, her seatmate gamed away on his tablet with his earbuds in. He reminded her of an older version of Will, her string bean, game-loving boyfriend, so handsome and fun—and soon to meet her at the airport.

"Just say yes," he had said to her the first time they had met—only three-ish months ago. She had been pouring herself a cup of punch at the church Christmas party when he appeared behind her for a refill.

She turned in surprise. "Excuse me?"

"I can read minds! Just say yes and I'll make your day! Then we'll *both* be happy!"

"Is that right? And what would I be saying yes to?"

"A moment ago I perceived that you were wishing I'd cross the room to introduce myself and ask you out. So here I am—and as I said, you can just say yes." He spread his arms, the empty punch cup still in hand.

Mari's brow rose. "An interesting gift—but you seem to have skipped the part about introducing yourself."

He set the cup on the plastic tablecloth and extended his hand. "William Wallace, cousin and guest of Mark Sargent. He dragged me here."

"Mari Coleman. My mother made me come."

"Pleased to meet you."

"Same." She smiled. "And sorry, but your perceptions were a mile off, William Wallace, *if* that's your real name. You haven't remotely been on my radar all evening. But since we've been officially introduced, I might take a chance and say yes anyway. That is, if you still intend to ask me out."

He grinned, thumping his chest with a heartfelt proclamation. "'*Freedom!*' It's in black ink on my birth certificate—William James Wallace—though I'm not in the least Scottish! Want to go on a date with me?"

She regarded him with amusement. If Mark had brought him, he must be an okay guy. And come on—how often did something like this happen? Wouldn't she regret saying no? "Sure. Why not?"

Will pumped his fist. "Dang, I'm good!"

Gingerly Mari stretched out her bum leg in the space between the seats, smiling to herself as she remembered their first date—at a pizza arcade, of all places, a fitting introduction to his goofball personality.

"Watch," he had proclaimed, twirling the ice in his soda with his straw. "Pretty soon it's bedtime for all these little kids. They'll go home, and we're gonna *own* this place!" He was right, and they had indeed had a blast.

The airplane gave a little shudder, and Mari craned her neck to see out the window, spying a grid of city lights below. She couldn't wait to see him. Technically they had only had a few actual dates since Christmas

26

because she had left for college again after New Year's, but they video chatted almost every day. And though their relationship was still new, she was fairly sure it was going somewhere. She could feel it. In fact, being with Will six weeks sooner than expected was the one consolation about going home mid-semester. Well, that and her job possibility. Perhaps her knee troubles were God's way of getting her home for a good reason. Or not, she mused. It was hard to see God in such a bummer of a situation.

Ahead of her, Mari suddenly observed her other seatmate sauntering back between the rows from the front of the plane. He paused to check in with his boys behind them before taking his seat beside her. As he belted himself in, he threw her a glance. "Get a little nap in?"

"A good one actually." She wondered where he had been for so long.

"Nice." He opened a slim volume and began reading.

She strained to make out the title but couldn't. Her eyes flicked to her fat backpack as she tried to remember what Marilee Montayne had written in her journal. Something about surrender. She was so exhausted she couldn't recall, and getting it now seemed like too much work. Plus, they were landing shortly. She heaved a tired sigh, and the man beside her looked over.

"Sorry," she said.

"No—my sentiments exactly! It's been a long trip for us, and I'm ready to be on the ground. Are you coming or going?"

"I'm on my way home."

"Nice. And where's home for you, Mari?"

He had remembered her name! She tried to recall his. "New Hampton."

"Ah, good old New Hampton! Let me guess—you're a Taiton student?"

Mari shook her head. "No. I live near the campus, but I could never go there."

"No? Why not?"

"It's kinda lame."

"Are you kidding me? Taiton's a *fine* school! I hear they have an exceptional history department!"

"Well, anything in your hometown is lame, right?"

"Oh, right, right. I get it." He observed her for a bit. "So where *do* you attend?"

She smiled sheepishly. "Is it that obvious I'm a student? I must have the look. I'm in my fourth year at Bourdette—back in Boston."

"Another fine private college."

"You know Bourdette?"

"Never visited, but I've heard of it. Okay, so you're finishing up there?"

"Sort of. I will eventually. I'm in my fourth year, but I injured my knee in March. I was trying to pick up an additional major in health and fitness, but I'm not physically able to complete the courses. So I'm going home."

"I see." He glanced briefly at her knees. "Bummer."

"Yeah." Mari nodded. "The department head called me in for a meeting Wednesday afternoon where he and the dean of students 'highly encouraged' me to try again in the fall." She held her fingers up in quotes. "It's too late in the semester to switch classes, so I'll have to wait. But they were kind enough to credit me the entire semester—thankfully. I'll start over with the same courses this fall—if the knee cooperates, that is. I'm supposed to rest it."

"Generous of them. Does it hurt much?"

"Yeah. Mostly when I bump or tweak it. If I wear my brace and take it easy, it behaves."

"I'll be extra careful! So this went down Wednesday, huh? Your meeting. Wasn't that the first? April Fool's Day? I bet that was nice."

Mari flayed her hands. "See? Thank you! Any normal person would get that! The dean—he was clueless! The whole time he was talking I was confused—like, was this some sort of joke? I thought maybe my roommate had set it up or something. But no, it wasn't a joke. So here I am with my tail between my legs. Not exactly kicked out of school, but it feels like it all the same."

"That's too bad. I'm sorry."

"Thanks." His sympathy felt sincere.

"So you'll have the one semester left then—after your knee heals?"

"Probably more. I still have to finish my original degree. And then fitness if I still want to double major. It makes sense to do it."

"Uh-huh. And your plans for after school? Any career goals?"

She laughed. "That's the golden question! I'm trying to figure out what to do without having to add yet more school." At his questioning look, she continued. "Well, I started out in business, but then reality smacked me in the face, so I dropped that and switched to health and fitness with a minor in sociology. Then I blew out my knee—the first time—and had to have surgery between my sophomore and junior year, so that dream went down the tubes. So I decided to go full on sociology with a women's studies focus. But in the meantime, my knee healed, and at the beginning of this year I realized I had enough previous credits to actually double major with health and fitness too, since I'll have to go an additional year anyway."

"Sounds like a reasonable plan."

"Right—but then my knee fritzed out again and I'm being sent home. But get this—out of the blue a job I've always wanted just opened up in New Hampton!"

"Interesting timing!"

"Yes! Ever since high school it's been my dream to work in a place like Sunlight Women's Center. I've worked there for about six summers in a row now, and just a few weeks ago, a director's position opened up. Initially I didn't apply because I thought I wouldn't be home until June, but now with my knee thing, I'll be home right away. I think I have a good shot at getting it! I'm experienced, and I know the center, and they know me. Plus, I'm close to finishing my degree. It'd be a dream come true!" She crossed her fingers. "But even if I don't get the director's position, I'll still have my old job, so that's nice."

"Sunlight, huh? That's commendable!"

"You've heard of it? It's a model in many states for comprehensive care and counseling for women in crisis. I'd love a counseling position, but I'd probably need more psychology classes. And someone else said a minor in business was a must to work in administration, but I'm not going down that road, and heavens, I'm not switching majors again!"

He nodded soberly. "And you've discussed this with your advisor?"

Mari shook her head. "Not yet."

"You should. It's what they're there for. And your parents—I'm assuming you've talked this out with them?"

"With my mom, yes. My dad's gone a lot. He's a construction manager for a hotel chain. So that's another benefit to going home. My mom could use the extra support."

"Sounds like an interesting profession!"

"Yeah. Sometimes he's gone a few months at a time until the project is done—although he flies home for weekends fairly often. And sometimes he'll have a month off."

He nodded again. "And how are you dealing with all this? Your knee and going home—that can't be easy."

"I'm trying to keep a positive attitude," she answered, grateful for someone to finally care, even if he was a stranger. "Thanks for asking.

Probably the worst is not knowing what I'm supposed to be doing in life."
She paused, suddenly embarrassed. The guy had probably already tallied
all the tuition she had forked out with nothing to show for it, pegging her
for one of those ultra-self-aware Gen Z-ers, or whatever she was, a young
person afraid of getting a real job and without a single realistic goal in life.
She shook her head in dismissal. "Anyway, I'll figure it out."

"Of course you will."

He turned back to the front. The plane banked smoothly left, then
leveled out, and Mari knew they were nearing the ground.

After a bit he looked back. "Have you ever asked God to show you
his plan for your life? I probably should have warned you I was religious,
but look—we're about to land, so don't worry. I'm not going to pound
something down your throat."

She smiled. "I'm not offended. I grew up in church."

Her answer seemed to energize him. "Yes? Then ask God to guide
you into his will for your life. He'll answer you!"

Her head bobbed in agreement. "Right. Good idea." He made it
sound so simple. Spiritually confident people like him always mystified
her. To Mari, God always seemed so far away, although admittedly much
of that feeling had surfaced since letting her family's unquestioned Sunday
routine lag in Boston. Studying and everything else had allowed no time for
church. Plus a person needed a day off too, and sleeping in on weekends
had been her sanity saver.

"So what do you do?" she asked. "Are you a counselor or a minister?"

"I'm an educator."

"Oh, a teacher! What do you teach?"

He held up a finger. "Pardon me. Would you hold that thought? I need
to brief my boys on this landing so it doesn't catch them by surprise."

"Sure," she said, watching him lean around his seat. When he was
back, she said, "It's too bad they couldn't put you all in the same row."

"Storm cancellations. We had to take what we could get. We're on
our way home from London—just a brief visit over spring break. I'm only
glad we're not stuck in Boston. That would have made our travels even
longer!"

"Right!" She was about to inquire more, but he pointed outside,
nodding toward the window as the tops of building and trees grew rapidly
closer.

"Here we are already!"

The tarmac appeared; then came the customary bump of the landing and the roar of engines to slow the plane. As they taxied in, the pilot came on the intercom to welcome their arrival and announce the local time and temperature.

Her companion shook his head. "Did you catch that temp? It's *April*, for heaven's sake!"

Mari frowned. "Did he say nine p.m.? Shoot! I told my boyfriend eight. He's not going to be happy about that!" She hooked her bag with her good foot, pulling it up to get her phone.

"At least you won't have to wait for *him*!"

She had to agree. She had already had her fill of waiting in an airport for the day!

But Will didn't answer his phone. She left him a message and then texted him too. When she looked up, she noticed her neighbor eyeing her.

"Okay, I didn't mean to spy, but I happened to see the name 'William Wallace' on your phone."

"My boyfriend."

"No way!"

"The one and only Scottish hero. 'You may take away our lives, but you'll never—'"

"'—take away our freedom,'" he finished with her. "My goodness! I'll have to tell my wife about this! She'll get a kick out of it! I'll bet he milks that for all it's worth."

Mari chuckled. "He usually goes by Will, but he can be a real ham when he gets going on his name! It's his favorite thing!"

"No doubt. 'Freedom!'" He lifted his fist and gave a little cry, gaining the attention of those in the seats around them, and they both laughed.

The plane jerked as it finally came to a stop, and seatbelts everywhere began popping. Passengers sprang up to collect their belongings. Mari's seatmate extended his hand to her where she sat with her backpack resting on her lap.

"Mari, it's been a pleasure."

"It's Mari Coleman. Yes, it has. Thank you for your advice."

"David Grant. Good luck to you. And give my regards to your parents."

He stood and collected his things, and then she watched in amazement as he and his family were expedited off the plane. Since when did *that* ever happen? *David Grant*. She made a mental note to do a search on him later.

On the escalator down into the baggage claim area, Mari had high hopes for finding Will waiting for her, but she could not spot him in the sea of people milling about the lower level. She scanned the doors for him as she waited beside the empty baggage conveyer. Had he tired of waiting for her and gone to sit in a café? She glanced around for any snack shops nearby, then checked her phone again for messages.

Their luggage carousel was malfunctioning. Wearily Mari shuffled with her fellow passengers to the next conveyer. She was starting to get concerned and more than a bit irritated that Will still had not called or texted her—even in response to her initial texts to him from Boston! She eyed the dwindling battery charge on her phone, debating. If she were going to implement a Plan *B*, perhaps now was the time to do it.

The new luggage carousel roared noisily to life right as she called her sister, Shannon. She moved around the other side of a large pillar in a futile attempt to mute the clatter.

"Where are you? Can you come pick me up?"

"Um, hello to you too! Isn't Will picking you up?" Shannon's voice was hushed, and Mari strained to hear her.

"He's not here yet, and he hasn't replied to any of my texts. Can you come get me?"

"No, I can't. I'm at the dinner theater with Colton and Mom on the other side of town. I wouldn't have answered, except that it's intermission. He'll come. He said he'd pick you up, didn't he? Call him!"

"I *have*. He should have been here by now, and he's not answering his phone!"

"Geez, Mari—I can hear you! You're talking really loudly! Call him again."

Mari glanced at the rumbling conveyer and lowered her voice. "I've called him, Shannon! Multiple times. I have zero battery left, and my phone's gonna die any second. Call him for me, will you? Then text me."

Shannon huffed. "Why are you dumping this on *me*? I'm on a date, for heaven's sake!"

"What else can I do?"

"Okay, I'll try, but if he's not answering your phone, I don't know why he'd answer mine. Who's he with?"

"I don't know!"

"Okay, bye," Shannon snapped, abruptly ending the call.

Mari let out a frustrated breath, sliding the phone back into her pocket.

She glanced through the crowd again, looking up right then as the tall figure of Peter Watkins strolled through the electronic doors from the street. She gave a cry of surprise. Peter Watkins! Here was someone she knew at least! Peter was the ultra-cute guy from church that she'd had a terrible crush on a few years back—until that ditzy new girl waltzed into his life to snatch him up. Mari was still struggling to get over that. Nevertheless, there he was, walking into the airport with several coats slung over his arm. What timing! She could ask *him* for a ride—or at minimum use his phone!

Excitedly Mari took a step forward, but right as she was about to hail him, Peter suddenly broke into a grin, lifting his hand to greet someone in the crowd. She watched in amazement as Peter approached the very man she had sat next to on the plane—the David Grant guy! The two of them shook hands and embraced like old friends, and even the man's young boys ran up to exchange hugs with him. Mari's mouth hung open. What were the odds that she would sit beside a stranger on a flight who was friends with someone she knew?

She observed them for a second, then right as she mustered up the courage to intercept them, a murmur went through the crowd. The mother and baby who had sat behind her on the flight, accompanied by a woman in a white blouse, jeans, and cobalt blue heels, walked up to receive the remaining coats from Peter, who eagerly reached for the infant, then embraced and kissed the baby's mother soundly on the lips. Oh, brother. Peter's *wife*! Mari shook her head. She had not recognized her on the plane. Mentally she connected the dots as the woman in the cobalt heels also gave Peter a hug, and after donning their coats, the little cluster turned for the exit with their luggage in tow. Through the glass doors she saw them load their bags into a waiting SUV.

Marilee Montayne. David Grant and his sons were undoubtedly *with* Marilee Montayne. And furthermore, Peter Watkins and his wife were friends with them. Unbelievable!

Her phone vibrated in her pocket. She pulled it out to find a text: "Can't find Will. Wait by first door. Sending someone."

Irritated, she slid the phone back into her pocket. Where was Will? Boy, was he going to hear it when he finally showed up! She turned back to hunt for her suitcases in the noisy river of luggage.

"Did you see her?" a woman nearby asked Mari. "That was Marilee Montayne! She was on our flight!"

"Really?" Mari asked dryly. "Are you sure?"

Heads bobbed all around. "Definitely! It was her all right! With her husband and their kids and nanny!"

"I thought she looked pregnant!" someone else remarked.

"Oh, she's definitely pregnant!" added another.

Who's Marilee Montayne? Mari bit her lip, remembering David Grant's response when she had confided her own exciting discovery with him. He had been baiting her the whole time! And "stretching his legs"— why, he had probably been up sitting with her in first class! Oh, he was smooth! David Grant—right, like that was his real name! She shook her head. He had made a fool out of her.

One of her suitcases came around the carousel at that moment, and she frowned at the jumbo neon tag banded to the handle. In a second she discovered what it meant when she pulled the bag off the conveyer: one of its rollers had been busted clean off. She groaned and laid it on its side, waiting for her remaining luggage.

$\cdot$ ———— ❖ ❖ ❖ ———— $\cdot$

Chapter Two

The swarm of travelers in the baggage claim area had long since dispersed, leaving the spacious walkway in a momentary lull until the next flight's frenetic burst. Will was beyond late. Gloomily, Mari acknowledged that the prospect of him still rushing breathlessly into the airport was slim and fading. She was likely at the mercy of Shannon. With her phone dead as predicted, she parked herself on a bench immediately inside the first door to the street, enduring the intermittent blasts of cold air as it opened and closed. She hoped she wouldn't have to wait through Shannon's entire show!

Perhaps it was better that Will wasn't there, she mused. Her exhaust-o-meter was nearing the irrational zone, and she would certainly snip at him. For now, the rigid bench took the brunt of her dour attitude. She shifted impatiently. Where *was* he? At noon when they had last talked, he said he couldn't wait to see her. This was so opposite of the joyous reunion she had imagined. Of course, she supposed it was *possible* something bad might have happened to him, but short of outright death or dismemberment, she wasn't feeling sympathetic toward any excuse, however extreme.

It figured. Just one more weird thing to add to an already odd year. She had started calling it her year of "firsts." Will was her first boyfriend—first *real* boyfriend. She had dated a few other guys before, but no one steady, and none had swept her off her feet like him. On the stroke of midnight on New Year's Eve they'd had their first kiss—technically January first.

On February first, a month later, she had her first—and hopefully last—mugging, resulting in having to change all her credit cards and acquire a new phone.

On March first Mari blew out her knee again. And if that weren't rotten enough, it was also the day her mom called with the shocking news of her maternal grandfather's stroke, from which he was recovering, thank goodness. She couldn't wait to see him.

Then this past Wednesday—April first—was the afternoon of her crazy meeting with the dean of students. Its freaky timing left her with trepidations for what she might expect in twenty-eight—no, twenty-seven more days. She wished for nothing more complicated than a cheery May basket, but time would tell. One thing was clear—Will and she were likely to have another first: their first fight! His explanation had better be good.

Unzipping her bag, she found her lip balm. Then since her bag was opened, she retrieved her journal once more, flipping back to Marilee Montayne's swirly signature to ponder the graceful lines of ink. *Mari, Sometimes surrender is the only way to win. God bless. —Marilee Montayne.* What a bewildering statement. Surrender—as in "quit"? Mari Coleman did not quit anything. And surrender *what*? The only thing that she was even slightly tempted to surrender was her fitness major, but at this point she wasn't letting go.

And *God bless*—? Was Ms. Montayne sincerely wishing it, or was the expression akin to the sentiment after a sneeze? *God bless you! Oh, thanks.* Mari decided she was too tired to think about it. With a wide yawn, she put the journal away and glanced at the crawling hands of the world map clock dominating the wall in front of her. It was goading her to self-pity.

She was probably dehydrated. Pausing to let her knee adjust to a standing position, she made her way to the drinking fountain beside a nearby restroom to refresh herself. Wiping her chin, she looked back at her pile of baggage around the bench. She had paid a hefty fee to lug those two monster suitcases home, plus her pudgy roller carry-on expanded to maximum capacity and a sizable cardboard box secured with a gross amount of tape. All her other college possessions were probably already neatly tucked away in Aunt Clara's garage until fall—that is, if they could squeak them in among the mountain of spendy wedding paraphernalia accumulating there for Missy's coronation in late July.

"Mari Coleman!"

At her name Mari twisted around, her mind racing to place the clean-shaven man in the blue jacket calling her. Oh, wow—Mr. Sinclair, her next-door neighbor! *Former* next-door neighbor. But then recalling that Mr. Sinclair had passed away, she immediately realized it was his son, McAllister, and whoa—did he ever look like his dad! A younger version, yes, but the spitting image of his father!

"Mac?"

He gave a nod. "How are you doing?"

She let out a breath of surprise. "Talk about a blast from the past! I haven't seen you for ages! I just flew in from Boston! Where are you coming from?"

"Work." He smiled.

"Really? What are you doing here? I've been waiting for my ride. How are you? It's been——" She shook her head trying to remember when she had seen him last.

"It's been a while!"

"Yeah! Wow, of all the places to run into each other! Good to see you!"

"Yeah, you too! So, hey—your mom called saying there was some sort of emergency—that no one was available to pick you up. She asked if I would do it. I apologize. This is the soonest I could get here."

Mari blinked. "My mom called you to pick me up?"

"I was running across town tonight anyway, and this is right on my way. It just took me longer than I expected to get out of work with the snow and all. But hey"—he gestured toward the door behind him—"my car's running, and I don't want to get towed. Do you have a bag?"

"Oh, right—yes! Yes, my bags are over there." Mari motioned with her arm, then seeing his expression, she added defensively, "I had to pack up my entire dorm room!"

He chuckled. "I see that!"

"Wow, thanks for coming!" She led him over to her stuff, shaking her head in amazement that her mom had sent Mac Sinclair to get her! What in the world had made her think to call him? "Geez, I would have never in a million years expected *you*, but thanks for doing this! Oh, wait, Mac—" She reached to stop him as he extended the handle on one of her bags. "The roller's broken on that one—courtesy of the airlines."

"Oh, isn't *that* nice?" He reinserted the handle and picked it up by the side strap, letting out a playful groan. "Holy cow! What's in here—bricks?"

"I know—sorry." She pulled on her backpack. "Probably my books. Or shoes." Carefully she hoisted the cardboard box from the bench, balancing it awkwardly as she reached for her carry-on handle. "This is everything. I've got these if you can get those two."

"All right." He glanced at her long-sleeved T-shirt. "Do you have a coat?"

"I left it in Boston. It's April. I figured I could get by with a lighter jacket."

"Which is where?"

"Buried in my suitcase." She smiled.

He shook his head, setting down the bags to unzip his coat. "It's crazy cold out there. We had one of those fluke spring storms this week that dumped half a foot of snow."

"Yeah, we got it after you in the form of ice. Don't bother, Mac. I'm all right."

But he insisted, handing it to her. "You'll thank me."

"What about you?" Hastily she removed her backpack to don the jacket.

He pulled on a pair of gloves. "I'm fine. Come on—let's go before I get a ticket!" He grabbed her backpack and slung it over his shoulder and turned for the door with her luggage.

The coat was huge on her, of course, but she zipped it anyway and followed to his vehicle, climbing in the front while he loaded her belongings in the rear.

"I really appreciate this," she told him as he got in.

"No problem." He buckled in and began to navigate the car through the maze of other vehicles coming and going to pick up other passengers.

As they exited the airport, she noticed the sloppy, wet snow piled at the edges of the road. And he was right—the air *was* chilly, and she was grateful for the coat.

"We live downtown now. My parents bought a condominium."

"Kingswood Place, right?"

She nodded. "Yes. We're on the side that faces the Green."

"Taiton side."

"Yes."

"Nice."

In the dark, the wet pavement glinted under the streetlights, as now on the main highway the traffic moved steadily along. Her parents' condominium was only twenty minutes from the airport, so it wouldn't be long until she was home, although it didn't feel quite like home yet to her, not like the house she had grown up in.

Her parents had purchased their condo during Mari's first year away at college—nearly four years ago already—and so she had stayed there only for Christmases and summers. Admittedly, the new place was sweet— they were luxury condominiums for sure—but all her fondest memories were attached to the quaint foursquare-style house tucked back near the end of Frost Street, where she had lived her whole childhood.

Mari rode quietly, watching for the highway exit to her former neighborhood, the Whitmore Street exit. There! She turned her head as they passed it, her heart automatically taking the familiar offramp into her old stomping grounds. She gave an inward sigh.

"Do you ever get back to the old neighborhood?" she asked. Mac's family's house had been at the end of the street right next to the field, and Mari's next door to his. On the other side of her had lived the Gordons— Gary and Susan and their large family.

Mac dipped his head. "Every day."

She threw him a look. "Really? I thought your mom moved after your dad passed away—which, by the way, I was very sorry to hear about. He was a great man, and I'll always remember him for his kindness."

"Thanks."

"That was, what—a year ago?"

"Two years now. And yes, my mom lives in an apartment on the north side of town, where I'm headed tonight. No yard to contend with. But I bought the house from her."

"No way!" She smiled at him in the dark. "Good for you, Mac! Oh, I *loved* that neighborhood! I miss it terribly! And how's your mom? Is she doing okay?"

"Oh, she's all right. It's a big change, you know. And for that matter, I'm sorry about your granddad's stroke too. It's such a bummer. But I'm glad he's improving."

"Thank you. Me too."

They were silent for a few moments.

Mari let out a breath. "I'm trying to remember when I saw you last. I must have been in, like, third grade or something!" He had certainly changed from the long-haired, wild rascal she remembered.

"Probably around then. I seem to recall your father scolding you and Shannon for poking your stubby fingers into my high school graduation cake!"

They both laughed.

"I don't remember that, but I don't doubt that it's true! So if you were eighteen then, I would have probably been—"

"Eight or nine, I'd guess," he interjected. "Because I remember having to babysit you when I was fourteen. You had just turned five and Shannon was three. Worst night of my life!"

"Oh, gosh—really?" Mari laughed. "That goes way back! I don't remember that either!"

"I only watched you once. The Gordons moved in that summer

and my job got bumped to Samantha—thankfully. You girls cried about everything."

"Oh, brother! And yes, Samantha Gordon! I loved her! She was such a great babysitter!" She smiled. "I still run into her now and then. When I'm home. They have a whole pack of kids now."

"Yes, I see her too. She stops in at her mom's quite often, so she gets back in the old neighborhood."

"They're a nice family."

"Yeah."

Another silence lapsed between them. She folded her arms, enjoying the softness of his coat.

Mac looked over. "So did Shannon blow you off tonight?"

Mari shook her head, a little embarrassed. "No, my boyfriend, Will. He didn't show up, and he hasn't answered my texts or calls. Of course, my flight was delayed like *ten* times, so he might have gotten confused—but still!"

"Are you worried?"

She cocked her brow. "You know, I've had plenty of time to think about this, and I've concluded that if something *had* happened to him, my phone—even dying—would have been blowing up with a dozen of his friends trying to reach me. Unless they were all in the same predicament, right? Like they *all* died in the same car crash. So *no*, I'm not worried. Upset? *That* I'm trying to manage!"

Mac chuckled. "I don't envy that fella!"

"No kidding!"

"Well, give him the benefit of the doubt."

"I suppose. I hope he has a stellar reason—like he ran over his phone or something. Or lost it in a snowbank. It'd be the *worst* if he actually did forget!"

"If your boyfriend forgot you, I'd give the dude the boot right now—that's my advice. Get it over with before your heart gets all entangled."

She glanced at him where he sat with his gloves on the wheel in the dark. "Well, I'm not planning to dump him over this. I'm sure whatever happened wasn't on purpose. But it is a jerk thing to do—if he *did* forget. It's not okay. But like you said, I should at least hear him out, right?"

He tipped his head. "Just saying—"

Mari gestured as they passed a street sign. "It's shorter if you take this first downtown exit. More direct."

"Then turn on Juniper?"

"Yes, Juniper. It takes you right up to the door."

Mac's vehicle wove around the curvy streets several blocks until arriving at the stately Kingswood Condominiums, towering five stories over the impressive first-floor main entrance below. He parked his vehicle by the curb in the horseshoe-shaped turnabout and helped Mari bring her things in through the main entrance. There she thanked him profusely and told him that she could get a cart and take it from there, but he insisted on continuing all the way upstairs with her to her door on the third floor. She unlocked it, and he set her luggage in their broad front hall in front of the louvred closet doors. Gratefully she returned his coat.

"Thanks so much, Mac. I know it was inconvenient and out of your way to bring me home, but I appreciate it. I'd pay you something, but I only have a debit card. I blew all my cash on overpriced food at the airport." At his indignance, she added, "Well, I *do* appreciate it!"

"You're welcome. Say hello to your mom and sister for me."

"I will. And likewise, greet your mother." She paused. "I just realized I never even asked about your brother and sister. Are they around?"

He shook his head, his lips a thin line.

"Not around? Or—"

"No, Lisa's off grid. Probably using. No one's heard from her for a while."

"Oh, I'm sorry. And your brother?"

"He's around. Currently out of jail and doing okay, but not great. Sober, I guess, so he *says*. But not working yet. He and his girlfriend live in an apartment across town. She's got a couple of kids."

She was a little sorry she had asked, but it was too late now. "Sorry to hear that. I hope things can get turned around for him. For both of them."

He shrugged. "Well, I should get going. Mom's probably waiting for me."

"Yeah. Thanks again, Mac."

"No problem. Sayonara!" He gave her a little salute and left toward the elevators.

Mac Sinclair! *How random,* she thought, watching him leave. She shut the door, glad to finally be home.

"Hello!" she called down the polished hall out of habit.

There was no answer, of course, since her mom and Shannon were still out, but the lack of response reminded her that her dad was gone too. On the heels of talking about him on the airplane, she found herself missing him. Hopefully they would have a chance to connect soon.

Immediately to the right in a little cove offset from the hallway were Mari's and her sister's bedrooms, with Mari's door to the left, Shannon's to the right, and a shared bathroom between the two, its door framed by matching built-in linen cupboards on either side. Leaving her bags, Mari went to her room and flicked on the light, stopping short at the sight of a zippered bridal gown bag hanging from her drapery rod. *Oh, great*—first Missy's wedding hype, now Shannon's!

Her bedroom was crammed to the corners with her sister's wedding stuff: fancy framed chalkboard easels, boxes of empty wine bottles, string lights still in their packages, bolts of white tulle. Tiredly Mari eyed the mountain of artificial flowers and sprigs of greenery piled atop her bed. Out of curiosity, she went to peek into her sister's bedroom opposite hers, finding it tidy and organized. It figured. She sighed and went to get something to eat.

The Kingswood Condominiums were an impressive-looking six-story building with four dwellings on each floor—two facing the front and two across the back, each with ample balconies around its perimeter. The stack of condos spanning the front faced Port Street, at the end of which the main thoroughfare ran through downtown New Hampton. The dwellings that stretched across the back of the building overlooked picturesque Taiton Green, a broad expanse of field owned by Taiton College that had both a manicured park on the west side and athletic fields on the east, separated by a sizable elliptical pond—or small lake, depending on one's definition and the water level each particular year. The grassy lawns of Taiton Green were a popular place for students to both relax in nature or work out and were often the location of not only large college events but also city festivals and outdoor concerts.

Upgrading to one of the tasteful Kingswood condos facing the Green had long been Mari's mother's dream, with its fine marble floors, stylish and roomy kitchen, and spectacular view of the college and the field. Her dad, though somewhat more reluctant to move, saw the sense in downsizing, and the idea of being finished with maintaining a yard was attractive, especially since he was gone for weeks at a time. He was growing less and less keen on mowing grass, raking leaves, or shoveling snow when he was finally home—or paying for the services when he wasn't.

Mari had been out of the loop when the deal went down, for she had been away at school, but their late-spring closing date had worked in her favor, giving her time over spring break to pack her own room for the move and say goodbye to her beloved childhood nest. She *did* like the new place, for it was beautiful and extravagant. Yet it could never offer the cozy warmth of her old home, especially around the holidays. And when she dreamed, the ethereal setting was always the house on Frost with its gorgeous, varnished woodwork and creaking hardwood floors. She had loved that house.

Mari found a bagel in the refrigerator and broiled it with some ham and provolone, then took her plate to sit in the spacious living room, which filled the whole corner of the condo. The entirety of its two exterior walls were full-length windows, now shrouded with closed draperies since it was dark out. She ate in silence, her eyes lingering on her father's open study area adjacent to the living room, his rugged desk and handsome bookshelves butting up against the backside of her bedroom wall. A plank sign reminding all to always give thanks hung above his workspace.

When finished with her snack, Mari left her plate on the breakfast bar in the kitchen and went to visit her parents' bedroom in the corner next to the dining room, its door opening off the living room. She plopped down onto the colorful quilt, noting the eight-by-ten photo from their last anniversary cruise on the nightstand. She picked it up, admiring her tall and beautiful mom. Likewise, her dad looked so handsome in his shirt and tie with his rich-toned skin next her mother's fair complexion. Her grandparents had been a biracial family too—her dad's parents—and Mari had inherited what her mother called the "gorgeous glow" of Coleman skin, a healthy-looking year-round tan, which Mari loved.

Crowded next to her mom's clock was a large box of tissues and her journal, atop of which was a greeting card from her dad—a handwritten love note, she discovered. Mari started reading it, then closed it and put it back, the motion causing her to catch a whiff of men's cologne. She pulled up the neck of her T-shirt, recognizing the lingering scent of Mac's coat, another reminder of her dad. And suddenly she found herself weepy. Probably her all-nighter finally catching up to her, she mused. It was time for bed.

Abandoning her luggage where Mac had parked it in the hall, she brushed her teeth and splashed her face with water. Then stripping down to her T-shirt, she fell into her sister's bed, leaving a note on the door: *Quiet, please! I'm sleeping with you tonight.*

In the morning Mari woke to a light tapping on the door. Her mother, Laura Coleman, greeted her softly as she stepped into the room. "Welcome home, sweetheart!"

Mari was glad to see her. "Thanks, Mom," she murmured sleepily.

"How was your trip?"

She stretched. "Long."

"And how's your knee?"

"Still there."

"Do we need to make an appointment?"

Mari shrugged, pulling herself out of bed to hug her. "My Boston doctor said it's a waiting game for what it does." She suddenly noticed that she was alone in the bed. "Where's Shannon?"

Her mom planted a kiss on her cheek. "She slept with me so she wouldn't wake you."

"Oh." She sat down on the side of the bed again, eyeing her mother's simple black knit dress with red poppies embroidered down one shoulder. "You look nice. Are you going somewhere? What time is it?"

"Thanks. Almost nine. I came to wake you 'cause there's a young man in the other room with a very worried look on his face. He's been waiting to talk to you."

Mari let out a breath and dropped her head.

"He feels pretty bad."

"As he *should*!"

Her mom smiled. "Well, you should go talk to him. Plus, there's a bridal shower this morning for Douglas Gordon's fiancé, and I think you ought to go with us. It starts at ten, so you'll need to hurry a little."

"Dougie Gordon's getting married? Wow—that's cool! This must be old home week! Is that why you sent Mac Sinclair to pick me up last night? Of all people on the planet! Your mind must have been in the old neighborhood!"

"Wasn't he a champ? I'm so grateful he could do it!"

"Yes, it was fun seeing him. He's really changed over the years." Mari moved the pillow in preparation for making the bed. "Wow! Dougie Gordon's getting married! To whom?"

"To JoyAnne Strang."

Mari's head snapped up. "Are you kidding me? No way!" JoyAnne Strang, her slime-bucket archenemy from Ford Brentwood Academy? There was no possible way! A sickening memory of one of her classmates handing Mari a nude photo of herself flashed through her mind, one that JoyAnne had secretly taken of Mari in the school showers and had posted with her phone number in the boys' locker room. Who else would have hung it there but her?

"Why is that such a surprise?"

Mari shook her head in disbelief. "They're from two different planets! He's such a decent guy, and she's—well, doesn't she have, like, four kids from different fathers? I *cannot* see those two together!"

Her mom dug a hand into her waist. "Mari!"

"Sorry! I just *can't*! She's always plastering sexy hey-look-at-my-body pictures all over social media and—"

"Marissa Jules Coleman! Honestly, listen to yourself! You're not in high school anymore and neither is she! You need to let the past go!"

"I know—and I *have*! It's just a total shock!" Truly, she preferred her train-wreck high school days to remain dead, buried, and gone forever. And they *had* been. Until now.

"Well, I think JoyAnne has matured since then. And it's none of your business who Douglas wants to marry!"

Mari looked away.

"And she has *two* children, not four. Now get up. Will's been waiting for you."

"Sorry, Mom. You're right. I shouldn't have said that." She sniffed, reaching for Shannon's robe on the arm of the nearby chair.

"Well, I'm surprised at you!"

"I know. Sorry. I'm—overtired or something. How's—how's Poppy?" JoyAnne Strang and Dougie Gordon! Truly, it was hard to fathom.

Mari's mother looked at her for a moment, then turned for the door as Mari belted her sister's robe. "He's improving. He's getting some extra physical therapy that's made all the difference in the world."

"Good. I'm hoping to see him today. And I'm sorry I said that about JoyAnne."

Her mom paused with her hand on the doorknob. "I certainly hope so. I don't want you to be rude at the shower. And yes, it would be helpful if you could visit your grandfather. I can't get over there today. As for Will—don't be too hard on him, sweetheart." She threw her a kiss before closing the door.

"I won't. Love you, Mom," she said. She stood there feeling stunned, embarrassed, and guilty all at once. JoyAnne Strang and Douglas Gordon—seriously? She shook her head. Good heavens—what had happened to Dougie Gordon?

Shannon was approaching as Mari came out of the bedroom. Two years younger than Mari, Shannon was a good four inches taller, favoring their mother. Her hands flew up. "I know! I meant to get my stuff out of your room yesterday, but something came up! I'll do it today. I promise!"

Mari nodded. "Okay. Good morning."

"Good morning." Shannon tossed her silky, bleached-blond hair over her shoulder, adding quietly, "Someone's here to see you—did Mom tell you? He's been here since seven this morning!"

"*Seven!* Why didn't you wake me!" Mari ran a hand through her own hair, but it wedged in a tangle of curls. "Do me a favor and bring my luggage into the bedroom, would you? I need my clothes." She turned for the bathroom, adding. "I saw your flowers on my bed. They're nice."

Shannon beamed. "Thanks! Wait till you see yours!"

"Mine?"

The moment Mari came within sight of the living room, Will sprang to his feet. "There you are—*finally*! Mari, I am *so* sorry! So, so, *so* sorry! A million times sorry!"

"You forgot me, didn't you?" She was surprised by how calm she was about it. Her eyes flicked over to the largest bouquet of red roses she had ever seen dominating the coffee table. Where had he found all of those before seven a.m.? The room smelled like the walk-in cooler of a florist shop.

Fervently Will shook his head. "Not exactly! It wasn't like I *forgot* you—I would never forget you! The time got away from me—that's all. It was—it was—well, I made a stupid mistake. There was a reason for what happened. I can explain."

Mari folded her arms as her tall and pencil-thin boyfriend approached. With his greenish-brown eyes and light-brown hair trimmed short, sometimes Mari thought he looked like Shane Coshak, the hot lead singer of Shade Maker, but Will didn't sing, although at the moment had she asked him to perform the National Anthem, he would have given it his best shot right then and there, no matter how pathetic it sounded.

"Okay, I was at Simon Baxter's house when I got your text about your flight. We were gaming in his basement, so I set an alarm to not forget, and then we got carried away saving the world. When I checked my phone, I realized I had set my alarm to *a.m.*, not p.m. Plus it was on silent, so I didn't hear your calls. I tried to call you right away, but it went straight to your messages—"

"My phone died, and I forgot my charger in Boston."

"I thought you wouldn't talk to me or something. I even went to the airport, but you weren't there."

"Mom found me a ride. An old neighbor."

"Well, I'm glad, but man, do I feel like a lump! I'm sorry!"

"Don't you ever look up during your video games—like take a breath or something? Or think, 'Geez, we've been playing for quite a while now'—?"

He shook his head. "Honestly, no. The time flew. It did. I'm sorry. Please, please, *please* forgive me! I was so looking forward to being together last night!"

What could she say? He hadn't done it on purpose. "Of course, Will, I forgive you. But it felt pretty weird to be dropped like that."

He threw his head back in relief. "Thank you! And I know—I'm sorry! I'll make it up to you—I promise on a stack of Bibles a mile high."

"I won't deny it, Will. It bugged the heck out of me," she restated. "But I *do* forgive you. You can let it go. And I"—she told herself out loud—"I'll let it go too."

"Thank God! Well, anyway, I'm happy to see you now. Can we go out for breakfast or something?"

She shook her head. "I'd like to, but a friend from my old neighborhood is getting married. The youngest of the Gordon family. They're having a bridal shower for his fiancé this morning."

His face fell. "How long will that take?"

Mari lifted a shoulder. "A couple hours maybe? I'm not sure. I'll text you from Shannon's phone when I'm free. Mine's still dead. I'm going to have to buy or borrow a charger."

He nodded. "Okay, text me. I'll pick you up for lunch, and we'll spend the afternoon together."

"Great! But I'd like to see my grandfather this afternoon. You could come with me."

"Your grandfather? Um, yeah. Yeah, sure. I could probably do that."

"I haven't seen him since his stroke, Will. You don't have to come if you'd rather not."

"No—that's fine! We could stop by for a little while. Maybe on our way to do something."

Mari nodded. "Okay. I'll text you when I'm free. But now I need to get ready for this party. I guess it starts at ten."

He glanced at the clock. "Okay. I'll wait to hear from you."

She smiled up at him. "And thanks for the flowers. They're pretty." There had to be at least three dozen roses crammed into that vase.

With a proud grin he leaned down to kiss her. "Later, Mars."

After a lightning shower, Mari threw on a sweater dress and grabbed her spring jacket. On her way out the door she transferred her makeup bag from her backpack to her coat pocket to finish her makeup in the car.

Shannon had the same idea, carefully brushing on her mascara via her compact mirror in the back seat, her mouth cocked at an odd angle. "So did you hear my news?" she asked Mari.

Mari glanced at her sister through the front visor mirror, where she had just finished with her lip color. She and her sister were such opposites. Shannon was tall, fake blond, and girly, with long manicured nails, whereas Mari had to stretch to reach five-foot-two and didn't bother with frivolities like hair colors and manicures. When it came to makeup and clothes and all that, Mari called herself a minimalist. She just wasn't into it the way Shannon was. But they got along well. Generally. Better than when they were kids.

"What's your news?" she asked.

"Colton and I put an offer on a house yesterday."

Mari turned in surprise. "Wow—you can afford that?"

Shannon paused, mascara wand in hand. "You must not have heard my other news. I just got a job at Sanford's Salon on Port Street, right downtown by the college. Hardly anybody gets in there unless they're really good."

"Shannon," their mother said, flicking her a look in the rear-view mirror.

Shannon merely raised her brow.

"Congratulations," Mari offered simply, turning back to the front. Why was it that some people had all the luck? To get a coveted job at an upscale salon like that—and right out of school! Shannon was like a Missy clone—finishing school early, landing a terrific job, marrying a guy established in his career. Everything was handed to them on a silver platter. "So where's this house?"

Shannon carefully drew her nail along her eyelid to remove a smear. "Blackwood Street. In the older section of town. It's small. Oh, and by the way, I told you that I had to quit my job at the Coffee Break, didn't I? Because of the new job. Well, I talked to my supervisor today, and he's going to let you take my place there if your knee can handle it. You can start on Monday. It's the morning shift—only through lunch."

Mari swung around in her seat. "I don't want your old job!"

"Why not? I'm doing you a favor, Mari."

"I'm not working at a coffee shop! Plus, I already have a job—

potentially."

Shannon opened a hand. "Fine then! Sorry! I didn't know."

"Where will you be working, hon?" her mother asked, looking over.

"I applied for the director position at Sunlight Women's Center. I'm pretty sure I'll get it. I've volunteered there since forever, and they know me. Plus, I'm almost finished with my degree. And if I don't get it, I'll take my old position from last summer."

Shannon snapped the compact shut and put her mascara away. "Why would they give it to you if you have to leave for school again in a few months? I think working at the Coffee Break would be perfect for you. It pays well, it's within walking distance, and Mom says that then you could stop in and visit Poppy."

Mari flashed a look at her mother. "Since when have I needed you two to plan out my life? I have as good a shot at the position as anybody!"

"Yes, you do. And you were supposed to be *asked* about the other job," her mother said, glancing at Shannon in the rear-view mirror. "It was just a suggestion. I didn't know you had your heart set on working at Sunlight."

Mari folded her arms.

"Why *wouldn't* you want to work at the Coffee Break?" Shannon muttered under her breath while she zipped her purse closed. "Plus then you could help cover Poppy."

"'Cover Poppy'?"

They were at a stoplight, and Mari's mother looked over. "We've been taking shifts so he's not alone at the facility. I've been taking a lot of personal time off work since he got sick, and now that it's not an emergency anymore, I need to get back. With her new job Shannon could run over after he's out of therapy in the morning and stay with him over lunch. Then if you could be there from then until about three, it'd be perfect, 'cause I'd stop over after school and stay with him for the rest of the day." She turned back to wait for the light. "It'd really help out a lot—*if* it works out. If it doesn't, that's okay. We'll figure it out."

Mari stared at the crossing traffic. "I haven't worked in a coffee shop since the summer I graduated from high school." She remembered the days of perpetual espresso-scented hair.

"It's like riding a bike," Shannon said.

"But working on Taiton campus? It would bug me to have cocky little freshmen in my face every morning!"

Her mom cast her a look. "*You* were once a cocky little freshman."

Shannon laughed. "I liked working there! You'd get to know some of the regulars."

"We'll see," Mari said. The only place she wanted to work was the women's shelter. It seemed logical since it was a career-building opportunity. It was the closest thing to where she wanted to go in life.

The bright sun glare on the melting snow was blinding. The roads were wet, the cars ahead of them spitting road spray onto their windshield. Mari gazed ahead unseeing, trying to wrap her mind around being at a party with JoyAnne Strang and her catty friends. She hadn't seen her since graduation. What would she even say to her? Everything she could think of sounded awkward. How that girl ever managed *not* to get kicked out of Ford Brentwood was a miracle. JoyAnne "Strange" was what Mari used to call her. She was loud, flirty, and wild. All boobs and teeth. Her gums showed when she smiled. But the boys hadn't seemed to mind. And now she was engaged to Dougie Gordon!

"So where is this bridal shower?" Mari asked.

"Brother Warren's," her mother answered. "Susan's sister, Jackie, is hosting it."

Well, that was *one* good thing, Mari mused, settling back in her seat. She adored Brother Warren, the white-haired retired minister from her church. There was no one kinder than that old man. Somehow she had always felt like his favorite girl. Yikes—it was hard imagining someone like JoyAnne even stepping foot inside Warren Glende's house for a party! It promised to be an interesting morning.

Chapter Three

The Glendes' door swung open before Mari's mother even knocked.

"Hello! Welcome, welcome! Please come in!" cried a middle-aged woman with long, brown hair before turning to shush the little yapping dog at her feet. "Angel! *Angel*—for heaven's sake!" She looked up. "Sorry about that, ladies! Do come in!"

The tantalizing aroma of coffee and food met them in the foyer. Across the room Mari heard a squeal of delight and spied her former neighbor making a beeline for them—Mrs. Gordon, who looked the same as ever with her caramel-colored bob, plump hips, and happy countenance.

"It's the Coleman girls! I'm so glad you made it! Welcome!"

"Susan—it's been too long!" her mother gushed, hugging her warmly. "How good to see you! We see each other at church, but we never talk."

"Too long, yes!" Mrs. Gordon beamed at them. "Shannon—hello! Another beautiful bride-to-be! And Mari!" She hugged them both. "Have you met my sister? Ladies—my sister, Jackie Burke. She's living here with Dad now. And Jackie—these are the Coleman girls, who lived next door to me on Frost until they had the audacity to move! I still miss them terribly!"

Jackie extended her hand. "It's a pleasure."

"Nice to meet you! Sorry we're late, but we're here," Mari's mother answered, slipping her arm out of her jacket.

"Oh, no worries," Susan assured. "We're off to a jerky start! JoyAnne and some of the other ladies were excited to go next door to see our neighbors' new house—the DeSotos. Have you met them? They're the sweetest couple! Anyway, then *everyone* decided they wanted to see it, so we're waiting a bit. But they'll be back in a jiffy." She hung their coats on a nearby rack.

Jackie gestured to the magnificent spread of food adorning the dining room table. "We'll be eating shortly, but can I get you some coffee? Punch?"

"Coffee would be nice," Mari's mother said, looking around. "Your home is lovely! So festive!"

"Thank you! Please make yourself comfortable. Mari? Shannon?"

"Punch for me," Shannon said.

"Coffee, thank you," Mari murmured, taking a seat on a hard-backed chair beside the same black studio piano at which the late Mrs. Glende had taught her piano lessons until seventh grade, when her parents had finally let her quit.

From around the corner a voice hooted, "What's all this commotion?"

Mari watched as Susan and Jackie's elderly father, Warren Glende, emerged from the hallway, his eyes a-twinkling. He used a cane now, she observed.

"My, my, my—don't we have a lineup of beauties here!" he called, eyeing them as they rose to greet him. "Mrs. Coleman, how are you? What do you hear from Nick?"

"Hello, Brother Warren!" her mother said, kissing his cheek. "He's doing well! Thank you for asking."

"Wonderful! And Shannon—look at you, lovely as ever! How are your wedding plans going, sweetheart?" He hugged her, nodding at her reply, and then turned to Mari, pausing to smile at her.

"Mari, Mari," he said softly. "You're a delight to your Father—you know that, don't you?" He stepped closer, lifting her chin with his finger. "Listen, sweetheart, God *knows* you. You'll find your path if you keep your eyes on him." He smiled kindly.

Before Mari could respond, they were suddenly interrupted by the patio door in the kitchen rumbling back with a burst of women's chatter as a group of ladies entered, doubtless returning from their jaunt next door.

Brother Warren's face brightened as he turned. "Goodness—listen to that cackling! Ladies! Y'all sound like seagulls in a fish market!"

A chorus of laughter resounded as he hobbled quickly toward them.

Mari sank onto her chair, watching the noisy throng of women crowding into the kitchen.

Shannon lowered herself to the piano bench beside her. "That was interesting. You okay?"

"Yeah," Mari said simply. Did she *look* like she was struggling to find her path? And just like that—dropped like a hot potato.

Jackie appeared with all their drinks carefully balanced in her hands. Shannon rose to take her punch and assisted in handing off the coffees, thanking her.

"You're welcome, dear. I hear congratulations is in order for you! When is your wedding?"

"Late July." Shannon replied happily. "One hundred eleven days!"

"How exciting!" Jackie turned toward Mari. "And I hear you'll be graduating from high school soon!"

Mari blinked. "*College*."

Jackie's hand flew to her chest. "My apologies! I misunderstood Susan! I'm so sorry!"

"I'm finishing up my sociology degree at Bourdette in Boston. I'm in my fourth year. But I'll probably graduate *next* year."

"Ah, I see! I'm so sorry. I didn't realize you were older than Shannon."

"Don't worry. It happens all the time," Shannon quipped amusedly. "She's my little big sister."

"But she's *secure*," their mother said, throwing a look at the two of them.

"It's okay," Mari returned with a polite smile. She brought the coffee up for a sip, then pulled it away to peek at the weak brew. She would need a lot more caffeine than this.

A cheer erupted from the kitchen, signaling that the woman of the hour had arrived. Mari felt a twinge of anxiety as a beaming JoyAnne Strang in a white, form-fitting dress and heels was led in from the deck and someone adorned her with a glitzy bridal sash and pinned a corsage on her. From where she sat, Mari thought she looked—well, *pretty*, she admitted reluctantly. Gorgeous, even. Like a bride. For once her dress wasn't hair-raising short. And her neckline was a graceful scoop instead of the customary showy plunge she was known for. Maybe she *had* matured some, now that she had kids. Or perhaps someone had set her some firm guidelines for the shower! She took a breath, mentally preparing herself for their meeting.

Then one of the ladies stepped up and raised her hands, calling over the crowd. Mari gawked in surprise. No way! The brown-haired girl from the airport the night before—Peter Watkins' wife! What a small world!

"Ladies! Ladies! Let's get started!" she called. "Since most of us are already gathered here in the kitchen, let's take a moment to pray over the party and the food before we eat. JoyAnne, anything you'd like to say first?" She waved toward the bride, and instantly the room became quiet.

She almost appeared shy, Mari observed, watching JoyAnne smile and greet her guests.

"Hi, everyone!" JoyAnne said. "Thanks for coming. It means a lot to me. And thank you, Jackie, for hosting, and to all who brought the food and made everything look so beautiful. But I want to give a special thanks to"—her eyes suddenly grew red and her mouth quivered—"to my friend Kyla for all you've done for me. You and Brother Warren." She tossed her head, blinking back her tears. "Sorry, everyone! Anyway—thanks."

The room gave a collective "Aww" as Kyla Watkins reached over to give JoyAnne a brief hug and a kiss. JoyAnne wiped her eyes and apologized again.

"Let's thank the Lord—shall we?" Kyla urged, bowing her head.

All Mari could do was stare. This was like the twilight zone. So strange, and as unlike JoyAnne Strang as you could possibly get! Plus, most of the ladies in the room were from Eagle Bluff Church, she noticed. How did JoyAnne even know these people? And furthermore, Mari was reminded that Kyla Watkins knew Marilee Montayne—knew her personally. How in the world did all this fit together?

When Kyla had finished praying, Mari watched her hug JoyAnne once more, and another girl around their same age came to throw her arms around them both. Then Susan Gordon approached their little cluster and urged JoyAnne to start the buffet line.

A woman balancing a blond, fuzzy-haired baby on her arm suddenly paused in front of Mari at the piano, the baby's chin shiny with drool. "Well, hey! Mari Coleman! Welcome back! How are you?"

It was Mrs. Gordon's daughter, Samantha.

Mari rose, careful of her knee. "Samantha! Nice to see you!" As she spoke, the baby broke into an enormous grin, revealing two little teeth. They both laughed in surprise. "What a charmer! Is this your newest little one? He's really cute!" Indeed, next to his tiny white sweater, his eyes were blueberries.

Samantha planted a kiss on the baby's head. "Oh, no! *My* baby is five! This is baby Kenny, Peter and Kyla Watkins' little guy. Isn't he adorable? Look how he's watching you!"

Then, spotting his mother coming, the baby began kicking excitedly, lunging for her as she arrived. "Thank you, Samantha! I can take him now," she said, swooping him up. "Hope he's been good for you." She smiled at Mari. "Hello. I don't think we've met. I'm Kyla Watkins."

"Mari Coleman."

Kyla gave an embarrassed smile as her baby burrowed his face into her shirt. "Oh, dear! Looks like he's ready for lunch too!" She pulled him away, frowning. "You look familiar. Were you—were you on our flight last night—?"

"A row ahead. Middle seat."

Samantha gave a cry of wonder, looking between the two of them as Kyla nodded. "I *thought* I recognized you! I'm so sorry if my baby disturbed you."

"He was fine," Mari assured. "I slept most of the flight anyway."

"Good for you! *I* didn't! I was stressing about this shower! And today I'm completely jet-lagged! What a small world! How do you know JoyAnne?"

And how do you know Marilee Montayne? she wanted to ask Kyla in return, but she didn't. "We were classmates at Ford Brentwood Academy, though not really friends. I mostly know the Gordons. We were next-door neighbors for years." She threw Samantha a quick smile.

"Cool!" Kyla hastily retrieved a business-sized card from her back pocket and handed it to her. "Well, *I* know JoyAnne through my church, and if you're ever looking for a good one, I'd highly recommend Eagle Bluff. I *love* it! And now I better go feed this ravenous child before he lets himself be heard!"

Mari glanced at Samantha as Kyla walked away.

"You've been away at college, Mari. She doesn't know you grew up at Eagle Bluff."

But Mari's brow crinkled. "Wait—did she just say she knows JoyAnne through our *church*?"

Mari felt a hand on her arm. Jackie Burke was back.

"Come now, ladies! There's all sorts of delicious treats waiting for you!" She waved them toward the elegant serving table. "Come! Fresh, lovely croissants! Come, Shannon—you too!"

"Let's try to get together soon," Samantha said. "We should catch up."

"Yeah," Mari agreed.

In the short distance across the room, both Samantha and Shannon got talking to different people, so Mari ended up in the buffet line by herself. She took a plate and waited as the woman ahead of her got her food.

The woman looked up. "Are you Shannon's sister?"

Mari nodded.

"I saw you sitting with her. I'm Leah DeSoto. Shannon did my hair for my wedding. She's really good! It was so beautiful! I loved it!"

"Nice. Congratulations!" Mari took the tongs and helped herself to a mini quiche. "Are you the next-door neighbor with the new house?"

The girl's face lit up. "Thanks, and yes! Have you heard my story? Out of the blue I inherited my grandparents' house, and God used my moving here to bring me out of the absolute *worst* pit of bitterness. It was a miracle! He restored me and my dad's relationship, and I met my husband here, and on top of that, my grandparents left me a big cache of money, so we built a house! Well, half a house. We added on to the existing one."

Mari still held the tongs. "Wow. That's, um—that's pretty unusual."

"Yes, it is! I'm so grateful to Jesus for saving me! How about you? Do you have a faith story?" She set a fancy fruit kabob on her plate and smiled questioningly at Mari.

Faith story? What kind of question was that for a buffet line? Mari didn't quite know what to say. "Um, yeah, I do. I grew up going to Eagle Bluff Church. It's the only church I've ever attended. My parents have been leaders there on and off since I've been young. And so—" She shrugged. "I guess that's my story."

Leah nodded. "Okay, great! Well, if you're interested, I host a Bible study on Saturday mornings. Kyla Watkins leads it. She's the girl who—"

"I know who she is."

"Oh—right. So if you'd ever want to come or anything—"

"Uh-huh. Well, I'll have to see—with my work schedule and everything."

Leah tipped her head. "Where do you work?"

"I'm hoping to get the—"

"How are you girls doing?" Jackie Burke asked, swinging in behind them. "Do I need to put out more of those stuffed jalapenos? That bacon wrap is *so* delicious!" She smiled. "I'm so glad you two are getting acquainted. Leah, Mari was Susan's next-door neighbor for years! And Mari, Leah lived here with Brother Warren and me for about eight months."

Mari's mouth fell open. "You *lived* here? With Brother Warren?"

Leah gave a giddy nod. "And Jackie. It was amazing!"

Jackie snatched her into a quick side hug. "Yes, this sweet girl lived here with us while they were remodeling their home. They're newlyweds— she and her husband. They got married on Valentine's Day right here in our living room!" She gazed affectionately at Leah. "Isn't she just glowing?"

"Yep." Mari gave another plastic smile, lifting her plate. "Look—I'm going to need two hands for this, so I'm going to have a seat." She motioned to her place beside the piano.

"Right—sure! Nice chatting with you," Leah said.

Mari took her seat on the hard chair, alone in the crowded room once again. Across the house she saw that Leah DeSoto had taken a place at the kitchen island where Kyla was nursing her baby. The two were close friends, she observed. Her eyes dropped to her plate. She didn't have her phone to see what time it was, but it didn't matter. The party had just gotten started, so there'd be no escaping it anytime soon. This might be worse than yesterday's flight delays, she thought glumly, poking into her quiche.

Lifting her head, she nodded to a girl passing in front of her, her hair dyed a stark jet black with straight, sheared off bangs. Then her eyes grew wide in recognition.

"Ariel!" she exclaimed. It was Ariel Marquette, the super-quiet girl from her old church youth group—though minus the mousey brown hair! Wow, had she changed, Mari observed, startled by the girl's hot-red lipstick and conspicuous pewter nose ring—the kind with tiny, round balls protruding downward from both nostrils.

"Oh, hi," Ariel breathed, pausing with her plate in her hand. Her ears were a constellation of piercings too.

After an uncomfortable moment of looking at each other, Mari waved toward Shannon's spot on the piano bench. "Um—care to join me?"

"Oh, thanks." Ariel sat and began to pick at her food.

Well, at least here was someone that Mari knew, even if she was a drastic contrast from the dowdy, melt-into-the-woodwork Ariel she remembered! Mari wondered why she was there. There was no way she and JoyAnne were old buds. JoyAnne had attended Ford Brentwood with Mari, whereas Ariel had gone to public high school. Mari wouldn't have known her but for Eagle Bluff youth group. Not that she and Ariel had been close friends. Or friends at all. Ariel had been the type of girl that everyone was friendly *to,* but no one was really friends *with.* Apparently she still had a connection to the church.

Mari waited a few seconds, then asked politely, "What are you up to nowadays, Ariel?"

"Um, nothing much. Just working." Her eyes locked awkwardly on Mari's, but she added nothing further.

The night shift, Mari guessed, by the dark rings under her eyes. "Where are you working?"

"Just custodial stuff." Another pause.

"And how's that going? Do you like the work?" Crazy. With that prominent nose ring, Mari didn't quite know where to look.

"It's okay."

Mari jerked her chin at the fresh ink and irritated skin on the inside of Ariel's forearm. "Did you get a new tattoo? What is it?"

"Um, a cobra," Ariel replied, holding it out for her.

Mari straightened, startled once more. Indeed, a scaly, greenish snake stared up at her—an evil-eyed cobra, with its hood spread and fangs extended, winding from wrist to elbow. As a college student, Mari was so beyond judging people's body art. Nearly everyone her age sported tatts nowadays, and she had seen some doozies. But goodness! A cobra—? For *Ariel*? Honestly, that tatt had regret written all over it! Had her mother approved of that creepy art?

"How, um—interesting," she stated with an obligatory flash of her own forearm's scroll of flowers.

"Yeah," Ariel said, examining her skin. Then she dropped her arm, facing Mari for a moment before returning her attention to her plate, her cheeks tinged pink.

That was Ariel, all right. The old Ariel. Mostly normal, but kinda not. "She's on the autism spectrum," their youth leader had explained back then. That hadn't meant much to Mari in high school, although now she had a better understanding. Back then Ariel had merely been the shy, skinny youth group girl who rarely brushed her hair and always smelled like corn chips. Mari studied her a second before resuming her own meal. A cobra! Whoa, had she changed!

Across the room there was a burst of laughter, and Mari glanced over to see that Brother Warren had joined Leah and Kyla in the kitchen, perching himself on one of the bar stools. She watched them, bewildered by her sudden stir of emotion. Why did his gush of attention over them make her feel like a friendless sixth-grader again?

Brother Warren had been such an influential person in her life. For as early as she could remember, he had always greeted her in the halls at church and stopped to ask her questions about her life. But it wasn't only that he talked to her; it was the *way* he talked to her—his sincerity in what he asked. She didn't only *feel* that he loved her—she *knew* it. It was Brother Warren who had drawn out how terribly she missed her dad in his absences, comforting her with a kind hug and always a prayer.

Mari reached back for her tiny cup of now-tepid coffee from its coaster on the piano—which reminded her of all the awkward piano lessons with his wife for which she had not practiced a lick. Her sweet conversations with Brother Warren afterward had been Mari's reward for enduring those painful half-hour sessions. But today Mari didn't exist.

Shannon stopped to get her purse. "I'm moving to the couch. How's it going? Enjoying yourself?"

Mari sent her a deadpan look. "Tremendously."

Then her sister greeted Ariel, and after exchanging a few pleasantries, she moved on.

Hearing loud giggling, Mari glanced toward the kitchen again, this time observing that JoyAnne had now joined the little visit-y cluster around the kitchen island. Standing next to Brother Warren, Leah DeSoto now held the baby with a burp cloth over her shoulder, patting his back while everyone watched Kyla animatedly tell a story, gesturing with both hands, her ponytail swinging back and forth. Every now and then Brother Warren would throw his head back in laughter.

And then Susan Gordon paused to chat, bringing her arm around JoyAnne and casting her soon-to-be daughter-in-law an adoring look. Mari bit her lip, marveling again at the unlikely pair. The Douglas Gordon *she* knew had been such a decent guy. She sighed. Eventually JoyAnne would mill through the room to greet her guests and they would have to acknowledge each other. In the meantime, Mari finished her plate and took an unhurried trip to the bathroom.

When Mari returned to her place on the hard chair beside Ariel, she saw that most of the ladies were relocating to the living room, as it was nearing the time for the shower games and opening of gifts. A decorated armchair was brought forth for the bride-to-be, who took her seat, flanked by Kyla and Leah. JoyAnne looked up to smile at the ladies in the room, her eyes growing round as she suddenly noticed Mari for the first time.

"Mari Coleman!"

Mari smiled politely. "Hello. Congratulations!"

That was as far as they got, for Susan Gordon went to stand behind JoyAnne's chair, calling the room to attention. "Excuse me, ladies! I have an announcement!"

The room grew quiet.

"Again, I'd like to thank you all for coming. This is a sweet day for us. I'm so delighted with JoyAnne and the woman she's becoming, and I'm thrilled she'll be my daughter-in-law!" She placed her hands on JoyAnne's shoulders, smiling down at her. "So, JoyAnne didn't want me to do this today—she didn't want to make a big deal of it—but I'm so stinking *proud* of her that I begged her to let me say something! So—this morning JoyAnne got a phone call from the Sunlight Women's Center. She's just been offered the position of director!"

Mari felt a cold stab as the room burst into a cheer. Everyone clapped, and several women called out their congratulations.

"Would you like to say anything about it?" Mrs. Gordon asked the blushing girl.

JoyAnne shifted modestly in the chair. "Thanks, everyone! Well, it seems to be a perfect fit for me, given my journey in life. And it fulfills a dream in my heart to help hurting women. I had no clue that God could use me, much less drop an opportunity like this into my lap!" She gave her giant all-teeth grin, and once again the room applauded.

Everything became a blur for Mari where she sat stiffly on the hard chair. How in the world was it even possible for a girl like JoyAnne to be chosen as director of any women's center, much less Sunlight? Mari couldn't even look at her.

Out of the corner of her eye she noticed Shannon across the room waggling her phone discretely near her lap. As their eyes met, Shannon jerked her head toward the door. Mari nodded, tapping her wrist. Then in a few minutes when the little half-sheets of paper were being circulated around the room for a shower game, Mari excused herself and made her way outside. Shannon met her on the front steps a few minutes later, promptly handing over her phone.

"Here—I figured you'd want to get out of here. I'm sorry, Mari. I know you had your heart set on Sunlight."

"I'm okay," Mari said, pretending to brush it off. "But yeah, I can't stay."

"Well, return my phone before you leave."

Mari waited until she was alone to call Will.

"I have *no idea* where that is," he said after she gave him the address of where to pick her up. "I've never even heard of Richmond Road!"

"Will," she said irritably, "you have a *phone*. Use your GPS!"

"Well, I'm kinda in the middle of something right now. I'll get there as soon as I can."

Mari's jacket was still in the house, but the powerful sun had warmed things up considerably outside, melting off any of the week's remaining snow. She stayed on the step under the eaves, away from the dripping edge of the roof, trying to breathe, trying to relax her shoulders, trying to judge the timing of when Will would arrive and when she should go back in for her purse and coat and to return Shannon's phone.

What a morning! She stared unseeing at the soggy lawn, stunned that Sunlight had given the position to JoyAnne. Of all people! It could only be sheer *luck*. She certainly wasn't super qualified for the job. Mari shook her head. Why did timely things like that happen to everyone else but her? They never happened to her. Never!

Plus all the wedding hype in that room. She could go a hundred years before attending another bridal shower. It seemed like *everyone* was getting married or had just gotten married—Missy, Shannon, Leah, JoyAnne. Why should their "glowing" bug her so much? But it did.

Mari had never been one of those hollow-headed, eye-batting girls obsessed with boys. She had always prided herself in being sensible and devoted to her studies, knowing her day for love would eventually come. And it had. She had Will now. She let out a long breath. Then why was she so irritated with those ladies inside? Was it because of Peter Watkins still? She had liked him a lot. A *lot*. She still felt the sting of rejection.

It wasn't as though they had even dated or anything before that Kyla girl came along, but she had been hopeful. Peter Watkins had been the nicest, most handsome guy Mari had ever met, having just shown up at church one summer on fire for God, almost three years ago now. She had been smitten, and every time they were together, he had been so friendly. But apparently it wasn't meant to be. Plus, they would have made an odd couple anyway if they *had* ended up together, with him so tall and her so— so *not* tall. Nevertheless, she'd had a flaming crush on him.

One night way back then, Mari had confided to her sister her sore disappointment of his engagement, at which Shannon had blurted back mercilessly, "Mari, Peter Watkins is nice to *everyone*!"

"I know! But it seemed like there was something there. A spark or something. I'm just bugged that this Kyla girl shows up out of nowhere and he falls for her."

Shannon's reply had been frank: "Mari, get over it!"

Get over it. That seemed to be the never-ending advice, applying even today with her women's center job prospects going down the drain. Now she would need to find a job, for she could no longer take her old position at Sunlight. There was no way she would report to JoyAnne as her superior!

She checked the time on Shannon's phone, then laid her hand on the door latch, steeling herself. She would go straight to get her purse, and then hopefully Shannon would come meet her at the coat rack so she didn't have to cross the center of the room to return her phone. Then she would wait in the car for Will.

Of course, Mari didn't factor in her mother seeing her quickly snatch up her purse, nor the corresponding concern her mom would have about where she was going and if some emergency had occurred. Neither did she factor in that her mother would call out such questions in front of the entire room. But Shannon came to the rescue.

"She's not feeling that great, Mom," she said discretely, crossing the room to join Mari at the coat rack. It was an excuse for which every woman was suddenly sympathetic. Mari definitely owed her one for that.

"Thanks for coming!" JoyAnne called out. She had just opened Leah DeSoto's gift and was holding up a set of old-fashioned embroidered dish towels.

Mari smiled apologetically. "Yeah. Congratulations again! Sorry that I have to leave."

Leah DeSoto met her at the door, a little breathless from hurrying after her. "Hey—I wanted to catch you before you left."

"Oh," Mari said. "Thanks for the invitation. It was a nice party, and it was nice meeting you."

"Thanks for coming. But hey, I wanted to give you my phone number in case you were interested in the Bible study some time." She handed Mari a little card.

Mari's head bobbed. "Thanks. Like I said, we'll see how it works out with my job and everything."

Lots of things were in the air, Mari mused as she headed to the car, but one thing was certain—she would not be going to Kyla Watkins' Bible study.

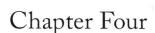

Chapter Four

Will was late. By the time he pulled up in his ultra-cool neon green classic Jeep, half of the vehicles around Warren Glende's house had already disappeared, and Mari's mother and Shannon were just leaving.

"You're *still* here?" Shannon asked as they arrived at the car.

"Leaving now! See you later!" Mari answered, shutting the car door and scooting across the road to hop into the passenger's side of Will's Jeep. She turned to him, drawing the seat belt across her lap. "Where *were* you? I texted you over an hour ago!"

"Stuck in a line at the car wash!" he answered, unfazed by her fuss. He removed his hat and tossed it into the back. "Did you notice how clean my Jeep is?"

"Seriously?" Mari screwed up her brow, plopping back in the seat. "You took forever!"

"I wanted it clean for you!" He glanced in his mirrors, then did a quick U-turn in the middle of the road. "Plus, it took me a while to find the place. Did you have fun at the shower?"

"It was the worst morning of my life!"

He flashed her a look. "What happened?"

"It was just—bad. Everything about it. I have *no* friends, Will. None."

"What's going on?"

"I don't want to talk about it." She folded her arms, now smelling the vinyl car polish.

He glanced at her again but remained silent. At the corner to the main highway, he tapped his signal and pulled into the parking lot of a convenience store.

"What are we doing?" Mari asked, looking around as the Jeep rolled to a stop.

He put the vehicle in park and turned in his seat.

"What's going on, Will?"

"Nothing. You need to decompress. Take your time."

"Don't guilt me!"

"I'm not! Relax! Look, Marzipan, I've waited exactly fifty-seven days to see you, and I blew it last night picking you up. Can I just look at you and tell you how glad I am you're back?"

Mari stared, then cracked a small smile.

"*There*," he said. "That's more like it! Okay—so what happened this morning?"

Mari gave a heavy sigh. "I don't know. I felt like an outsider the whole time. I mean, I *know* people—like my *mom's* friends and everything—but *my* old friends have all moved away, and there's all these new girls with their dreamboat husbands and babies and winning careers. And then this quiet girl, Ariel, from my old youth group was there, and she's gone all weird with a nose ring and a big old snake tattooed on her arm—with red eyes! And I'm like—okaaay, what happened to you? And even the bride—I knew her back at Ford Brentwood, and let me tell you, she was *not* someone you'd want to hang out with. She was one of those devious, naughty girls, and now she's all—" She waggled her hands. "I don't know. She's really changed. It was so weird. I felt so alone. Plus one of the ladies thought I was in high school!"

Will studied her quietly. "So nothing actually happened?"

"I just *told* you what happened!"

"You told me how you *felt* about a lot of things, but did anything actually happen?"

She looked away. "Well, even Brother Warren was right in there with them—all the new girls. He barely said hello to me, and when he did, he had this stern word for me. And then he just walked away!"

"Who's Brother Warren?"

"A retired minister from church. It was at his house."

"Well, blow him off!" Then he frowned. "A retired minister hosted a bridal shower?"

"His daughter hosted the shower, and *no one* blows off Brother Warren, Will."

"Okay—so what did he say?"

Mari paused, trying to remember. "I don't know. Something about God showing me my path in life."

Will cocked an eyebrow. "Now *that* is hardcore stern!"

Mari shot him a look, but he opened his hands. "I don't get it! Why are you so upset? Why waste your emotional energy on two hours of a Saturday morning with some 'new girls'? You're home, Maribelle! Relax! No one's requiring you to be friends with them. And don't compare yourself! You have your own dreamboat boyfriend,"—he threw her a sportive look—"and soon you'll have your own winning career, once you hear back from the women's shelter."

"That's another thing. The bride got the position at Sunlight!"

He pulled back in surprise, and Mari turned to look out the windshield.

"So *that's* what happened!"

They sat together in silence.

"I'll need to figure out another job," she said after a while.

"That's the easy part. It's the disappointment part that's the bummer."

She nodded glumly. "It's been a rough day."

"I can see that. But hey—'She turned the page and started a new chapter.'"

She huffed, glancing at him. "What's that—some kind of 'Life moves on' platitude?"

"Well, yes, but I'm trying to be poetic about it. It always does, you know. You'll do something else, and that'll be that."

"Will, I've had a sucky day. Don't tell me to get over it!'"

He hesitated a moment, then reached down to rummage through his console. He brought up a wrinkled receipt and waved it in the air. "See this? This is one genuine sucky day—no denying it! Now watch this—" He wadded up the paper, rolled down his window, and tossed it out. "There it went, just like that!"

"You littered the parking lot."

"For good reason! Come on, Marigold—let it go! You can breathe now! You're with me, the studly guy who's crazy about you!" He tapped her on the arm. "Smile!"

She didn't want to, but for his sake she forced herself to do it.

He flayed his hands. "'And suddenly her day changed!' And it's going to get even better when I do what I've been waiting for months to do." He grinned, leaning over to kiss her. Then he kissed her again. And again.

It took a minute to relax enough to kiss him back—especially with the stick shift between them—but once she did, it felt like a stress valve finally gave way. She rested her forehead dreamily against his. "Okay, you are absolved of your sin."

He leaned back. "From what sin am I absolved?"

"Forgetting me at the airport."

"Hey"—he shook his head—"I did *not* forget you!"

"Yes, you did, Will! But I get that it was an accident. And at any rate, I forgive you!" She smiled and raised her chin.

He gave up the argument and kissed her again. "Well, I'm glad to be absolved. All right, let's get some lunch. I've saved my appetite, and I'm starved!"

Mari frowned. "Weren't we going to see my grandfather first?"

"No, we're going out for lunch first."

"The shower was a brunch. I just ate. I thought we talked about this."

He shook his head. "No, we specifically talked about *lunch*, so I waited. I thought we were seeing your grandfather later."

Mari paused, scratching her eyebrow. "Well, fine then. Want to go to Bob's Burgers? I'd have an ice cream."

His brow wrinkled. "Their burgers are lame. I was kinda thinking Chinese."

"The Wok? I don't care for their desserts."

The two looked at each other.

"Okay," Mari relented, "we can do Chinese."

"What's wrong with their desserts?" asked Will. "I think they're great! I'm really in the mood for Chinese. There has to be *something* you could eat."

"That's fine. I don't need anything anyway."

In his typical fashion, Will moved seamlessly from subject to subject over lunch, dominating the conversation, but Mari didn't mind, as she was still feeling blue from the shower and overtired from traveling after her dorm-packing all-nighter. She was simply glad to see him, and he didn't seem to notice that she was quiet. She leaned on her arms, nursing her ice water through her straw while Will devoured second and third helpings of spicy General Tso's chicken, egg rolls, and lo mein, chatting between mouthfuls.

When they left the restaurant, both were surprised that they had been there for almost two hours. Then as they were about to get into the Jeep, Will noticed that the cinema next door was playing an early-bird matinee of a much-anticipated movie release.

"No way! Do you see that?" he exclaimed. "I've been waiting for *Griffin* to come out for months! We could get in for the very first matinee! This is crazy!"

Those begging eyes. Mari was learning about her boyfriend's

obsession with medieval sci-fi movies. How could she refuse? Plus, there was something gratifying about being deemed "best girlfriend ever" with her yes.

"Best out of how many?" she asked curiously.

"Well, only two," he admitted. "But my first girlfriend dumped me after a week."

"Now that's some fierce competition!" she returned, and they both laughed.

By the time the two of them got out of the movie theater and finally made the trek to Riverview Care Center, Mari's grandfather was shuffling out of his room with his walker on his way to dinner.

"Hi, Poppy!" Mari called to him from the end of the hallway.

"Ah, Mr. Jones—look!" the attending aide exclaimed. "You've got company!"

Her grandfather's eyes twinkled as he recognized her. "Maarrr!"

"Hi, Pop Pop!" Mari said, plopping a kiss on his cleanshaven cheek and hugging him warmly. "It's good to see you! I'm home from school for a few months so I'll be around more. Do you remember my boyfriend, Will? Will Wallace. You met him at Christmas."

The old man's eyes rose to Will, who acknowledged him with a nod. "Sir."

"You must be Shannon's sister," the aide guessed, offering his hand. "I just came on shift, and we're heading to the dining room. Would you like to take him down?"

Eagerly Mari nodded. "Let me get rid of my coat." Quickly she threw it onto a chair in her grandfather's room.

The aide motioned to the left. "It's straight down this hall and left at the end. Follow it all the way down. It'll open up to the dining hall on your left."

"Geriatric NASCAR," Will murmured under his breath. "Left, left, left."

Mari ignored him, nodding to the staffer. "And what do we do when we get there?"

"They'll be ready for him. But ma'am, I need to tell you—your grandad is learning to feed himself again. You're going to want to help him, but you need to let him do the work." He smiled kindly. "It's tough to watch, but it's best to let him figure it out."

His warning, however, did not quell the discomfort of watching her grandfather painstakingly chase his green beans and chunks of creamed chicken breast around his plate and struggle to bring them to his mouth. Everything in her wanted to assist him. She finally tucked her hands under her thighs. While he labored to eat, Mari rattled on to him about her meeting with the dean a few days prior, buying her ticket home, packing up her room during the night, and journeying through the ice storm to get to the airport.

Will sat with them, but after a while he adjusted his chair toward the television set in the far corner. "I can't take that," he confessed, nodding to her grandfather's messy efforts.

Eventually the original staff worker came to get them. Back in the room, he helped her grandfather get ready for bed, another lengthy process.

"He's working so hard," the aide told Mari as he guided the old man to the bathroom. "All the little things—brushing his teeth, washing his face, toileting himself—all those are major hurdles right now. But he's gaining ground. You're working hard, aren't you, Mr. Jones?"

Her grandpa grinned, meeting Mari's eyes in the bathroom mirror. "Harrdly worrking."

She smiled at his joke, reaching for the door lever. "Very funny, Poppy! Okay, I'll let you keep your dignity while you finish up. There's just some things a granddaughter oughtn't see!"

Closing the door, she came out to find Will stretched out on the armchair. He leaned his head back. "How're you doing?"

"I'm good. How are *you* doing?"

He shrugged. "Fine."

She realized how bored he must be. "Thanks for being here, Will. It means a lot."

"Of course. When was his stroke again?"

"March first. It takes a long time to recover. We're lucky that it's going as well as it is."

"I guess."

Mari moved to sit on one of his knees, and he quickly sat up to let her. "My mom and sister take turns coming here every day so he's not alone."

"Aren't you paying all these people to care for him? He's not alone."

She jabbed him with her elbow. "You know what I mean. Shannon got a new job, and they want me to take her old one at the Taiton Coffee Break, 'cause the schedule works out perfectly for me to come here between when Shannon leaves and when Mom gets off work." She gave a thoughtful sigh. "I suppose I could take it. I mean—I'll *need* a job. It just feels like such a high school job, like I'm going backwards in life."

"Says who? No one's evaluating you, Marzipan."

"You know what I mean. Although it kinda cuts up the day. I'd probably need to get another job at night. I don't know."

They sat quietly together until the bathroom door opened and her grandfather emerged in his pajamas, carefully wheeling his walker across his room. He rotated, backing against the bed before he sat.

"Excellent!" the tech praised. "You've worked hard today, Mr. Jones! Let's get you into bed so you can rest!"

With a little more effort, her grandfather was soon beneath the sheets. The tech wrapped the call button around the guard rail and held it up for him to see, then set it on top of the sheet.

"You're welcome to hang out," he told Mari. "Here's the remote if you care to watch TV, although your mother prefers to have it off. She reads to him a lot."

"Thanks."

"Anything else I can do for you?" he asked.

She shook her head, her throat feeling tight. "Thank you for taking care of him."

"Why, of course, Miss Coleman! I'll be back in a little while." With a modest smile, he left.

Now without the staff present, Mari didn't quite know what to do with her grandfather. She slid onto the edge of the bed, twisting her good knee up so that she could face him, her back to Will.

"Maarrrr—" her grandfather began.

She brightened. "*Ee!* Mar—*ee.*"

"Maarrrr—" he repeated, tagging on a feeble, "—*ee.* Maarrrr—*ee.*"

Mari bobbed her head in delight. "Yes! You said it! Did you hear that, Will? He said my name!"

Will opened his eyes, raising his head from where he was sprawled out on the chair. "I did! I heard it! Good job, Mr. Jones!"

She turned back. "Want me to read to you, Poppy?" She noted a few hardcover books on the bedside table and paged through one that looked interesting, reading him excerpts. Before long, she heard her grandfather's breathing change. With the crisp white bedsheets pulled up around his neck he looked more like a child than an old man. She watched him sleep for a minute before she put the book away.

Will sat up and stretched.

"You've been very patient," Mari commented.

His brow rose. "I might be nearing the end of my threshold."

"Well, he's asleep. We can go."

69

His arm dropped to snatch up Mari's coat from the floor beside the chair. "I'm not gonna lie—that's music to my ears!" He tossed it to her and scooped up his own jacket. "Let's get out of here!"

Silently they passed through the hall toward the main entrance. As they neared the front doors, Will took a couple swift steps ahead to activate the electronic doors.

"After you, ma'am" he said smugly with a bow.

Mari chuckled, pulling her gloves out of her pocket as they exited into the cool, fresh air. "It's really hard to see Poppy like that. He seemed so healthy before the stroke, given his age and everything. I know he's making progress, but he's got a long way to go."

"You're not kidding," Will agreed, indicating to where his Jeep was parked. "It's more than hard—it's pathetic!"

"What?"

"I don't know if I could live like that! I don't think I could. Seriously, Mars, if that ever happens to me—if I would ever get like that, I'd want you to promise me you'd pull the plug."

Mari swung her head toward him in surprise.

"I feel sorry for the guy! That's no life!"

She stopped short on the pavement. "Will! That's my grandfather!"

"I know." He nodded, pausing with her. "And that's his—that's *your* choice and all. You and your family. That's fine. I'm just saying for *me*—I don't know if I would want to live like that."

She gave him a bewildered look.

"Sorry, but that's the way I feel. For *me*. I mean, somewhere down the line you gotta start thinking about quality of life. *I* wouldn't want to live like that. I couldn't do it. I would ask you to mercifully put me out."

"'Put you out'?"

"Well, let me go. Let nature take its course. The guy can barely eat or go to the bathroom by himself! I mean, sheesh—his granddaughter's reading him bedtime stories. What kind of life is that?"

She furled her brow. "Are you saying my mom shouldn't have called 911? That we should have just let him die in our condominium?"

"*No*,"—he shook his head—"I didn't say that! I'm talking about *me*. You guys made your choice. You can do whatever you want."

"He's *recovering*, Will. He's getting better."

"Yeah, but is it worth it?"

She stared at him in disbelief. "Wow! Now *that* shows a lot of heartfelt sympathy for what we're going through as a family! Thank you for your very educated opinion, William Wallace." She swung on her heel, heading back the way they had come.

Will caught her arm. "Whoa, now—hold on! I was talking about *myself*, okay? Don't be offended." At her lack of response, he continued. "Hey, I'm *sorry*! I didn't mean for you to take it personally."

She yanked her arm away. "How can I *not* be offended? You just insinuated that we should have let my grandfather die! I can't believe you said that!"

"Mars, come on! You know I wasn't jabbing you! Come on—I'm sorry!" He followed her into the care center. "Mari!"

Mari simply pointed to the parking lot. "You can walk your butt out to your squeaky-clean Jeep."

"Well, let me take you home! At least let me take you home!" He gave an angry grunt, following her down the hallway. "Mari, knock it off! How are you going to get home?"

"I'll figure it out!" she shot over her shoulder, marching swiftly to her grandfather's room.

"Mari—dang it! You're overreacting! Talk to me!"

She let herself in quietly, wishing she could slam the door behind her, but she didn't dare. Outside in the hall she heard an aide intercept Will, whose voice now rose in frustration at not being let in the room. Mari stood poised for trouble, sick of the prospect of waking her grandfather in a fight with her boyfriend. She threw a quick glance at him snoring quietly in his bed. The nerve of Will to say those things! How could he be such a jerk? *Yeah, but is it worth it?* She could have smacked him!

Behind her the door squeaked, and she whirled, ready for round two. But it was the staff, poking his head in. "You okay, miss? The young man— he wants to come in, but I stopped him."

Mari tossed her head, trying to look under control. "I'm all right. But I'd like to be alone."

He gave an understanding nod. "All right, miss. I'll take care of it."

She could have hugged that fellow.

Then it was quiet.

At first, she couldn't even feel. She stood motionless in the center of the room, her thoughts a monstrous, tangled, knotted mess. Where did she even begin? It wasn't just Will. Everything in her life was going haywire. Everything! Her bum knee and resulting freakish school demise, JoyAnne and Dougie, the snatched-away Sunlight job, and now breaking up with the one friend she thought she had had—because certainly that's where things were going with Will, she speculated. But better to find out now what he was really like. Nevertheless, what a disappointment! What a bitter disappointment!

Then that miserable ache began to pulse in her chest, as if the admission had triggered an emotional landslide. She buried her face in her hands, holding her breath, trying her hardest not to cry. Silly, lanky Will. They had gotten along so well—so well. He had been so much fun. She had cared for him a lot. She gave a doleful groan. Breaking up was the *worst*. She absolutely hated it. Plus it just plain stunk that everyone else had all the breaks in life—Shannon, Missy, Kyla Watkins—even JoyAnne Strang. When would it ever be *her* turn?

She slid out of her coat and tossed it onto the armchair again. Then kicking off her boots, she padded across the room to study the space beside her grandfather on the bed. Slowly and carefully, she sat onto the mattress and lay on her side, hypercautious of her knee as she wiggled in beside him, pressing her stomach against his back with the bed rail cold against hers. It was a snug fit, but next to his warm but frail body, the weight of every burden tumbled forth in silent weeping, the kind of crying one stifled in the dark with roommates present. She couldn't wake Poppy, nor did she want a concerned visit from the staff. Then, when she was emotionally spent, she closed her eyes to take a nap.

Later when the aide peeked in, Mari heard him chuckle at the sight of her spooning with her grandfather. "Now there's a couple of sardines!" he quipped softly as not to wake the old man.

She turned her head, admitting in an embarrassed whisper, "I'm *stuck*." And not only that, her knee was scolding her for her awkward pose.

He laughed. "Your mother called looking for you. I came to check if you were still here."

"I can't budge. I'm here until you help me off the bed."

The staffer unhooked the rail, then supported her until she could stand.

"Thanks. It was cozy while it lasted," she told him, stabilizing her knee as she straightened her dress. "Wish I could have stayed there all night. It's been one of those days, you know." She glanced fondly at her grandfather's back. "But yeah—I'll go call my mom. She'll need to pick me up."

"There are options for staying, you know," he said in a hushed voice, gently adjusting the blankets around her grandfather. "But not in this bed. We have a foam chair that unfolds into a thick sleeping mat. If you'd like, I could bring it in for you. I've heard it offers tolerable comfort."

She raised her brow. "What's your name? You deserve a raise! Bring it in! I'd love a sleepover with my poppy!"

"Thank you. The name's Norman, and I'll go get it. But you should still call your mother. She was quite concerned about you."

Of course she was. Mari learned that her cell phone had been going off like crazy at home for the last hour.

"It's Will, Mom. Have Shannon put it on silent. I'll deal with him tomorrow."

"What's going on, honey?" her mother asked. "I'm worried about you! Did you two have an argument?"

"Yes. I'll talk to him tomorrow." Yeah, they would talk, all right. She was not looking forward to that.

"Not tonight? He seems pretty persistent about trying to reach you."

"No, definitely not tonight," she answered firmly. She gave her a vague explanation of what had happened, adding that she intended to spend the night at the nursing home. "It feels good to be here with Poppy."

Her mother understood, having used the fold-out chair a time or two herself. "Okay. If that's what you need to do, darling, that's fine. I'll swing by to pick you up in the morning."

Norman was a champ, delivering not only the foam chair, but also accompanying sheets, blanket, and pillow. Together they moved the armchair so that Mari's bed stretched lengthwise along the wall. Then he brought her a handful of cheese-and-pretzel snack packs with a foil-covered cup of apple juice. It was the first she had eaten since the morning brunch.

"Norman, you're one of the kindest men I know. Thanks for all you do here."

"My pleasure, ma'am. Sleep well. Lord willing, you'll be undisturbed 'til morning."

Chapter Five

Away from her cell phone and blissfully unaware of incoming calls or texts, Mari slept hard, not stirring until morning. She stretched, then quietly arose before her grandfather, tiptoeing to the bathroom to brush her teeth with his minty toothpaste on her finger. Miraculously, most of her makeup survived the night, though her mascara had smeared some from her crying the previous evening. She splashed her face with water and found a cotton swab to clean up the smudges. Stepping back from the mirror, she noted the sweater dress that had served as her pajamas was a tad wrinkled and sweaty. But what could she do about it?

On the other side of the bathroom door she heard the first of the staff enter her grandfather's room to cheerfully greet him. Close call! She was relieved that she had gotten up when she had. Apparently mornings started early at Riverview.

"Morning, Del!" she heard the aide say. "Let's get those feet on the floor and walk you to the lav. It's going to be an excellent day!"

Good timing, she told herself, glad to be finished in the restroom. And it sounded as though the staff this morning was another win for Riverview. She'd been so impressed with Norman for his kindness the night before. Quickly she primped the flat side of her hair on which she had slept. On the way out, she called a warning greeting as she opened the door; nevertheless, the aide threw a surprised glance over his shoulder from where he helped her grandfather out of bed.

"Good morning!" he returned, giving an additional start. "Why— Mari Coleman! I surely didn't expect to see *you* walk out of there!"

She stared, just as shocked. "Mac Sinclair! What are *you* doing here? Do you work here?"

"Sort of. You're here early!" His eyes dropped to her stocking feet. "Really early!"

"I slept here." She gestured to the makeshift bed.

"Then mystery solved!" He turned back to her grandfather, who was gazing at Mari with sparkling eyes. "Well, how about that, Delbert? You've got company already!"

He pointed. "Marree!"

Mac glanced back in amazement. "Did you hear that? He said your name!"

"I did! Good morning, Poppy!" She went to plop a quick kiss on his cheek.

Mac steadied her grandfather's walker. "Well, this is a fun surprise! As you can probably guess, we're about to take care of some business." He jerked his head in the direction of the bathroom. "Remarkably he's able to go all night without voiding, but time is of the essence."

Mari made a face. "*Way* too much information—thank you! I'll get out of your way. Poppy, did you know we had a slumber party last night? I slept right here in your room!" She waved to her bed.

Her grandfather looked absolutely delighted.

Mac winked, guiding the old man across the room. "Give us a sec!"

"Close the door, please!" she urged.

Balancing on the edge of the armchair, she pulled on her boots, then found her makeup bag in her coat pocket. After a few facial touchups in the reflection of the glass of a picture on the wall, she reshaped the bulky foam mattress into a chair, leaving the bedding neatly folded on top.

"You should have mentioned the other night that you work here!" she called so he would hear. "I had no idea!"

The bathroom door opened immediately. "I don't," Mac said, attending her grandfather back to his bed. "But I know how critical therapy is early on, so after the stroke I offered to come in for some extra support. I've been stopping in early on my way to work. Not every single day, but as often as I can." He stood by as the old man backed in and seated himself. "I want him to get as much help as possible."

"Does my mom know about this?"

"Of course! It's all coordinated with his doctor."

"Well, that's nice of you!" She suddenly noticed his dress slacks and crisp button-down shirt, in contrast to the medical smocks worn by the Riverview Center staff. "So where *do* you work?"

"Revere. The sports clinic. For about five years now. It's not too far from here." He motioned toward the window.

"Is that right? Well, we're really grateful for your help."

"You're welcome. So if you don't mind, I'd like to go through our routine."

She straightened. "Oh! Do you need me to step out?"

"I'd rather you watched so you could help him practice."

Mari lowered herself into the armchair, observing as they began a series of exercises—simple ones at first, then gradually increasing to movements that took some concentration.

Mac looked very pleased. "When we started, I had to help him with everything. But look what he can do on his own now!"

Mari applauded. "Very nice, Poppy!"

Her grandfather smiled, bringing his arm up to make a muscle.

Mac chuckled. "He hasn't lost his sense of humor! Even his speech has improved." He turned back to his patient. "All right, my man, let's move on to our next set." He gave him his arm to assist him into bed, where they began another series of exercises, first with legs, then arms and core.

When they were finished, Mac passed him his water from his bedside table, orientating the straw toward him. He patted the man's shoulder. "Excellent work today! If you continue like this, it won't be long until you're out of here!"

Mari rose to join them. "That's fantastic! Way to go, Poppy!"

Her grandfather swallowed and handed back the water. "Yesss!"

They both laughed.

Mac glanced at the clock, then reached for his jacket draped over the foot of the bed. "Well, it's great to run into you again, but I need to keep moving. The staff will be in shortly to finish getting him dressed and ready for breakfast, and you *will* want to step out for that. Are you staying? Can I offer you a ride somewhere?"

"Mom's coming to get me, but I'll walk out with you. Be right back, Poppy!" she told her granddad. She turned to Mac in the hall. "What you're doing for him is so kind. Thank you so much! I don't know what to say!"

He gave a modest grunt. "Well, *he's* the one doing the work! Wish I could do more. If there's anything else that you can think of, let me know. I'm glad to help."

"You've done a lot already."

He reached to shake her hand. "Have a great day, Mari!"

After a few seconds of watching him saunter toward the lobby, she called after him. "Mac!"

He turned.

"I know you have to go, but since you offered, can I ask a favor?"

"Yeah?"

"My life has been so crazy lately. It's hard to wrap my mind around all the changes, with my school and work and Poppy and—well, a lot of things. Then yesterday was—I don't know—it was like the worst day of my life, and—"

"Dump him."

Mari jerked her head in surprise.

"Is this about that loser who forgot you in the airport?"

"No!" she said defensively. "Why would you think that?"

He cocked his brow. "Well, who spends their Saturday night on a foam mattress in a nursing home?" He shrugged. "Okay, what were you going to ask?"

Now her cheeks were warm. "All I wanted to ask was if I could come sit on your porch once in a while, just to hang out in the old neighborhood and think. I can't exactly go back to my old house anymore, but I'd kinda like that connection to the past. If you wouldn't mind."

"Absolutely. Any time."

"Just the porch. And I wouldn't bother you—I promise."

"Sure. Any time." Then he chuckled. "Honestly, you could come over *every* day if you want—every day between three and five-thirty! It'd solve a huge childcare issue for me! I'm kidding, of course."

Her mouth opened. "You have kids? Wow, I had no idea! But then you are, well—*older*. Older than me, at least. Sorry—that sounded bad! I only meant that you've been a grown-up a lot longer than I have. I still think of you as this intimidating high school senior."

Another laugh. "Right! And yes, I have a kid—a daughter who just turned eight."

"And you need someone to watch her?"

"After school, yes, but I was only joking. I wouldn't expect you to do that."

Mari frowned, her mind whirling through new possibilities. "And it's just for two hours?"

"More like two and a half. Three if traffic is bad or I get out of there late. Right now she rides the bus to my mom's every day, but she's on the north side of the city, and it gets late by the time I drive all the way across town after work and then back home. I'm looking for something closer. But I'm not asking you to do it. It's not an emergency. I just need to take the time to call around."

"You know what? That might work with my schedule!"

"I was *kidding*, Mari."

"Yes, but I could probably do it! It's just a few hours."

He looked at her.

"Shannon set it up so I could have her old job at the Taiton Coffee Break—which I initially didn't want, but then some other things happened, and anyway, if I took it, I could work there through lunch, and then come here for a few hours until Mom gets off work. Then I could go to your house. What time does she get home?"

"Three-fifteen."

Mari flayed her hands. "That'd be perfect! Honestly, it ends up helping me too, because then I'd have evenings free." As she spoke, she realized she was thinking of spending them with Will. Crud. There was still *that* to work out.

Mac looked stunned. "I'd pay you, of course. I'd pay you well."

"Okay." She grinned and shrugged.

He smiled in return, extending his hand. "That was *way* too easy! Are you sure about this?"

Mari shook it. "Absolutely! So how do we work this? When do I start?"

"Well—tomorrow? How about 3:15 at the bus stop?"

"Is it still at the corner of—"

"Still at Dixie's. Same as when we were kids. Mari, are you *sure* about this? You'll be watching my daughter. Your thinking time on my porch just became nonexistent!"

"I'm good at multi-tasking. But shouldn't I meet her first? What's her name?"

"Aubrey Michelle. Yes, I'll come home early and join you for the first day."

"Great! It's a deal!"

He threw his head back with a laugh. "Wow! Thanks, Mari Coleman!"

"And thank *you*."

He motioned to the parking lot. "And speaking of Aubrey—I'm on my way to pick her up for church. You're sure you don't need a ride somewhere—?"

"I've made you late—sorry! And no. Mom will be here soon."

"Well, tomorrow then."

"See you tomorrow." She waved, watching him through the lobby doors as he crossed the parking lot to the same vehicle with which he had picked her up the night before last. He was on his way to church. Now *that* was a wild thought! There was surely a story there, for the Sinclairs, she remembered, were not religious. Probably his wife's influence, she mused. Well, good for him. What a crazy coincidence, running into him twice in the space of a few days! But now she had a job—*two* jobs, since she had just unofficially committed herself to the coffee shop. It was only for the summer, she reasoned. She could endure it for a few months.

When her mother arrived, Mari was in the dining room having a one-sided conversation with her grandfather as he labored over his omelet breakfast.

"Good morning, honey!" she said, setting her purse on the table and planting a kiss on her father's head. "Good morning, Dad! Did you two get any sleep last night?" She handed Mari her phone.

"Slept great, actually," Mari answered, pocketing it. She would deal with Will's calls later.

Her mom slid onto a chair across from her. "I looked all over for your makeup bag, but I couldn't find it."

"I have it. You didn't happen to bring me some clothes, did you?"

"I thought what you wore yesterday was very nice. I figured you could go to church in that. You look fine."

"Mom!" she protested. "Every woman at the thing yesterday saw me in this! Plus, it smells like my deodorant."

"Then keep your coat on, and no one will notice. Dad, were you surprised to see Mari yesterday? You got to have a slumber party! Here— let me help you with that." She grabbed his fork and scraped his omelet scraps together into a more accessible pile. "There you go! You're doing so well!" She put the fork back into his hand and turned to her daughter. "So what's going on with Will, Mari? Your phone wouldn't settle down last night, and he was at our door again at seven a.m. with roses in hand—nice ones."

Mari simply shook her head.

Her mother gave her a knowing look. "He wouldn't believe me when I told him you weren't there. I said he could try to talk to you after church. So that's two days in a row that you've had a disagreement. I have some concerns about that! What's going on?"

"I told you last night. He said some things he shouldn't have." Her eyes flicked to her grandfather and back. "I don't know. I think we might be done."

Her mother searched her face. "And how do you feel about that?"

Mari fidgeted, picking at a fingernail. "I don't know. I like him a lot.

It's just that—" She shrugged. "I don't know. He was a jerk to say what he said."

Mrs. Coleman pushed her purse to the side. "Well, I won't ask what it was, but I *will* say that if you're not meant to be together, then you need to let him go. The sooner the better."

"I honestly don't know. I *do* like him. I feel sick about it."

She nodded. "Well, pray. If you're meant to be together—and you need to figure that out—then maybe the two of you should get some help on communication." At Mari's silence she continued: "Honey, guys make mistakes. People say things they shouldn't. It's not that uncommon. You learn from those things and move on. But you need to ask the Lord which way to move."

The dining room aide suddenly appeared, greeting them cheerfully. "Mr. Jones, look at how you polished up your plate! You must have been hungry this morning!" The woman smiled at Mari and her mother as she removed the man's soiled napkin from his chest. "Everyone's so proud of how he's doing!"

Mrs. Coleman bumped his arm. "Did you hear that, Dad?"

The old man beamed, pointing a gnarled finger toward the kitchen. "Taasty!"

The aide grinned and nodded. "I'll give your compliments to the chef! And how are you ladies this morning?"

"Wonderful!" Mari's mother answered kindly, reaching for her purse. "I wish we could stay, but we need to leave for church or we'll be late. Dad, Mari and I are heading out." She straightened his flannel shirt collar as she rose. "See you this afternoon."

He tipped his head, indicating that he understood.

Mari kissed him. "Bye! See you tomorrow, Poppy!" She slipped her coat off the back of her chair, letting her mother know she had everything with her and was ready to go.

The aide gathered up the dirty dishes. "See you this afternoon, Mrs. Coleman. More coffee, Mr. Jones?"

As they made their way toward the entrance, Mari turned to her mother. "Guess who I saw this morning? Mac Sinclair! You never told me he was coming in to help Poppy!"

Her mom was buttoning her coat. "Didn't I? He's been such a hero—coming in on his own time to do extra physical therapy with him. It's made such a big difference. I can't thank him enough."

"So *that's* why you called him to pick me up at the airport! I was wondering what made you think of Mac. It seemed so random. What's the connection with Poppy?"

"The Sinclairs were our neighbors, honey."

"Right, but why's he helping him so much?"

The electronic doors hissed open and closed as they exited to the parking lot.

"Grandpa was Mac's mentor. He helped him through his custody battle for his daughter a few years ago, back when he was going to therapy for his shoulder at Revere. They've gone out for coffee almost every week since. Well, until the stroke."

"Seriously? How come I've never heard about any of this?" Custody. Okay, question answered: Mac was divorced.

"Probably because you've been in Boston!"

"His daughter's *eight*, Mom."

"He only got her a few years ago, when she was three or maybe four—I'm not sure."

"Geez, what else have I missed?" Mari paused, waiting for her mother to unlock the vehicle. "Well, I offered to do his daycare."

Her mom threw a startled look over their car.

"It works out with my schedule to watch her after school, and he's offered to pay me." She climbed in and pulled on her seatbelt. "Plus, I'm taking the job at Taiton. After my shift I'll be able to spend a few hours with Poppy before going to Mac's. It works out perfectly."

"Oh, that's wonderful! And what about this summer when school lets out? Will you watch her then?"

"Oh. We didn't talk about that."

Mrs. Coleman twisted to look over her shoulder as she backed out of the parking spot. "Well, Grandpa's doctors have been so impressed with his progress that he may be able to go back to his assisted living apartment soon."

"That's what Mac said. If he keeps regaining mobility."

"Yes. So everything could change by then."

Mari smoothed her dress and settled back in the seat. So many changes.

Mari recognized the lime green Jeep facing the church parking lot entrance the moment they turned in.

"There he is," her mother said in a sing-songy voice as they glided by, as if it weren't already obvious. She parked and reached for her purse. "I'll remind you that church starts at ten. I'd ask that any discussion you and Mr. Wallace need to have honors that start time. There's nothing so important that you can't work things out after church somewhere."

Will was going to love hearing that, Mari thought, pulling the visor down to check her makeup in the mirror. "All right."

"I'll be praying for you, hon," her mom added, getting out of the car.

Before Mari could even move, Will was there opening the door on her side, his countenance miserable and contrite.

"Okay, I don't blame you for being angry, Mari. What I said was terrible. I wasn't thinking. Not at all. Please forgive me." He had on a navy windbreaker with a gray stocking cap pulled down over his forehead.

There was something about apologies like this that bugged her. Of course, she *wanted* to forgive him, but if she said that she did, then everything would be done in an instant. She didn't want to gloss over what happened. She wanted him to know how he had hurt her. But if she said anything about it, then she felt like a jerk for belaboring her point.

She pivoted in her seat. "You're entitled to your opinion, Will, but I was hurt that you thought so little of me and my grandfather as to throw your words out there without caring about their effect. That was super insensitive!"

He nodded. "You're absolutely right. I was wrong. What I said was uncalled for."

"You basically insinuated that we should have let my grandpa die."

His hands shot up. "Hey, I clearly did *not* say that! But I understand how you might have *heard* that. And I should have probably kept my mouth shut from the beginning. Mari, I'm very sorry. Will you please forgive me?"

Mari didn't know what to say.

"Marseilles, I'm dying here! You're my best friend! I was awake all night afraid you'd dump me over this. Please, please, *please* forgive me!"

She let out a long breath. "Okay, I forgive you, Will. But it was disturbing to me that those things came out of you."

"It was disturbing to me too! Truly, I'm sorry! I'll make it up to you somehow."

She gestured to the building. "Well, we're going to have to finish this conversation later. It's ten o'clock. My mom insists that we not be late."

He huffed, glancing over his shoulder. "As if that takes priority over this! You're important to me, Mars. More important than anything!"

"Can't you just call me Mari? It's my name, you know."

Will spread his hands. "Oh, come on! It's my way to have fun with you!"

She slid out of the car and closed the door, jerking her head. "Let's go. We'll talk about this after church. And lose the hat. You're not the stocking cap type, Will."

As if properly baited, he swiped the knit hat off his head, revealing large, dark letters inked across his forehead: I-D-I-O-T.

Mari gasped, her hands flying to her mouth. "*Will!* What did you do?"

"I'm owning it, Maribelle!"

"Is that permanent marker? Oh, my goodness!" She burst into laughter, doubling over. "How are you going to get that off?"

He grinned. "It's just ink. I have some wet wipes in my Jeep that'll do the trick. I hope."

She howled out a laugh. "Well, you'd better hurry up! What if someone sees you?"

"I would suffer the humiliation all for you."

"You nut!" She shook her head, noting the curious glances of a few latecomers hurrying toward the building. "What about *my* humiliation from being seen with you?"

"Hey, now—let's show a little respect!" He eyed himself proudly in the side mirror of her car. "You have *no idea* how difficult it is to write while looking into a mirror!"

"Seriously, Will—wipe that off! I'll wait if you hurry."

He gave a happy nod. "Your wish is my command."

The service was already twenty minutes in progress when the two of them entered the church, slipping quietly into a back row where Mari recognized Ariel Marquette sitting by herself at the opposite end, her long sleeves concealing her edgy tattoo. What an anomaly—such a timid girl going for such bold look—tattoo, hair, and the whole package. At Mari's nod, Ariel quickly returned her gaze to the front. Before long, however, Mari had to excuse herself to the restroom to quash a giggle fit. She couldn't stop thinking of Will's ridiculous act of penance.

Will was eager to leave directly after the service. Self-conscious of her rerun outfit, Mari was only happy to comply, though it was very un-Coleman of her, as her family typically stayed "till the last dog died," as her father put it. On their way through the lobby, however, a few family friends stopped to greet them, welcoming her back from school and asking about her grandfather. Will hung by her side as she talked with them, his forehead still pink from all his scrubbing.

Hearing a familiar laugh, Mari peered across the foyer to the coffee bar, spotting JoyAnne Strang with a pair of curly-haired, pink-clad preschoolers clinging to her legs while she talked with a foursome of women. Her children. And so it was true—JoyAnne went to Eagle Bluff now. Unbelievable. She watched as the girl gestured with her hands, apparently introducing her very nervous-looking friends to Kyla Watkins, whose ponytail swung back and forth as she tipped her head in greeting. JoyAnne's friends wore that awkward deer-in-the-headlights expression, as though they had never stepped foot inside a church before and likely never intended to again. Mari turned back to finish her conversation.

When her friends said goodbye, Mari glanced around for Will, who was straightening up from the nearby drinking fountain.

"I'm ready," she told him.

Another chorus of laughter rose from beside the coffee bar, automatically drawing their gaze. The cluster of ladies had now more than doubled in size, with their attention fixed on a grinning Kyla Watkins, who held her arms extended toward the hallway. Right then Peter Watkins appeared into view carrying their baby, who was flapping and kicking and squealing with happiness at the sight of his mother. At the group's sudden cheer, the baby jerked with a start, his face slowly puckering. Shortly he let out a loud wail, to the further delight of the ladies gathered.

"Nancy Drew and her entourage," Mari quipped dryly, turning for the door.

Will shot her a look. "What? Who's that?"

Mari lifted her chin toward Kyla. "Oh, you've heard all the drama, haven't you? How Kyla Watkins supposedly found a secret treasure in her house. And that girl, Leah, too. She said she stumbled upon a chunk of money her grandparents had left her. Must be nice!"

Will blinked. "I have not a clue what you're talking about!"

"Never mind. Let's go."

They had barely made it outside to the sidewalk when Mari heard her name called behind them. She turned to see Mac Sinclair hailing her, his other arm holding the glass door for a thick-bodied, dark-haired child with him.

Mari stopped short. "What? You're *everywhere*!"

Mac laughed, coming to join them. "We've got to stop meeting like this! Hey—glad I caught you!"

"I didn't know you went to church here!"

"Oh, well, I'm new." He gave Will a polite glance.

Mari waved. "Will, this is my old neighbor, Mac."

Will drew himself up taller, offering his hand. "William Wallace."

Mac met his eyes. "McAllister Sinclair."

"My boyfriend," Mari explained, to which Mac gave a nod. "Mac's family lived next door to us in the old neighborhood," she told Will. "He's helping my grandfather with physical therapy, and I just agreed to watch his daughter." She smiled down at the curly-headed girl curiously eyeing her. "You must be Aubrey! Hello!"

Mac placed his hands on her shoulders. "Yes, this is my daughter. And Aubrey—this is Miss Coleman. She's going to watch you after school until I get home from work—at our house."

Aubrey twisted to look at her dad. Will, too, glanced between them, utterly confused.

"I'm looking forward to getting to know you," Mari offered sweetly. "And I realize ten-year-olds don't need a sitter, so don't worry—we'll probably just hang out."

The girl's eyes flicked back to Mari. "I'm *eight*."

"Oh. Well, you look older. We'll figure it out."

Mac smiled as Aubrey looked away. "I was also surprised your family comes to Eagle Bluff."

"I grew up here. How long have *you* been coming?"

"Not long—just since Christmas. A high school coach invited me."

"That's when *you* started coming, isn't it, Will?" Mari elbowed him, turning back to Mac. "We met at a Christmas party here. His cousin brought him."

"Nice!" Mac said. "Well, hey—I'm glad to have run into you. As it turns out, I can't meet you at the bus tomorrow. After we talked this morning, I checked my schedule and found I'm booked tight with afternoon appointments. Plus I didn't get your phone number, and you should probably have mine."

"Oh, right." Mari pulled her phone out of her pocket, noting as she woke it up that she had eighteen missed calls from Will and twenty-seven unanswered texts. She shot him a look. *Sheesh!*

"I might be able to pull away Tuesday afternoon," Mac said, typing into his phone.

Mari nodded. "That works. But really"—she smiled down at Aubrey—"since we've been officially introduced, I think we could figure things out on the fly. I'm already familiar with the neighborhood. We grew up next door to each other," she reiterated to Will, then turned back to Mac, "although I never really knew you, since you were so much older."

"Likewise, only younger." He handed her his phone and took hers.

She entered her number and handed it back. "I'm up for it if you are."

Mac made a little sound. "Mari Coleman, you must be the most accommodating human on the planet! That would be awesome! Here—thank you."

She smiled, pocketing her phone. "It's not like I have a crowded schedule. Anyway,"—she looked warmly at Aubrey—"I'll meet you tomorrow afternoon, sweetie. I'll be there the moment you step off the bus."

Aubrey looked away without smiling.

Mac raised a finger. "Ah, the *bus*! Thank you! I'll have to arrange *that* this afternoon! Well, I'll let you two go then." He turned to Will, extending his hand. "William—pleasure to meet you. And Mari—'til tomorrow."

Aubrey's voice carried as Mac guided her back toward the church. "I *hate* that bus! Why can't I go to Grandma's? I'd rather go to Grandma's! And what's 'commodating'? Why did you call her that? I don't even know her!"

Mac said something unintelligible in reply.

Will flayed his hands. "What the heck! When did this go down? I knew absolutely *nothing* about any of this!"

"It just happened this morning. Come on—let's go." Abruptly she turned and headed across the parking lot toward his vehicle.

He followed. "Who is this guy? I never heard of him before, and all of a sudden you're watching his kid—?"

Mari paused at the Jeep, throwing him an amused look. "You were like a dog with your hackles up over there! I already told you—Mac's my old neighbor. He's been doing physical therapy with my grandfather to help him recover from the stroke. Do you have a problem with that? I'd watch his kid for free."

"Of course not! It's just so out of nowhere!"

"No kidding! But you needn't be threatened by Mac Sinclair. He's old, and he's got an eight-year-old, for heaven's sake. And I'm watching *her*, not him! Get over it!"

He stared at her a moment. "Well, it took me by surprise is all. But yeah, it's nice of him to help you, and nice of you to watch his kid."

He was backpedaling for sure. Mari lifted her chin. "Thanks. You're forgiven."

"So I don't have to get out the marker again?"

"I hope not!" She gave a loud sigh. "You know what we need, Will?

We need to do something fun."

He gave an exaggerated nod. "I'm with you there! I propose we start with lunch."

"Where are you taking me?"

He tapped his jaw. "Hmm. How 'bout The Wok again?"

"You just had Chinese yesterday!"

"Yeah, but I didn't have any of their wontons."

"Will, you're terrible! No, we're not going to The Wok!"

"Where do *you* want to go?"

"How about that sandwich shop downtown? We could walk there from my place."

He shook his head. "I've eaten there a few times, and I didn't like their bread."

"Then what do *you* like? I'll do anything but Chinese."

He opened her door, motioning. "Get in, you most accommodating human on the planet! I'll try to think of something. Are you absolutely sure you won't do Chinese?"

She threw him an incredulous look.

His hands flew up. "I'm *joking*! We'll go to the sandwich place. They do have good wraps."

He closed her door, and she waited for him to come around. As they were leaving the parking lot, she turned to him. "Okay, I might have misled you back there."

His brow rose. "So now you *do* want to go to The Wok?"

She snickered. "No, that's not it. I said I'd watch Aubrey Sinclair for free, but he *is* paying me. Still, I'm doing it because I'm grateful."

"Well, he better make it worth your while. That'd be the *last* thing I'd ever want to do on my afternoons. Here—" He handed her his phone. "Put on some tunes!"

Chapter Six

After a nearly perfect lunch date at the sandwich shop near her home, Will tried to convince Mari to walk several blocks farther to the old downtown bowling alley, since he had been on a bowling league in college. He bet Mari a *million bucks* he could whoop her butt, and although not an avid bowler, her competitive nature almost compelled her to accept the challenge. But she resisted.

"Will, my knee—remember?" she said, gesturing. "I can't bowl." She suggested they go to an arcade instead, where the two then clashed in a retro pinball game for the same bet. She lost, but not by much, and though the contest had been intense, so had their enjoyment of being together— both a relief and refreshment to Mari. It was what she had needed.

"If it weren't for this knee, you'd *so* owe me," she declared. "I'd be rich!"

"Oh, right!" Will jabbed in return, his face flushed from exertion. "Like you need your knee for pinball! And I was playing with half my brain tied behind my back!"

They held hands on the walk back to the condominium. Mari tried to convince him to keep going for a leisurely stroll around the lake on Taiton Green, but he declined.

"I just dropped a wad on these," he protested, indicating his new sneakers. "I want to keep them white."

"For real? The trail's paved, Will," she said.

But he insisted it was too wet. "One splash of mud and they're toast!"

Instead, he suggested asking if Shannon and her fiancé would want to play board games together. When they arrived at Mari's condo, however, Colton was already engrossed in an online video game while Shannon putzed with wedding crafts. He tossed Will another controller, and the two were soon lost in play, so Mari sat beside him on the couch and watched.

After a while she got bored and went to make some of Will's favorite cookies, scoring high when she delivered a plateful to the coffee table, as both he and Colton devoured more than half a dozen each.

When it was time to go, Will brought her with to the hallway outside so that he could kiss her in private.

"I had fun with you today, Marinara. Can you come over tomorrow?"

She smiled. "Me too. Probably. I don't know yet. It's my first day for both jobs."

"Okay, call me right away after work. We could order pizza or something. Or make a frozen one. It's cheaper."

"I'll definitely call. Good night, Will."

She returned to the kitchen, glad to have that dreamy feeling back.

Dinner was simple that evening. As this was the first night the three of them had been home together since Mari's return from college, they sat at the dining room table enjoying tuna melts while discussing their week's schedules and the logistics of who would use which car and when. Shannon was trying to sell hers and wanted it parked at a prominent corner downtown with a "for sale" sign on it. She had been driving their dad's car, but that left Mari without a vehicle. Shannon offered to give Mari a ride to work in the morning and then pick her up again in the afternoon, after which Mari could then drop *her* off and use the car until after she got back from the Sinclairs', stopping again to get Shannon on her way home.

"Honey, I'm sorry, but that's way too complicated," their mother broke in. "I think you're just going to have to use your own car and let Mari use Dad's. Besides, people are going to see the 'for sale' sign no matter where you park it."

"That's not true! A lot less people see it in the work parking lot."

Mari swiped some melted cheese with her finger. "Why not just buy your new car and trade your old one in at a dealer?"

Shannon shook her head. "Colt says I'd get a lot more selling it private party. I think we could make this work."

"Shannon, we're *all* sacrificing right now," their mother said.

At the edge in her voice, Mari's eyes darted upward. Her mother looked tired.

"I'll walk," she said quickly. "You can keep your car parked wherever you want. We can text at lunch and figure the ride thing out from there."

Shannon set her napkin on her plate. "No, it's fine. You can have Dad's vehicle. I'll see if I can maybe use Colt's."

"Thanks. But I'll probably still walk."

The Coleman household was in a flurry the next morning with the three women hustling in their separate directions for the day. Mrs. Coleman was the first to leave, looking sharp in her office dress and heels. She threw Mari a kiss going out the door, calling out a goodbye to her other daughter, who was still in the shower. Mari kissed the air back at her. Less than a minute later, Shannon came bursting out of the bathroom with her hair wrapped in a towel.

"Can you get my lunch out of the fridge?" she called, flying into her bedroom. "I can't be late!"

Mari slipped on her shoes and met Shannon at the door, handing off the pre-packed lunch.

"Thanks!" her sister said, rushing toward the elevator. "Hurry if you're going down with me!"

"I'll take the stairs," Mari said, forgetting about her knee. She took the next elevator down.

The cold spell that had dumped the foot of snow on New Hampton the previous week had entirely moved on, and today the weather was back to typical April—breezy and mild with spots of sunshine and an occasional threat of showers. Mari enjoyed her brisk trek across Taiton Green on her way to the Campus Center, where an attractive windowed cove on the south side of the spacious building housed the Coffee Break. She imagined that some shriveled, gray-haired soul on the Board of Regents had proposed its cliché-ish name, but the Taiton student body apparently wasn't turned off by it, for there always seemed to be a line at the counter. Granted, specialty coffees were a college staple. But even a segment of "townies" frequented the place, finding there a quiet spot to read their e-books or browse the news on their phones or tablets while sipping their preferred recipes of the dark brew.

Mari arrived early, threading through the clusters of square tables in the dining room to the front counter, where she asked to speak to John, the manager, as instructed by Shannon. After she explained who she was, he shook her hand and indicated for her to join him behind the counter, directing her to hang her jacket in the back. Glancing approvingly at the logoed work shirt of Shannon's she had donned, he threw her an apron and set about the task of training her in on everything she already knew but would need to be executed exactly *their* way.

As the process wore on through the morning, she was introduced to the other employees on her shift one by one, most of them students and younger than her. Carefully Mari noted their names. First, quiet *A-plus* Alyssa, who scored high for pleasantness and for filling Mari in on important details that John missed in her training. Next was motor-mouth Mark with the re-*mark*-ably scraggly beard, whose running statements were laced with grand exaggerations and excessively more detail than necessary. *Can-do* Candace was down-to-business, sporting fuchsia hair and a gap between her teeth. Then Boris, the suave Russian exchange student with his flashy red eyeglasses and mop of curly hair. Mari mentally paired him with Natasha of Rocky and Bullwinkle.

And then there was high-strung Tatum, the thirty-something alpha dog to whom everyone gave way. Observing her interaction with several employees, Mari was left with the impression that she was either the manager's right-hand man or his daily migraine. Possibly both. Tall with severe eyes, she barked out orders and opinions without reserve, especially to Mark regarding his incessant dialogue. Mari settled on *Hate-him Tatum* to lock in her name.

After mastering the machines, Mari was assigned to assemble and wrap the half dozen or so sandwiches offered on their limited menu, with Candace and Tatum as her partners. Candace was watchful and diligent to correct Mari's mistakes, taking time to answer her questions. Tatum, on the other hand, stood aloof in her black uniform with her tight, white, long-sleeved undershirt, constructing her sandwiches like a master and filling a whole tub of them for the cooler before Candace and she had done half that amount, though Mari knew she was the one who had slowed them down.

"This seems like a lot!" Mari mused. "Are you sure we need this many?"

"Just wait 'til the first rush," Candace commented, disposing of her hairnet when they had finished their food prep.

Mari discovered what she meant promptly at 9:52 when a sudden surge of students doubled the line at the front counter. Every barista sprang into action, knowing exactly his or her position in the little workspace to efficiently take and fill orders.

"Class just got out," Alyssa explained over the hiss of the steamer. "It'll be steady now through lunch."

"What should I do?" Mari asked, requesting a task.

"You can get out of the way to start with!" Tatum growled behind her.

Mari squeezed against the counter to let her pass.

"Keep an eye on the front case," Alyssa suggested, twirling a long spoon through the liquid before pouring it into a cup. "The fruit cups and sandwiches go fast."

Right then Mari flinched at the slap of a cold, wet rag on her neck. She gasped, pulling it off, whirling to face Tatum, who jerked her head toward the dining room.

"*I've* got the front case. Go bus tables." With a flip of her chin, she turned back to the latte she was constructing.

With her jaw still hanging, Mari looked down at the dark blotch the sopping rag had left on her shirt, but her coworkers carried on with their duties as if nothing out of the ordinary had occurred. Mari surmised they were either too consumed with managing the line snaking out the door or too afraid to challenge Tatum. Both scenarios seemed equally plausible. But since it was only her first day on the job, she pulled herself together and went to collect dirty dishes and wipe tables.

The customer area of the Coffee Break was made up of two main sections. The front half, where the service counter was located, was filled with square tables surrounded by sturdy wooden chairs, the atmosphere resembling the dining area of a fast-food restaurant, where students came to get their coffees and accompanying eats or treats and got down to business to enjoy them. It was busy and noisy there, as the tables were constantly pushed together or apart to accommodate the varying sizes of each party.

The back half of the Coffee Break was where patrons came to linger, the space partitioned into several smaller sections furnished with a variety of eclectic couch and patterned armchair sets and corresponding side and coffee tables. Down the center of the room dividing the two contrasting seating areas was a high counter with a privacy screen down its middle on which were installed multiple charging stations for electronics. Most students frequenting this tall counter sat solo on the cushioned barstools to navigate their laptops undisturbed.

With her wet cloth, Mari started in the back, moving between the clustered furniture settings to clean end tables and gather up miscellaneous trash and dirty dishes left behind, working her way toward the high counter divider, filling the dish bin on the corner trash and recycle center as she moved along. Then she hefted the bin back to the kitchen, rinsed her rag, and returned with an empty tub, starting the process over again, this time in the front room, although by now many of the tables were crowded with students. She worked quickly, wiping down what she could.

On her way back to the bin clutching together five partially filled water glasses, Mari passed a forty-something man with dark, wiry hair reading at one of the square tables beside the windows, a neat stack of papers next to his coffee mug. He looked up to nod politely at her, then paused to turn in his seat, his eyes narrowing.

"I know you! You're new here, but I *know* you from somewhere!"

She paused at the dish bin, noting him to be familiar too.

"For the life of me, all I can think of is 'William Wallace,' but I'm confident that's *not* your name!" he said.

The guy on the plane. Mari smiled and said, "William Wallace is my—"

"—Your boyfriend!" he chimed in synch as recognition dawned. "Yes, yes—the young lady on our flight! As I recall, you were a little concerned about my boys kicking your seat."

Instantly her cheeks grew warm. "And as *I* recall, you had absolutely no clue who Marilee Montayne was!"

His lip curled in amusement, and he gave a nod of concession. "Touché. But let's keep that tidbit under wraps, shall we? You have no idea how weird people get when they connect those dots. It's Mari, isn't it?" He extended his hand. "Dr. David Grant, professor of history."

So that *was* his name. Impressed that he remembered hers and a little wowed that Marilee Montayne's husband wanted to shake her hand, she approached, placing her damp hand in his, now observing that his tidy pile of papers were student essays.

"Welcome to the Coffee Break!" He waved as though the place were his. "I'm surprised to see you here, Miss Mari. From the sound of it the other day, I was sure you'd never darken the doorstep of a lame school like Taiton College! What gives?" He winked at her surprise. "Now, now— don't get all weirded out! I simply make it a habit to remember details about my students. It builds connection."

"Apparently! I had no idea I'd made such an impression!"

"One never does, huh? Now, weren't you working at some women's center—or hoping to?"

Once more Mari shook her head in amazement. "Correct again! And sad to say, that job didn't pan out. My childhood nemesis stole the position from under me."

He leaned away. "*Childhood nemesis!* My goodness! There's history, mystery, and pain packed in a statement like that! Tell me—does Childhood Nemesis have a name?"

"Yes. JoyAnne Strang. You wouldn't know her."

His brow shot up. "Au contraire! JoyAnne is friends with our nanny,

Kyla Watkins! So *she* got the position, huh? What a small world!"

Oh, yeah. She forgot. Mari shifted uncomfortably. "Then that's all I'll say about that."

"Fair enough." He nodded back. "So here you are!"

"Yes, here I am. So—is this what you do?" She gestured to his table. "You hang out here memorizing details of people's lives?"

He glanced at his papers and back at her. "Oh, I find the Break a handy little place to pass a few hours between classes. Good coffee. Great atmosphere. I get a little work done, and I have a little out-of-the-classroom interaction with my students and other interesting folks like you."

"I saw you reading."

"Finest history book ever written!" He flopped the cover closed to show her. "Are you familiar with it?"

Mari blinked. Was he joking? It was a Bible. "Is it legal for you to have that here?"

He drew back. "Legal? What kind of question is that? Of course, it's legal! Why wouldn't it be?"

"Well, we're in a school."

"We're in a *coffee shop*!" He tapped his mug. "I can read what I want here! How about you? Have *you* ever read it?"

She glanced around her. "Parts."

He eyed her curiously. "You look uncomfortable. Are you offended that I have a Bible?"

"Well, no. But some people might be."

"Some people. How about you?"

"I'm okay with it, I guess. I grew up going to church."

"That's what you said on the plane. So do you mind if I ask you a question?"

"About what?"

"Are you familiar with the Bible story of the prodigal son? You know, the young man who asked his father for his inheritance and went out and squandered it. Do you know that story? Came to his senses and went home. His father threw him a party with a fatted calf and all that."

"Yes, I've read it," she responded hesitantly.

"Great! That's what I was reading just now. Part of my philosophy in education is to challenge my students with thought-provoking questions that help them focus on important things in their lives. I have one for *you*, if you're game!"

"What kind of question?" Again, she glanced around. Was he

seriously talking about the Bible in a public coffee shop?

"No pressure, Mari. Opting out is fine with me."

"What's your question?"

"All right. Don't answer me now. I'll ask my question. You think about it and bring me your answer tomorrow—if you want, that is, okay? So here you go: Of our characters in the prodigal son story—the father, the prodigal, or the older brother—with which do you most closely identify?"

"*Pfft*—none of them!"

He held up a finger. "Ach—*tomorrow!* I'll ask for your answer tomorrow! So go find your Bible and brush up on the story."

Mari stared at him.

"And now I should probably apologize for keeping you from your work. You're getting quite the stink-eye from the boss lady over there." He jerked his chin in the direction of the front counter.

Glancing over her shoulder, she met Tatum's steely glare as the woman handed a beverage to a waiting customer. Mari turned back to the professor. "What is her problem? If I get fired, I won't be here to answer your question."

"If you get fired, find me. I'll go to bat for you. Pleasure visiting with you, Miss Mari. Have an excellent day!" He dropped his hand heavily on the stack of essays and slid them forward.

"Same. See you tomorrow."

After another quick pass through the tables, Mari returned to the kitchen with the next bin of dirty dishes. While unloading them into the dishwasher, she got an earful from Tatum, who told her in no uncertain terms that freshman ought not to be brown-nosing with the professors while they're supposed to be working. Knowing that nothing she said would make a difference to Tatum, Mari reined herself in and zipped her lip—though it took every ounce of self-control for her to do it—while the woman ground in her point multiple times.

"I like Professor Grant," Alyssa told her quietly when Tatum was out of earshot. "He always remembers my name and asks me about my family."

"He's a creep," Candace stated, walking by at that moment, who also had overheard the scolding. "I call him 'The Reverend.' He's always trying to bait people, like he's recruiting for a cult or something worse. Take my advice—stay away from him!"

Mari eyed her, startled by her bitter tone.

"Who are you talking about?" Boris asked in his endearing Russian accent.

Candace gestured. "Dr. Grant, the professor who sits at the end of the row by the windows."

Boris craned his head to see. "Yeah, him. We talk once. He is friendly man. He has been to Moscow."

Mari, too, glanced toward the professor, wondering if he ever gave her coworkers Bible assignments. She didn't exactly want to ask, especially since re-*mark*-able Mark had spied their cluster and was on his way, unwilling to miss an opportunity to display his vast and superior knowledge of whatever he would discover their topic to be.

Suddenly Tatum appeared, as if perceiving their discussion. "People like him live in a bubble with their perfect lives and try to tell others what they should think and believe. It irks me. He shouldn't be allowed to do it."

At Tatum's pronouncement the topic was closed, and everyone scooted back to work.

Mari's shift at the Coffee Break ended later than she had expected, but after she got off, she was not sorry she had walked there, for she needed the exercise and fresh air on her trek home to help divert her sour thoughts from *Hate-em* Tatum. Thank God the job was only part-time! Shannon had texted earlier that she had left their dad's car for her, so Mari went straight to the parking garage below the condominiums to get it. Carefully she navigated the vehicle to the exit and soon was on the highway heading toward Riverview.

Her grandfather was resting when she arrived. Two care center staffers were just leaving his room and gave a good report on the morning. One of the nurses praised Mari for how involved their family was in helping their grandfather, but she also added that physical rest was important for his recovery as well. Mari was relieved to hear it, for it meant an hour of guilt-free relaxation for herself while her grandfather napped.

When he awoke, he greeted her by name, and Mari came to sit with him on the bed. With his gnarled hand, he was quick to point out a pot of yellow jonquils on his tray table.

"Aren't those cheerful!" Mari exclaimed. "Who brought those in, Pop?"

"Shaannn!"

"Shannon? Well, that was nice of her! I guess she's your best girl today!"

"Two," he said. "Two bessst!" He pointed toward Mari.

"Two best girls?" she asked.

"Yesss!"

Mari laughed. "You got it, Poppy!"

Then she settled in and gave him the rundown on her day—minus the complicated parts of coworker drama and Dr. Grant's intriguing assignment. She did, however, tell him about the professor and whom he was married to and how they had previously met on her flight home. Then she reviewed her college saga with him and showed him the scars on her knee to refresh his memory of the surgery she had had a few years ago.

And before she knew it, it was time to go.

"See you tomorrow, Pop Pop," she said, kissing his cheek. "Mom will be here soon."

On her way down the hall, she donned her jacket, patting her side pocket to make sure her dad's vehicle key was still there. As she skirted a custodial cart parked beside a resident's door, a young woman exited the room with a trash bag. Both women looked up at the same time, and Mari started.

"Ariel—hey!"

"Oh, hi," the girl breathed, standing to attention.

Mari noted her uniform. "You work here?"

"Yeah." She nodded, holding Mari's gaze.

"Really? Wow! My grandfather is here—did you know that?" She motioned down the hall. "He's in 108!"

"Yeah. I clean his room."

Mari blinked in surprise. "What? You never said anything on Saturday!"

"It, um—never worked out to tell you." Color crept into her pale cheeks. She curled a strand of black hair around her ear with her snake-tattooed arm.

"Oh. Sorry. Well, this is cool! I'll have to let Mom and Shannon know you work here."

"I see them sometimes."

"Oh. I didn't know that either." Mari paused guiltily. Here she had seen Ariel twice over the weekend and she had practically ignored her both times. "Well, thanks for all you do, Ariel. It means a lot to our family."

She dropped her eyes. "No problem."

She looked tired, Mari thought. So tired. As if she were coming down with something. Or as if she were depressed. Lonely, perhaps. Should she ask her to do something? Go have coffee? She eyed the windy reptile adorning the slender girl's arms. What in the world would they talk about? She cleared her throat. "So when do you get off? When's your shift over?"

"Um, it varies."

Another long pause.

Mari nodded. "All right. Well, if you ever need a ride or anything, give me a call, okay?"

"Okay, thanks."

"I need to get going, but nice seeing you, Ariel."

"Yeah. Bye!" Immediately she turned to pull a new trash bag from a box on the cart and shake it out, as if the door to the conversation had fallen shut.

Mari felt a little bad as she continued down the hall, but she couldn't do it. She just couldn't bring herself to invite Ariel out. It was easier to converse with her struggling grandfather than that girl. Plus she had changed so much. Her look. That nose ring was so distracting. And that tasteless tatt—! What was going on with her?

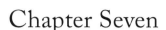

Chapter Seven

The mid-afternoon traffic was mild that day, affording Mari an early arrival to her old neighborhood. Happily, she turned off at the Whitmore exit and took a right at the "T" before the Oakwood Cemetery, gliding onto Frost Street as she had done hundreds of times throughout her childhood. If she had stayed on Whitmore, the street would have curved the other way around the cemetery into an older section of New Hampton, continuing for many blocks until reaching the Whitmore Complex, a series of six identical four-story apartment buildings dominating one side of the street, an affordable housing project of a previous New Hampton era.

But Mari never went that way, as instructed by her father who had deemed the area "unstable" back in her driver's training. As a naive fifteen-year-old, Mari had thought "unstable" meant the propensity of earthquakes in that area or something. Her "duh" moment came when their local evening news reported a record-breaking drug bust that had occurred in the Whitmore neighborhood. The revelation opened up a deeper level of discussion with her father about safety and awareness. Plus, she never had a reason to go that way anyway.

For Mari, driving into the secluded Frost neighborhood was like entering a private sanctuary, for it offered the aura of country living despite being tucked in the center of the metropolis. As she wound her way past familiar homes, her mind replayed fond images from her childhood: young friends riding bikes and shooting hoops on basketball court driveways, old men and dads on lawn mowers or leaning under car hoods, moms buckling children into family minivans, grandmas with shopping bags and yappy lap dogs. So many memories.

Without thinking, she automatically pulled into her former driveway near the end of the street, then caught herself and moved her car next door to Mac's, parking at the curb rather than in the driveway of his detached garage. His was the last house on the block before Frost Park, a broad, pie-shaped grassy meadow hemmed in on one side by a crescent-shaped wooded ridge curling eastward, and the Whitmore apartments on the far opposite side, the backside of the cemetery becoming the "crust" of the pie. Due to the breadth of the park, Whitmore residents rarely traveled Mari's old neighborhood by foot; nor did they visit by car, for Frost was a dead-end street and separated from Whitmore by the cemetery and the park.

By most Frost Street residents, the flat, open acreage of Frost Park was simply dubbed "the field," as there was nothing "park" about it—no playground equipment or even a ball diamond there and mowed by the city only a few times a summer. Nevertheless, the space was prized for its primitive dirt walking paths, as well as its woodsy charm, as deer, raccoons, and other curious critters often ventured down from the thick foliage on the hill to enjoy the rich, green plain—or neighborhood trash cans, to her father's chagrin.

Exiting her car, Mari gazed wistfully at her grand, old two-story house from Mac's sidewalk. The most notable change was the tall wooden fence erected around the property by the new owners, separating their yard from both the Sinclairs' and the Gordons'. Though tastefully done, the lumber barrier seemed out of place, lending a formidable air to such a friendly setting. Yet the place hadn't been neglected, she observed, as evidenced by the mowed lawn and neatly trimmed front bushes. The porch sported a fresh coat of white paint, and her mother's tulip bed beside the steps was weeded for their imminent bloom. Part of her wanted to run up those stairs to knock and ask to see the inside of the house. Yet *Why,* she asked herself. It would never compare to the way she remembered it.

She checked the time, not wanting to be late to the bus stop. Aubrey Michelle. It was time to get in gear for watching an eight-year-old. Would the girl be into dolls and dresses and hair? Was she a reader? Did she take piano lessons? Dance lessons? Did she like sports? Mari would find out in about seven minutes. Glancing back at Mac's house, a sudden thought hit her. Quickly she shot him a text.

"I have no key to your house!"

That could be an issue.

The walk to the bus stop took less than five minutes. Mari sat alone on the narrow bench in the children's wind shelter, her eyes resting on Dixie's, the old ma and pa convenience store across the street. She was amazed it was still there. She wondered how old Mr. Dixie was nowadays.

Mr. Dixie's name was actually Carl Fordunger, but he called the store after his wife, Dixie, rather than their last name—understandably so, given the word *dung* in it. Over the years Dixie Fordunger became simply "Mrs. Dixie," after which young patrons logically dubbed Carl "Mr. Dixie," and the names stuck. The Dixies—er, Fordungers—were good people, known for their diligent watch over the children at the bus stop across the street, coming to the rescue of many a kid who had missed the bus. They were also known for their hawk-eyed vigilance of their store, although they had a unique way of dealing with grabby-fingered offenders.

Mari had once experienced Mr. Dixie's expertise firsthand when she was ten. That day she had set two packs of bubble gum onto his counter with the corresponding coins for purchase while two over-sized Snickers bars lay secretly tucked deeply in her backpack. She stared at the gum, unable to lift her eyes to look at Mr. Dixie, who had come to wait on her.

"Miss Mari Coleman, how are you?" he said cheerfully.

"Good," she replied. Crud. He knew her.

"And how are your folks? I talked to your father the other day. He came in to pick up milk for your mother."

And her parents. Mari swallowed. "They're g-good."

"Wonderful."

He smiled, opening the till to dispense her change. Hastily she turned to leave, but he called her name. She turned, her heart pounding out of her chest.

He looked kindly at her. "Miss Mari, I care about your family, and I care about you. So for that reason, I'm going to *give* you the candy bars you put in your bag today. That way you can go to bed tonight without feeling guilty for stealing—because I'm *giving* them to you."

Mari remembered nearly fainting right then and there. She had no idea what she said to him, but she was so flustered that she almost stepped in front of a passing car when she crossed the street, the driver, in turn, laying on his horn and calling out a scolding. She had learned her lesson that day, returning the chocolate bars to Mr. Dixie in a paper bag the next morning before school with a note of apology. As far as she knew, her parents had never found out about her sin, nor had she been tempted to steal again.

Now where she sat, Mari heard the roar of the bus before she could see it, but soon it appeared, grinding noisily to a halt in front of her with a squeak and hiss of its brakes. Its skinny double doors popped open, and Mari stood, watching a brightly dressed little girl delicately navigate each step and hop out, her pigtails flopping with the jump. Behind her came a little boy with a backpack half as big as him. Then another handful of kids slightly older deboarded, also dispersing toward their homes. As Mari waited for Aubrey, she could hear the ruckus of obvious fighting on the bus. After the space of a few seconds, a bigger boy cut into view, yelling something back over his shoulder as he bounded clumsily out of the bus, taking a run for it—from Aubrey, who came charging noisily out after him.

"Give it back, you stupid-head!" she demanded angrily, flinging her pink-and-silver backpack onto the boulevard.

The boy turned, taunting her with a sporty stocking cap. "Come and get it, Dumpy-lumpy!" He tossed it high from one hand to the other.

"I said give it back!" She jumped, trying to grab it, but he held it over her head.

Immediately Mari stepped in. "Hey, hey—kids!"

It caused enough distraction for Aubrey to wrench the hat from the boy. "You pig!" she spat. With both hands she gave him a shove that landed him on his seat.

"*You're* a pig!" he retorted from the ground. "And your mom's an ugly pig too!" He shot a look of disdain toward Mari.

"Hey—that's enough!" Shocked at their behavior, Mari whirled to the bus driver for support, but the woman shook her head as if she had had more than enough of dealing with them herself. She closed the bus doors, and the motor revved to life as the bus drove away.

The boy had scrambled to his feet, hollering back from his retreat down the sidewalk, "Ugly-buggly! You're uglier than a dead toad!"

"Shut up, you stupid-head!" Aubrey spouted. "You're a big bully!"

"Come back here!" Mari called after the boy. "Young man, you come back here and apologize!"

"*No!*" Aubrey huffed, pulling the hat firmly over her poofy hair. "Don't make him come back! I don't want to talk to him! He's so dumb!" She marched over to scoop up her backpack and turned to tromp toward home.

Mari glanced back at the departing boy, then hurried to catch up with Aubrey.

"So, uh, hi," she said, looking down at her. "My name's Mari, in case you don't remember."

Aubrey gave a dark glance upward.

"How was school today?"

"I *hate* school," she sputtered, "and I *hate* Connor Haddington!"

"I see. And that was Connor Haddington?"

"Well, *duh!*" She tossed her head, quickening her pace.

Okay, someone needed space. Deliberately Mari paused, letting the girl walk ahead. Her phone buzzed in her pocket. Mac had responded to her text.

"A has a key. Good luck!"

Her brow went up. *Right.* Heavens, was she always like this? Mari sighed, breathing a silent prayer.

Calmly she trailed her charge, but when she got to her old block, she slowed, taking her time to reminisce. So many memories. Someday soon she would visit Miss Susan, she thought while strolling past the Gordons' house—perhaps with Aubrey, depending on how things sorted out after today.

Then she turned toward her home—*former* home—pausing long to take in the beloved American foursquare architecture with its updated vinyl siding her dad had hung once upon a time. Everything in her wished she lived there again. She craned her neck, straining to see through the three-season porch screens, curious at how the new occupants had set it up. She had been in third grade the year her dad had erected those screens—slightly older than Aubrey was now, who, as indicated by the telltale banging of the Sinclairs' screen door, had just let herself into her house. Good—the key was a non-issue.

She pivoted to study Mac's house, a mirror-image of her family's old dwelling, a full two stories with the same predictable template, except that his porch was open. A sturdy wooden swing hung from the ceiling by chains on the far side next to the field. She smiled, recognizing that the swing was why she was here in the first place. As she had requested of Mac, she would soon park herself on that seat to think, with the added pleasure of overlooking the field and the soon-to-bloom lilacs alongside his driveway. But first she had an angry eight-year-old to contend with. She set off resolutely down the walk, psyching herself up for the job.

Entering the house, she stepped over Aubrey's backpack, sweatshirt, and shoes chucked onto the smooth varnished floor of the wide foyer. Immediately her gaze lifted to the anticipated oak staircase to her left, its lovely carved spindles turning at a landing, where a floral stained-glass window similar to theirs at her old home graced the Sinclairs' exterior wall on the field side of their house. To her right, Aubrey bounced on the edge of a brown leather couch in the living room while aiming the remote control at the television mounted above the mantle. She glanced back, briefly acknowledging Mari's entrance.

"Hello again," Mari said. "Doing any better?"

The girl shrugged. "What's for snack?"

Mari temporarily ignored her, whisking the girl's coat off the floor to hang it on a decorative hook in a cove at the bottom of the stairs. She placed the backpack in one of the handsome oak cubbies and set her shoes onto the mat, leaving her own beside them. A wave of homesickness washed in as she glanced down the hallway that she knew led to the kitchen. So many similarities.

Admiring the multi-colored rug on which Mac's furniture was arranged, she joined Aubrey, seating herself at the opposite end of the couch that faced the fireplace, the tall windows on either side of it providing an ample view of the neighbors' new boarded fence. To her left, an airy dining room adjoined the living room, the rooms separated by matching colonnades on either side, with glass-doored cabinets at the base of each pillar. The dining room table was set parallel to a lovely bay window with a band of clear, diamond-shaped leaded glass panes across the top, the window's perimeter adorned with sheer curtains and tiebacks, offering a similar panorama of the dismal new fence. In the olden days the Sinclairs would have viewed her parents' fine landscaping from that table. Mentally Mari found herself planting clematis and hydrangea bushes along that entire barricade.

"Do you have any homework?" she asked Aubrey, but the young girl was busy springing on her seat to the beat of a commercial jingle. "Aubrey, do you have any homework?" she repeated.

"No," she said without glancing up.

"What are you watching?"

No response.

Mari repeated the question.

"My *show*!" She motioned to the television, as if it were obvious. "I'm super hungry! Can you get me something to eat? And I *don't* want salad."

"Salad?" Mari threw her a look.

"My grandma makes me eat salad for snack. She says I'm fat."

Mari jerked. "What? Okay. What would you like to eat?"

She turned from the screen to flash a smile. "Ice cream—?"

"Ah! Well, we're not having that! I'll see if I can scratch up something for a smoothie."

"I don't like smoothies. They make me puke."

She blinked. "Fine. I'll make one for myself then. Let me know if you change your mind."

Mari cut through the dining room to the kitchen but stopped short upon entering, staring in delight at the stylish new countertops and cupboards and roomy center island. Nice! The Sinclairs had redone their kitchen! Mari drew out her phone to snap pictures of the spacious room from various angles. Her mother was going to drool! An update like this had been her dream, though she had chosen the condo route instead. If only. Mari sighed.

"Hey!" Aubrey called from the living room. "Can you bring me some chips instead? Please?"

Mari shook her head. Wow, that was going to get old fast. She had better have a talk with Mac. At least the girl had said, *Please*. Quickly Mari gave herself a self-guided tour of the Sinclair kitchen to find a blender. While gathering items from the refrigerator and freezer, she was surprised to discover a bag of fresh kale in the veggie drawer. Perfect!

"Impressive, Mac," she murmured, setting it on the counter next to the frozen strawberries.

After some chopping and blending, Mari returned to her spot on the couch beside Aubrey to sip her fruity smoothie through a metal straw. She set a second one on a coaster on the coffee table beside a small plate with a peanut butter sandwich.

"This is all I could come up with today," she said. "It's okay with me if you pass. I don't mind. So tell me about school."

Aubrey looked at her choices, then grabbed the remote to pause her show, lifting her eyes in a challenge. "Grandma lets me have ice cream after school."

Mari frowned. "I thought you said she made you eat salad!"

"Well, my *dad* lets me have ice cream."

"Oh. Okay. We'll talk about that when he gets home. In the meantime, just try a sip." She gestured to the smoothie. "Or not. I don't really care."

The girl hesitated, and Mari guessed she was weighing out her odds of success to hold out for ice cream or not. But then she gave a little wiggle and reached for the glass.

Immediately Mari looked away, asking very matter-of-factly, "Is Conner Haddington always mean to you?"

Aubrey curiously sucked the straw while crafting her answer. "He and another boy tease me. They always wait for me at recess—he and Ty West."

"In a mean way? Do they say bad things to you? Or do they just want attention because they like you? Sometimes boys do that, you know."

She shrugged, licking her lips. "Sometimes they say bad things."

"Like today—that wasn't nice."

Aubrey said nothing, eyeing the sandwich. In a moment she succumbed and took a bite.

"Do you tell the teacher when that happens?"

"Sometimes," she mumbled through her mouthful.

"Well, you should tell the teacher if someone says mean things to you. Or if they hit you or anything. And you should tell your dad too."

Aubrey bounced on her seat a few times, then took another bite.

"And what Connor Haddington said today about your mom—that was very unkind. I'm sorry he said that about her."

The girl threw her a strange look.

"That your mom is ugly," Mari reminded her. "That wasn't nice. No one should call someone ugly. Nor should anyone call someone a 'pig' or a 'stupid-head.'" She cocked an eyebrow.

Aubrey blinked. "He was talking about *you*. I don't have a mom. My mom died."

Mari caught up her jaw. "I'm—I'm *so* sorry to hear that, Aubrey!" Oh, brother! That would have been a handy piece of information to know ahead of time! She would be talking to Mac. Mentally she was already making a list.

But Aubrey merely chomped another bite of the sandwich and began to bounce again. In mid-chew she took a long slurp of her smoothie, gasping as she pulled the straw from her lips. "Can I watch my show now?"

Mari shook her head. "Not quite yet. I want to talk to you. Tell me what your day was like at school."

She shrugged. "I don't know."

"Did you do anything interesting? Anything fun?"

She furled her brow. "Hmm—not really."

"Okay. What's your favorite subject?"

"Recess."

A classic kid answer. "And what do you like to do during recess?"

"Um, swing. Or play kickball—but only without Connor Haddington. He is *so* annoying!"

"Ah, I see. And your favorite subject besides recess? You know—like math, science, art?"

She shook her head. "I don't like *any* subjects."

Mari remained quiet, waiting, but the young girl simply finished the sandwich.

"What do you usually do after school?"

"Watch my shows."

"Okay. What else?"

She rolled her shoulders, making a sound that communicated that she didn't know.

"Do you play with dolls? Or Barbies?"

Aubrey screwed up her face. "I'm not a baby!"

"Then tell me what you like to do! Do you like to read?"

Her face brightened. "I like it when my dad reads to me!"

Mari nodded. "That's good! What kind of books does he read to you?"

She gave a bounce. "Long books with lots of chapters. Stories about animals that have adventures. They're like people—only they're animals."

"Cool! What else do you do with your dad?"

"I don't know. Lots of things." She hung her head back. "*Now* can I watch my show?"

"Not quite yet. Do you have any chores that you're supposed to do after school?"

Aubrey shook her head from side to side. "Nope!" She raised the smoothie for one last cold slurp, sucking long and noisily for every last drop.

"I'm glad you liked the smoothie."

Aubrey drew her sleeve across her mouth. "It was okay."

"Well, if you have to puke, do it in the bathroom. All right, before you can watch your show, you need to ask me two questions about my life."

Aubrey frowned. "Why?"

"Don't you want to know me? Just two questions!"

Aubrey's eyes dropped to Mari's black shirt and slacks. "Okay. Why are you dressed so ugly? You look like a bad guy or something. And your shirt is dirty."

Mari glanced down at the dried smear of whipped cream across her belly. "Golly, you're right! I guess I goobed myself at work. This is my uniform. I work at a coffee shop in the morning and forgot to bring a change of clothes."

A bounce. "Is that why you smell weird too?"

"Do I smell weird?"

"Yeah. You smell like,"—she leaned in, sniffing the air—"I don't know—like cake or something. It smells weird."

Mari gave a sheepish smile. "That's probably why."

Aubrey sighed loudly. "Now can I please, please, *please* watch my show?"

"One more question."

The girl shook her head, flicking up two fingers. "Nope, I already asked two!"

Mari paused. The girl was smart; she had to give her credit for that.

"Fair enough. But first, can I tell you something cool about me?"

"Will it take long to tell it?"

"I used to live in the house right next door." Mari pointed out the window. "You could see it better before that fence was put in."

"My dad already told me that. He said you were a snotty baby who cried a lot."

"Did he?" Mari folded her arms. "Well, I'm not now! Have you met the family who lives there? Do they have any kids?"

Aubrey shook her head. "Nope. Only Mr. Eden, but I don't like him. He's evil."

"*Evil?* Goodness, Aubrey! Why would you say that?"

"He keeps mean dogs, and once I seen him do something really bad: he dug a hole in his backyard and buried a dead body in it! I seen him do it!"

Mari gave a cry. "Aubrey! Did you tell your dad?"

"Yes—but he doesn't believe me! He *never* does." She gave a loud sigh. "Can we be done now?"

Mari stared at her, not sure of what else to say. "All right—you may watch your show."

With a happy bounce Aubrey snatched up the remote to un-pause the DVR. "I *love* this cartoon! Wanna watch it with me?"

"Sure." Mari settled back into the warm leather, grateful that she was at least invited into one part of Aubrey's world. Candidly she watched the child, her list of topics to discuss with Mac growing moment by moment.

When Mac walked in from work that night, Mari was tending a pot of chili at the stove.

"I apologize," she said hastily at his surprise. "I didn't ask if we could cook, but it was the only activity I could think of to do together! And I'm sorry if you don't like chili, but could you *pretend* to like it just for tonight? Aubrey did most of it herself, and she's really proud of it!" She found herself self-conscious of wearing his apron, a navy one with the name *Mac* embroidered on it, but it was all she could find.

"Not a problem," he returned. "Make yourself at home! It smells amazing in here." He threw his jacket over a chair and went to plug in his phone. "How'd it go? And where's Aubs?" His eyes dropped to the apron.

Mari could hear Aubrey on the stairs. "She's coming. It went well, but I was hoping to talk to you tonight before I leave. In private please."

His head shot up. "Is everything all right?"

"Nothing's wrong! I just have some questions and some requests that I don't want—" She trailed off, smiling as Aubrey entered the room and ran to greet him with a hug.

"Hey, Chubbers! I hear you made supper tonight! Way to go! How was school?"

Chubbers? Mari threw him a look.

Aubrey slapped him a high-five. "Good."

"Anything exciting happen? How was the bus?"

"Nope. Fine."

He nodded happily. "And have you been nice to Mari—cooperative and everything?"

"Yep." She lowered her eyes, turning away.

He glanced at Mari in approval. "I see you've managed."

Mari tipped her head in return. "So far so good. Aubrey, would you find us some bowls please?"

"Nice," Mac said. He loosened his collar and began rolling up his sleeves to wash his hands in the sink.

Aubrey got a chair to fetch the bowls.

After drying his hands and setting the towel aside, Mac straddled a stool at the island counter. "Finished with your homework, Chubbers?"

"Not all of it," she replied with her back toward him.

Mari glanced at her in surprise, then at Mac. "Any homework rules I should be aware of?"

"Yes, ma'am! Homework and chores before TV. Right, Aubs?"

"Yep."

Mari's brow rose. "I see. And where might that list of chores be?"

Mac pointed to a colorful chart hung by a pair of daisy magnets on the side of the refrigerator. "Two jobs daily, which I gather didn't happen today. So what'd you two do this afternoon?"

Mari turned to Aubrey. "Care to answer that?" She was curious to see how the girl would frame two hours of television and making a pot of chili.

Aubrey lifted her shoulders. "Um, talked mostly. And she made smoothies. And then we cooked supper."

Mac looked pleased. "That's great! Honestly, Mari, I can't tell you how grateful I am that you'd do this for us."

Mari simply smiled, giving the counter a final wipe down with her cloth as Aubrey arranged the silverware around the bowls. She offered Aubrey the ladle, supervising as she served up their food. Then as Aubrey transferred the bowls to the island, Mari slid onto a stool across from Mac, feeling it would be impolite not to partake of Aubrey's creation. Mac grabbed the sour cream from the fridge and led a brief prayer over the meal, after which he complimented Aubrey on the delicious-looking food.

Starting in on his supper, he turned to Mari. "Your granddad was extra chipper this morning. He got out of bed entirely by himself!"

Mari's brow went up. "Really? That's awesome! I caught him during a nap, but we talked afterward. He pointed out some jonquils on his tray and told me they were from Shannon!"

"Nice! He's turned a corner for sure. Even his speech is improving. He seems pretty happy that you're back from school. And speaking of— how is it that you're here before the end of your semester?"

She chuckled, pausing before her bite. "Are you sure you want to know? It's a loaded subject!"

Thus began the telling of her surprise meeting with the dean of students and her grand knee saga, and for the duration of the meal the discussion centered around her damaged meniscus and cortisone shots and torn ACLs and surgeries. As a physical therapist, Mac was thoroughly engaged in the subject, firing off question after question, then fielding Aubrey's confused queries too, building makeshift models from his silverware and napkins to explain the anatomy of the knee.

"Your school did the right thing," he reassured when they had exhausted the subject. "You've got to let it heal. I have a few exercises I could show you, but for the most part you need to rest it."

Mari sighed. "I know. But it still feels like getting kicked out of school."

Aubrey swung her head to look at her. "You got kicked out of school?"

"No, she said it *felt* like it," Mac clarified. "She had to leave because she hurt her knee. Weren't you listening?"

Aubrey's arm flopped onto the table. "Everything you're talking about is so complicated and *boring*!"

"Aubrey Michelle!"

Mari set her spoon in her empty bowl, pushing it forward. "Sorry— that's my fault! It *is* boring."

"Not so boring! And *I* started it," Mac said. He laid his napkin in his bowl, sitting back. "Great chili, Aubs! Did Grandma teach you how to make this?"

Her brow crinkled. "No, Mari did!"

Mac sent Mari a knowing wink. "Well, this was quite a step up from *my* dinner plans! I was going to throw in a frozen pizza!"

Frozen pizza. Mari brought her hand to her forehead. She had forgotten all about Will! She stood, pulling off the apron to set it on the counter. "I should go. Aubrey, thank you for the wonderful afternoon. I'm looking forward to tomorrow."

Aubrey's eyes flicked up and returned to the table. "Okay. Bye."

Mac had already pushed back from the counter. "I'll walk you out. Aubs, I'd like you to finish your homework. I'll be back in a minute."

Mac closed the door behind them on the porch. "All right, what happened?" he asked.

Mari shook her head. "Nothing huge. But I have a few questions for you. And some requests. And some concerns."

He straightened, as if defensive. "Okay, what?"

"First, kudos for the kale and other vegetables in the fridge! Seriously, Mac, that floored me! I can see you're making obvious healthy choices for yourself and your daughter, so good job on that."

His brow rose. "So frozen pizza doesn't nullify that?"

"Well, having kale builds a little food equity, if you ask me. And you had berries in the freezer too. It made a great smoothie. So I was wondering if I could pick up a few groceries—like fruit and stuff. And maybe a little protein mix for our smoothies, if you'd allow that."

He nodded. "Sure."

"Thanks. And then about Aubrey's hair. Would you mind if I picked up some hair product that works better for her hair type? I've got some great stuff for curls that would bring down the frizz. Plus some hair bands that don't rip her hair when she pulls them out."

"Of course."

"Good. Now—TV boundaries."

"Right. I've recorded some cartoon classics on DVR. She knows which she can and can't watch. Half an hour or so is plenty."

"Thank you. That helps. Now, you can say no to my next request— it's okay—but I'd like to ask if I could buy Aubrey some new tennis shoes."

He gestured back inside. "She's got tennis shoes. They're around somewhere. She needs them for school."

"Right. But kids tend to run faster and jump higher in new ones, if you know what I mean. It might help us get outside. If it's in the budget.

And it's okay if it's not."

Mac stared at her a moment, then pulled a money clip from his pocket to wiggle out a card. "Be smart."

"No, just reimburse me when you pay me."

He shook his head. "Take it. I trust you. Is that all?"

"Well, there's another thing. I made the mistake of bringing up her mother, not realizing that she had passed away. I'm so sorry! I didn't know, and I hope it didn't cause any problems. I didn't mean to be insensitive, but it probably wouldn't hurt if you talked to her about it. It wasn't like we had a big discussion or anything, but still I thought I should mention it. Just in case it came up later."

He gave a crooked smile. "I assure you Aubrey's mother is very much alive."

Mari drew back. "*She is?*"

"That little imp!" He chuckled, shaking his head. "Mari, sometimes my daughter makes up stories. I'm not sure if it's her age or just *her*. But it's something you should know."

"So your neighbor burying a body in his yard—?" She jerked her thumb toward her old house.

"Case in point!"

She breathed out in relief. "Okay, I get it. So is Aubrey's mother in her life? Do you share custody?"

He shook his head. "No. We're praying that she could be in her life. But don't worry—she's not going to show up or anything."

"Good to know. Thanks."

"Anything else?"

"Well—"

He gave a little laugh, shoving a hand in his pocket. "Shoot!"

"Okay, this nickname 'Chubbers'—I'm sorry, Mac, but it's gotta go."

"Hey, now—it's all in fun!"

"I know, but she's getting to the age when she's starting to think about her weight, and you need to understand girls and how they think. I was thick like her, and kids in school are cruel. Plus, she said your mom makes her eat salad after school because she's fat."

His face crinkled. "What? No! My mom was into these salad kits for a while, but it had nothing to do with Aubrey!"

"Well, regardless, 'Chubbers' has to go. I insist. And 'Aubs' is cute, but I think you can do better. You're the man in her life, Mac. Make it count. Make her feel beautiful about herself."

He threw up his hands. "Fine. Noted. What else?"

"Just one more thing—"

"Just one, huh?"

"Yes. She's had a rough day, Mac. When you go back in there you should probe a little. See if you can coax it out of her. Particularly the school bus and a boy she says is mean to her. She needs someone safe to talk to, and that person wasn't me."

He made a sound, looking away, and the two stood together in silence.

"This is the hardest thing I've ever done," he said at last.

"I can't imagine."

"I'm clueless, and I'm terrified I'm going to mess up her life."

Mari nodded sympathetically. "Well, don't beat yourself up. She's a normal kid, and you're a good dad. You have *kale* in your fridge, for heaven's sake!"

They both laughed.

She motioned toward her car. "I should go. I was supposed to connect with my boyfriend a couple hours ago."

"Ah, the boyfriend. William Wallace!" He spoke the name with amusement.

"Yes," she said simply. "Good night."

"Thanks, Mari. Good night."

Chapter Eight

The girl Aubrey consumed Mari's thoughts her entire drive home from Mac's house. She recalled all too well what it was like to be short and pudgy as a child. She couldn't imagine having to go through that awkward stage without a mother and while being bullied at school. The girl's behavior obviously reflected her stress. Mari wracked her brain for feasible ways to help. Maybe if they did some activities together Aubrey would learn to trust her. Maybe doing something outside could get her to talk, like planting a garden together. But her knee. That wouldn't work. Maybe walks around the field that weren't too aggressive. Or perhaps—

As she neared her exit, her eyes grew wide as out of the blue she suddenly remembered she had promised to phone Will when she left Mac's! *Shoot!* He was probably wondering why she hadn't called. Immediately she pulled him up on her dad's Bluetooth.

He answered on the first ring. "Mars, where *are* you? Why didn't you answer your phone?"

"Did you call me?"

"I called you a hundred times!"

"What? Oh, sorry. I didn't check my phone. I'm just now getting home from Mac's. It was a long afternoon, and we got to talking."

"Talking? I thought he was at work!"

"He was! I was watching Aubrey and helping her cook. And then Mac came home from work and we—" She huffed, confused that he was upset. "It was my first day there, Will! We had a lot to talk about!"

"Is it going to be like this every night?"

"No!" She signaled and took the Juniper exit toward Kingswood. "Well, *maybe*. I don't know! Sometimes it might. What's going on? Why the interrogation?"

"I was trying to call you! I wanted to surprise you, and I ordered in for the both of us. Plus I got some wine. The sweet kind that you like. I've been texting and calling, but you never responded. The food's already cold."

She scrunched her face. "We didn't plan this! I didn't know! I never checked my phone. You know that about me. I didn't even *think* about my phone."

"So are you coming over?"

The sunset's reflection on the Kingswood windows was already in view. She cringed. "I'm sorry, Will. I can't. Not tonight. I'm just beat!"

"Mariachi!"

"I know—sorry. I'm already here at the condominium, and I need to wash my uniform for the morning. Besides, I already ate, and I'm just plain worn out. Can we do it tomorrow? Let's do dinner tomorrow. I'll buy."

He groaned. "*Fine.* Tomorrow. Don't forget!"

"I won't forget! Geez, Will!"

"Well, I don't like this job of yours. That guy is preying on you!"

"He's my grandfather's physical therapist! How is that preying on me?"

"*Exactly.* He shouldn't have asked you to watch his kid!"

"He didn't ask me—I offered! Honestly, Mac, what's wrong with you? You're acting like an eighth-grader! You haven't asked me *one* question about my day!" She wrenched her visor down to jab the Kingswood parking garage opener.

"You just called me Mac."

"What?"

"You called me *Mac*!"

Mari gave a long blink, glancing to where the Bluetooth lit up the dash. "It was an accident, Will, and you know it. Are you kidding me?"

"Fine. It doesn't matter! So how was your first day at the coffee shop?"

She pulled into her parking space, staring at the concrete wall through her windshield. Right now having a boyfriend seemed like so dang much work.

Apparently Will felt her vibes, for he began retreating quickly. "I'm just a little bugged—that's all. Sorry, Mari. Don't hang up!"

"Work was *fine*," she offered stiffly.

She didn't want to talk to him about anything anymore, but eventually he schmoozed her enough to pull it out of her, and starting from the coffee shop and continuing all the way to her conversation with Mac, she gave him

118

a brief rundown of her day.

Will grunted. "A kid who lies—? I'd have absolutely no patience for that!"

"It was only the first day," she said. "I'm still getting to know her, and I have a ton to learn."

"Suit yourself!" he responded. "Some people put themselves in the most bizarre and complicated situations and then complain about how hard they have it."

"Some people?"

"Yeah, Mari—like this girl I love! I care about her a lot and don't want to see her get all stressed and worn out running everywhere spinning plates for everyone else. You're important too, you know. You don't need to make life easier for everybody at the expense of yourself. I'm not trying to tell you what to do. I only want what's best for you—because I *love* you. I love you times a million!"

Mari swallowed, her hands still resting on the steering wheel. Sometimes it felt as if they were from two different worlds, but she believed him when he said he loved her. "Thanks, Will," she said simply. "I'd appreciate your patience right now. Things *are* complicated, and I just can't help it."

"You have a lot more control over your circumstances than you realize," he countered, "but yes, I can chill. So can I bore you with *my* day?"

Will then proceeded to detail out the technicalities of the computer programming project he was working on. Midway into his story Mari glanced at the clock on the dash, gathered up her belongings, then left her vehicle to take the elevator to her floor, where she lingered in the hall outside her door until he finished. When they said goodbye, she promised to head straight to his apartment after work the next day and call him when she was on her way.

"Great! See you tomorrow, Maribelle. I love you."

"Love you too," she echoed automatically. She stood staring at her phone after she hung up. What just happened? Why did she feel so deflated?

Shannon was sorting laundry in the broad hallway when she walked in, the louvred panels spread wide to reveal the washer and dryer set. Greeting her briefly, Mari turned for her bedroom, then stopped, eyeing the mound of clothes on the floor.

"Are those darks? Can I throw these in?" She began untucking her shirt.

Shannon replaced the cap on the laundry detergent and slid it on a shelf. "Sure. How was work this morning?"

Mari cocked a brow. "Need you ask? You could have warned me!"

Shannon gave a knowing smile. "Tatum's a character, isn't she? It takes her a while to trust people, but she'll get used to you. She's just dealing with a nasty mean ex right now. But Mark, now—good luck!"

Mari popped into her room to change into her pajamas, then delivered her uniform to her sister. "Is Mom home?"

"Yep."

Mari padded down the hallway, calling over her shoulder. "Hey— nice flowers this morning! Poppy said they were from you! And thanks for leaving me the car."

"Cool!" Shannon closed the washer and tapped a button, bringing it to life. "Yeah, he was pretty jazzed about them." She pulled the louvered doors shut. "There's chicken in the fridge. Did you eat?"

"I ate at Mac's—thanks," she replied, tapping on her mother's door frame. "Hi, Mom." She went to kiss her where she was folding a pile of clothes on the bed.

"Hello, sweetie! You ate at Mac's?"

Mari sat on her dad's side of the bed and elevated her leg. Her knee ached from the long day. "Yeah. Chili. That was my activity with Aubrey, his daughter."

"Great idea! How'd it go?" She lifted a stack of sweaters and disappeared into her closet.

Mari shrugged, rubbing her hand over the quilt. "Good, mostly. We've got some challenges, but I think things will work themselves out." She wasn't quite sure how to transition to Will.

"Well, you're just getting to know one another."

"Yeah. How was *your* day?"

"Productive!" She returned for another armful of clothes. Then, casting a glance at her daughter, she straightened. "Goodness, what's that gloomy look about? Did it *not* go well at Mac's? Or is the coffee shop a 'no'? You don't have to work there, Mari."

Mari sighed, pulling a pillow onto her lap. "It's Will. He's being weird."

"Weird?"

"Yeah. It bugs him that I'm watching Aubrey. He says Mac is preying on me."

Her mom's face crinkled. "Preying on you? What's that supposed to mean?"

"I know! That was my reaction too! Our whole conversation was just strange. It wasn't exactly a fight, but it was close. I don't get it."

"Is he jealous?"

"Of Mac?" Mari spread her hands. "Mom! Come on!"

"Did you talk about it?"

"Yeah, and we're okay. It's just—weird, that's all." She let out a long breath. "Everything was good until I came home from school, and now it's—" She shrugged, not knowing how to finish. "I don't know. Sorry—I just need to talk."

Her mother sat on the edge of the bed.

Mari shook her head. "It makes *no* sense."

"Maybe he needs a little time. Did things go okay at the coffee shop?"

"Yes. More challenges, but it'll be okay. I *did* meet a professor this morning, which was interesting—well, met him *again*." She rolled onto her arm, telling her mother of her encounters with Dr. Grant, which morphed into describing the rest of the crew at the Coffee Break.

Overhearing them, Shannon came to join the conversation, and before long the three were lying across the bed laughing as Shannon entertained them with her humorous dealings with Coffee Break patrons and employees. Eventually the stories shifted to mundane reports of the day, punctuated by yawns. Then Shannon suddenly remembered she hadn't put the clothes into the dryer yet, and their little trio broke as they headed tiredly to their beds.

Spring was fickle, pummeling Mari with a biting wind as she set off to work the next morning. With a shiver, she pulled her collar snugly around her neck, but after a third of a block she turned back for the parking garage, opting to take her dad's vehicle instead. Not only was she freezing, but minus a hair binder, her curls were whipped about uncontrollably.

The Taiton student center was within sight of Kingswood, but the pathway across the Green took some time by foot. Yet driving was no shorter, for Mari had to take Juniper Street back out to the main highway, go south to the first exit, and then thread her way back through the entire Taiton campus to the student center parking lot. Even so, she arrived at the Coffee Break early and hung her jacket in the back, grabbing her apron on her way to join the gang up front waiting on the line of early-bird students.

"Scones!" Tatum hollered in her face right out of the gate.

Mari drew herself up, popping her an imaginary punch, but *A-plus* Alyssa laid a hand on her arm. "Morning, Mari! We're low on scones. Can you throw some in the oven quick?"

Red-faced, Mari plopped the cold dough on the baking sheets in the kitchen, her thoughts churning. There was no excuse for rudeness like that. She wouldn't tolerate it. She was going to the manager—who that very moment appeared from the backside of the kitchen with two hot pans of quiche.

"Good morning," he stated briskly. "Cut these in eighths and take them up front." He glanced at her. "You've cut quiche before, right? Wet the knife so you don't mangle it." He snatched the trays of scones, adding, "I heard you did good yesterday. It's pretty tough to replace Shannon, so I'm glad. She was a fantastic employee." He turned hastily for the oven.

Being compared to her sister grated her. He hadn't meant the compliment to sting, she assured herself. Nevertheless, she couldn't wait for her first break when she would download a countdown on her phone for her college departure. Resigned that now was not the time to bring up *Irri*-Tatum's offensive attitude, she faced the quiche and raised the knife, praying she wouldn't botch it.

Midmorning Mari was paired with re-*mark*-able Mark for replenishing sandwiches in the front case. As they labored side by side, she learned more than she ever cared to know about the intricacies of how pastrami was made—the various cuts of beef used, the methods by which it was dried, smoked, and steamed, the unique combinations of spices used to make it, and how lamb or turkey could be substituted for the beef. Mark was just beginning his verbal tutorial on how it differed from corned beef when a call went out for someone to bus tables.

Mari's hand shot up. "I'll go!" She would have been willing to scrub toilets.

Starting in the back, she quickly breezed through the dining areas collecting miscellaneous coffee mugs and plates left behind, wiping down tables and pushing in chairs, readying the room for the next wave of customers.

This morning Professor Grant was seated at a table in the center of the room, his papers to his right, folders to his left, and laptop behind his Bible, which took prominence front and center. Alyssa had just delivered him blueberry bread and a coffee, chatting for a minute before rejoining her fellow baristas behind the counter. Mari's heart beat faster as she neared his table. What was this supposed to look like? Would he notice her? Would she initiate the conversation, or should she?

He turned, smiling broadly. "Good morning, Miss Mari! You're still employed, I see!"

"I am. Good morning!" Whew, that was simple! She wiped the crumbs off a chair, pushing it to the table. "The buzz back there is that you're not in your usual spot today!"

"Indeed!" He leaned forward, lowering his voice. "Don't look now, but I was cued this morning that there's a brand-new security camera aimed at my regular table. It appears I've created a controversy in our little Taiton world. Some anonymous folks are apparently taking issue with a professor having a Bible in public—like it's a crime or something."

Mari's eyes automatically searched the ceiling. "Wouldn't a place like this already have cameras?"

"Correct. So why the new one over my seat?"

"Well, it wasn't me!"

His lip curled up. "I'm not accusing you! I'm like—let's go! Bring it on! But whatever. On another note, I have some great news! My wife and I found out we're having another boy. Number three."

"Congratulations!"

He raised his coffee as in a toast. "Thank you! It's a bit more exciting for me, as she was hoping for a girl, but we're both grateful for whomever God chooses to give us." He took a sip. "Have we done our homework, Miss Mari?"

She straightened, wet cloth in hand.

"I know you were secretly hoping I'd forget, but I haven't, and I'm looking forward to your answer!" His eyes narrowed, the mug poised before his mouth. "You *did* do your homework, yes? There are severe penalties you don't even want to know about for those who forget!"

She returned his smile. "I'd take stocks over guillotine if there's a choice. True confessions: I *did* forget—although not right away. But I already had an answer yesterday, if I'm allowed to share it."

He shook his head in faux disappointment. "Mari, Mari! All right, I'll let you off this time, but *only* if you remember what my question was. If I have to reiterate the question, then stocks it is—period! So, what'll it be—the prodigal, the father, or the older brother? And tell me why!"

"I've opted for letter *D*—none of the above. I'm going to say I relate best with the fatted calf, whose happiness is sacrificed at the expense of everyone else." She folded her arms smugly.

Dr. Grant tipped his head in surprise.

"I don't mean it as dark as it sounds," she added. "I couldn't relate to anyone in the story, and it was the best I could come up with given the options."

He chuckled. "Fair enough! That's a first for me, but I get it. I'll count that as acceptable. Perhaps some other time when we have more time to talk, you could share why you feel that way." His eyes flicked over her shoulder and back to her. "And now before we're shut down, here's your next assignment: Do you think the way the father treated his wayward son was fair?"

Mari glanced back to spy Tatum with her own dishcloth in hand working strategically through the dining room toward them.

Dr. Grant continued, "Well, you know what happens. The prodigal son comes to his senses and returns home, his father receives him, and so forth. But that's not the end. There's an older brother who has a reaction. So in light of where *he's* coming from, do you think the father was fair in the way he treated his rebel son?"

Mari opened her mouth to answer, but Dr. Grant cut her off. "*Tomorrow*, my dear! Read it again and mull it through. Hello, Miss Tatum!" He raised his head, calling to Mari's coworker. "And how are you on this fine day?"

Tatum gave a brisk nod. "Professor." She cast a dark glance at Mari.

Dr. Grant brought his mug up. "Miss Mari and I were just discussing joyous family celebrations—the kind where you go all out to have a feast for the black sheep of the family. Maybe serve—I don't know—something extravagant like *veal* or something." His eyes sparkled as he sipped his coffee.

Mari smiled, turning away. "I'd better keep moving."

"Indeed. It's been a pleasure." He turned back to the other woman. "Miss Tatum, how is your son? Is he doing any better in school?"

Hefting the bin of dirty dishes from its place atop the trash receptacle, Mari carried it back to load the dishwasher, finishing right in time for the first frenzied lunch rush, from which point the day passed quickly.

When her shift was over, she clocked out, then changed into jeans and a navy and bright yellow Bourdette T-shirt in the restroom, proud to sport it on Taiton territory, even if only for a minute on her way out of there. Reaching for her coat, she discovered that someone had inadvertently— or not—hung a sopping wet towel over top of it, and her collar and one shoulder were completely soaked.

Her grandfather was not in his room when she arrived at Riverview. "It's spa day for this corridor," one of the staff told her. To her confused look he added, "Haircuts, manicures, pedicures—all that sort of thing. It's a bigger deal for the women, but the men need the service too. He'll be back around three."

Mari checked the time, then went to leave a note for her mother. She would miss seeing her grandfather that day, but she was just gifted a few hours to complete her shopping list from the previous evening. Troubleshooting Aubrey Sinclair's life had kept her up half the night, but she did get a few ideas. The girl was smart but obviously in need of an adult in her life she couldn't manipulate. Granted, the kid had some valid issues—being motherless and raised by a single dad—but her bad habits would only grow if not curtailed. The challenge would be to affirm her while steering her behavior.

As she hurried back toward the main entrance, Mari suddenly heard the unmistakable sound of someone retching in the hallway restroom. She paused in alarm, casting an uncomfortable glance at the door, feeling sorry for the person within, whose misery was clear. What if it was a resident who needed help? She lingered until she heard the toilet flush, followed by the whir of an electric hand-dryer. Proceeding a few face-saving steps down the hallway, she waited for the heavy door to open, then twisted to look back over her shoulder. Recognizing the pale-faced girl coming out, she gave a cry.

"Ariel!"

Ariel dropped her hand from her mouth. "Uh, hi."

"Are you sick?"

"I'm okay."

Mari motioned to the bathroom. "No, you're not—you're sick!"

The girl's shoulders slumped as she nodded miserably. "I know."

"What's going on? Did you eat something bad?"

"I—uh—I think I might be—" Her cheeks were blazing now. "Uh—might be sick with a stomach bug or something."

"What are you doing here? You should go home!"

"I'm thinking about it. I thought I might try to stick it out."

Mari's brow rose. "Ariel, you're in a nursing home! You could give it to these people!"

She shifted uncomfortably. "I, um—yeah. I was just thinking about that."

"Let's go sit down!" Mari gestured toward a nearby lounge, but again Ariel shook her head.

"I'll be okay."

"No, my dear. Let me walk you to your car."

"I was dropped off today."

"Then let me call your mom—"

"No!" Her hand went to her forehead, pulling back her crisp, black bangs. "No, don't call my mom! I think if I rest for a few minutes—"

Mari eyed her, still getting used to her new look. "Honey, if you have the stomach flu you should go home—period." Again, she waved toward the lounge. "Are you *sure* you don't want to sit down? Look—you need to go home. Your employer would *want* you to go home. Truly! I'll give you a ride!"

She met Mari's eyes. "Okay."

Mari dipped her head. "Let's go! Should I tell your supervisor you're leaving?"

"I'll tell her on our way out."

In all their youth group years together, Mari had never been to Ariel's house, so it was a complete surprise to discover that Ariel and her mother lived in Whitmore, on the other side of Frost Park. Here all along they had been neighbors—sort of—although it wasn't too strange that they hadn't known it, since Mari never went there, whether by car, bike, or on foot, as Mari's parents had always urged her and Shannon to stay on the Frost side of the cemetery. Plus, going to different schools and having a principal for a mom, Mari never had to ride the bus to school either. So it was with great curiosity that Mari turned into the infamous Whitmore neighborhood, with Ariel barely holding it together in the passenger's seat.

Mari remained silent, eyeing the older, rundown homes with neglected landscaping and scabby lawns, while ahead loomed the blocky Whitmore Complex apartments where mothers sat at picnic tables in the side yards, smoking, while their toddlers played on their kiddie bikes in the littered street. It was undeniably an economically depressed area, she observed. It made her thankful for her hardworking mom and dad.

"Right here," Ariel murmured, indicating a humble home across from one of the mammoth apartment buildings.

Mari pulled in the tiny driveway. "Are you going to be all right?" She reached to check Ariel's forehead. She didn't appear to be feverish. "Maybe try some chicken soup," she encouraged. "Do you have any? I could bring you some."

Ariel placed her hand on the door handle. "I'm okay. Thanks again for the ride."

As she slipped out of the car, a small rectangular box dropped out of her coat pocket onto the seat. Handing it to her, Mari recognized a pregnancy test kit. Her eyes shot to Ariel's, who quickly snatched it and shoved it back into her pocket.

"Ariel, hon, let's talk. Can we talk? I think you should get in. Let's go for a drive."

She shook her head weakly. "I can't. I feel—I think I might be sick again." She brought her hand over her mouth. "I need to lie down."

Mari turned off the car and popped her seatbelt. "Okay, I'm coming in with you."

"No! No, don't come in! You can't—come in."

Mari eyed her warily. "Have you opened that yet? Are you pregnant?"

"I was going to at work, but I got sick."

"Have you told your mom?" She glanced at the house. Red front door. Blinds drawn.

"She can't find out."

"Ariel! We need to talk! I'm coming in."

"No! My mom's boyfriend might be there. We can't wake him up."

"Okay. Then get in." She patted the seat.

Ariel shook her head. "I need to lie down. We can talk tomorrow."

"Okay. What's your phone number? I want your phone number."

Ariel breathed out her number as Mari quickly transcribed it onto a napkin.

"Okay. You go inside and take that test. I'm going to text you in a little while for the results. And then I can come over, or we can talk on the phone—whatever you need. And don't worry—I won't embarrass you."

"Okay. Thanks for the ride." She hurried away to a side door along the driveway.

Dazedly Mari sat back in her seat, waiting until she was inside. Ariel had a boyfriend. Who would have guessed it? At least she *hoped* Ariel had a boyfriend and that she hadn't been preyed upon or something worse. And why was that girl so terrified of her mother finding out she was pregnant? With someone like Ariel, her mother should absolutely know what was going on! One thing was clear—she needed to talk to Ariel again very soon.

Chapter Nine

After two hours of running errands with Ariel's dilemma spinning through her brain, Mari arrived at Mac's more than a little frazzled, but she pulled herself together, for today she was determined to nip any of Connor Haddington's rascally shenanigans in the bud. A stern boss look is what he needed, she decided. She arrived at the bus stop right as the school bus rumbled around the corner and hissed to a halt at the curb. Stepping up in plain view of the swinging door, Mari folded her arms, drawing herself up as tall as her scant five-foot two frame would allow. No one was getting away with foolishness today!

As before, the youngest kids got off the bus first, their small hands gripping the railing as they navigated the tall steps. Then came the middle group. And finally—here she came—Aubrey, in her mint green sweatshirt with a bright pink lollipop in her fist, laughing as she leaped out of the bus—with Connor Haddington exiting right behind her, a matching sucker in his hand.

"See you tomorrow, Slime-face!" Aubrey bellowed cheerfully.

"Bye, Grime-face!" Connor echoed. "Shime-dime-lime-face!" He hiked his backpack onto his shoulder, popped the sucker into his mouth, and took off in the opposite direction.

Aubrey scowled at Mari hovering so close. "Are you going to come here every day? I *do* know my way home!"

Mari blinked, keeping her voice pleasant. "Well, *that's* a relief! I was going to tell you this was my last time doing it. How was school?"

Aubrey tossed her head. "Fine." She swung up her girly backpack and started home at a brisk pace.

"Looks like things with Connor got worked out," Mari observed, keeping stride in spite of her knee.

The girl's shoulders rose and fell.

"Did you two talk?" Mari asked.

Aubrey made an *I-don't-know* sound and pulled the lollipop out of her mouth. "What's for snack? Can you make me a smoothie again?"

"Well, I have a better idea. How about going to Smoothie Q for deluxe smoothies?"

Her face shot up as she stopped short. "For real? Did you ask my dad?"

Mari nodded. "Yep. And he said yes, if your chores and homework are done."

"I don't have any homework."

Mari gave Aubrey a knowing look. "Okay. But it'd be a game-changer if you *did,* and I found out later that you 'accidentally' forgot about it."

"Um, I'll check my backpack." She popped the sucker back in, continuing for the house.

Up ahead a car pulled to the curb in front of the Gordons' house, and a woman got out, waving to them. Leah DeSoto. The woman with the remodeled house next to Brother Warren's.

"Hi, Aubrey!" she called.

The lollipop came out. "Hi!"

She hoisted a tote bag over her shoulder and closed her door. "How are you? Did you have a good day at school?" Her eyes rose to Mari. "And it's—uh—*Lynn?*"

"Mari."

"*Mari*—from the shower—sorry! How are you? And it's Leah."

Mari nodded her greeting as Leah joined her on the sidewalk. Aubrey kept walking, however, calling over her shoulder that she had chores to do.

"How do you know Aubrey?" Mari asked.

"I have her in Sunday school at church. Plus my husband is friends with Mac. We hang out a lot."

"Ah. I watch her after school." She gestured to her former house. "I grew up here. Family friends with the Sinclairs."

"Nice." Leah waved toward the Gordons'. "I get together with Susan on Tuesdays. She's helping me work through some of my issues from my perfect childhood, if you know what I mean." She laughed.

Leah cocked her head. "What?"

"Oh, just some crazy mother stuff. And father stuff too, I guess. And sister stuff. You name it, I have it—all fallout from a dysfunctional family! You have no idea how it shapes you as a person. But look at me—blabbing. Sorry. I suppose you didn't need to hear all that. I'm working on personal boundaries."

Mari lifted her chin. "Oh. Okay."

Quickly Leah retrieved a small card from her purse. "Have I given you one of these? I host a Bible study on Saturdays. It's so good. It's mostly girls our age, and we're always looking for more to join us. It'd be a great way for you to get to know some people from the church."

"I'm not new. I grew up at Eagle Bluff."

Leah threw up a hand. "Right—sorry, I forgot. *I'm* new—new to New Hampton even. I grew up in Bridgewater. But anyway, we'd love to have you. Then us new people can get to know *you*!"

Mari glanced at the card. "Yeah, I'm pretty sure you already invited me at the shower, but thanks."

"Did I? Sorry. Anyway"—Leah motioned to the Gordons'—"I should keep moving. It was nice to run into you again, Mari. My phone number is on the back if you change your mind. Or just want to call."

"Thanks. Nice to see you too." She waved, watching Leah head up the walk to the Gordons'. In all the years Mari had lived there, she had never once been invited to Susan Gordon's to chat about her family issues. Probably because she didn't have any. Her parents were great. Her mom was her best friend, and her dad was kind and wonderful. When he was home.

Mari found Aubrey in the dining room busily scrawling answers on a math worksheet, her tongue protruding as she concentrated. Mac's books were spread out on the other side of the table—what looked like medical textbooks, his Bible, a journal.

"Done!" Aubrey slammed her pencil down and shoved the paper into the pocket of a bright orange folder.

Mari extended her hand. "I should probably check that. Any other homework?"

Aubrey slid the folder across the table. "Just to read for twenty minutes, but I do that with Daddy at night. Can we go now?"

"Chores?"

She groaned, scooting off the chair and heading for the kitchen. While perusing the math sheet, Mari heard the bumping of bar stools being pushed out of the way as Aubrey swept the kitchen.

"We're not in a hurry," she called. "Do a good job!"

After approving the math homework, Mari went to wait in the foyer while Aubrey rushed through the house emptying wastebaskets. Several framed photos were on display on the skinny table against the wall at the foot of the stairs, one of which caught her attention. Aubrey's mother, she speculated.

In a couple minutes Aubrey raced up to receive Mari's very jubilant fist bump. "Well done, little lady! Let's go!"

While Aubrey donned her shoes, Mari gestured to the photo. "Your mom is pretty. What's her name?"

Aubrey glanced up, apparently forgetting her claim that her mother was deceased. "Guess!"

"Maria?"

"Nope!"

"Sofia?"

"Nope. It's Elena Maria Sofia!" she spurted, then laughed. "Just kidding! It's only Elena. I don't know her middle name."

Mari held the door open for her. "Well, she's pretty, and I like her name."

Stepping onto the porch, Aubrey immediately tensed. "Nooo! Oh, I *hate* those dogs! Can we wait here 'til he's gone?" She shuddered.

Ah, the alleged Mr. Eden, Mari observed, spying the sharply dressed fifty-something man coming from the field. He was passing by on their sidewalk, keeping a firm grip on two sleek rottweilers straining at their leashes. As the screen door dropped noisily shut behind her, the man looked over to nod a curt greeting. Immediately Mari was conflicted. Like Aubrey, she was inclined to let him pass, but this could be her ticket into her former house someday. She figured she should at least introduce herself.

"Hello there, neighbor!" she called with a wave, her attempt to hurry down the porch steps rewarded by an abrupt jab of pain. *Dang*, she had forgotten her knee.

The man gave a sharp command, pulling the muscular dogs to a stop.

Mari paused, partly from pain but mostly to provide ample space between them. "Hi. I'm Mari Coleman. I grew up in your house. And I watch Mac Sinclair's daughter, Aubrey."

He tipped his head. "Margaret. Roger Eden. Yes, it's a nice little place. I enjoy it." His eyes darted to Aubrey, standing behind her.

It didn't seem the time to correct him. "Your dogs—they're rather intimidating!"

"Yes. Loki and Thor."

"Ah—brothers?"

"Yes." He glanced at the animals and back to Mari, offering nothing more.

Mari motioned toward the car. "Well, we're running into town. It was nice meeting you. Enjoy your walk."

"Ma'am." With another crisp nod, he proceeded toward the gate on his driveway.

She would give their exchange a *C minus*, she mused. He was not a conversationalist. Plus she didn't like the cranky way he had looked at Aubrey. Like he was warning her to stay off his lawn or something.

"He lets his dogs run in the field every day," Aubrey declared, getting into the car. "But he never picks up their poop!"

Mari sighed, clipping on her seatbelt. "Why can't all dogs be like cats?"

Aubrey spun her head in surprise. "Yeah—then Mr. Eden would have to *drag* them down the sidewalk by their leashes!" She threw her head back, giggling as if she thought the image hilarious.

Mari smiled, pulling the car in a broad U-turn to head out of the neighborhood.

And then the most miraculous thing happened. On the drive to the smoothie shop, Aubrey's day began to trickle out, and Mari learned a lot. She learned that lunch that day had been rubbery chicken nuggets with crinkly-cut carrot sticks on the side, but both dipping sauces had been gross. She learned that stern Mrs. Poppen made all the kids follow her instructions *exactly* in art class and that no one could ever pick his or her *own* colors for art projects unless the colors were practically the same as the teacher's, *and then what was the point?* She learned that Aubrey's best friends at school were Hailey Cross and Cami Pitt, and the three of them liked to play pet orphanage in the corner of the playground at recess.

Then later while slurping their frozen strawberry drinks, Aubrey also revealed that Hailey's mom had cancer and had to wear fake hair. It also came out that her classmate Ty West was sent to the principal's office for swearing at the hall monitor—again—and that Connor Haddington had to move his seat away from Ty to the other side of the classroom, and now he sits by her. The two of them were put into the same reading group.

"How is that going?" Mari asked. "Do you mind that he's in your group now?"

Aubrey wiggled her straw around. "Not really. He can't read good, so I helped him, and he was nice to me after that."

"Well, I'm glad to hear it! It was kind of you to help him. And I'm sorry to hear about Hailey's mom. Does that make her sad?"

"Yeah. Plus her dad had to go live in a different apartment. Her mom kicked him out for having naughty pictures on his computer. Pictures of girls' private parts. It's so gross! Now she can't stay overnight with me anymore. Her mom won't let her."

Mari set her cup aside. "Wow, Aubrey—those are big issues! I'm sure Hailey's mom only wants to protect her, and that's the right thing to do." After a quiet pause, Mari asked, "Has Hailey's dad ever done anything bad to her?"

"Like what—yell at her? He yelled at her once because she spilled milk on the couch."

"Yeah, that. Or anything else that would seem inappropriate—or be gross."

Aubrey shrugged. "I don't know."

"Well, I know you already know this, but if anyone shows you raunchy pictures of naked people, tell your dad right away, okay? Or me. Even if it seems to be funny. It's important!"

Aubrey stared awkwardly at the table. "Can we not talk about this anymore? And don't tell my dad about what Hailey's dad did. It's too embarrassing!"

"I won't embarrass you," Mari promised.

When Mac arrived home that afternoon, Aubrey flew to hug him as he entered the kitchen.

"Dad! Guess what we did today? We played kickball on the field and nine kids came to play with us! And look—" She held up her foot. "New shoes! Mari bought them for me! And guess what else? We got to go to Smoothie Q!"

Mac muffed her hair, casting an amazed look at Mari, who raised her brow and smiled where she stood over a griddle at the island. He dropped the mail onto the counter and spent a few moments admiring his daughter's new shoes and hearing about their adventures.

"Even Connor Haddington came to play! And guess what else? I'm done with all my chores!"

"Impressive!" He bumped her fist. "And what smells so wonderful? Were you cooking again?"

"Grilled sandwiches! *I* made them, but Mari has to flip them. I tried, but mine fell apart."

Mac faced Mari appreciatively. "I see someone has turned a corner today! And this"—he nodded to indicate the sandwiches—"that's two for two! I don't expect you to cook, you know. That wasn't part of the deal."

Mari nodded. "I know. But it's a great activity, and we had plenty of time."

"Time. Yeah, sorry I'm late. We had a last-minute shoulder dislocation. It's hard to turn away someone in pain like that." He pushed up his sleeves to wash his hands. "It was either stay or send him over to the ER—which would give him pain meds and send him back to us tomorrow."

"Ouch. Glad you stayed." She turned the griddle off. "Aubrey, we need three plates and our salad from the fridge, please." She slid Mac his credit card and receipts when he took the stool at the counter.

"Kickball, huh?" He cocked an eyebrow, wiggling the card into his money clip. "Is that your idea of resting a knee?"

"All-time pitcher," she chirped, sliding a hot sandwich onto his plate. He grunted, checking his phone.

She cut the remaining sandwich in half, splitting it with Aubrey.

Mac prayed to bless the food and thanked the two of them for cooking, then crunched into his sandwich.

"What'd you learn in school today, little flower?" he asked Aubrey.

Aubrey shot him a confused look. "Little flower?" She looked at Mari and laughed out loud. "My dad called me a little flower!"

Mac glanced at Mari. "Let me rephrase that. What'd you learn in school today, squirt?"

She laughed again. "Flower! Why'd you call me that?"

"Because you smell! Now answer my question—did you learn anything in school today?"

"Nope!" She threw her head back. "*Little flower!*"

"*I* learned something today," Mari broke in. "All these years I thought Mac was short for McAllister, but I stand corrected. Aubrey tells me your first name is actually 'Macaroni.'"

Mac scowled at his daughter. "Aubrey Michelle! Why are you telling our family secrets?"

The girl slapped the table, erupting into a giggle fit.

Mac lifted his sandwich, smiling at Mari. "These are great! And by the way, my mom says hi and thanks you for watching her."

"Cool! I'm happy to," Mari said. "And the sandwich is just a club. I made dozens of them today at the Coffee Break. Just decided to grill it."

"Nice. And you really had nine kids join you in kickball?"

"In minutes! It was the neighborhood rage, I guess! We had a lot of fun."

"Hey—hey, all right, Aubs! Settle down now!" Mac redirected Aubrey to her plate and turned back to Mari. "How are things with your other job?"

"Good. Although there *is* a bit of drama. There's one boss lady who does *not* like me whatsoever. I don't know what her problem is, but she treats me like dirt. It really grinds her when I talk to a certain professor who hangs out there." She proceeded to tell him of Dr. Grant.

"I've met him," Mac commented. "Nice guy. Did you know that he's married to actress Marilee Montayne?"

"As a matter of fact, I did know that! I bumped into her in an airport restroom just last week! I have a picture with her on my phone!"

"No kidding! That's crazy!"

"I know! She seemed nice. So anyway, Dr. Grant has this thing about asking Coffee Break patrons Bible questions—right out in the open in the dining room. And I've become one of his subjects."

"Oh, yeah? Questions like what?"

She relayed their two encounters about the prodigal son story and the questions she had been asked.

"That's interesting! How did you answer?"

"I told him I best related to the fatted calf, who sacrifices himself for everyone else." She laughed at his surprised expression. "He had the same reaction as you! I haven't told him my second answer yet, but I have some thoughts about it. Every Sunday school class I've ever been in teaches the story the traditional way—with the older brother as the jerk, but you know what? I think the father could have done things much better. And yeah, I get that the father represents God, and he loved his wayward son and longed for his return and all that, but the homecoming *did* seem a little over the top for someone who had trashed his whole inheritance. I mean, think of that happening in real life—it's not realistic. And prostitutes? Come on! The prodigal kid was a loser, and shouldn't there be consequences for a person's actions?"

"What are prostitutes?" Aubrey piped up over her sandwich.

Mari glanced over. "It's when people are paid for—uh—when two people are doing married-people stuff, but they're *not* married."

Aubrey frowned. "Cami's parents aren't married."

"Well, it's more than that."

"—Look, Aubs," Mac cut in, casting Mari a look. "We'll talk about this later. I want to let Mari finish telling me about her conversation with Dr. Grant. As you were saying—?"

"Sorry about that," Mari said lightly. "Okay—well, honestly, when someone acts that stupid, I really can't blame the older brother for freaking out. After all, he was probably the one who held everything together at home—and single-handedly. Granted, the guy could have loosened up a little and welcomed his rebellious brother home more cordially. That would have been more noble of him. Yet I get his reaction. So *no*, I don't think the father was fair."

"Huh," Mac said simply.

"How about you? What's your opinion?" She liked talking to him, she realized. She felt respected and completely at ease.

He shrugged. "I'm a boring traditionalist, I guess. But I'm more interested in hearing your faith story."

Mari spread her hands. "What is this term 'faith story'? Leah DeSoto asked me the very same question over the weekend."

"Did she?"

"In the buffet line, of all places! What are you asking when you want to know my 'faith story'?"

"Well, was there ever a time when you consciously chose to put your trust in Christ as your Savior?"

"Every year of my life since I've been a toddler! I've *always* known that Jesus died on the cross for my sins, Mac. I grew up at Eagle Bluff. I *do* know all that."

"Don't be offended! I'm not accusing you of anything!"

"Well, I'm just not fanatical about my faith like some people are. You know what they say—'all things in moderation.'"

He laughed. "Right! To love the Lord your God with a *reasonable* amount of your heart, mind, soul, and strength. I think you'll find that verse in Second Opinions."

She let his jab pass. "Then what about *you*? What's your 'faith story'? I know you have one! You're certainly not the rascal who lived next door when I was growing up!"

"And I'd be happy to share it with you!" He paused to take a drink of water. "So you already know what I was like in high school, and it only got worse. My first year of college I got stuck with the most annoying roommate. He was a Christian who perpetually asked me questions that made me both *think* about God and *mad* at him all at the same time. I made his life miserable.

"My sophomore year I had a new roommate, but all those questions still ate at me. My junior year I decided it was time to grow up. I straightened myself out and got clean—no drugs, no drinking, no girls. And yet those questions still didn't go away. I found I couldn't clean myself up enough. My problem was *in* me, and it owned me. Then after graduation I found out about her." He looked at his daughter. "My world was rocked."

Aubrey's eyes darted from Mari to her dad. "Is that a good thing or a bad thing?"

He smiled warmly. "Best thing ever!" His gaze returned to Mari. "But life-changing, nonetheless. She went back and forth between us for a while until a patient of mine helped me go for full custody. Best choice I ever made." He paused a moment. "He and I became great friends, meeting for coffee almost every week until he had a stroke."

Mari gawked at him. "Wait—are you talking about my grandfather?"

"The same! He was the one who showed me in the Word that I'm a slave to sin. I could never be good enough to earn my salvation, but Jesus Christ broke sin's power over me at the cross. And now I'm a son of God."

She stared for several moments. "I—I had no idea! Wow! We almost need to say a benediction after that! So how'd you end up at Eagle Bluff?"

"Dan DeSoto invited me. Leah's husband. He's a high school coach and accompanied a student to the clinic. The rest was history."

"That's crazy!" Mari suddenly noticed Aubrey soaking up every word. She smiled at her. "Well, I'm glad that all happened; otherwise I might not have met you!" She turned back to Mac. "But while we're on the subject—or near it—just today I happened upon an acquaintance of mine who works at the nursing home. She happens to find herself in the same predicament as—you know—her mother did with her." She inclined her head toward Aubrey. "She's terribly sick and terrified. I wish I could help her."

Mac straightened. "Really? You should connect her to JoyAnne at the Sunlight Women's Center—Susan's soon-to-be daughter-in-law. Do you know her?"

"What are you talking about?" Aubrey asked. "Are you talking code about me?"

Mac turned to her. "No, another girl who needs help."

"Help with what?"

"Some medical things," Mari cut in. "Yes, I know JoyAnne."

"Does she need a doctor?" Aubrey wanted to know.

"Yes."

Mac nodded. "Yes, get her connected with JoyAnne. She'll get the help she needs. I can get her number from Susan."

Mari made a sound. JoyAnne and Ariel together? Yeah, right. "I don't know, Mac. I went to school with JoyAnne, and I don't think she's the one to be helping girls in crisis. At least not *this* girl!"

"What?" He looked surprised. "Why would you say that? *Of course* she's the one to help her!"

Mari shook her head. "I *know* JoyAnne, and I have no idea how she was ever chosen as director of that center."

"What are you saying?"

"She's so immature! That girl is all about her face, her pouty lips, and her cleavage! She's obsessed with herself! You can't even go on social media without seeing her boobs on display!"

Aubrey's mouth dropped. "Daddy, she said *boobs*!" She held her hand over her mouth to stifle her giggling.

Mac spread his hands.

"I probably shouldn't have said that," Mari offered meekly.

"Yeah, maybe!" He glanced at his daughter.

"I mean—JoyAnne *is* a girl, and that does come with the package, but you don't have to flaunt yourself in front of everyone. Everyone already knows what's there!"

He shook his head. "I can't believe we're talking about this! Are you saying she's unqualified for her job because she's had an off-colored past?"

"Off-colored? Yeah, a little! Geez, Mac!"

"So—*her* life can't be changed by the power of the cross? She's come to Christ, you know. Did you know that? She's going to church. She's been meeting regularly with Kyla Watkins."

"Well, of course she can change! But wouldn't you want to see that change *first*? I mean—it must be nice to waltz right into a position like that with no qualifications!"

"'Must be nice'—? What's that about? And what do you know about her qualifications? Did you interview her? Oh, I get it—you're jealous of her!"

"I'm not jealous of JoyAnne Strang! I only know what she's like."

He laughed. "Yes, you are! Anyone who plays the 'must be nice' card is only advertising their envy! You're mad because *she* got that job, and *you* didn't."

She waggled her head. "*No*, I'm not! I just think I was better qualified. First of all, I have a *degree*—almost. And second—"

"You are totally judging her for her past!"

"I'm only stating the truth!"

Mac shook his head. "All right. Look, Mari—this is *not* the time or place to discuss this."

Aubrey broke in. "Are you guys arguing?"

"We're just talking, Aubrey," Mac said. He turned back to Mari. "Speaking of immature, can I ask you a personal question? Do you even have a Bible?"

"What kind of question is that? Of course I have a Bible!"

"Do you ever read it? I thought you grew up going to church!"

She huffed indignantly. "What's that supposed to mean? Are you saying *I'm* immature? I have a busy life, Mac! I've been in school. And now I have two jobs, and I'm visiting Poppy every day. I don't have time to sit around reading the Bible all day like some people do. I seriously have no time."

He waved his hand. "Well, you have time tonight. Go home, find your Bible, and read it. It'll do you good. Trust me."

"Right." She shook her head. "Not tonight. I can't."

"Why not?"

"Because I'm getting together with—" She stopped short, throwing her hands to her head. "Oh, my word—what's *wrong* with me?" She groaned, pushing in her plate. "I forgot about Will *again*! He's going to kill me! Please, Mac, go slash my tires or something so I have a valid excuse for being late!"

Aubrey looked back and forth between them. "Who's Will? Why do you want to cut your tires?"

"My boyfriend—William Wallace."

Mac leaned in, pointing. "A name which means *nothing* to her. Your boyfriend's got a case of 'little guy syndrome' if I ever saw it!"

Mari's jaw went slack. "I beg your pardon! He's not little. He's thin, but he's tall. He's at least as tall as *you*!"

"He's little on the inside. You'll have to slash your own tires. I'm not covering for you. If you can't remember your Willy Wally, that says something about your relationship! But I'll stand in for your dad and tell you that that young man had better behave himself when he's with you!"

Mari stared while Aubrey screeched in laughter. "*Willy Wally!* Sounds like the name of a *cat*! Here, Willy Wally, Willy Wally!"

The stool squeaked across the floor as Mari got up to leave.

Mac threw his napkin onto the table. "Be right back, Aubs," he said, following her out.

She faced him on the porch. "Look, Mac—I like watching your kid, but can we keep my personal life out of this? My boyfriend is none of your business!"

He dug his hands into his waist. "Fine! But likewise, could we use a little discretion in what we talk about with my daughter sitting right there? I'm going to have to explain all that to her!"

"*Fine*—I'll work on that!"

"And you're entitled to your opinion on JoyAnne—but so am I, and I think she's going to do just fine."

"Noted. I disagree."

They stared at each other in silence.

Mac let out a long breath. "Okay. Mari, what I said about your dad—"

"Yeah, about that. You can *never* stand in for my dad, Mac! Never! Don't ever do that again!"

"I know. I apologize. I apologize for *all* of that. I shouldn't have—"

She lifted a hand. "Just stop! I need—I just need to go." She turned to hurry off the porch as fast as her bum knee would allow. When she opened her car door, she saw him draw a hand through his hair as he stood watching her leave.

❖ ❖ ❖

Chapter Ten

Will was slouched on his couch playing video games when Mari finally arrived at his apartment.

"I ate," he announced in a defeated tone, barely looking up. "I gave up waiting. The leftovers are in the fridge."

"Sorry, Will," she said, kicking off her shoes by the door. It was out of the question to tell him she had already eaten too.

She waited beside the sofa, but he remained engrossed in his battle.

Oh, brother. She had rushed across town for this—? She was already battling her *own* mood. But as his cold-shoulder treatment continued, Mari retreated to the kitchen. Will was one of those strong feelers, she was learning. She would give him space. Once he "emotioned through" everything, his sullenness would blow over. Plus she wasn't ready to talk to him anyway. Her cheeks were still flushed from being so perturbed with Mac. *Little guy syndrome.* That was so incredibly mean of him! And Willy Wally—?

Numbly she scanned the fridge for the leftovers, replaying her exchange with Mac. *Speaking of immature—do you even have a Bible?* Like it was obvious to the whole world what a spiritual ignoramus she was! Her pride stung like crazy. Did she look that stupid? It made her mad. She shouldn't have to deal with insulting treatment like that! She didn't need that in her life. She had half a mind to quit.

Though not hungry in the least, she filled her plate anyway, intending to stir her food around ala elementary-school-lunchroom fashion to appear that she was eating. *Speaking of immature—do you even have a Bible?* Had Mac seriously asked her that? Agitated, she cleaned Will's microwave before heating her food. No doubt Mac thought her take on Dr. Grant's questions was dumb too. And JoyAnne Strang was a hero, of course. Of course! Just like in her dad's eyes. It figured! It both bugged and disappointed her. Vigorously she rinsed the dishcloth with fresh water and wrung it out. How had that conversation careened so out of control?

The problem was that she didn't want to quit. She admired Mac. To have him think less of her—or worse, think she could be a bad influence on his daughter—smarted. It smarted a great deal.

She glanced at the back of Will's head over the couch. "Mac had to work late," she told him, trying to snuff Mac's barbed comments about him from her mind.

"Figured it was something like that," Will said.

She wiped down his countertops, waiting for the microwave to chime in completion. Only then, when she took her spaghetti to the table, did she notice a tiny gift-wrapped box with a miniature gold bow tucked beside a full wine glass on her placemat. Her heart sank. *Great.* She had wrecked not only his dinner plans but also an apparent surprise. With all her might she rallied her mind to focus. She was *here* now—with Will. Her sense of duty made her finish every last noodle on her plate. She wished she hadn't taken so much.

"There's garlic toast on the counter!" he called when she was almost through.

"Yeah—found it!" she said. She was so stuffed she could pop.

When finished, she deposited her plate into the sink and went to sit beside him, watching him slash zombies until his character conquered the level. Victoriously, he placed the controllers on the coffee table and turned to her.

"So what was it this time?"

She answered calmly. "The clinic had a client with a dislocated shoulder walk in right at closing, and Mac stayed to help. Then we had to talk about some stuff. Time just got away from me." It was an incomplete explanation, yes, but knowing how sensitive he was, it was all she could give.

"Why didn't they go to the ER? But whatever."

She simply shrugged.

"I suppose he can stay as late as he wants if you're there. Sheesh, must be nice! That guy has it made."

Must be nice. Her head popped up in surprise. "Why would you say that? He's a single dad with a daughter!"

"Right—living in a huge house with a maid coming in for him to watch his kid. I suppose you're doing his laundry too. Like I'm supposed to feel sorry for him."

"I'm not doing his laundry! Will, what is this about? I've told you before—don't be jealous of Mac!"

He huffed. "Why is it when we talk about this, *I* always end up being the bad guy? Old Will, the jealous idiot boyfriend!"

"Stop it, Mac!" She closed her eyes. "*Will.* I'm sorry."

"Case in point."

"I'm serious. Knock it off! Mac was in puberty before I was out of diapers! Plus, I've made it clear to him that my personal life is off limits. Why do we keep going round and round on this? If you want to dump me, Will, just do it! If not, stop guilting me for my job!"

Will stared at her, but she wasn't finished.

"Lately every time we're together something weird happens. What's happened to us, Will? Are we done? Do you want to break up?"

"Do *you*?"

"No! But I don't want a whiny boyfriend! Quit acting like this! There's no reason to be jealous! I want a boyfriend I can have fun with. Someone who gives me a little gift with my glass of wine." Dang. What a dumb thing to say! She hoped she hadn't stepped over the line.

His eyes flicked to the table and back. He gave a long sigh, then went to get the present, returning to stand in front of her. "Okay, you're right. I apologize. Let's call a truce. I'd like to put everything behind us and do a complete reset. Here—open this." He handed it off with both hands, as if making a ceremonial presentation.

It was a ring. She looked up, stunned. "Will! Is this—is this a *proposal*?"

He shook his head. "Not yet. It's a promise ring. And I couldn't afford a diamond, so I got a sapphire instead 'cause I like the color. It's my birthstone."

"A promise ring?" She fingered it, admiring the setting. Wasn't that a high school thing?

"Don't you want it? You're looking at it funny."

"Well—yes. I'm just surprised."

"It's my way of saying I'd like this relationship to go somewhere."

The band was too big, so she slipped it onto her middle finger. "Thank you. So do I."

"I didn't know your size."

"It's okay. I know how to twist thread around it to make it fit. Thank you!" She looked up at him. "Will, you know you can trust me, don't you?"

"Yeah, I know. And I *do*. I don't know what's wrong with me. Sorry."

"Well, you're forgiven."

"Thanks." He shifted his feet as an awkward silence passed. "So what should we do now?"

That was a good question. She wasn't sure they were done talking, but she didn't know what else to say. She shrugged. "What did you have in mind originally?"

"Well, I was thinking of watching a romantic movie. Or—" He paused, a sheepish look on his face.

"What, Will? What would *you* like to do?"

He gestured to the controllers on the coffee table. "Mari, this new game is super fun. I think you'd like it."

"Fine." At this point anything would have to do.

"Yes!" He pumped his fist. "Marzipan, you're the absolute *best*! Plus I bought these specialty beers—let me get them!"

And then she wasn't sure if it was their talk, the ring, the wine, the beer, the exhilarating video game, the cozy couch, or the combination of everything—whatever it was, hours later the conditions were all too ripe for getting a little too intimate that evening, and that's exactly what happened. Not that she wasn't willing. She was—and would have been more so if not for Mac Sinclair dragging her father into the room. Her conscience tugged at her, for it was as though both of them were standing watching them the whole time, their arms folded in disapproval. At one point she tried to stop things—sort of—but Will assured her that he loved her and that they'd probably be getting married someday anyway. But it was too far.

All she could think about on the dark drive home was Ariel in her predicament. Ariel and Mac standing in for her dad with his piece about Will behaving. She bit her lip at the irony as she rode the elevator to her floor, alone and weighted with regret. How had she let that happen? Her only consolation was that it was at least late enough that her mother and sister would be in bed.

But the hall lights were still on when Mari opened the front door.

Shannon stepped out of the bathroom. "Where've you been? We just got off a video chat with Dad, and he asked about you." Then she spied Mari's bra protruding from her pocket and made a face. "Geez, Mari!"

Mari simply cut to her room. She changed and stood in her pajamas on the cold floor. Okay, it wasn't how her parents had raised her, but it wasn't like she was an eighth-grader who was going to get into trouble. She was an adult, for heaven's sake! She could make up her own mind for who she wanted to sleep with. But still, she wished she hadn't done it. She let out a long breath, then padded to her mother's room.

Her mom was in bed reaching for the lamp. "Oh, hi! You're out late! With Will, I'll presume. You just missed Dad! He forgot the time zone difference—again."

"We lost track of time. Video games."

Her mother eyed her, then patted the mattress. "What happened? Did you break up?"

She shook her head. "No, things are—good." She sat heavily on the bed wondering where to begin.

"What's going on?"

"Nothing. I'm just disappointed that I missed Dad. How is he?"

"Great. He sends his love. Said he had us on his mind all night. But I don't believe you for a second."

Mari looked away. "It's been a confusing day."

"With—?"

"With Will. And Mac."

Her mother flashed her a look. "Mac? What happened?"

"Nothing. Just a weird conversation. Nothing bad, but I can't stop thinking about it."

"About what? Honey, what's going on?"

"Nothing's wrong. We talked some about my knee. And about God. It's just been a weird day." She realized she didn't want to tell her mom about her talk with Mac. Or about anything regarding Will. Or Ariel. Or JoyAnne. Why had she even come to her mother's room?

They sat together for a moment before her mom spoke: "Mari, hon, can I give you a word of caution about this job of yours? Mac's a great guy, and Aubrey is a wonderful little girl, but be careful. You're coming into their world in a mom-like role, and I don't want to see things get—you know—awkward. You might start to feel like a family. Only you're not."

"What? Are you referring to *me* going down that path? Or Mac?"

"Well, either! Just be careful. I'd hate for either of you to get hurt."

"Don't worry—that's not *remotely* my issue."

"Well, better to say something now than have something happen later."

"Mom, it's my second day! All I wanted was a job so I could help out with Poppy!"

Her mother made an impatient sound. "Don't snap at me! Why are you so crabby? I think you need to go to bed!"

"*Fine*, I will!" Mari pulled herself to her feet.

"Goodness, Mari! What's going on? Why won't you talk to me?"

Mari shook her head. "It's—nothing."

"Right!" She waved. "Okay, sit down—although I'll remind you of how late it is. I need to work in the morning."

"So do I." Mari paused but remained standing. But what could she say? After a few moments she asked, "Mom, do you know Ariel Marquette? That super-quiet girl from church with the ultra-black hair and that creepy snake tattoo?"

"Yes, Ariel. She works at Riverview now. Did she get a tattoo?"

"Yeah, her. Do you know her mom?"

"No, I've never met her. Susan says she works at that bar downtown—Cooley's or something. Why?"

"Just thinking about Ariel today. I ran into her leaving the nursing home."

"She seems to be doing well there. It seems like a good fit for a girl like her."

"Yeah, I guess so."

Her mother waited, regarding her silently.

Mari sighed. "Okay, you're right—I'm tired. We can talk tomorrow. I'm going to bed. Good night."

"Okay then. Good night, Mari."

She heard the click of the light as she left her mother's room.

Mari was late for work the next morning—partly because she hadn't slept well with Will, Ariel, and Mac cycling through her brain all night long. But mostly because Shannon forgot to tell her she needed their dad's car all day due to hers being repaired, and Mari hadn't planned enough time to walk to work. After a brief but unpleasant squabble between the two of them at the front door, Shannon finally offered Mari a ride—though begrudgingly, since the jaunt to Taiton campus would cost her even more minutes, making *her* late for work too. When she dropped her off, she practically drove off before Mari had shut the car door. They were both overtired, Mari reminded herself.

As she hurriedly slipped behind the counter, Candace raised her brow. "Someone should be making sandwiches right now."

"I know—sorry," Mari said. "Let me quick drop my bag in the back."

But on her way for her work apron, she overheard the manager speaking sternly in the kitchen right around the corner.

"This is the *last* time, Tatum. Not once more—do you hear me? If this happens again, we are calling the police! Stop pretending you have everything under control!"

Mari's hand froze in mid-reach.

"You know nothing about my life," Tatum shot in reply.

"I don't care! What's happening is *wrong*! I have given you every benefit of the doubt—"

"—You have no proof, so you can leave me the heck alone!"

Tatum's voice had suddenly grown louder, as though she was turning to leave the kitchen, and Mari knew they'd be face to face in a second. In a desperate move, she snatched her apron from the hook and charged hastily around the corner—smacking straight into her and giving her best startled cry.

"Tatum!" she sputtered, drawing back. "I'm so sorry! I didn't know you were there!" Breathlessly she turned to the manager. "Sorry—I was just coming back to apologize for being late. I'm sorry, and I promise it won't happen again!"

Tatum was too stunned to speak. The manager simply blinked and bobbed his head. "See that it doesn't. And slow down, for heaven's sake!"

"Thank you. It won't." She knotted the apron around her waist. "And I'll—get to work." She would have surely outdone JoyAnne Strang in theater, she thought smugly, giving herself an *A plus* for the performance.

"Did you forget something?" Candace asked when she returned up front. "Like—the sandwiches?"

"Give me a sec," Mari told her. "I need to check a few things."

She hovered attentively over the front case for a few minutes, moving beverages around to look busy, making pretend mental notes until she saw the manager had returned to his regular duties. Then snagging Boris to help her, the two of them returned to an empty kitchen to make the sandwiches.

Professor Grant had set himself up in a new spot and was quietly reading when Mari went out to bus tables.

He nodded his greeting. "Late night?"

She looked at him in amazement. "How would you know that?" Were her eyes bloodshot?

"You rushed into this place like you had barely gotten your last shoe on. Being tardy is one of my pet peeves, you know. Everyone gets all in a tizzy and blames it on this or that when it primarily boils down to one thing—poor planning." He paused. "But lucky you—you're not on my class roster."

She eyed him briefly. "Let me guess—I'm not the only one who's sleep deprived this morning."

His lip curled in amusement. "I gotta hand it to you, Miss Coleman. You're one sharp cookie, and I like you." He chuckled. "All right, Sunshine, let's talk about our homework, shall we? I asked you if you thought the way the father treated his wayward son was fair."

Mari paused with a cluster of mugs in her hands. "You know, I had this all thought out yesterday. I even talked it over with Mac Sinclair. Do you know Mac? I watch his daughter. Anyway, I had concluded that the father might have gone a little nuts when his son returned. And considering the extent to which the younger brother blew his entire inheritance, I can't blame the older brother for having an issue with that."

"But—?"

"Well, now that you ask the question again—was it *fair*?—that changes things. *Fair* implies equal treatment or equal endowment, and I wonder if there's *anything* that's fair in life. In just my family alone, there's hardly anything that's fair. My sister is tall and gorgeous—and then there's me. But we're not talking about my family."

"On the contrary! This story is about a family, so it's fine if you want to talk about yours. Although as a father, I'll say that you're not lacking in looks. If your father never affirmed you in that, he should have."

Not the way he had affirmed Shannon, she mused. "Anyway—"

"Yes, anyway—bravo for your answer! This concept of fairness—you're on to something there! Technically, the father treated neither of those two boys *fairly*, did he?" He cleared his throat. "Maybe juggle those dishes around a little. We're under scrutiny again."

She set the mugs in her bin and gathered up the plates. "Well, I'd like my next question."

"I'm not sure we're done with this one. So let me ask you—what would fairness have looked like for that wayward boy?"

"I have no idea, but I think I see what you're getting at: there was a whole lot of mercy extended to him, which isn't particularly fair."

He nodded approvingly. "Bingo! Mercy is not fair. No one deserves mercy, do they? So here's tomorrow's question: Why did the father rush to meet that prodigal child?"

"Because he loved him."

He spread his hands. "Have we not gone over this? Let's talk tomorrow!"

"I'm ready to talk about it now!"

"You're out of time, dearie." He raised his head. "Miss Tatum! Would that everyone had a work ethic like you! Do you mind if I ask your ethnic origin?"

Without looking back, Mari gave one last swipe over the table with her dish cloth, then hefted the loaded tote to haul it to the kitchen.

As it turned out, Tatum left before her shift was over that morning, informing the crew that she was taking a sick day. For Mari, her departure was like storm clouds giving way to sun, although she couldn't help but wonder if her "sickness" was related to her previous kitchen scolding. It appeared some kind of trouble was brewing at the Coffee Break with Tatum at the center of it, whatever it was. Had there been money missing from the cash register? Mari found her gaze often drawn to it.

With Tatum's absence, pink-haired and proficient Candace stepped into the lead dog role, managing well, though the added responsibilities made her considerably busier, which had its advantages. Noting she was occupied with a project in the kitchen, Mari grabbed her bucket and went for another pass through the dining room, hoping for further conversation with Dr. Grant, who was now typing studiously on his laptop.

He glanced up as Mari happened by, seeming pleased to see her. "Back for more, eh?"

Mari smiled. "The father rushed to meet his son because he loved him. He loved him deeply."

"Ah, jumping right in, are we? All right." He slid his chair back a little. "That's certainly true. But if that father loved him so deeply, why did he let that kid leave in the first place? Why did he give him his inheritance and let him go? Answer that, Miss Coleman! Surely he wasn't naive as to what might happen!"

Mari regarded him thoughtfully. "Maybe that was part of love— letting him do what he wanted to do."

"Yeah? Is it love to give your kid whatever he wants?"

"I'd say it was more about letting him make his choices."

"What do you mean by that?"

She fingered the wet cloth. "Well, you can't make someone love you back. If you could, it wouldn't be love. And sometimes people make up their minds to do what they're going to do. I'd have to look at the story again, but I wonder if that isn't the case here. The father knew his son had made up his mind to leave, and he let him go. Maybe that was love."

"All right. But do you think it was *wise* to leave that young man to his choices?" He brought his fingertips together. "They weren't particularly healthy choices. That father had to know it would be the end of the boy's inheritance!"

Mari made a little sound. "You're making this difficult!"

The professor simply waited.

"Okay. Since the father represents God, I know it had to be wise. It's just a matter of figuring out why!" She sighed. "I don't know. I'm sure the father *did* care about the family inheritance, but maybe he cared *more* about his relationship with his son. Maybe he was willing to risk losing his wealth on the chance that his son would decide to come home. Maybe he knew he'd come home eventually."

"How could he possibly have known that?"

"Then maybe he *hoped* he'd come home."

"Ah! Or prayed to that end? *Believed* to that end, maybe?"

"Yeah—that. Maybe it was faith."

He nodded. "Right. So if the father loved his son that much, why would that kid want to leave? Why would a young man who was so loved want to take his inheritance and break away from his father to go live a life of 'wanton pleasure'?"

"Stupidity. And free will."

Dr. Grant tipped his head.

"Those are the most obvious answers, but"—Mari said while squirming a bit—"well, 'wanton pleasure' *is*—you know—pleasurable. There's something appealing about sin. Otherwise, why would we do it?" As she spoke, her cheeks grew warm as her previous evening with Will came to mind. "Plus maybe he didn't understand how much his father loved him."

"So you're saying it's possible to be deeply loved and entirely clueless about it?"

"Apparently it is." She paused reflectively, adding, "And maybe it's possible to know you're deeply loved but be entirely *unmoved* by it. Like to know it, but not really *know* it."

Dr. Grant observed her quietly.

Suddenly Mari glanced around. "Well, thank you for your time, but I should get back to work. Is there a question for tomorrow?"

He straightened in his chair. "I'd like to know what made that young man decide to come home."

"Got it." She gave him a discreet thumbs up. "See you tomorrow."

"God bless your day, Miss Coleman!"

Candace met her at the counter. "I know what you're doing out there," she said.

Mari returned her bucket and rag to the lower shelf. "He's a chatty customer, and I'm being polite."

"More like naive! Why are you taking Bible questions from a *history* professor? You should be careful of guys like that. Every day he sits there trolling for spiritual conversations with unsuspecting folks like you—young vulnerable folks. Why do you think he does that?"

"He says he wants to help students think about important things in life."

"Right. Think again!"

Mari already knew Candace's opinion on why Dr. Grant was there, but she preferred not to get into it with her. She was about to walk away, but at the last minute turned back. "Candace, why is talking about God so threatening to you?"

The woman's eyes grew round. "Oh, I have no problem with God. God is all around me for whatever I need." She waved her arm, as if encompassing the universe. "It's creeps like *him* that I'm wary of."

"Creeps?" She shot a look back at the professor.

Candace leaned in, lowering her voice. "When I was fourteen, I found myself pregnant by the neighborhood 'evangelist.' He'd been luring in girls for his Bible studies for years! I can recognize a predator a mile away."

Mari's mouth dropped. "Candace! That's terrible! I hope he was prosecuted!"

"Eventually."

"Oh, my goodness! That must have been so scary having a baby so young!"

She huffed. "Are you kidding? I was only fourteen! My parents helped me get rid of it."

Mari brought her hand to her chest. "Candace, I'm so sorry for what you've been through! Have you ever gotten help for that?"

She frowned. "Help?"

"Counseling. For what he did to you. And for losing your baby."

Instantly she stiffened. "Look, missy—don't go condescending on me like I'm some messed-up piece of trash! I'm just fine, thank you. This is about gullible girls like *you* who think they've got the world by the tail. Everything's going great for you, isn't it? Well, I'm warning you–be careful!"

Mari drew back, shaking her head. "I wasn't trying to put you down or anything."

"Well, I think you're pretty naive! You should get back to work. You've wasted enough of your employer's time!"

Mari nodded. "Right. Okay. I appreciate your concern for me, Candace. And for the record, I am *not* judging you."

With a curt nod, Candace headed for the kitchen.

In a blur, Mari turned to face the morning rush that had begun streaming in. Candace. Wow. What a shocking drop of information! She bit her lip as she started her next order. Who would have guessed the crater of pain that lay inside that girl? Her stomach hurt at the thought of it. No wonder Candace took issue with Dr. Grant's interaction with Coffee Break patrons!

Mari struggled to remain diligently on task for the rest of her shift, now ultra-conscious of the number of students—both men and women—who paused at the cheerful professor's table to visit. Candace's suspicion was outrageous! There was nothing remotely sinister about Dr. Grant. And yet the intensity of the girl's dire warning had opened Mari to the possibility, which was why she couldn't disregard it—although the thought of the professor having a dark side made Mari sick from every angle.

Candace. Stirring her current order, Mari shot a look at the pink-haired girl, now at the cash register. Like Ariel, Candace would be a perfect candidate for counseling through the Sunlight Women's Center. Mari knew that Sunlight had a whole department of staff who dealt with that kind of trauma. But that would mean Candace would have to go through JoyAnne, which took Mari back to her train-wreck conversation with Mac the previous evening.

She sighed. Part of her knew Mac was right. JoyAnne *had* changed. And yet it bugged her so to have Mac take her side. Dang it. Mari wished someone would notice what *she* could have brought to the center, had she been hired instead. But the worst thing—there was no one she could talk to about it. At any rate, Mari concluded that she would simply have to try to help those two women herself. It appeared to be the only option left.

Chapter Eleven

After work Mari was so consumed with Candace's disturbing disclosure that she wandered the Taiton Student Center parking lot for several minutes trying to find where she had parked—until she recalled that Shannon had dropped her off that morning. Rolling her eyes at herself, she phoned her sister. When she didn't answer, she called Will, who promptly urged her to call Shannon, for he was in a crucial step of an important project and it was impossible for him to help her. Mari was about to phone Mac when Shannon called back, declaring she was on her way.

"Just take me back to the salon," Shannon directed, letting her have the car. "Colt's picking me up after work."

"Tell him thanks," Mari said.

While her grandfather rested, Mari scoured the halls of Riverview to find Ariel, only to learn later at the office that she had called in sick that day. Mari wasn't surprised. As she ambled back to her grandfather's room, she debated delivering a care package to her before going to Mac's. Soda crackers and ginger ale, maybe? Yet recalling how adamant Ariel had been about her mother not getting wind of her condition, Mari decided against the risk. What if Ariel's mother or her boyfriend were there? So she simply texted her again, but as with the previous day, Ariel did not respond. Mari sighed. Someone like Ariel needed guidance. It was crucial she got a hold of her.

When her grandfather awoke, Mari asked the staff if she could take him out to the courtyard to enjoy the lovely day, and given the green light, an aide walked them out, hovering near until her grandfather was securely seated on his walker in the shade of a newly leafed maple. Then alone, Mari surprised him by revealing she had brought out his Bible.

"Mind if I read to you, Poppy?" she asked, at which his face registered delight.

But it didn't turn out to be as nourishing a time in the Word as she imagined it should have been, as egged on by Mac the last evening. First, she was still steeped with guilt for having gone too far with Will. Second, she had to search the concordance to even locate the parable of the prodigal son. And then reading it, she had to fight to keep her thoughts on the actual story, for Candace's warning about Dr. Grant had now entangled itself with all her previous spiritual discussions with him. Plus she couldn't stop thinking about Candace herself and all the trauma she had been through as a teenager. It polluted everything. No wonder she bristled at Dr. Grant! Mari found herself so angry for all the woman's pain that she had to take a break from reading halfway through the story.

As she paused, her grandfather moved his gaze from the peaceful courtyard back to her. She smiled at him, consciously yanking her mind to the present, back to the beautiful, loving man she was with and the gorgeous day she had with him. She was so thankful she still had him. They sat together quietly, listening to the chittering birds.

"Poppy, did Mac visit you this morning?" she asked for conversation's sake, knowing he likely had.

"Yesss, Mac," he replied, fumbling with his flannel shirt pocket, as if suddenly remembering something. He handed her a small card. "Mac!"

Her name—Marissa—was inked across the envelope. She looked at him, bewildered. "Is this from Mac?" No one called her Marissa—no one except her mother when she was angry.

Another nod. "From Mac—yesss!"

Breaking its seal, she found inside a little card with stamped lettering that said, "For You." As she opened it, her breath caught in surprise as a delicate bouquet of tiny, colorful flowers fanned out toward her. A miniature pop-up card! And one that had its origins in an art shop, she guessed, studying the intricate, paper blooms so skillfully folded together. She turned it over. *No more boyfriend jabs or treating you like a child—I promise,* it said, with his name scrawled below.

She looked up to see her grandfather watching her.

She held the card out. "Look, Poppy! Isn't this the sweetest thing you've ever seen?"

"Mac!" he stated, his eyes twinkling.

"Yes, from Mac." *Oh, brother.* Who knew what her grandfather was thinking? Nevertheless, the card made her happy. She didn't want things weird with anybody, most of all Mac. And now she felt so much better about seeing him again. She tucked the card into her back pocket and checked the time.

"All right, back to our story," she said, finding her place in the Bible.

She returned to the beginning, reading the entire parable to him again. This time, however, thoughts of Mac and his faith story overshadowed the gloom of Candace's dark past. Mac, a real-life prodigal who had come home. She paused in reflection. In comparison to Mac's, her faith looked stiff and uncaring. Like it or not, she had to admit that she was more like the older brother in the Bible story than she had previously believed. Not entirely, no. She wasn't *that* bad. But she saw herself enough to have to change her answer to Dr. Grant.

And Dr. Grant. She closed the Bible, preparing to walk her grandfather back into the building. What should she do about him? Was it naive of her to trust the professor? However, a glance at the clock indicated she couldn't think about that now. She had to keep moving or she would be late to Frost.

When Aubrey got home from school, she rushed into the house in a panic, dumping her belongings in the center of the foyer. "Mari, quick! We have to hurry! They're all going there—all the kids are going straight to the field! I'm supposed to bring the ball!"

"Whoa, whoa, whoa!" Mari said, appearing from the kitchen. "Not so fast! You know the rule: homework and chores first."

Aubrey's mouth fell open in a cry.

"It's your dad's rule. And come here—look." Mari waved to the cubbies near the stairway. "Every day after school, I'd like you to put your things where they belong. Shoes on the mat, coat on the hook, backpack here." She tapped the oak panel.

The girl's shoulders slumped as she complied. Then quickly she returned to the door to check the park. "See—I told you! They're all there!" She moaned, her face puckered in distress.

"Would you like a smoothie while you do your homework?"

"Can I just have something quick? Like a nature bar or a banana?" She dragged herself from the door to unzip the silver pocket on her backpack.

Mari eyed her. Was Aubrey blinking back tears? Classic manipulation, she told herself. But then she considered that the girl was trying to *hide* her tears, not use them to get her way. And wasn't outdoor activity one of her reasons for buying her new shoes? Quickly Mari whipped out an alternate plan.

"Young lady, I've changed my mind. Homework and chores can wait. We're going to the field."

Aubrey's head snapped up. "For real?" She threw her arms around

Mari's waist, jarring her knee. "Thank you! Can we hurry?"

Mari winced, gritting her teeth. "Yes! Get your tennis shoes on! I'll get you a banana." She needed a second to breathe before turning for the kitchen, where on a whim she also grabbed two boxes of nature bars from Mac's pantry, just in case.

The previous day's kickball gathering had clearly been a success, for instead of nine, Mari now counted fifteen children waiting for them at the field. Most of the new kids were siblings or friends of yesterday's gang, but Connor Haddington had brought his buddy Ty West home with him on the bus—who immediately set the stage for conflict when he wrenched the ball from Aubrey's arms and booted it half a mile down the field for a "field goal." It took both skill and self-control for Mari to simultaneously correct the offender and calm Aubrey's freak-out, while sending Connor on a jog to fetch the rubber ball. Doubtless, she would need to keep Ty West close.

With Aubrey now making an even sixteen players, Mari split the group down the middle, sending the "Badgers" to the outfield and the "Boa Constrictors" up to kick first, the names chosen after a much-heated debate as to which was the "baddest" animal each team could think of. From there the game unfolded relatively smoothly, with only minor squabbles over a few of her referee calls. And then after each team had been up to kick six times and the players were beginning to lag, Mari called the game, deflecting the arguments over which team had won by doling out the nature bars and asking if anyone had any funny jokes.

"Whoa—hey—*clean* jokes," she specified after a brow-raising humor attempt by Ty. She glanced worriedly at the other children, thankful that his raunchy story had gone over most of their heads. The last thing she needed was parents calling Mac about their park gathering. Then a fourth-grader stepped up with a stream of knock-knock funnies that had everybody giggling and groaning.

Crumpling her wrapper after her snack, one of the girls asked, "Do you have any water?"

Just like that *everyone* was thirsty, and it was time to go.

"See you tomorrow!" Mari called as the group dispersed toward their homes. She held up a sweatshirt. "Connor, is this yours? Kids, look around! Make sure you have everything!"

Connor ran back to fetch it, then snagged Ty's camouflage backpack from the ground.

"Bye!" Mari called as they took off for Connor's house.

Aubrey sidled up to Mari. "I hope Ty West doesn't come tomorrow."

Mari wrapped her arm around her shoulders and squeezed. "I am so proud of how you handled yourself today! Great job!" She smiled down at her, then leaned in to give her a sniff. "Whoa, girl—you need a shower!"

Aubrey giggled. "It's my new perfume!"

"Yeah—'Ode of Dead Socks'!"

They both laughed.

"Can I use my new shampoo?"

Mari nodded, pleased that she was excited about it. "Yes! But remember what I said—if you use too much conditioner, you'll be rinsing it out all night!"

"Can I do it now?"

"Yes, go take your shower. Then it's homework time!"

Aubrey took off for the house, but Mari stayed to take a turn through their little matted grass kickball diamond to collect left-behind items and trash, stuffing the latter into the empty snack box. As she worked her way across the scrubby grass toward Mac's, she suddenly recognized two women in front of his house, power walking toward the field. No way. JoyAnne Strang with Kyla Watkins! Was there no place on the planet to escape that girl?

Kyla spied Mari too and immediately waved, calling, "Hey! It's the girl from the airplane!" Her hair was in a ponytail.

As she approached them on Mac's driveway, Mari heard JoyAnne hastily tell Kyla under her breath, "That's *her*—that's Mari Coleman."

"Hi," Mari said, walking up. "Yes, it's me—Mari Coleman." She met JoyAnne's eyes briefly.

"We're out for a walk," Kyla said. "Minus kids. It's great!"

"Doug and I eat with his folks on Wednesdays," JoyAnne added, her cheeks flushed. "I left my girls with Susan."

"—And it's a perfect neighborhood to meet in the middle for a walk beforehand," Kyla finished. "It's our time for checking in with each other. What are *you* up to?"

Mari gestured. "I watch Mac's daughter after school. I grew up here. Right between his house and the Gordons'."

"Ah, lucky you!" Kyla exclaimed. "I adore Miss Susan! She has helped me so much! I don't know where I'd be without her!"

Mari smiled.

Kyla then turned toward JoyAnne, giving a barely perceptible tip of her head toward Mari.

JoyAnne shifted her feet, as though self-conscious. "Um, hey. I wanted to thank you for coming to my bridal shower last weekend. That was nice of you." She dropped her eyes.

"Sure. Congratulations on your engagement. Dougie's a great guy." She couldn't bring herself to offer her congratulations on the Sunlight job.

"Thanks. I was wondering if, um—if you'd ever want to get together sometime?"

Nope. Never, Mari answered to herself—simultaneously noticing Kyla's face swing back toward her, as if judging her response. What was *that* about?

"Oh, uh—sure," she said, opting for a polite but evasive response. "Although right now I'm pretty busy. I work at Taiton through lunch and then here after school. And then I've been helping my grandfather a lot. And I have a boyfriend. So I'm not sure when."

JoyAnne nodded. "Right. Well, maybe sometime."

"Yeah. We should. Sometime." Sure, as if they were old pals or something! She started loading a mental warehouse of ways she would be busy all summer.

An awkward silence followed.

Kyla motioned toward the field. "Well, we should keep moving so we're back in time for dinner."

"Yes. Nice to run into you," JoyAnne chimed, baring her gums with her smile.

"Nice to see you both," Mari echoed.

She cut across Mac's lawn toward his porch steps, relieved to have dodged a bullet. She was not having another talk with JoyAnne. No way. Been there, done that. Yet something felt strange about that conversation. Had they been discussing her? She glanced back, eyeing the girls as they resumed their walk. As if in answer to her question, JoyAnne twisted right then to look over her shoulder toward *her*. Mari snapped her face forward, quickening her step, her gut revisited with an unpleasant twinge of buried teenage tension. Well, well! Had someone told them she was upset about the Sunlight job? She wondered who. Mac? Shannon?

Inside, she closed the door, standing in Mac's foyer to let out a long breath. This was so crazy. How was it that all these new girls were so gushy over Mrs. Gordon? *I don't know where I'd be without her!* Now she even felt like an outsider in her own neighborhood!

Suddenly from upstairs came an ear-piercing shriek of terror. Mari's heart dropped. *Aubrey!* At the detriment of her knee, she topped the stairs in a flash, flying past the open bathroom door to find the hysterical girl wrapped in a towel in her bedroom, urgently pointing out her window.

"They're getting out!" she cried. "Look!"

"Who are?" Mari asked, rushing to the window. "What's the matter?"

"The *dogs!* They're getting out!"

"What?" Mari looked down in confusion.

"They're digging! They're getting into our yard! Nooo!" She threw her head back in a panic.

"Hey—settle down! Aubrey! Hey—it's okay!" Mari peered downward to see that indeed, one of the neighbor's dogs was furiously digging under the fence, his paws scratching and head poking sideways through a freshly scooped-out hole under the vertical boards.

"They're getting into our yard!" Aubrey wailed. "Call my dad! Quick! Call my dad!" She stamped her feet, beginning to cry. "I want my dad to come home!"

Mari touched her arm. "Get a grip, Aubrey! Those dogs are not going to hurt you!"

"*Now!* Call him!"

Mari watched the girl's meltdown in disbelief. There was no way she was going to call Mac about the neighbor's dogs! That would be ridiculous. But Aubrey was out of control. Mari looked back at the burrowing animal, wondering if there was something she could do. Could she block the hole?

"All right—stay here," she commanded, turning to take the stairs to the kitchen. Quickly she scanned the inside of the refrigerator, then pulled open the freezer, grabbing the first thing she saw—a bag of frozen meatballs. She ripped it open on her way out the back door.

"Hey, pup," she murmured, cautiously approaching the tunneling animal, which immediately growled, baring its teeth. In a surge of adrenaline, Mari snatched a couple of the meatballs and chucked them to the dirt near the animal, who then snapped and snarled but quickly withdrew. She waited. As anticipated, its sniffing muzzle returned before gobbling up the nuggets. In a moment its big head reappeared under the fence in full snuffling mode—along with the second dog's.

"That's right. Here you go, fellas," she crooned softly, tossing them a few more. And another few. Then she took a handful and gently lobbed them over the top of the fence. Promptly the Rottweilers disappeared, scrambling after the meat. Dropping the bag, Mari hurried to fetch a hefty piece of firewood from Mac's backyard pit, wedging it tightly in the gap under the fence. She added a couple more logs on top and beside it, then straightened, waiting for the awful throb in her knee to subside. Today had not been kind to it.

Shakily she retrieved the meatball bag, but as she walked away, she became aware of whining and scratching on the other side of the fence. She paused, looking back. After a moment of consideration, she relented, skillfully launching the remaining meatballs handful by handful over the fence. Then on her way into the house, she had another idea.

Returning with an aluminum cake pan, she dragged the garden hose over to the fence. Removing part of her barricade, she slid the cake pan three fourths of the way under the fence and filled it with water. Immediately two dog snouts appeared, noisily lapping it up. When they had finished, Mari retrieved her pan and replaced the log.

Aubrey was still wrapped in the towel when Mari returned upstairs, though this time she was in her dad's bedroom, which apparently offered a better view of the drama below.

"All right—you're safe," Mari announced. "I blocked the hole."

Aubrey glanced warily out her dad's window. "What if they dig a different one?"

"I don't think that's going to happen," she replied simply. "Good heavens, girl! You scared me half to death when you screamed! Why on earth are you so afraid of those dogs? Did one snap at you or something?"

"I hate them because they're *mean*. And so is Mr. Eden!"

Mari shook her head. "Now, now! Just because you don't like his dogs doesn't mean that your neighbor is mean. Don't be acting like that."

"He *is*! He's mean! He makes mean faces at me!"

"Are you telling the truth? Does Mr. Eden really make faces at you?"

"Once he did—when I seen him bury the dead body in his yard! He looked up and made a mean face at me."

"Aubrey, for real? Did that really happen?"

"Yes!"

Mari folded her arms. "Are you sure? Where? Show me where you saw this."

Aubrey beckoned her to the window. "Look! See over there—in the back toward the fence! That's where he buried it!"

Indeed, the sod looked turned over where Aubrey had indicated, though not freshly so. Mari turned to her. "How do you know it was a body?"

She shrugged. "I just know it. He dug the hole, then put black garbage bags in it and covered it up! I seen him do it!"

"*Saw* him. And several bags? How do you know it wasn't garbage?"

"Because he puts his trash in the bins beside his garage, like my daddy does."

"And he looked up at you?"

"I accidentally bumped my head on the window, and he looked up and went like this—" Aubrey contorted her face and shook her fist in a threatening way.

Mari shuddered. "And you told your dad this—all of it?"

"Yes, but he thinks I'm lying."

Mari stared out at her former yard where the neighbor's dogs now panted peacefully in the shade of her old maple. "Well, I'll talk to him. But for now, you need to get dressed. You have homework—remember? And chores. Go on—get dressed and I'll help you with your hair. And when you come down, bring your dirty laundry."

With a loud sigh, Aubrey padded out of the room.

Mari glanced outside again, then turned, suddenly aware of being in Mac's room—his loosely made bed, open closet doors, dress slacks over the arm of an upholstered chair. She shut his door on her way out.

When Mac arrived home, he found the two of them on the porch, Aubrey on a low stool in front of Mari, who sat on the swing behind her, fixing her hair. They had been talking about ways to show kindness to Aubrey's friend Hailey's mom because she was in cancer treatment. They had just decided on making banana bread for them tomorrow after school.

"Is it that time already?" Mari asked when he came up the steps. She was glad to see him, though more than a bit anxious with last night's weird argument still hanging between them.

"My last appointment cancelled," he said. "I'm a little early." Seeing what was happening, he set his hands on his waist, shaking his head. "My, my, someone is getting the royal treatment!"

"Like it?" Proudly Aubrey turned her head side to side.

Mari's hands followed her movements fluidly. "Hold still, girl! Almost done!"

"Love it!" Mac's eyes flicked to Mari's. "Gee, thanks a lot! The bar is officially topped out. I can't possibly do her hair like that!" His gaze. Was it her imagination, or did he look nervous too?

She shook her head. "You don't have to. It just felt like the thing to do today. We had a crazy afternoon, didn't we, Aubrey?"

Aubrey perked up. "Daddy, guess what happened!"

Mari raised her brow at Mac while Aubrey plunged into the dog incident by detail, her hands flying wildly in the telling.

"Are you kidding me?" He glanced next door in disbelief.

"I owe you a bag of meatballs," Mari admitted humbly.

"One of them even hit a dog on the head," Aubrey declared with a giggle. "I seen it from upstairs!"

"You *saw* it. All I intended was to plug the hole," Mari said. "But then they were so eager, like they hadn't been fed. And when I gave them water, they drank and drank—like they were terribly thirsty. I felt a little sorry for them. Okay, all done!" Mari tapped Aubrey on the shoulders, who hopped up to hug her dad.

"It's best if you left those dogs alone," Mac said. "How was school today, squirt?"

Aubrey beamed. "Good. I got to be Mrs. K's assistant during library!"

"Nice!"

"And I'm almost done with my homework—just one tiny part left."

"Great!"

"Plus your chores yet," Mari reminded from the swing.

"Yep!" Aubrey said. "Guess what, Dad? Mari let me play kickball on the field *first* before homework!"

"—Which you should go finish so we can play kickball again *tomorrow*," Mari added sweetly.

Aubrey smiled. "Can you come with me?"

"We're going to visit a bit," Mac said, squaring his daughter's shoulders toward the door. "I'll be in soon."

"Mac, I apologize," Mari said as soon as Aubrey was in the house. "I *know* the homework rule, but all the kids were already at the field—fifteen today! I just couldn't disappoint her!"

He settled on the ledge of the porch with his back to the street.

"Sixteen with Aubrey," she added. "And sorry—I owe you a couple of boxes of nature bars too. It seemed like the right thing to do—to give them all a snack. I'll pay you back."

"No, that's fine. How's the knee?"

"Well, wrenching it in the dog drama didn't help it any."

He made a sound through his teeth. "You gotta be careful. And fifteen—? That's amazing! That's like a little club!"

"I know! They're all good kids—well, except for Ty West. He's one of those nine-going-on-nineteen boys who knows *way* more than a nine-year-old should, if you catch my drift. He's a bit of a bully, and his language—yikes! But anyway—" She took a breath, changing the subject. "I wanted to talk to you about Aubrey and the dog thing. Mac, are you aware that your daughter is absolutely terrified of those dogs next door? Terrified!"

"Oh, I'm aware of it!"

"And your neighbor—this Roger Eden—what do you know about him?"

"He's an okay guy. An exterminator. Kind of reminds me of your dad—always an interesting story to tell."

"Well, Aubrey's terrified of him too. She says he's made threatening gestures toward her."

Mac threw back his head. "Aww, no. She's not going down that dead-body road again, is she? I've told her she needs to knock it off!"

"She says you won't believe her! She's absolutely convinced that he's done something really bad!"

"I thought we talked about this! She tells stories."

"Mac, she's convinced."

"I know! Look, Marissa—this is how it went down: I came home from work one evening to have Roger Eden show up on my porch asking if I had a power digger of some sort to till a spot in his yard for some asparagus he was transplanting. While the two of us were in my garage, he told me he respected me as a single dad, but I should know that my daughter has a habit of staring out the window at him and sticking out her tongue."

Mari brushed away a fly, regarding him thoughtfully. "So where's the asparagus? I didn't see any in his yard."

Mac shook his head. "Okay, you're not helping! I don't know, but *please* don't encourage her in this!"

"I'm just saying—why won't you believe her? If it didn't happen, where did she come up with this? She's *eight*! This isn't normal for an eight-year-old—talking about burying body parts in plastic bags! Where is she getting this? Do you let her watch scary movies?"

"No! Although"—he dipped his head—"my mom was somewhat lax in her supervision, so it's possible she happened on some bad show by accident. Which is why I'm glad I have *you*." He smiled.

"You're diverting the subject."

He let out a breath. "What do you want me to do? Call the police to come dig up his yard? Yeah, right! She's eight and she tells stories! I'd like her *and you* to leave Roger Eden and his dogs alone. Period. Subject closed. So how was the coffee shop this morning?"

"Fine, we will. But I still think your daughter should know you take her seriously. You gotta have trust in your relationship, Mac. She won't talk to you if you don't listen to her."

"I *do* listen to her! And Roger Eden doesn't owe me an explanation for his asparagus. Maybe he ditched his plan. Maybe it all died. Maybe it's planted alongside the fence where you can't see it. Is that possible?"

Mari eyed him a moment. "Okay. You're right. Fine." She tossed her head, moving on. "Work was good, mostly. I happened to walk in on my grumpy coworker getting a tongue-lashing from the manager. I suspect she was caught stealing from the cash register, and I don't know why he didn't just fire her. She's not the most pleasant person in the world. And I had a really great talk with Dr. Grant. And by the way, Mac, I read the Bible today—just so you know."

"Did you?"

"Yes. With Poppy. Only a little, but it's something."

He looked both surprised and pleased. "Way to go, Marissa!"

"Yeah, well, I'm learning." She tapped her foot for a gentle push on the swing. "Anyway, I wanted to tell you something else. After my talk with the professor, another coworker pulled me aside and warned me about him. She thinks he's a predator!"

Mac laughed. "Dr. Grant? Why would she think that?"

Mari spread her hands.

"There's no way!"

"But how would you know?"

He paused, regarding her. "Fine. I'll run a background check on him."

She sat back in surprise. "Seriously?"

"Consider it done."

"Oh. Well, um—thank you." He was calling her by her given name, she noticed. But she didn't mind. In fact, she kind of liked it. "I got your card," she said. "Thanks."

Mac looked pleased. "He remembered to give it to you, eh? That's great! I think your grandfather is still mentally sharp. Leaving it with him was partly a test. Although I *did* owe you the apology, and I meant what I said. I was *way* out of line last night."

"Apology accepted. And likewise, me too. I said some stupid things, and I'm sorry." She paused, not knowing what else to say. "But, um—the card was beautiful!"

"Did you like that? Our receptionist makes those on the side. She's quite talented."

"It was amazing!"

"I thought so."

Then neither spoke.

Again Mari pushed off to rock the swing. "I didn't have time to make anything for supper tonight."

He shook his head. "Not expecting it. Wednesdays I have my group and she has her club at church, so sometimes we go out before. Would you like to join us?"

"Oh, no—that's your special time with her! And besides, I forgot Will two days in a row. I can't do it a third time!"

He smiled. "Right!"

Nearby the screen door creaked open, and Aubrey leaned out. "Hey, Mari, I think the dryer is done. It keeps buzzing. Can you help me fold my clothes?"

"Be right there!" Mari replied. She turned to Mac as she wiggled off the swing. "Sorry. I should have asked, but I took the liberty of teaching Aubrey how to do her own laundry so I could wash my uniform here. It seemed like a good time-efficient thing to do."

He made a sound, also rising to his feet.

"Don't worry—I didn't touch anything of yours. I promise."

"I—that's fine. Thank you."

She paused by the door. "Oh, and one more thing. Aubrey's had a super-packed afternoon, so I wouldn't be surprised if she's extra tired tonight."

Mac nodded. "Okay."

She eyed him for a moment, adding, "Mac, that's code for 'cut her slack if she's an emotional mess this evening.' She might be a little fragile."

"Right. Noted. Thanks."

"You're welcome." She smiled. The air was cleared. It felt like a weight off her shoulders.

Chapter Twelve

Driving out of the neighborhood from Mac's, Mari paused at the stop sign near the entrance to the cemetery where Frost Street met Whitmore, as she had done hundreds of times before, waiting as a half-dozen vehicles zoomed around the curve heading into the Whitmore neighborhood, their occupants likely busy folks hurrying home for their suppers after work. This evening as her eyes followed the vehicles, she couldn't help but think of Ariel again, likely pregnant and alone. What was going on with her? Why wouldn't she text her back? If it were any other girl, Mari could easily let the matter go, but Ariel—Ariel was—well, she was practically a vulnerable adult. Only not. But close.

They had never really been friends. Ariel was younger than Shannon, for one thing. But it was mostly because of the way Ariel was—so socially challenged. Still, Mari's heart went out to her. She thought of how scared she must be. Was *anyone* helping her? And who was the father of this baby? That question alone took Mari's mind down several disturbing paths.

Glancing at the time on the console, Mari calculated that Mac's early arrival home from work gave her an extra half hour before Will was expecting her at his apartment. At minimum. What if she just drove by? She wouldn't stop, she decided, but only drive by Ariel's house. Her best-case scenario would be if Ariel were outdoors and they could talk. That was unlikely, of course, but if the place looked deserted, she might dare to go to the door to see if she were home. Maybe. Even observing any cars in the driveway would be helpful, possibly providing clues of what the girl might be dealing with—or who had influenced such a drastic change in her.

So instead of turning left to the highway, Mari went straight, winding her way quickly through the narrow avenues on her mission, following it all the way back until up ahead the expansive Whitmore Complex came into view. Its six apartment buildings, four stories each, spanned three entire blocks. Their patchy lawns bordered Ariel's street on one side, and in the back, their parking lots and garages butted up to the far edge of Frost Park, opposite Mari's former neighborhood.

Unlike previously that week when the area had been quiet, as Mari approached Ariel's block today, she was surprised to see the neighborhood crawling with people. Obnoxious rap music blasted from someone's car, the system's woofers maxed, vibrating Mari's whole vehicle and her body in it, while nearby a mix of teenagers and twenty- or thirty-somethings congregated on Whitmore's picnic tables and the pavement. Something was going on—a party or festival of some sort. A neighborhood barbeque? It felt odd for a Wednesday.

Then as she drew closer, she began to observe how rowdy the crowd was, as if a massive beer bash had just commenced and a giant toast was about to occur—or the fourth or fifth toast—for there was a beer bottle or plastic cup in every hand, with plenty of raucous hollering to accompany whatever celebration was going down. She observed the tight T-shirts; slouchy, saggy pants; black hoods; and thug caps. Even in the open air she could smell pot. Crud. She had driven into something crazy, nothing she wanted to be a part of. Tapping her brakes, she debated turning around, and yet she was almost there. She could practically see Ariel's house now, and she had already decided she was only driving by. This was a public street. *Act like you own the place,* she told herself. Eyes straight ahead. The mob would surely part, and she would be on her way.

As expected, the crowd did give way for her vehicle as she slowly advanced toward the Marquettes' little bungalow, but what she didn't count on was trying to see past all the people loitering in the street to view it. Braking, she craned her neck to look around them—to be rewarded by spying a handsome twenty-something on Ariel's front steps, holding his beer, yucking it up with the rest of the gang. The baby daddy? *Could be,* she mused, trying to get a good look at him. Dark hair, medium build. Her eyes flicked to the driveway. No cars. Was Ariel home alone with this guy? Was Ariel even home?

For a split second she debated turning in, and after she nixed that idea, the thought crossed her mind to take a photo of the man to ask Ariel about him later. However, before she could even reach for her phone, someone yelled at her.

"What the hell *you* looking at?"

Mari's attention jerked to a cluster of rough-looking young men all huddled together on Ariel's boulevard right beside Mari's car, one of whom had twisted around to hurl the challenge. He looked barely out of high school, if that. At the same time, she became abruptly aware of several small packages being covertly exchanged for cash.

"I said what you looking at?" he repeated.

She met his eyes and instantly looked away. Crud! A deal going down right under her nose, and the guy thought she had been staring at *them*! Time to go. This was *not* where she wanted to be! Swiftly she reached over to tap the lock button on the door.

Wrong move. At the telltale pop, the whole group swung to look at her.

Now intent on getting out of there, Mari faced forward and began inching her car through the crowd, acting as though she hadn't seen anything, but before she had driven even a yard, the group's watchdog had taken his stance in front of her, forcing her to brake. He folded his arms, staring at her as if he dared her to proceed. Crud. She laid on the horn, hoping he would get the message.

Another wrong move.

Like lightning her car was swarmed by a half-dozen beer-toting, scruffy-bearded thugs making a lot of noise. Her breath caught in her throat as she eyed the next intersection, yards ahead. Okay, she'd learned her lesson, and they had made their point. Now how on earth was she going to get out of there? In a panic she fumbled to get her phone out of her purse.

Right then a bald and burly-looking man appeared at her window, flashing an obscene gesture with his free hand, his bare muscular arms a collage of tattooed flames and skulls. Next to him another fellow whipped the contents of his plastic cup onto her windshield, crowing with delight as Mari flinched and the amber brew sprayed onto those nearby.

Unbelievable. Straight ahead, Mari told herself. Eyes straight ahead. With a feigned confidence she pointed down the street. "Just driving through," she called, flicking the bald brute beside her the barest glance and trying to ignore the cocky and now shirtless dude showing off his muscles at her hood.

The guy beside her smacked his knuckles on the window. "This is *our* street. Who said you could drive on it?" He had flames tattooed around his neck too.

She raised her phone, as if declaring both her innocence and a warning. "Let me pass! I don't want to call the police."

"I asked you a question!" he snarled, striking the window again and calling her a vulgar name.

"Burne, let her go! Let her go, Burne!" someone called from the other side of her vehicle. "Trey, make him stop!"

"She's a cop!" someone else yelled. "Hey, coppy lady, over here!" The air was filled with hoots and whistles, but Mari didn't look.

"Trey! Let her go! Let her pass!"

The man beside her began to pound her window with his fist. *Oh, God, make it stop!* Fighting hard to keep from completely losing it, Mari nimbly dialed 911, but before the emergency dispatch could answer, the little gang began rocking her vehicle side to side.

"Hurry!" she pleaded into the phone, cringing as she sputtered out her information. Any second that glass was going to shatter. If it hadn't been for the hoodlum at her window, she would have guessed that the group would have let her go after sufficient harassment. But this guy—this dude was nuts! Why were all the bystanders allowing this?

Suddenly the rocking stopped, and a chant began—someone's name, which Mari couldn't understand—and as everyone turned to look in the same direction, she followed suit, watching as one of the young men jogged out from a nearby driveway to give the thug at her window a baseball bat. A burst of cheers went up, and the chant resumed as he tapped it on his palm, smiling menacingly at her.

"Oh, my God! One of them has a club now!" Mari cried to the dispatcher. "Help me! Hurry!"

"Stay in your vehicle, ma'am. The police are on the way!"

But before the lout with the bat could do anything, a boy suddenly raced out from the Whitmore side into the street, screaming and charging the shirtless hotshot in front of her car, pummeling him with his fists and yelling at him to get out of her way and let her pass. Mari felt a stab in her chest as she recognized him from only hours previously—that rascal kid, Ty West! What was *he* doing here?

She watched as the infuriated young man in front of her car shoved Ty to the ground, but the kid bounced up after him again, shouting, "Let her go, Trey! She's a *teacher*! She's my kickball teacher! Let her go!" And then seeing the older kid hurl an angry fist at the boy, Mari screamed, laying on the horn, startling everyone enough for Ty to ditch at least some of the blows.

And then just like that, everyone scattered.

Terrified and confused, Mari watched as the young thugs and Ty scrambled away, leaving the remaining crowd of beer-brandishing bystanders staring at her clutching the steering wheel in her car—until the whirring of sirens registered in her brain. The police. The police had arrived. *Oh, thank God!*

She didn't want to get out of the car, but one of the officers made her, and she plodded through her statement on the curb in front of Ariel's house.

"It looked like some sort of gathering," she told them. "I don't understand what I drove into."

The officer raised an eyebrow. "It's called a Whitmore funeral. A gang leader overdosed the other night, and it's their customary send-off. You picked the wrong evening to visit your friend. Next time you'd do well to stay on your side of the cemetery."

Mari cast an astounded, albeit enlightening glance back at Ariel's house. This was her front yard. This was what she looked out at every day. This was where she had grown up. These were her friends. She'd had no idea what Ariel's life was like. No idea.

Of course, as the police performed their due diligence, none of the questioned witnesses had recognized any of the perpetrators. They had never seen them before. Nor could they describe them. The only officially identifiable people were the flame-tattooed bald guy named Burne and the kid Trey, because Ty had shouted their names. But they were nowhere to be found, and strangely, no one else had noticed if either of them had been there.

"Oh, they're around," one of the officers assured Mari. "We're quite familiar with Burne. Burne Batson. You don't want to mess with him."

"And a kid named Trey," she added. "He was the one beating on Ty West in front of my car."

"We know Trey too. Trey West, Ty's older brother."

When one of the officers offered her a ride to the station in the squad car, Mari easily relented, too shaken to drive. Another officer volunteered to follow behind in her vehicle. On the way out of the neighborhood, she searched the line of curious onlookers for Ty, but he was not to be found.

Her mother and Will arrived at the police station at the same time.

"What the *heck* were you doing?" Will called from the far end of the hall.

Her mom rushed down the corridor to embrace her. "Honey, are you all right?"

Mari clutched her mom's neck. "I'm all right."

"Your call scared the daylights out of me!" she cried. "What happened?"

Mari broke from her mother to hug Will.

"Mars! What in the *heck* were you doing in Whitmore? Especially this time of day!"

His tone made her defensive. "I was only driving by my friend's house—just driving by, and then all these men surrounded my car and—"

"Who lives in Whitmore?" her mother asked.

"Ariel Marquette. She lives across from the apartments."

"You went to see *Ariel?* Why?"

"Because—because she works at Riverview now."

Will huffed. "Well, that was dumb! Only an idiot would drive in *that* part of town! Why didn't you just talk to her at work?"

Mari blinked. Had he just called her an idiot? "Because she was *sick*!" she snapped. "She wasn't *at* work!"

"Sweetheart!" her mom exclaimed, resting her hand on Mari's arm. "You must have been so scared! Tell us what happened!"

"I was in the wrong place at the wrong time." She took a deep breath to calm her irritation with Will before launching into her saga. He paced jerkily during her telling, while her mother crooned in sympathy.

"So what does the car look like?" Will cut in. "Did they scratch the heck out of it?"

Mrs. Coleman shot him a look. "That's the least of our concerns right now, Will."

Mari let out a tired breath. "Look—I'm released to go. Can we finish this at home?"

"I'm taking you," Will declared, refusing Mari's insistence that she could drive herself.

"Then how will we get *my* car home?" she asked.

"We'll work it out," her mother said gently. "Let him take you, hon."

It didn't really matter. She just wanted to get out of there.

In the parking lot Mari's phone rang. It was Mac.

"Marissa, I just got word! Good heavens! Are you all right? Were you hurt?"

"I'm all right," she answered, a little confused. "How did *you* find out?"

"We just got to the church for my group and Aubrey's club. The pastor said your mom called for urgent prayer. You're really okay? You weren't hurt?"

Mari whirled to look at her mother. "No, I'm fine, apart from acute embarrassment! But I expect I'll live."

"Is there anything I can do?"

"Thanks, Mac, but no." She stopped. "Wait—where are you? Are you still at the church? We need to get my dad's car home from the police station."

"I was on my way to Kingswood."

"Kingswood? So are we! When we get there, could you take Will or my mom back to get the car?"

"Absolutely! And you're taking tomorrow off. I'll come home early for Aubrey."

She shook her head. "No, I'm fine. Don't do that."

"You're staying home!"

Mari was suddenly conscious of Will and her mother watching her. "We'll talk about it," she said. "I should go."

Will frowned, having obviously overheard the call. "He was coming to Kingswood?"

Mari ignored his question, digging her hand into her hip. "Mom, what did you tell Pastor Keith? Now word's out, and everyone's gonna think I got shot or something!"

Her mother held up her hand. "Don't blame me, young lady! You were in full panic when you called! You gave me *no* information!"

"You didn't even call *me*," Will glowered. "I didn't know *anything* until your mom called!"

Mari paused, putting a hand to her forehead. "Look—can we just go home?"

Will waved to his Jeep. "Let's go."

On the drive to the condominium they were quiet. She couldn't talk. She still saw that thug trying to smash her window with his fist. She sighed, pulling her phone out of her pocket.

"Don't leave work early," she texted Mac. "I want to be there for kickball after school. Plus Aubrey and I have plans."

As she put her phone away Will looked over. "Why was Mac driving to Kingswood?"

"He didn't say. I'd guess he was concerned."

"You're not wearing my ring."

She turned to stare at him. Really? With all that had happened that evening, *that* was foremost on his mind? "Will, for the millionth time, don't worry about Mac! The ring is in my pocket. I didn't want to lose it playing kickball." She leaned to wiggle it out and slip it on her middle finger. "See?"

"Just checking. Are you hungry? Want to stop somewhere? I'm assuming you don't want to come over."

As if she could eat right now. "Yeah, sorry—I'll pass. And no, I'll get something at home."

They drove the rest of the way in silence. When Will pulled over at Kingswood's curb, Mari finally spoke. "Know what's wild? I recognized one of those Whitmore kids. He played kickball with us after school today."

Will turned in his seat. "So then he knows where you work."

Mari looked at him. "Well, yes, but that wasn't my point. My point was that he *lives* in that neighborhood. I can't imagine what it'd be like growing up there."

Will let out a breath. "I don't get you, Marigold. One of those hoodlums knows where you work, and that doesn't alarm you? You could be in danger! I don't like that at all!"

Ty wasn't a threat to her, but what could she say? Mari laid her head back on the seat pondering Ty and Ariel at home in that environment. Ty West with a flame-tattooed, bat-wielding neighbor. No wonder the kid was nine-going-on-nineteen! The brief but terrifying scene in her car flashed through her mind again with another thought: *Who knew—one of those gangsters could have been Ariel's boyfriend!*

The pings of several incoming texts jarred Mari out of slumber the next morning. Groggily she fumbled for her phone, wondering who was texting her at 5:30 a.m.

It was Mac. Mac, sending Professor Grant's background results.

Shaking herself awake, she propped herself up on one elbow to swipe through multiple screenshots, zooming in to study each page carefully. No criminal history, she noted, a welcomed weight off her shoulders! He *did* have an impressive scholarly profile, however. She scrolled through his credentials wondering how a school like Taiton had acquired such a gem.

"Good morning, Mac," she texted back. "Thanks. This helps a lot."

Mac sent her a thumbs-up. "Still doing okay? The offer's still open for the day off."

"Doing good," she returned. "See you this afternoon."

She set her phone on the bedside table, relieved to have an official "all clear" for her intriguing micro-discussions with Dr. Grant. Nevertheless, she realized it wouldn't change pink-haired Candace's perspective. Nothing would change what that girl had experienced in her childhood. Her warning to Mari about the professor had been so sincere, as seen through the lens of her trauma. Mari wished there were some way to talk to her about her past, some way to get her some support and healing for what she had been through. Candace had some major wounds.

With a long stretch she sat up in bed, her thoughts abuzz with the day ahead, problem-solving for so many people! A week ago she had been concerned with only three people: Will, her grandfather, and herself—probably in the inverse order. Now she had Ariel, Aubrey, Ty, and Candace living in her brain—with a stinging side of JoyAnne Strang and Kyla Watkins. Plus there was Aubrey's friend Hailey's mom going through cancer treatments and a divorce. And then Dr. Grant. And Mac. And a kickball club. She dropped her head in her hands. All these people! And her desire to help Ariel, Aubrey, and Candace was becoming an obsession. She couldn't turn it off! But what could she do? She felt so powerless. Especially now that she wasn't working at Sunlight.

She bit her lip at the thought. Of course, Sunlight would be able to give Ariel the help and support she needed. They would walk with her through her pregnancy and help her care for her child or find the baby a loving home—if indeed she were pregnant. Counseling would be available for Candace too. Even Hailey's mom, she realized. But they would have to go through JoyAnne, and—well, that nixed the option for Mari. She would do her best to help them herself.

She glanced down at her phone, remembering how the topic had set off that weird conversation with Mac the other night when he had urged her to get Ariel in touch with JoyAnne. She wished she had someone to talk to about the dynamics with JoyAnne who wouldn't immediately jump down the jealousy road, which always seemed to happen. If only they could know JoyAnne's dark history. If only they could see their dark history *together*. Then they would understand. But meanwhile, what was Mari to do with all these people weighing on her heart? She eyed her phone beside her on the bed, thinking of Mac. What would *he* do? She sighed, knowing *one* thing he would advise: to pray for them. But she was terrible at prayer. She resigned to read her Bible instead.

Clicking on the bedside lamp, she scooted off her bed to scrounge through her closet in search of her compact version. Finally locating it, she returned to the bed, flipping through the pages to find a place to begin. She had never been a good Bible reader. Nothing ever seemed to relate to real life. Well, some parts did, but she had to hunt to find those spots. Yet Mac had so urged her to read it, and something in her wanted to do it for his sake. Maybe she needed to prove something to him. But not only Mac. Dr. Grant too. He had dubbed it the finest history book ever written.

She was obviously missing something. So here she was, staring into an overwhelming book. But she had to start somewhere.

One chapter a day, she finally decided. Jotting her goals onto a bookmark, she turned to the book of Matthew and began reading, finding herself tripling her target on her first day.

Chapter Thirteen

Tatum was back at work that morning, dressed in her usual layers and barking out orders left and right with—thankfully—Mark's chatter the current target of her ire. Enjoying the momentary reprieve, Mari stayed busy and kept clear of her as much as possible so as not to divert the woman's attention back to her. She did find it perplexing how kind the manager was to her, however. It was as though his and Tatum's head-to-head in the kitchen the previous morning had never happened. Mari could only presume that they had talked everything out, possibly that morning before she had arrived.

Interestingly, to the same degree that Mari avoided Tatum, she found herself drawn to work near Candace, although every minute of it she feverishly debated how, when, or *whether* to tell her about Dr. Grant's clean background check. Yet whenever an opportunity arose to do so, it never felt right to take the plunge. She couldn't do it. She even hesitated when the dining room needed bussing, now aware of Candace's slanted scrutiny. Yesterday's conversation about her past had built a tiny bridge between them. Would Mari's visits with the professor demolish it?

Ironically, it was the manager who made the call, beckoning Mari aside to tell her not to wait to be asked to do everything and that it was customary for the newbies to do the grunt work. In other words, until they hired another employee, bussing tables was considered her job.

Now with a green light to talk with the professor, Mari zipped quickly through the lounge half of the Break and then slowed to a normal pace once she reached the front dining room. Seeing that Dr. Grant was on the phone, she worked the perimeter tables first, saving his area for last.

"Miss Coleman, how are you today?" he said finally, setting down his phone.

"Fine. How are you?"

"Fine," he returned.

It was a simple question, but she felt the heat creep up her neck. It was the way he looked at her. He was either tired or—or had someone told him about her Whitmore misadventure last evening? Had the church grapevine stretched all the way to him? Via Kyla Watkins, perhaps? No doubt with a critical slant borrowed from JoyAnne. She certainly didn't owe him an explanation for anything—she knew that—but it looked as if he were expecting her to say something. And she wanted to. Something about his openness to talk with her begged her to tell, begged her to dump everything that was on her mind.

"Actually, I'm *not* fine," she said. "I had a bummer of an evening last night."

His brow shot up. "Oh?"

But now, judging by his expression, maybe he *didn't* know about it. Now where did she start? With Ariel's dilemma? But the professor knew JoyAnne, so that could take the same turn as when she had talked to Mac, with him directing Ariel to Sunlight. But maybe if she gave him some of the back story about JoyAnne—maybe then he could give her some advice. Yet how could she possibly explain it all right now under Candace's scrutiny? She didn't want to jeopardize her trust. Of course, Tatum's hawk eyes followed her too, but Tatum wasn't coming from a past like Candace. Her grouchy opinion didn't really matter to Mari; she was simply irritating. Oh, why was everything so complicated?

"It's a long story," she said, folding the damp rag over in her hand. "Dr. Grant, would you ever be available to talk sometime? I have a lot of questions, and there's some people I've been with recently who are in tough spots. I wouldn't mind some advice. Could we maybe meet on Taiton Green some afternoon? There are some nice benches by the pond."

He sat up slowly. "Nothing personal, Miss Coleman, but I have a policy of not meeting with women alone in places that aren't public like this. I'm sorry."

Mari was immediately embarrassed. "Oh—right. I suppose people could accuse you of things."

"That's one of many reasons. I'd certainly meet with you if a third party were with us, preferably my wife, but then you'd be all googly-eyed and distracted. However—"

"I could bring Shannon," she offered.

He tipped his head. "Shannon, yes—excellent idea! Bring her, and we'll meet right here some afternoon when you're off work. Or perhaps—"

He paused, eyeing her.

"Yes?"

"I *was* going to suggest our nanny, Kyla Watkins, and her friend JoyAnne, but then I remembered—"

"—That wouldn't work for me," Mari cut in.

"Right. Your childhood nemesis. Then perhaps Kyla alone, if Shannon can't do it. I'm sure she'd be willing."

Mari raised her brow, shaking her head.

"No? Why not?"

"There were, um—there were some things with her. In the past."

"There were some *things* with her," he echoed.

"Yeah. A couple summers ago. I'd prefer it wasn't Kyla."

"She's only been around a couple of summers. I wasn't aware that you two knew each other back then."

"We didn't. But some things happened and—" She stopped, unable to continue.

He cast her a long look. "This wouldn't by chance have anything to do with her husband, Peter Watkins, would it?"

Her cheeks grew warm, and there was no need for her to answer.

"You were dating Peter?"

Mari shook her head. "No, but we *might* have if she hadn't—you know—swept in like a hurricane."

"I see!" He nodded, regarding her thoughtfully. "Well, I'm sorry for your disappointment."

She shifted uncomfortably. "Well, there's other things too."

"What's going on?"

"Nothing."

He frowned, folding his arms.

"Well, it's just that both of those girls—her and JoyAnne—it's like they have it made. Everything always works out for them."

"But not for you—? I thought you already had a boyfriend! Aren't you dating the legendary William Wallace? But you wanted Peter instead."

"No! I mean—well, back *then* I did, but that was before. Look—this is *not* about Peter, okay? I'm not *that* shallow!"

"What's it about then?"

Oh, brother. Mari glanced back toward the serving counter. Where was *Irri*-Tatum's steely gaze when she needed it?

At her silence, the professor shifted in his chair. "Miss Mari, I'm not going to corner you, but I'd like to help you think this through. Are you willing to do that? Come on—let's lower the deflector shields, shall we? I'm on your side." Without waiting for her response, he continued: "How big is God to you?"

She looked at him in confusion. "What?"

"I want you to think about something. Look out this window." He pointed to the campus grounds. "Look at those trees, bursting forth with life! God designed the sap to know exactly when to flow upward from the ground. Every spring those little buds form and leaf out just the way they're meant to, every tree with its unique leaves. And think about how those trees thrive on light and give us oxygen to breathe—the wonder of photosynthesis. And glorious chlorophyll, the welcome green after the gray of winter. And the splendor of autumn's colors. Who designed all those systems? How big is your God, Mari?"

Her shoulder twitched. Was she supposed to answer?

"I'm having another son," he continued. "When I rest my hand on my wife's belly, I can feel him inside of her—a whole and separate person, though he's still growing. Have you ever thought about the absolute miracle of human conception and birth? My wife's body was designed to grow a baby, give birth, and feed him!" He paused. "I could go on, but my point is that this infinitely creative God is the God who cares for you, Mari. He is an excellent manager of all he made. This is the God who loves you and knows who you are on the inside. Do you believe this?"

"Well—yes."

"Then why is Kyla Watkins' blessing a point of contention for you? How big is *your* God, Mari? Isn't he big enough to bless you too? Or do you think that God is stingy with his goodness—like he only has a few special people that he blesses? Wouldn't you rather trust him for what he has for *you* than to sit around moping that you didn't get Kyla Watkins' blessing? But oh, yeah—I forgot. Her life is perfect."

Mari protested: "I'm not moping!"

"No? You're bummed because she got what you wanted and she's happy. That's called jealousy."

"People always say that! I'm not jealous of her! I think you've misunderstood."

"Ah, okay, okay." He nodded. "Okay. Then let's talk about JoyAnne. Why is JoyAnne's achievement your demise?"

"My what?"

"Why is her success your loss? Why does her getting that Sunlight position mean you're the loser? Isn't God big enough to have something for you too? Or does he have a shortage of work in his kingdom?"

"Well, I *know* I'll find another job! It's just that I felt I deserved the Sunlight job more than her. I was more qualified. Look—I'm not feeling like you're on my side right now!"

"I *assure* you I am."

Mari simply looked at him.

"All right, I'll give you the benefit of the doubt. Let's say they made a mistake. Perhaps you *were* supposed to have that Sunlight job, but through an error in judgment they gave it to her instead. What are you going to do now?"

She flayed her hands. "That's exactly where I'm at!"

In the silence that followed, Mari suddenly became aware of the din of the morning rush. Glancing around, she saw the line of students curling from the front counter all the way out into the student center hall. Surely by now Tatum or Candace were poised to reprimand her. Maybe both. She looked back, gesturing. "I should go."

He nodded. "All right. Listen, Mari Coleman. God *loves* you. You can trust him. He's big enough to both know the desires of your heart and to give them to you, but you can't be sucking your thumb about what you think you *should* have gotten from him. You've got to move forward."

Her cheeks were flaming. What could she say? "I—I understand. Thanks," she replied, starting jerkily for the bin of dirty dishes waiting for her. He called her back.

"One more thing: I'll not be here tomorrow, except for my classes. I wanted to let you know that, lest you think it was about *you*. Kyla just learned that her birth father is dying from cancer. That was her on the phone just now. She and Peter are going down tomorrow to help transfer him from the state penitentiary to a secured hospice facility in New Hampton." He raised his brow. "How's that for a perfect life?"

Mari's shoulders drooped. "I apologize. I didn't know. Will you please tell her that I'm sorry?"

He gave a curt nod. "I will."

Thanks to the current surge of Taiton students, the Coffee Break staff remained in constant hustle, providing Mari opportunity to slip unnoticed into the kitchen with her heaping crate of soiled dishes. Numbly she packed them into the dishwasher, her pride stinging from Dr. Grant's rebuke. Part of her wanted to be mad. She hadn't deserved that. She hadn't asked for a science lecture on the greatness versus the puniness of God—in regard to the subject of jealousy, no less! Geez, how in the world had they even gotten on that subject? And suckin' her thumb—? How insulting! And yet—

Dang. He was right. She knew it. It was a kick in the butt—the butt-kicking warm-up before Tatum's inevitable scolding for talking to him in the first place. *I assure you I am on your side.* Was he? She knew he was, but it stung. He was obviously disappointed in her. Plus to hear Kyla's father was dying—now Mari felt like a lump for all her whining about her.

The flurry of activity didn't slow down when Mari joined the crew up front. She worked diligently alongside everyone, glancing occasionally out to where Dr. Grant sat, wishing she could dash out there to end with him in a better way, but there was no lull in the Coffee Break action. Then she noticed him close his laptop and gather up his papers. As he packed his briefcase, her heart sank. He was leaving, which meant she wouldn't be able to talk to him until Monday.

On a whim, she poured a to-go cup of orange juice and pressed on its lid. Then she lifted her chin and walked straight out to his table, as if delivering his order.

"Okay, it wasn't fun to hear, but maybe I *do* have an issue with jealousy. I just wouldn't have defined it that way."

He smiled, rising to his feet. "No, of course not. It's the problem no one has! Everyone can spot it in others but never in themselves. But we all have our blind spots, don't we? I apologize if our conversation got too personal and I embarrassed you. I was pretty hard on you."

"I'm all right. I wanted to at least tell you that before you left so I didn't feel like an idiot all weekend."

He laughed, slipping on his sports coat. "It's been a privilege talking with you, Miss Coleman. I'd be honored to chat about whatever you had in mind some afternoon next week."

"Thanks. I'll figure things out with Shannon and let you know."

He tipped his head. "Until Monday. Oh, and by the way—" He held up the juice. "Good ploy, but I'm not an OJ fan, and most of the staff back there know it. But black coffee—any time." He winked.

She smiled. "See you Monday."

On the drive from Taiton campus to Riverview, Mari swung through the grocery store to collect a few comfort items for Ariel in case she was back at work. While there, she also snatched up some ingredients for a quick batch of crispy rice bars as a kickball treat, determining that if she left for Mac's ten minutes sooner, she could hastily assemble them before

Aubrey got home from school.

She was still shuffling her afternoon's events into the most efficient order when she parked at the nursing home. As she hurried toward the electronic doors, a sharp catcall whistle suddenly cut through the air. She glanced behind her, halting at the familiar lanky figure pushing off his lime-colored Jeep.

"Will! What are you doing here?"

Grinning, he crossed the pavement. "Hi, gorgeous! I took an extended lunch to see you."

"Really? That's so sweet! I wish I'd known you were coming! I wouldn't have stopped at the store!" She hugged him.

"That's okay. We still have almost an hour. I wanted to make sure you're all right after last night."

She squeezed him again and planted a kiss on his cheek. "Thank you! I'm all right. Trying not to think about it too much. It was all so unexpected, and it happened so fast. Thank God the police arrived when they did! I mean—what if they hadn't?" She shuddered.

"Yeah, what if they hadn't?"

Mari jerked her head. "Let's talk inside. I can't wait for you to see how much my grandfather has improved!"

First, however, she went straight to the office to inquire about Ariel. As suspected, she was still out sick.

"What do you want with her?" Will asked. "Isn't she the one—"

"Yes, Will, she's who I was trying to visit in Whitmore last night. She's been sick and hasn't been to work for a few days. I have some stuff for her." She held up the plastic bag from the store.

"I thought you barely knew her!"

"I know. But I still want to help her."

"Why?"

"Because I do!"

"Do you help everyone who's sick? Well, it's fine if she shows up here, but you're *not* taking that to her house! I hope you learned your lesson with that! Better yet—how about *calling* her to ask how she's doing?"

"I have. She's not answering." She eyed him, debating whether to tell him the whole story. He was her boyfriend—why wouldn't she? And yet it felt like breaking a confidence to do so. So instead, she smiled. "Let's go see Poppy."

Mari noticed her grandfather's eyes brighten when they entered his room, as though he recognized Will. Immediately he said hello, but he was unable to say Will's name. At Mari's suggestion, she and Will walked her grandfather out to enjoy the sunshine in the courtyard again—minus staff this time.

"See how good he's doing?" she asked Will as they strolled to a shady spot a little farther away than yesterday's perch. "Every day he's making progress!"

Will gave an exaggerated nod. "Yep! No need to rub it in."

She felt a little guilty that he'd gotten her point so quickly. But only a little. She kinda wanted it to sting.

"So what do you do with him?" he asked, settling on the bench. "He can't talk."

"He can too! And he understands everything—don't you, Poppy?"

"Yesss!" the old man said, turning to smile at Will, who shifted uncomfortably.

"I usually tell him about my day. And yesterday I read to him. From the Bible."

"Oh, right. Reading—that's a good idea."

"But sometimes we just sit together." Mari reached to squeeze her grandfather's arm. "We listen to the birds."

"Birrrds," her grandfather echoed.

Both Mari and Will chuckled.

She took a deep breath. "Just smell that air! It's so beautiful here! I love spring. You gotta rest and take it all in."

Indeed, it was a peaceful hideaway, with the grass recently mowed and landscaping freshly tended. Across the courtyard a sizeable boulder dominated an area planted with squatty, mound-like bushes, around which bloomed colorful clusters of fragrant hyacinths, daffodils, and tulips.

"Mind if we talk a little?" Will asked.

Mari looked at him. "You and me? About what?"

He cleared his throat. "I found you a job."

"I *have* a job. I have two jobs."

"I found you a *better* job. I stopped at the HR department at work this morning to inquire about any openings, and guess what? The main receptionist put in her notice today. Just today! It's like a God thing! I asked them to email you an application for the position, and if you can get it in right away, it's practically a done deal."

She stared at him.

"I guarantee it's better pay than both of your jobs now!"

"How do you know that?"

"Okay, how much does that Sinclair fellow pay you an hour?"

"I don't know. I've not been paid yet."

He spread his hands. "How do you *not* know that? He didn't tell you?"

She shrugged. "It never came up. He said he'd make it worth my time, and I trust him. Will, I like my jobs."

"No, you don't! You *hated* the idea of working at a coffee shop! You said it was a loser job! And this way you'd be out of that neighborhood."

Her eyes darted to her grandfather and back to Will. "Mac doesn't live in Whitmore! That's way on the opposite side of the field, and you have to drive all the way around a big cemetery to get there! It's several blocks. Frost Street is safe."

"Close enough. Too close for my comfort."

"Will, it's safe. I should know. I grew up there!"

"Yeah, like twenty years ago!"

"We moved *four* years ago."

"Why do you think your parents wanted to move out of there? Times are changing, Mari."

Mari blinked. "Because my mom's dream was to live at Kingswood! She's *always* wanted to."

Will groaned. "Mariachi! Why are you being so difficult? This is a huge break—getting into a good company like this! There'd be decent hours and benefits. Plus we'd be working in the same building. We could go to work and get off at the same time. I can't think of anything more perfect!"

Mari folded her arms, drawing a hand over her mouth.

"Okay, I probably should have given you some advanced warning," he said.

"Will, I don't want to be a receptionist! Besides, I can't see that it would pay that well!"

One of Will's eyebrows popped up. "But you *do* want to be a barista?"

"No! It's more than that! There's this professor at the Break. We talk every day. We talk about spiritual stuff, and it's making me think. And this other lady, Candace. Plus Aubrey. I don't want to leave her."

"The brat kid who lies?"

"She responds to me! I like her! Will, I appreciate that you care. I can see you're only trying to help, but I'm fine where I am right now. Really, I am."

Will bit his lip and shook his head. After a space of quiet, he sighed in resignation. "Well, would you do one thing then? Would you at least sleep on it for a night? Maybe ask your mom what she thinks. Please—would you do that for me, Mars? I *do* care."

She nodded. "Fine. I will."

"Thank you." He was quiet, looking out at the courtyard; then he shook his head again. "Man, I was so excited at the thought of having lunch with you every day! I can't believe you wouldn't want this!"

"Will, I'm not rejecting *you*. But I can't leave Aubrey right now."

"And that's a little weird to me. But whatever." He checked the time on his phone and stood. "I should get going. Are you coming over tonight?"

"I have a few things I need to do at home this evening. Plus I'll talk to my mom about this."

"*Tomorrow* night then?"

"Are you asking me on a date?"

"Well, who else would you spend your Friday night with?"

She smiled. "Okay. I'll be over after work tomorrow."

"I'll call you tonight. Bye!" He kissed her forehead and turned on his heel, leaving the two of them alone in the shade of the tree.

Mari met her grandfather's gaze, feeling a little embarrassed he'd been privy to that exchange. "Sorry, Poppy. You've been completely ignored." As she spoke her throat grew tight. The unexpected job proposal combined with already feeling tender from her morning discussion with Professor Grant had made her almost weepy. She fought to shake it off, adding, "Well, you heard all that. Any advice for a floundering granddaughter?"

He was fiddling with his pocket. "Mac," he said.

It was so out of the blue, she giggled. "You're funny, Pop!"

He patted his chest. "Mac."

She tipped her head reflectively. "I wish you could talk to me. Are you saying to keep the job with Mac? Or are you just remembering yesterday?"

Again, he fidgeted with his breast pocket, tapping it. "In here."

Frowning, she stretched to tuck a couple fingers into his pocket, touching a folded paper stuck on a seam. With an exclamation, she tugged it out. Sure enough—another note from Mac! *Aubrey needs one sheet of white tagboard for a school assignment. If you get this, could you pick one up on your way? Thanks.*

Mari held it up to her grandfather. "A school project. Mac asked me to stop at the store for his daughter. For supplies." Mari wondered if Poppy had waited until Will was gone to pat that pocket.

He smiled. "Mac!"

She kissed his cheek. "Well, how about that! Most people call or text, but Mac has his own courier! You're like his carrier pigeon!"

At that, her grandfather drew back his head to howl out in laughter. Surprised, Mari laughed out loud with him.

"Fun-ny!" he said. "Fun-ny, Marree!"

Hearing him talk and laugh like that made her so happy her heart could burst. She couldn't wait to tell Mac.

Chapter Fourteen

Aubrey gave a fist pump when Mari and she arrived at the field that afternoon. "*Yes!* Ty's not here! I'm *so* glad!"

"Hey now—be kind," Mari returned, also scanning for him in the crowd of children. But she was disappointed.

Behind them a handful of new kids timidly strolled up asking to play, and learning their names, Mari welcomed them in. Bouncing her fingers in the air, she counted by twos, discovering that with Ty gone, they now had an odd number of players, making the teams uneven. It didn't really matter that much, but on a whim, she beckoned Connor over to ask if he would be willing to pitch full time. Beaming, he accepted the assignment.

Aubrey gave a cry. "You never asked *me*! I could pitch!"

Mari leaned down to whisper, "That's 'cause you're my best kicker! Don't tell anyone."

Aubrey tossed her head, shooting a look at Connor.

Dividing the remaining children into two groups, Mari assigned the kindergarteners to pick the team names for the day. She knew it would take them some deliberating, and meanwhile she coached Connor on the finer points of rolling the rubber ball to home plate—which was merely cover for asking about Ty.

"So where's your friend today, Connor?"

The boy shrugged. "I don't know. He wasn't in school."

"Huh. Is that unusual? Or does Ty miss school a lot?"

Another shrug. "Sometimes."

Mari threw him the ball for another practice pitch, glancing over toward the Whitmore side of the field. With a double take, she paused to peer closer. Was that a kid running across the field?

"Connor—look! Is that Ty?"

Connor squinted. "Yeah, that's him! Cool!"

Yes! Mari smiled to herself and set about adjusting the teams.

"We're making a change, Connor," she told him. "But you still get to pitch."

When Ty arrived, she greeted him, but he wouldn't look at her. He milled around with the others, doubtless embarrassed of his glaring shiner. Mari was so glad she had reported his brother's abuse to the police. She simply pretended she didn't see the bruise and called all the kids together to start the game.

"We're doing something different today," she announced. "Each team will have their own pitcher now! Ty, I'll have you pitch for the, um"— quickly she scanned the teams for Aubrey so they weren't together—"for the Woodland Fairies. Connor, you've got the Giraffes."

Ty's face puckered. "I ain't gonna be a stupid fairy!"

"It's your team today. Giraffes are up first, so you're on." She threw him the ball, but he popped it right back at her.

"I'm not playing for no stinkin' fairies!"

Mari dug her hand into her waist. "Ty, this is what it is! If you don't want to play, you can sit out." She nodded toward the grass.

"What happened to his eye?" one of the girls asked loudly, at which Ty twitched and glanced around.

Mari answered so everyone could hear, "I'm not sure, but I'll bet he did something brave. Okay, is everyone ready? Here!" She tossed Ty the ball.

For some odd reason she had imagined that her accolade would transform Ty West into a happy, cooperative kid. In reality, just the opposite happened. During their hour or so of play, his obnoxious behavior escalated, consuming her attention, and Mari found herself harping on him to the point that she wished he hadn't come.

The last straw was when the Fairies were heading out to the field and the Giraffes were up to kick. Preparing to pitch, Ty grabbed the ball, and goofing around, lobbed it in the air to fist-punch it volleyball-style—right onto Aubrey's face—which then ricocheted sideways to smack bullseye against Mari's bad knee. With a cry, Mari doubled over to clutch it, while beside her, Aubrey erupted into screech-bawling. Everyone else stood gawking at Ty, wondering what Mari would do. The only thing she wanted to do was writhe on the ground, but she commanded herself to be the adult. Blinking back her tears, she beckoned Aubrey. Putting her arm around her, the two stood together until Aubrey calmed down some and Mari was able to speak.

"It was an accident. It's okay, Ty," she croaked. At least she wanted to believe it was. "Come on, everybody—let's have snacks." She waved everyone in. It was almost time to quit anyway.

Someone brought her the pan of crispy rice bars, and she held it while the pack rushed up, pressing in for their treats.

"You too, Ty," Mari urged, motioning him over. "Come on!"

He came, but he would not meet her eyes.

"Here," she said quietly, extending the pan to him. "You get two."

"Why does *he* get two?" someone asked.

"Because," she said simply.

Connor perked up. "Because he was pitcher? Do *I* get two?"

Mari nodded. "Yes. Pitcher's privilege."

Ty snatched his bars and disappeared to the group's fringe. Connor took his and joined him.

Her knee was pulsing. It was time to move this party along and go home.

She signaled Aubrey. "Aubrey, hon, go fetch that garbage bag I brought." When she returned with it, Mari held it up. "Children! Look here! Before you go, I'd like you to pick up all your trash. And make sure you have all your jackets and backpacks!" She handed off the bar pan to Aubrey and shook open the bag.

"Do you have any water?" asked the same thirsty girl from yesterday.

"I'm sorry, hon—I don't. But tomorrow you can bring your own water bottle, okay?"

And then before long their little group began disbanding as pairs and threesomes trotted off toward their homes. Mari tied up the trash, realizing she hadn't budged an inch from the spot where she stood. She turned to eye Mac's house. It would be a painful hobble to get there.

Suddenly behind her, Aubrey shrieked. "You pig! You big fat pig! I *hate* you!"

Mari twisted to see Ty running away in the direction of Whitmore.

Aubrey promptly burst into tears, holding out the empty bar pan. "He stole them *all*! He took all the ones that were left!"

Mari shook her head in disbelief. Once again, she beckoned. "Come here!"

Aubrey dropped the pan at Mari's feet and sobbed into her chest. "I hate him! I hate him so much!"

Mari stroked her hair, watching Ty's retreat over her head. "Shhh!"

Then with Aubrey's help carrying all their stuff, Mari managed to limp to the house. Holding the railing, she hopped up the porch steps and carefully navigated to the kitchen, where she found a perch and propped up her leg. This became her command-and-control center for instructing Aubrey on how to make an icepack, then for supervising her homework and chores, and finally for step-by-step coaching on the promised banana bread project—although Mari did get up to put the loaf into the oven for her.

"Do you have any notecards?" she asked Aubrey. "Let's write Hailey's mom an encouraging note."

"Uh—I think. My dad keeps some by his books." She disappeared into the dining room and returned to drop a thick pile of blank index cards onto the table.

"We only need one."

"What if I goof it up?" Scooping up her pencil, the girl went to work, her lips twisting as she concentrated. "Is this good? It says, 'We hope you feel better soon.'"

"It's perfect."

"Can I decorate it with my sparkle markers?"

"Great idea!"

While Aubrey ran upstairs, Mari went to put the cards back on Mac's end of the dining room table. Noting both his Bible and journal lying open, she paused. *You're a terrible snoop,* she chided herself, peeking at his writing, which were mostly notes on what he had read. But up in the corner under the words "Daily Prayer" she spied the name "Elena," after which was written, "reconciliation and healing of marriage." She nodded to herself. Mac was a decent guy. He wanted their relationship restored.

The banana bread was just coming out of the oven when Mac got home. His eyes brightened.

"Whoa—my favorite!" he exclaimed as Mari set the loaf onto the hot pad.

"It's not for you!" Aubrey squealed, running to him. "It's for Hailey's mom. I'm giving it to Hailey at school tomorrow!"

"Oh, bait and switch on me!" He dropped the mail on the counter.

"Sorry!" Mari smiled apologetically as she turned the oven off, set another timer, then hobbled toward her chair.

"Guess what, Dad? We put chocolate chips in it!" Aubrey said. "I even made a card! See?" She snatched it off the counter to hold it out.

"Yum! I see!" Mac replied. He cocked his head at Mari. "Are you limping?"

Aubrey drew herself up, declaring, "Ty West hit her in the knee with the kickball—on *purpose*! She *cried* even! But first he hit me in the face, and I cried too."

His eyes flicked back to Mari.

"That about sums it up," she admitted. "I've been icing it."

He motioned to the chair. "Sit down. Let's take a look."

Hastily she shook her head. "I'm all right."

"Come on—this is what I do."

"I know. But I'd feel funny having you look at my knee."

"Why? Would you like to make an appointment and have me look at it in my office? This is way cheaper!" He patted the chair. "Have a seat."

She winced as he touched it.

"I think we're finished with kickball," he said.

Mari shook her head. "I'll just be more careful."

"Oh, I think you're done!"

"No, Mac. We can't quit. I'm careful. I'm only standing there coaching."

He opened his hand toward her knee. "I beg to differ!"

"It was an *accident*, and that could happen anywhere—even here in this kitchen! There's no rule against standing, is there?"

He looked at her in amazement. "And what about this kid who's slamming the two of you with the ball—?"

"I don't think he meant to hurt us. We're not stopping our kickball group, Mac."

Audrey sidled up to Mari. "*I* still want to play. It's fun, Dad. But it's funner without Ty West."

"*More fun.* But we can handle Ty, right?" Mari drew her arm around the girl.

"Well, well! I see someone has a stubborn side!" Mac commented.

The kitchen timer went off.

"I prefer to call it determination," Mari said, stretching across the counter for the pan of banana bread. In one smooth motion she inverted it onto a cooling rack, then lifted her gaze to him. "I really want to keep my connection with Ty West. How else would I have an opportunity to be around him?"

Mac grunted, raising his hands. "Poor William Wallace—that's all I can say!"

"Hey, no boyfriend jabs! You promised!"

"I'm jabbing *you*!"

She laughed with him.

Aubrey looked between them. "Does this mean we can still play kickball? Mari says I'm her best kicker!"

Mac tapped her chin. "Yes, but you're going to have to be extra careful! Be right back." He set his phone on the counter and went into the back entryway. In a moment he returned to drop a few different knee braces onto the counter.

"See if one of these works for you."

"Mac, wearing a brace has become a way of life for me. I have a whole assortment of them at home."

"You need one with a little more support. Do you have crutches?"

Mari scrunched her face. "Oh, please no! Crutches are such a pain!"

"Just for the weekend."

She sighed. "Yes, I have crutches."

"Well, dust them off."

"Aye aye, Captain," she said, and Aubrey giggled, echoing—

"Aye aye, Captain!"

Mac poked her in the belly. "That's Supremo Father to you, squirt! Come here, little flower! What'd you do today besides kickball?" He pulled her into a hug from behind.

Aubrey shrugged. "I don't know. Made that." She pointed to the loaf on the table.

"Homework and chores done?"

"Yep!" She looked up at him. "Can I watch a show before dinner?"

He gave a nod. "Sure."

When Aubrey was gone, Mac glanced down at the banana bread and let out a heavy breath. "Yeah. Dinner."

Mari smiled. "I saw you had some chicken thawed in the fridge. You could grill some veggies with it."

He pointed. "You're hired!"

They both laughed.

"Can you stay? I'd like to hear what happened last night."

She gave a timid shrug. "For a little while, yes."

"You won't be in trouble with your boyfriend—?"

"It's fine. We have no plans this evening."

"Good." Then he chuckled. "And speaking of trouble—oh, boy, did I get an earful from our Mr. Roger Eden last night! He charged over here in a tizzy upset that *someone* was throwing rocks at his dogs!"

Mari gave a cry. "What! I wasn't throwing rocks at them!"

"I know! I corrected him! But apparently the meatballs looked like

196

rocks on his security camera!" He grinned.

"Oh, my word—he *saw* the whole thing?" She laughed, burying her face in her hands. "What did you say?"

"Well, I started with the truth, but he was grinding in his point so dang hard that I told him he should make a plan to feed and water his dogs when he's gone. That part didn't go over so well."

"Oh, brother. I'm sorry. That's my fault."

"No, that's *his* fault! His dogs were getting out—remember? Anyway, I couldn't stop laughing about it all night!"

They chuckled together.

Mari drew a breath, launching in. "So about last night. My friend Ariel's been gone from work for a few days, so I swung through Whitmore looking for her."

"That's noble of you to check on her."

"Mac, I think she's pregnant. I'm pretty certain she's pregnant."

He drew back. "Wait—are we talking about the Ariel at Riverview? Black hair? One of the custodians?"

"Yes, with the crazy snake tatt. And she goes to Eagle Bluff too. She's been around for years, but I've never gotten to know her. She was sick at work on Tuesday, and I gave her a ride home, and a pregnancy test fell out of her pocket."

"Ah—so *she's* the one you were referring to the other night!"

She nodded. "Yes. She hasn't responded to any of my calls or texts, so I thought I'd drive by her house. I guess I was a little naive. The whole street was packed with people—some morbid party for a gang leader who overdosed. I didn't know! And then I was caught staring at some thugs." She shook her head. "It just went south from there. This Burne Batson guy all tattooed with flames was trying to break my window, and—well, anyway, it was so crazy!"

"Glad you're okay. Did you see her?"

"Ariel? No. But I *did* see Ty West, the boy who clobbered Aubrey with the kickball this afternoon. He *lives* over there!"

"Clobbered *both* of you."

"Mac, he ran right in there to stop what was happening. He got a big black eye from his brother smacking him. I saw him do it. His brother's name is Trey, and he's a real jerk. Not a good role model at all. Anyway, Ty didn't go to school today, but he came to kickball with a big shiner. That's why we can't stop playing. I'm concerned about him living in such a rough neighborhood, and I'm concerned about Ariel too. She was *so* sick the other day and terrified of her mother finding out. Who knows who is influencing her over there! I don't want her to do something stupid like—you know—"

He blew out his breath. "Yeah. Wow."

They sat together quietly.

"I suppose I could inquire at the Riverview office," he offered.

"Already have. They wouldn't tell me anything. Mac, she looked so scared. I have to find her."

"I'll see what I can do. Maybe I'll drive over there myself—maybe take my friend, Dan. He'll be here tomorrow evening."

"Well, it would be wonderful if you could. But be careful. And thanks for not calling me a fool."

"Why on earth would I do that? I thought it was courageous of you to—"

A loud shriek suddenly cut the air, and Mac bolted off the stool to the living room.

"Look—they're getting out again!" Aubrey screeched. "No! No! No!"

By the time Mari had limped to the doorway, Mac was looking over his hysterical daughter's shoulder as she pointed out the window.

"The dogs—they're digging! They're getting out!"

"Settle down—settle down, Aubrey! Hey!" Mac exclaimed, tapping her on the arm. "They're *outside*! They're not going to hurt you!" He shook his head, throwing a glance back at Mari. "Well, would you look at that! Those little buggers are in our yard! They tunneled themselves right under the fence! Aubrey—hey, *enough* now! Stop your screaming!"

As Aubrey attempted to stifle her crying, Mac turned to open one of the glass doors under the colonnade dividing the two rooms. He moved a few things around, and then after a few beeps and the crunch of a lock release, Mari saw him bring up a handgun.

Her jaw dropped. "*Mac!* What are you *doing*? Are you going to shoot his dogs?"

"What? *No*, I'm not shooting his dogs! But I'm not going out there without some kind of protection!" He spun on his heel toward his daughter. "Aubrey Michelle! I said *enough*! Stop crying now! They're not going to hurt you!"

"You're not going out there at all!" Mari declared. "Put that away!"

He turned back in surprise.

"Put that away right now! How could that possibly end well? If they attack, you'll shoot. Even if they miraculously come when you call, what'll you do with them—bring the dogs in here? No, Mac. Put it away. You're going to call Roger Eden and tell him his dogs are out!"

He stared at her incredulously, then slowly returned his gun to the safe and closed the cabinet. "Back in a moment," he said, slipping past her into the kitchen, where he retrieved his phone and exited the back door.

Mari swallowed, her cheeks burning. Aubrey came sniffling to her side.

"Your dad's taking care of it," she said simply.

She met him in the kitchen when he came back in.

"They're out running loose in the field now, but Roger's on his way." Mac cast a look at his daughter. "Kid, you gotta get a grip! Those dogs can't hurt you if you're in the house! I don't want you screaming like that again! Do you hear me?"

Aubrey dropped her eyes, but Mari patted her shoulder. "It's all right, hon. You're safe. You can go finish your show."

Mac shook his head as she retreated to the living room. "Such a drama queen! And so *obsessed* with those dogs!"

Mari huffed. "As if pulling out a pistol isn't dramatic—? Mac, she's eight! She doesn't need that in her life! What are you doing with a gun in the house?"

He opened his hands. "What? I'm a gun owner! I'm a *responsible* gun owner! I wasn't going to shoot those dogs, Marissa. I was going to call him!"

"Then why did you get your gun?"

"In case one of them came after me! But I was going to *call* him."

"But *still*! It's not smart to have a gun if you're a hothead!"

They stared at each other.

Mari let out a breath. "Mac, I apologize—"

"Okay, I apologize," he said at the exact same time. He laughed, but she plunged ahead.

"I shouldn't have said that. This is *your* house, and you have your opinions. I shouldn't have bossed you like that. I just—I couldn't help it."

His lip curled. "Yeah, you *are* a little bossy! My goodness! I was planning to call him all along—honest! All I was thinking about was one of those dogs chomping into my leg if I went outside. Sorry I scared you, but I *promise you* I didn't intend to kill his dogs!"

They looked at each other again.

Mac gave an embarrassed laugh. "Well, now, if this isn't the most awkward moment I can recall in a long time!"

"Oh, my word—I'd have to agree." She rubbed her forehead. "I can't believe that just happened. I'd like to die right now—I feel so stupid. Please don't fire me!"

"Seriously, I *was* going to call him. Plan *A*."

She lifted her hands. "Okay. Can we please move on and never talk about this again? You should probably feed your daughter. I'm sure she's hungry. I'll prep the veggies if you start the grill." She swiped a nearby dishtowel, turning hastily away to fold it.

"Done," he said, but he lingered beside the island. "I see you got my note about the tagboard."

She looked back, breaking into a smile. "I did! Poppy was delighted to pass it on! It's really sweet of you to give him a job. We're having fun with it, Mac."

"Good. Okay, I'll start the grill."

Mari was perched on a stool in her pajamas mixing up a batch of chocolate chip cookies when Will called that evening. They had texted back and forth during the afternoon, so he had already heard her whole knee saga, which only solidified his mission for her to take the new job.

"I know. I'm thinking about it," she told him. "Mom just got home from visiting Poppy, so we'll talk about it soon." Of course, changing jobs wasn't an option for her, but saying she would consider it seemed the courteous thing to do.

"And I don't know why you put up with that Ty rascal! I'd teach him a lesson. And the Rottweilers? Geez, Marzipan—get *out* of there!"

"Mac's taking care of it," she told him. "But enough about that. How's your big project going?"

The diversion worked, as he began a detailed exposition of his day's accomplishment.

Meanwhile Mari's mother entered the kitchen to plop a bagel into the toaster. She tapped Mari's shoulder on the way out of the room, pointing to the appliance. After dumping her last ingredient in the cookie bowl, Mari cradled the phone to mix the dough. However, most of Will's story was lost when she suddenly became aware of plumes of smoke pouring from the toaster slots. Hurriedly she grabbed the bamboo tongs to yank out the bagel, now a charred puck. The kitchen reeked.

"Something's burning—" she heard Shannon call across the house, her voice cut by the sudden blare of the hallway smoke detector. Mari stuffed the phone against her shirt, yelling, "Got it!" while Shannon ran to stop the alarm and opened a patio door to clear the haze. Shaking the crumbs out of the toaster, Mari adjusted the setting and tried for round two with another bagel, the whole time of which Will carried on with his software project technicalities without interruption, unaware of the kitchen excitement. She was about to report what happened when he veered into a new subject.

"So something else happened today, and I'll bet you had something to do with it!" he said.

"Yeah? What's that?" She cast a watchful eye back at the toaster.

"You told Mac to call me, didn't you?"

"Mac called you? For what?"

"Right, like you don't know."

"I know nothing about this, Will. What?" She began scooping mounds of dough onto the cookie sheet.

"He invited me to his men's group on Wednesday nights."

"His men's group? Are you going?"

"You didn't set that up?"

"I knew nothing about it! Honest! Maybe you should go." The idea of him being a part of a group of guys like Mac was very attractive.

"And what about you?"

The question startled her. She—join a group—? "Um—I've been invited a few times."

"And—? I'd only do it if you did too."

Now she was cornered. Doubtless JoyAnne Strang would be at Kyla Watkins' Bible study. "We could think about it," she said evasively. She slipped the cookie sheet in the oven, her conversation with Dr. Grant swirling through her mind. *Why is her success your loss? How big is your God?*

"Let me know what you decide. Anyway, he paid me a compliment. You too, I guess. Said you're a class act, and anyone you date must be a good guy."

"He said that? Well, it's true. You're a good one, Will."

Then someone came to his door, and Will had to go. Mari shifted on the stool, waiting for the cookies to finish baking. *A class act.* She smiled at the compliment. Watching Mac's daughter was playing out differently than she expected, but she liked the job and was glad for his approval. His phoning Will was a surprise, but it had the potential for some very good results. She would be thrilled to have some of Mac's maturity rub off on him. Maybe Mac could help Will understand where she was coming from regarding Ty. And Ariel. Indeed, that Mac had offered to help find Ariel meant a lot. She bit her lip, then opened her phone to text him.

"Hi, Mac. So, about Ariel. Thanks for not going down the JoyAnne track with me again. I know I have issues with her. I'm working on them." She sighed as she sent it off. She *should* be working on them. Why was it so dang hard to let it all go?

He texted back within a few minutes. "We already had that conversation. How's the knee?"

"Much better, thanks to pain meds." She smiled, adding, "I'm considering soccer with the kids tomorrow."

He shot back a laughing icon. "Why not rugby? Btw, Aubrey was out in seconds tonight. All this activity has done her good."

"Nice! Don't let her forget the banana bread in the morning."

"It's beside her backpack. I love that you're doing that with her."

She sent a thumbs up. "Thx. Good night."

"See you tomorrow, Marissa."

Mari was waiting for the last batch to come out of the oven when her mother returned her plate to the kitchen sink.

She stopped, observing her daughter. "My, aren't you chipper this evening—sitting here happily baking cookies! You must have had a good day. Who are these for?"

"Treats for kickball tomorrow. And yes, it *was* a good day—apart from my knee getting crunched. But I iced it, and Mac looked at it. It's starting to settle down."

"Good. How's Will?" She got a glass from the cupboard and filled it with water.

"Great! We just talked. He visited me at Riverview over lunch. Actually, he came to tell me he found a new job for me, but I think I'm sticking with what I have. Shannon was right about getting to know people at the Break. And things are going well at Mac's."

"What's the job?"

"A receptionist position at his company. It's full time. He wants me to take it."

Her mother paused. "Well, if it's less stressful on your knee, maybe you should consider it."

"But what about Poppy?" The timer went off, and Mari removed the pan from the oven.

Mrs. Coleman tipped her head reflectively. "It *is* nice you're there, but your knee is important. There are other options." She still held the glass.

"Well, I love being with him. And I'm not being stupid with my knee."

"All right. It was thoughtful of Will to consider you. Are you two getting things worked out?"

Mari nodded, testing the edge of a cookie with her spatula. "Yes. I think he's finally getting over his thing with Mac."

"And you have good boundaries there—with Mac?"

"Totally! Mac and I have an understanding. There'll be absolutely no boyfriend jabs! Want one?" She held out a cookie.

"Glad to hear it, and no thank you. I'm about to brush my teeth. Good night, sweetheart!" She raised the glass as she turned.

Mari blew her a kiss as she left.

Chapter Fifteen

Mari's knee was not happy when she awoke the next morning, but by the time she got through the shower it had loosened up, so that with ibuprofen and her brace she felt confident enough to forfeit the crutches. Otherwise her Coffee Break job would have been impossible, and she dared not call in on such short notice. Nevertheless, she stashed the crutches in the car in case she needed them after her shift. Or in case Mac freaked out that she wasn't using them.

At work, Dr. Grant's absence from the dining room was conspicuous, producing questions from several of the staff. Though privileged to have the inside scoop, Mari kept the professor's information to herself, lest she appear to have fallen to his vices in Candace's eyes. It was probably best he wasn't there anyway, as the Break was horrendously busy that morning. She surely would have had to dodge her responsibilities to visit with him.

Surprisingly Candace was extra chatty as they rubbed shoulders behind the counter, offering Mari little glimpses into her life as a mother of a four-year-old. She said that she and her partner were about to take a trip to Hawaii in the coming weeks and were debating whose parents the little girl should stay with, as they didn't care for either. Mari simply listened and asked benign questions. When they chanced to be paired in the kitchen making sandwiches, she decided to bring up the subject of Dr. Grant, letting Candace know about Mac's background check.

"Oh, I've run one too," she returned. "I still don't trust him. But *you* sure seem to enjoy talking to him. I don't understand it."

Mari shrugged. "I guess I have a different frame of reference. I grew up in a good church with positive role models and people I respect. His questions and advice seem in synch with all that."

Candace paused with her spatula. "So do you just believe everything they say? How do you know what's legit and what's bogus? The creep who molested me was a Bible-thumper. If you ask me, it's *all* baloney." She went back to spreading mayo.

Mari was doling out cheese slices. "I respect where you're coming from, Candace, but I think you're making blanket judgments. You're disregarding *all* of Christianity because you got hurt by a predator—a genuine predator whose life, I guarantee you, was a million miles away from what the Bible teaches. What he did was wrong, and I hope no one ever has to go through what you experienced. But the Christians I know aren't like that, even with all their stuff. In fact, your sense of wanting justice for what he did—that's from the Bible. God *will* bring justice and punish wrongdoers. If people followed God's ways, Candace, we'd have a good society."

"Yeah, right!"

"No, really! Everything you would want a good society to look like— it's all in the Bible."

The woman snapped the lid onto the tub of mayonnaise. "But how do you know what's true?"

Mari eyed her, proceeding cautiously, "Well, I'm not the greatest Bible scholar, but if you'd like, I'd be willing to get you one, and maybe we could both read it and talk about it. You could ask me any questions you want, and if I don't know the answer, I'd tell you. Then you'd at least know what it says."

Candace hesitated, her eyes flicking to the clock. "We should get these sandwiches up front."

"Right. I'll stay and put this away." She gestured to the sandwich fixings. "You can think about the other stuff. Whatever you decide is fine. And just so you know, I would never want to mislead you or hurt you in any way."

As Candace left with the sandwiches, Mari threw a hand to her chest. What just happened? Had she really just proposed reading the Bible with Candace? Where had that idea come from? Good heavens, what if Candace took her up on it? She was clueless as to what she would do! It scared the daylights out of her! But Mac would know. He would help her. Or Mrs. Gordon. She could ask her too.

After slipping the last of the meat and cheese into the refrigerator, Mari returned to take her place behind the counter, this time next to Tatum, who was as cross as ever. Thankfully, she had to leave early before her shift was finished—over some urgent matter with her son. Mari watched her clock out, marveling at how much energy it likely took for a person like her to stay perpetually mad. Tatum, the personification of entitlement. The whole world owed her. It was beyond what Mari could fathom. And now with the woman leaving early, it appeared Mari had escaped one of her daily rebukes, and for that she was grateful.

It was raining when she got off work. As Mari scampered for her car, her phone rang. Quickly she climbed into her vehicle, discovering the call was from Mac.

"Mari, where are you?"

His tone alarmed her. "About to head to Riverview. What's going on? Is Aubrey all right?"

"Yes and no. There's been a little crisis, and I need your help if you're available."

"What happened?" She snapped her seatbelt and started the car, ready to rush anywhere necessary.

"She's okay, but there was an incident at school. A couple of boys found the banana bread and things got out of hand in the hallway. Apparently it became a football."

"Oh, no!" Her hands popped to her face.

"Oh, *yes*! As you can imagine, both it and Aubrey are destroyed. And worse, she knew the boys that did it—that Haddington kid and the other one you were talking about yesterday."

"No! Please not Connor and Ty!"

"Bingo. They're still in the principal's office with their parents, and I just picked up Aubrey."

She nodded. "And you have appointments this afternoon."

"Yes. I *could* cancel them, but—"

"No, I'll watch her. Oh, she must be a mess!"

"We're on our way to Smoothie Q for a consolation treat—just the two of us. But if you're willing, could I drop her off afterward?"

"Yes, of course! I'll be with Poppy. I'm so sorry, Mac." She glanced in the rearview mirror, preparing to back out.

"Thanks. Be there shortly."

Mari shook her head as she hung up. Those stinkin' rascals! Maybe Will was right. Maybe both of those boys needed to learn a lesson! But what did such a lesson look like? She had no idea.

The drama started over from the beginning when Aubrey arrived at the nursing home, the girl dissolving into tears as soon as she saw Mari. Mac flayed his hands apologetically, indicating he was at a loss with her and needed to get back to the clinic.

"I can handle it," she said, patting Aubrey's back as the girl sobbed into her chest.

"I'm not playing kickball anymore!" she announced when she was able to talk. "I *hate* kickball! I want to stay in the house and watch my shows."

Mari made a sympathetic sound.

"And I hate Connor Haddington and Ty West!"

"I know."

"I wish I could go to my grandma's house! *She* doesn't make me play *stupid* kickball games!"

Mari stroked her hair, remaining silent.

After a while Aubrey sniffed and pulled away. She wiped her eyes, casting a sullen look around. "Do you work here too?"

"No. My grandfather lives here, and I visit him every day. Would you like to meet him?"

"Not really. Is he old?"

"Yes."

"Does he smell bad?"

Mari blinked.

"I don't want to see him. Can I sit in the car?"

"That's not an option. This way please." Mari waved her down the hall.

Aubrey raised her chin in a challenge. "I don't want to go with you."

"That's fine. I'd like you to come anyway."

"No! I want to go to Grandma's! I hate you!"

Mari dug her hand into her waist, eyeing the girl as she reined in the temptation to march her straight out to her vehicle. She took a breath. "Aubrey, are you sad or are you mad?"

Her brow seemed permanently puckered. "I'm *mad*! Ty and Connor wreck *everything*! I wish they would *die*!" She brought a fist up to wipe her cheek.

Mari nodded. "I'm mad at them too! What they did was wrong. And I'm *sad* that our plan for Hailey's mom fell through. It was a good plan, and I'm *disappointed* for what happened. Are you disappointed?"

The girl's lip quavered.

"Look, I'm not going to make you play kickball if that's your concern. But if Ty and Connor show up on the field today, you can be sure that I'll have a few words with them! Now come along. You can't sit in the car, but you can wait in the waiting room while I'm with my grandfather. Do you have a book to read? It'll probably be a long time. Unless you change your mind. My grandfather's really nice. But it's *your* choice. I'm okay with whatever you decide."

She started down the hall, relieved that Aubrey trailed behind. She motioned to the waiting room. "Here you go. I'll be right over there in 108. The bathrooms are right—"

"I'll come with," Aubrey muttered.

Mari raised her brow. "Are you sure? You don't have to."

She sniffed. "I'll come."

Of course, Mari's grandfather was delighted to have a child as a guest. Immediately he pointed to a plastic baggie of hard candy on his tray, which caused Aubrey to lower her guard a few notches. He couldn't pronounce her name, but Aubrey was pleased with "Bree" and laughed at the way he said "Mac's girrrl" a dozen times.

"Do you have anything for me today, Poppy?" Mari asked him playfully.

With twinkling eyes, he handed her a folded note from his shirt pocket—a cartoony pencil drawing of her on crutches deflecting a soccer ball with her head. She laughed, showing it to him.

"It's a joke, Poppy," she said, explaining what it meant.

He nodded, his eyes dropping to her knee. "Care-ful."

"Yes, I'm careful."

Aubrey pressed against her, craning to see the drawing. "My daddy did that?"

"Yes. It's me," Mari said.

She frowned. "I don't get it. Why do you have crutches? And that's not a kickball."

Mari shrugged. "It's just a joke." Happily, she slipped the note into her pocket. "We can't go outside today, Poppy. It's raining."

Her grandfather turned to smile at Aubrey. "Okay. Nice right here."

The sky was still heavily overcast when Mari and Aubrey drove into the old neighborhood. The rain had stopped—which was good—but now it meant that Mari had to deal with the kickball dilemma after all. The bus had already come and gone, and parking her car in front of Mac's, she spied the after-school crew beginning to congregate on the field, laughing and jostling about while they waited for them, with Ty West prominently among the bunch. Oh, brother. She needed to talk to that kid.

Determined never to play the sport again for the rest of her life, Aubrey tromped straight into the house to flop onto the couch. "I'm not going," she declared, dour-faced, with her arms folded tightly. "And you need to stay here because you have to watch me!"

"All right, but we should at least tell them we're not coming," Mari said. She paused, adding, "Connor isn't there, you know. I checked. Are you sure you don't want to play?"

She shook her head no. "*Ty* is there."

"Just come and say hello to your friends."

"You like Ty better than me!"

Mari laughed. "Baloney! I've not made Ty even *one* smoothie!" She opened the door, lingering. "You know, if you sat on the porch steps you could at least see what's happening. But it's up to you." She tipped her head in question.

Another no.

So Mari headed out herself—bumping directly into Roger Eden, who was in the street also on his way to the field with his dogs, their nails clicking rhythmically on the dusty pavement. He gave her a polite nod, and she said hello, following him to the edge of the field. *Great.* She envisioned his dogs running loose with the children there. What if one of the kids tried to pet one?

"Mr. Eden!" she called. Everything about him made her nervous.

He turned, pulling the sleek dogs to a halt.

"Nice to see you. I'm assuming you're here for your dogs—?"

He looked as though he didn't understand the question. "Do you have a problem with that?"

"Well—" She motioned to the growing group of children. "We've been playing kickball here after school. I was going to ask if you could keep Loki and Thor on the leash today. Just so nothing—you know—happens." She shrugged.

"Are you accusing me of something?"

"Not remotely. It's just that Mac's daughter is terrified of the dogs, which you're fully aware of, I'm sure. I'd rather not make it worse, if you know what I mean. Or have one of the little ones out there try to pet one and—and hurt it or something." Her cheeks were hot.

"Last I heard this was a public area. I wasn't aware I needed your approval for exercising my dogs."

"You don't. Look, Mr. Eden—I don't mean to cause problems. I'm actually on my way to tell the kids I don't think it's going to work out to play today. So could you maybe hold off for a little bit, *then* bring your dogs out—? They're beautiful animals, but they're intimidating if you don't know them. Please."

He eyed her, then turned, craning his head to scan the field. "How long you thinking?"

"An hour max *if* they even play. It's complicated. Also, I want to apologize for the meatball thing the other day. That was me. I didn't have your phone number—otherwise I would have called you directly. But Mac wrote it down for me, and I put it in my phone."

His jaw twitched. "Right. Loki's a young dog. I'm still working with him. But let me tell you—if that happens again, I'm calling the police!"

If it happens again, I'm calling the police too, she returned silently. She nodded. "Understood."

As Mr. Eden turned toward home, Mari noticed a strange car pull up into Mac's driveway, parking in front of his detached garage. She hesitated, observing a woman getting out of the driver's side. Exiting the opposite side of the car was a boy with an aluminum foil-wrapped bundle in his hands. Connor Haddington. He glanced briefly toward the kids on the field as the woman came around. Together they headed up the front walk for the house. Oh, brother! Seeing what was about to transpire, Mari anxiously turned on her heel and hurried back, arriving on the porch steps as they knocked on the screen door.

"Hello," Mari said behind them at the same time that Aubrey appeared at the door.

The woman turned. "Mrs. Sinclair? Tess Haddington. My son, Connor, would like to talk to your daughter, please."

It didn't seem like the appropriate time to correct her. Mari topped the steps, simply gesturing to wide-eyed Aubrey in the doorway.

Connor's cheeks and neck were aflame. "Er, I'm s-sorry for what I did. It was mean, and I wish I wouldn't of done it." He shifted his feet, awkwardly handing her the foil package. "Here."

"It's banana bread, and it's still warm," Connor's mom broke in. "Although I'm sure it won't be as good as your mother's. Connor's sorry, hon. I hope you can forgive him." She swung toward Mari. "I apologize for his behavior, Mrs. Sinclair, and I promise you it *won't* happen again. Plus, I want to thank you for what you're doing with these kids. Connor has absolutely loved coming here after school this week. I hope you will still allow him to play. But if not, we understand."

Mari shot a look at Aubrey. "Well, thank you for the apology. It was quite a disappoi—"

"Hellooo!" a voice behind her suddenly hailed from the sidewalk. "Yoo-hoo! Mari! Hello!"

Mari twisted to see Susan Gordon on the boulevard waving to her. With her were a dark-haired gentleman, two young boys, and Leah DeSoto with a baby in a stroller.

"Can the boys join your game?" she called, motioning to the field.

Excitedly Aubrey waved. "It's my church friends, Hank and Howie!"

Goodness, all kinds of interruptions! Mari held up a finger, calling to Mrs. Gordon, "Hang on *one* moment please!" She turned back to Connor's mom. "Sorry. I'm sure she didn't see you. Aubrey, hon, what do you think? Are you willing to let Connor back on the team?"

The girl gave Connor a squirmy shrug. "I guess."

Connor looked enormously relieved. He turned to his mother. "Can we go? The other kids are already there. Come on," he said to Aubrey, who followed without coaxing.

"Can Hank and Howie play too?" she asked eagerly.

Mari nodded, waving them off the porch. "Yes, of course! Go on, and we'll meet you there. Mrs. Haddington, would you like to come watch us?"

"Call me Tess. Sure, I'll come!"

Mari snatched up the kickball from the corner of the porch.

The two new boys were running off with Connor and Aubrey when Mari joined Mrs. Gordon and company on the boulevard.

"I apologize," the older woman said. "I didn't know you had a guest."

Mari smiled. "No worries. This is Tess Haddington, one of the kickball moms."

"Oh, we know the Haddingtons!" Mrs. Gordon replied. "How are you, dear? Have you two met the DeSotos? Dan and Leah."

The man extended his hand. "So you're the famous Marissa I've heard so much about!" He shook her hand and Connor's mom's. "Mrs. Haddington."

Mari shot him a curious glance. "It's Mari, please, and hardly famous. Nice to meet you." Only Mac called her that. She wondered if he had been at the church during her mom's emergency prayer call the other night.

Leah bent to adjust the colorful chain of toys in front of the drooling baby. "Nice to see you again, Mari. We've got the Grant brothers and baby Kenny for the weekend—Kyla and Peter's little guy. Kyla's had a family emergency, and Susan took the kids until we got off work."

"The Grant brothers?" Mari looked toward the field.

"Professor Grant's boys, Howie and Hank," Susan said. "I've noticed you out there with the kids all week, and I thought they might like to play too."

"Of course! The more the merrier!" Dr. Grant's boys! How crazy!

Leah's husband glanced down at Mari's knee. "How are *you* doing? Mac said you got beaned pretty good with the kickball yesterday."

Mari also looked down at it. "Oh. It's, uh—better."

"Good. Well, let me know if there's any way I can help. I'd be happy to."

Leah beamed, adding proudly, "He's a coach. At Ford Brentwood Academy."

Mari straightened in astonishment. "Ford Brentwood? My mother works there! She's the assistant principal! That's where I went to school!"

His face brightened. "Ah—Mrs. *Coleman*! I'm connecting the dots! She's a wonderful lady!"

"Yes—that's my mom!"

"What a small world!" Leah exclaimed.

"No kidding!" Mari said. She waved to the field. "Well, let's walk. The kids are waiting."

Since the ground at the field was uneven, Dan DeSoto pulled the stroller by the front while Leah pushed it across the grass, parking it near the colorful assortment of backpacks and sweatshirts strewn off to the side of home base. Susan Gordon and Connor's mother followed behind, chatting amiably while Mari headed to the pitcher's mound to gather the children in.

"Goodness, look at all these kids!" Susan exclaimed.

"Yes, it's quite a pack," Mari agreed, self-conscious that she now had an audience.

"Hey, all—come on in!" she called, starting her customary headcount, noting Ty hovering near the back as usual. It made her both glad and nervous to see him.

The group had grown *again*, she discovered. Where were all these children coming from? But now, having waited so long for Mari to come to the field, many of them were distracted, playing in little clusters. She raised her voice, trying to organize the teams, but several kids weren't listening.

Aubrey appeared, yanking her arm. "Tell Ty to go home! He can't be on the team. I don't want him to play!"

Mari looked down at her. "Aubrey, I get it, but it's not that simple. I can't just tell him that. I'll need to *talk* to him, and that won't be quick. All these kids have been waiting for us already. Can you let him play this time, and we'll talk to him after?"

"Then I'm not playing!" She folded her arms, jutting out her chin.

"Teacher, look!" one of the boys called, pointing across the field.

Mari raised her eyes to spy a half dozen kids coming across the field toward them. Wow, even more kids now. That made the teams even larger. How was she going to—she stopped, frowning as she peered at the approaching group. These weren't kids, she realized. They were adults. Were they parents? Their walk looked angry. They looked like—oh, *no*! Her stomach lurched. Ty's brother! It was Trey West and four accompanying thugs walking fast. Oh, crud. What was this about?

Aubrey huffed, "You're not listening to me!"

"Fine. Go stand with the adults. We'll talk about this later." Mari steered her shoulders in their direction, then with a brief glance at Leah's husband, turned back, taking a deep breath as she braced for Trey's arrival. Will had predicted this. Sure enough, Ty had told his brother where she was, and now they were back for more.

But they never even looked at her. The angry pack strode straight for Ty, who hadn't seen them coming until they were upon him. His eyes grew wide with fright as his brother gave him a shove.

"What'd you do with my stuff, punk?"

Ty caught his balance. "Trey! Get out of here!"

"I said, what'd you do with it, you little twerp—" He clutched him by the neck of his shirt while all his muscle friends hovered menacingly around.

"What?" Ty whimpered. "What do you want?"

"You know what I'm talking about! Where's my stuff?"

"Let me go! I don't have it! I don't have nothing of yours!"

"You lyin' punk! If you don't give me that money, Burne's going to kill me! All of it! What did you do with it?"

"Hey, *you*!" Without thinking Mari marched straight across the grass to shake her finger in Trey West's face. "You let him go right now!"

His head snapped to appraise her. "What's it to you, you—" Without releasing his grip, he unleashed a string of vulgar names.

It only fueled her fury. "I *said* let him go!"

"And I said *stay out of it*!" He dropped Ty to get in her face. "*My* brother, *my* business!"

She shook her head. "Oh, no—*my* kickball field, *my* business! You can take your little power posse right back to where you came from!" As she flung her arm to point across the field, she bumped against Dan DeSoto, who had just stepped up beside her.

"What's going on here?"

Trey spread his hands. "Nothin'! Just having a talk with my brother—that's all. There's nothin' wrong with that."

Dan nodded, speaking quietly. "Well, we're getting ready to play some ball here. Do you think you could take this somewhere else? They're just kids. They don't need to see a fight." He motioned to the crowd of slack-jawed grade-schoolers staring at them.

After a sweeping glance, Trey turned to his brother. "Come on, punk—let's go!" He jerked his head, indicating they were leaving, but Mari caught Ty's sleeve, pulling him back.

"Ty *stays*." Boldly she met Trey's eyes. "He's my team captain, and I need him."

Trey slowly drew himself taller, but Dan held out his hand.

"*Please*," he said simply.

Trey narrowed his eyes at Mari. "You haven't seen the last of me!" Then he shot Ty a venomous look. "You know what you need to have when you come home. I'll be waiting! Come on, men!" He turned on his heel and strode off, his rabble strutting cockily after him.

Ty wrenched his arm away from Mari and backed a few steps.

"Are you all right?" she asked him.

He feigned an indifferent shrug. "He don't bother me none."

Then Aubrey appeared, throwing her arms around Mari with a force that jolted her knee and nearly knocked her to the ground. She winced at the zing of pain, patting Aubrey while still addressing Ty.

"Well, okay then," she said. "It's a good thing because I need you to focus. You're one of my best players, Ty." She turned to the other children. "Okay, let's gather up around the pitcher's mound!" Separating from Aubrey, she took her hand. "Everything's all right, Aubrey. It's okay."

Dan was staring at her with an astonished look on his face. "What's going on? What was *that* about?"

Her legs felt like jelly, and her knee was pulsing. "I'm not entirely sure. But I feel like I could pass out!"

He motioned toward the sidelines. "Please—go sit down!"

She shook her head. "No—no, I got this."

He shook his head right back. "No, *I* got this! Let me take it today, Mari. You go catch your breath!" He opened his hand, revealing a chrome coach's whistle.

She didn't protest. "Okay. Call 'em in, please."

Dan gave two short whistle bursts. "Gather up!"

In a second there was an army of children at attention. Mari held up her hands. "Sorry about the disruption, everyone, but everything's okay, and we're finally ready to get started. This is my friend, Coach DeSoto! He's helping us out today. Our team captains today are Ty West and—"

"Ty was captain yesterday!" a girl interjected loudly.

"—and *you*," Mari said, pointing to her. "Now we've wasted enough time—let's play! Coach, it's all yours!" She waved her hand, turning the group over to him. And taking Aubrey's hand, the two left to join the ladies observing from the sidelines while Coach DeSoto took the helm.

Chapter Sixteen

"Oh, my dear girl!" Mrs. Gordon exclaimed as Mari and Aubrey withdrew from the kickball game to join the onlookers on the sidelines. "Are you all right? Who were those boys? They looked like trouble all around!"

"We were ready to call the police!" Leah chimed. "My goodness! I can't believe you got in that young man's face like that! We were freaking out over here!"

"Me neither," Mari said, still in a daze. She bent to rub her knee. "It was a brother of one of my kickball boys, Ty West. I felt I had to defend him, I guess."

Mrs. Gordon shook her head. "Good gracious—has this happened before? I'm not sure it's safe for the kids to be playing out here if there's—"

"It's safe!" Mari cut in lightly. "I *assure* you this was the only time this has occurred! But I happened to recognize Ty's brother from another unfortunate incident this week, which I won't go into."

"Well, it's a good thing Leah's husband was here to handle it!" Connor's mother said.

"Yes, what a godsend!" Mrs. Gordon agreed.

Startled, Mari glanced at them. Hadn't *she* handled it?

Aubrey clenched Mari's hand more tightly.

"Go play," she urged, nudging her.

But Aubrey shook her head, remaining glued to her side. The girl was a mixed bag of emotions, having been terrified for Mari in her encounter with Ty's brother but also completely offended that Ty was not only permitted to play kickball but also allowed to be captain two days in a row. Mari simply slung her arm around her and continued visiting with the ladies, glad their afternoon drama was finally fading. As the game unfolded, Aubrey eventually decided to forsake her power pout and knelt to entertain the baby, playing peek-a-boo with a blanket and making him giggle.

Then as the teams again switched from infield to outfield, Coach Dan gave a sharp burst of the whistle. "Aubrey Sinclair, you're needed on the field!" He pointed to home base. "You're up!"

Aubrey cast him a look of surprise, then rose and walked herself into the game.

Mari turned wide-eyed to Leah. "Nicely done!"

"He's the best!" she answered, lifting baby Kenny out of the stroller, now fussing from Aubrey's absence.

Connor's mother sidled over to Mari. "I apologize. I called you Mrs. Sinclair earlier. I thought you were Mac's wife. Susan corrected me."

Mari laughed. "No worries! There wasn't opportunity to say anything." But out of the corner of her eye, she noticed Mrs. Gordon look her way. Mari glanced at her and smiled. The older woman returned her smile and moved her gaze toward the field.

As it turned out, Leah's husband was a fun coach and great with kids, able to act silly while still maintaining control of the players. He designated a hop-on-one-foot inning and a run-with-your-hands-in-the-air inning, even a run-the-bases-backward inning, which created a pandemonium of giggling as kids shouted wildly in correction when their teammates automatically took the normal route, only then to curl their paths back across the pitcher's mound on their way to third.

Then sometime later Hank Grant skinned his knee, and Leah handed off the baby to Mari while she tended his wound.

"It wouldn't hurt to have a first aid kit out here," Mrs. Gordon suggested.

"You're probably right," Mari agreed. "I'm still amazed at how this whole thing has ballooned! I just took the ball out with Aubrey one afternoon, and all of a sudden, it's this!"

"I love it!" Connor's mom said. "Good old-fashioned fun. And outdoors! That's what we need nowadays. Thank you for doing it. But we might want to keep an eye on the sky. I just felt some sprinkles. Looks like it could rain at any moment."

"So did I," Leah said, brushing her arm.

As Mari glanced at the clouds, she suddenly noticed a car barreling up Frost Street. She turned in alarm, watching it speed in—all the way to the edge of the field, where it braked and parked at a cocked angle. Abruptly a woman popped out, making a determined beeline toward the kickball crew. *Oh, now what's this?* Mari wondered nervously, shifting baby Kenny on her arm. Automatically she started in the woman's direction to intercept her, but then gasped in disbelief as she recognized her. How in the world—? It was *Tatum*—Tatum from the Coffee Break! And looking as ornery as ever!

"*Ty!*" the woman barked. "Ty West, you get your lousy butt over here, young man!" She pointed sharply to the ground beside her.

All heads turned to gawk. Mari shook her head in amazement. No stinkin' way. Was this his *mother*?

Ty stood mortified on second base, while Tatum shook her finger again.

"You heard me! Get over here right now!"

Coach DeSoto halted the play while Ty slunk forward.

Mari approached the woman. "Er—Tatum! What a surprise!"

Tatum drew back in mutual shock, her eyes dropping to the baby in her arms.

"You're here for Ty?" Mari asked.

"*Get* in the car!" Tatum commanded as the lad walked up. She faced Mari. "What are *you* doing here?"

Mari tried to catch Ty's eye as he scooted past, but he kept his head down. She gestured. "I watch a friend's child after school. Tatum, your son is welcome to play with us."

"Not today, he ain't! He was *not* to leave the house!"

Ah. Mari had an immediate suspicion that her sudden appearance had something to do with Aubrey's banana bread. She nodded knowingly. "Right. But when he's not grounded, we'd like him to come, if you'd allow it."

Tatum simply spun toward her car.

While she watched her march away, Mari felt the first of the cold raindrops. In her arms baby Kenny caught his breath, flinching in surprise. Then in an instant, the clouds burst forth in a sudden furious downpour, and a collective shriek went up from every child in attendance, including baby Kenny, who let out a frightened screech.

"Everyone—quick! Everyone to my house!" Mari yelled, pointing the way. "Everyone—grab something and go! Run!"

Leah raced to snatch the baby and make a dash for it, while Susan Gordon and Mrs. Haddington herded the stampede of screaming children through the pounding deluge behind her. Meanwhile Mari and Coach DeSoto heaped the remaining backpacks and left-behind debris into the stroller, pulling up the rear. Then at the house, the two of them had to finagle the heavy stroller up the steps onto the porch. When it was finally parked,

Mari straightened, shaking out her arms with a laugh.

"Holy cow—I am completely *soaked*! I'm drenched to the bone!"

"Won't *this* be a memorable day!" Dan said, running a hand over his dripping hair.

"Quite!" She laughed, pointing over her shoulder to the chaos of kids' excited chatter in the house, along with the baby's crying. "Listen to that! Sounds like a chicken coop! Oh, man—Mac's poor house! I can't imagine what his floors are going to look like!" She squeezed out a handful of wet hair.

"Oh, those kids are loving this!"

"Yes, they are! And speaking of kids—Mr. DeSoto, you are stellar with children! Thank you for standing in for me today. You were wonderful! Those kids will never want me again!"

He laughed. "It's Dan. But rumor has it you're pretty good with kids yourself! How's the knee? I hope you didn't stress it hurrying over here."

"I'm okay. It's perpetually sore anyway. But truly—thanks for helping."

"I'm happy to give you a break. Although I'll confess—that hoodlum kid beating on his brother was a little unnerving! I wasn't entirely sure where that was going!"

"It *was* a little intense!"

"Well, it was super brave to stand up to him, but don't ever do that again, okay? Unstable people like that—you never know what they might do!"

Mari smiled sheepishly. "I just reacted. I wasn't thinking."

"Right! But it's when people like *him* react that things can get scary! You do have guts, though, I'll credit you that!"

"Well, let's hope there's never a next time!"

"Exactly!" He began unloading the stroller, leaning the dripping backpacks along the wall. "You've gathered quite a gang out there! How many kids were there? Twenty-five? Thirty?"

Mari shrugged. "We were running late, and I didn't even finish counting today."

"Well, good for you! You've got yourself a captive audience. What are you doing with that?"

Her brow went up. "Playing kickball—? What do you mean?"

"God's given you influence! How are you going to steward that? They're wide open! What's your message?"

"I have *no* idea! I mean, I do remind them to do their homework every day, but there's no way to enforce that."

"Well, pray about it. God will show you. It'd be a shame to waste an opportunity like this!"

"Huh. Right. Okay. Thanks." She handed him another wet backpack. "How long have you been at Ford Brentwood?"

"Only since fall. I teach history and phys-ed. Just finished coaching basketball, and I'm starting women's track."

"Nice!" She wiped her wet hands on her belly. "I can't wait to tell my mom we met."

Hearing a burst of collective laughter inside, he gestured. "You should go. I'll take care of this."

She smiled. "Thanks."

Mari entered the house to find every room on the main floor crowded with wet and giggling children overjoyed with their predicament—apart from baby Kenny, who had not yet recovered from the deluge or the dash to the house. Discarded shoes and wet zip-up sweatshirts littered the foyer where Leah bounced the inconsolable infant, now stripped down to his diaper. He cast a wary look at Mari when she came near, baring two tiny teeth as he let out another mournful wail.

Leah nuzzled his head, cooing, "Shhh—shhh! It's okay!"

"Poor baby!" Mari murmured.

"Oh, he'll be all right once we get him in some dry clothes. How are *you*? How's your knee?"

"It's all right—thanks. It was super sweet of your husband to help me. Not just with the rain but with everything!"

"Oh, he loves kids! And fun timing! We were coming over here for dinner after picking up the Grant brothers from Susan's. Dan and Mac are great friends. Hey now, sweet baby—shhh! It's all right, little Kenny! Shhh!" She kissed his head, swaying side to side. "I'm waiting for Dan to bring me the diaper bag from the stroller."

"Want me to get you one of Mac's shirts?"

"Oh, my outer sweatshirt was soaked, but this shirt is okay. It's my jeans that bug me, but I'll dry. And look—Susan's putting towels over the furniture." She nodded toward the living room.

Mari followed her glance. "Smart thinking. Well, excuse me. I'm going to resurrect my work uniform. Back in a bit."

After a quick change of clothes, Mari snatched the tub of her chocolate chip cookies and made the rounds from the kitchen through the dining room and living room and back, making a point of learning the names of newcomers as she went.

"What a spectacular host!" Mrs. Haddington exclaimed from the corner of the living room where she and Susan Gordon visited.

"Oh, it's fun to have some treats," Mari said modestly.

Aubrey suddenly appeared to throw her arms around Mari's waist. "Thank you, thank you, thank you! This is so much fun! I love you!"

Mari squeezed her back. "Careful of my knee, hon. But yes, this *is* fun, isn't it?" She took her by the chin. "And you made it through with both Connor and Ty there! I'm so proud of you!"

Her voice grew sullen. "Ty never even said sorry!"

Mari nodded. "I know, but Connor did. And guess what—I think Ty was supposed to be grounded, so that's at least something. Some kids don't know how to say they're sorry, but we'll talk about that later. Now go play!" She kissed the air toward her.

Aubrey spun happily away to join her friends.

"You're really good with her," Mrs. Haddington commented.

Mari smiled. "Thanks. I like her a lot."

Mrs. Gordon smiled too, her eyes following Aubrey across the room.

Mari was putting the cookies away in the kitchen when Mac walked in, looking very confused at the commotion. His glance moved from her wet hair to her uniform.

She laughed. "We got poured on at the field! I had all the kids shelter here 'til the rain stops."

"I was wondering! It smells like wet dog in here. I thought it was some mistaken birthday surprise!" He cast an amazed look toward the front of the house. "That many kids for kickball, huh?"

"There's a lot, yes! Cookie?" She extended the tub.

"Thanks. Who brought these?" He took a bite, holding it up in approval.

"I made them last night." As his eyes dropped to her leg, she added, "Yes, it hurts, but I think the brace is sufficient."

He grunted, still eating, and she continued, "Aubrey seems to have recovered from the school incident. Connor's mother brought him over to apologize with a fresh loaf of banana bread. And miracle of miracles, she even went out to the field to play! And Dan and Leah DeSoto are here, plus Susan Gordon and Connor's mom. You should go say hello."

"Thanks. I will. Hey—stick around. I have something to tell you later." He snatched a few more of the cookies.

"Same," she returned. "And sorry about your floors."

When Mari returned to Leah in the foyer, baby Kenny was adorned in fuzzy pajamas, making worried noises as he sucked furiously on his pacifier, his fair hair lightening as it dried. He gave a jerky breath, looking around. Mac and Dan stood together facing into the living room.

"I have seatbelts for five," Dan said, counting heads. "But we could squeeze in more. It's only a few blocks."

"Same here," Mac said. To Mari's inquiring look, he answered, "We're organizing rides. Their parents are probably wondering about them."

"Nice. There's my car too," she volunteered.

"I think we're good if Dan and I each take two trips."

"I'll take the ones who live by me," Connor's mother offered, overhearing as she entered the foyer with Susan Gordon. "That's at least four."

"Don't count me, of course," Susan said. "I'll walk when it lightens up."

Mac nodded. "Sounds good."

In a few minutes Mrs. Haddington left with the first carload. Soon after, Mac called out a handful of children to send with Dan and another group to pack into his car, most of whom called out their thanks to Mari on the way out the door.

"You have the best mom ever," one boy said to Aubrey.

"*Childcare giver*," Mari corrected, waving him off. "See you Monday!" The title sounded rather sterile, she thought, but "babysitter" might embarrass Aubrey, and "nanny" had the connotation of way more than three hours a day.

With the mass exodus of kids, she now noticed the full condition of the foyer floor, but Susan Gordon beat her to the broom. So Mari helped straighten what she could.

"Go have a seat, dear!" the older woman urged.

Leah patted the couch. "Here! Come put your leg up! Baby Kenny's almost out."

In a few minutes both men were back for a second batch of kids, and Aubrey was left with only the Grant brothers.

"Can we play in my room?" she asked.

"Of course!" Mari answered. "But remember, whatever we get out we put away."

"We know."

And then it was quiet.

Leah adjusted the sleeping baby on her shoulder. "Aubrey adores you."

Mari chuckled. "Maybe this moment. A couple hours ago she hated me! But yeah—I love her too. She's pretty special." She gave a sigh. "I'm still wowed at the timing of you showing up today! I appreciated the extra support when Ty's brother showed up like that. Plus, I think it's amazing that your husband works with my mom. What a wild connection!"

"I know! And speaking of connections, Mac and I just found out our grandmothers knew each other. *His* grandmother was *my* grandmother's mentor! Isn't that amazing? Mary McAllister. His mom named him after her. He would have been 'Mary,' but since he wasn't a girl, 'McAllister' was as close as they could get."

"How on earth did you discover that?"

"My grandmother kept journals, and I happened to ask Mac about his name. Who knows—my grandma might have even held him as a baby!" She smiled, kissing baby Kenny's head. "My grandma had a tough time of it in her early years, and her mentor helped her a lot, which is why I've been meeting with Susan and Jackie—because my childhood was quite dysfunctional too, and I need their input in my life. I got saved in high school but then totally walked away from God—a classic prodigal. But *you*—it sounds like you had a great upbringing from what Shannon says. And your parents are still together."

Mari nodded. "Yeah, my family is pretty normal, I guess."

"Well, mine was quite the opposite. Honestly, Susan is my voice of reason. She's been a lifesaver for me!"

Mari gave a little smile. "I wish I had someone like that."

Leah snorted. "What do you mean? You do! A healthy home, growing up in church, the Gordons next door—you've *always* had that!"

"Yeah. Sort of. So how did you and Dan meet?"

"We met at Bible camp when I was sixteen. He and his brother put a snake on my bunk 'cause he had a crush on me! It took us ten years, but we finally got together. It's been an interesting journey, but I'm grateful God saw us through. We're truly soul mates!"

"That's sweet!"

Leah smiled. "Thanks. He's so wonderful! And super supportive of me while I work out stuff from my past. There's been a lot of layers of forgiveness, including forgiving myself! I've carried a lot of guilt from walking away from God. I used to blame others for that, but it was *my* choice completely. I think it's a dangerous place when you know about God and his ways and then choose to disregard him. I was totally living for myself, and yet I had this sick attitude that I had the right to judge others for what *they* did wrong. Anyway, I'm back, and God's restoring my heart. I'm learning to live from an attitude of pleasing God rather than just trying to be good." She looked up as Susan Gordon suddenly entered the room, making her way to an armchair. "And there she is in the flesh! I've been telling Mari how amazing you are, Susan!"

Mrs. Gordon threw her a kiss. "Right back at you! What are you making for supper, hon?"

"I made Jackie's crockpot chicken and rice. It's still in the car all wrapped up. You're welcome to stay! You too, Mari!"

Mari shook her head. "Thank you, but no. I have—I have a date."

"Ah! With that tall fellow you were with on Sunday?"

"Yes—with Will. Will Wallace." As she spoke, Mari was aware of Aubrey and the Grant brothers rushing down the stairs. Soon the girl appeared at her side, pressing in while the boys hovered near.

"What's going on?" Mari asked.

"The dogs are out!" Aubrey whispered urgently. "They're in the field!"

"That's where Mr. Eden takes his dogs to run. Is he with them?"

"Yes. But he won't pick up after them."

"Aubrey, hon, what has your daddy told you about Mr. Eden and his dogs? They're not your business!"

"Yeah, but what if they bite him when he comes home?"

Mari threw up a hand. "Fine. I'll text him. Now *stop watching them* and go play!"

With a loud sigh Aubrey skulked off, heading back upstairs with the Grant brothers close behind.

Mari shook her head, looking at the ladies. "Goodness! That girl is so fixated on the neighbor's dogs! She's terrified of them! Of course, it didn't help that one got out this week. Have you had any problems with them, Susan?"

Mrs. Gordon adjusted a pillow behind her. "Oh, that younger one is a digger! He's gotten under the fence and into our trash a number of times, but Roger's working with him, and we're careful. I certainly wouldn't throw anything at it or anything!"

Mari's mouth opened in surprise, but before she could reply, Mac and Dan walked through the door, chatting happily, both of their shirts mottled from the rain. She turned to face them, her cheeks burning.

"Wouldn't you know it, the moment I dropped the last kid off it stops raining!" Mac announced. "My windshield was completely dry coming home! They could have all run home!"

"But what a day!" Dan exclaimed. "It'll make for great memories! And I was able to intercept a few parents on their way out to get them."

"Oh, good!" Mrs. Gordon said. "I was hoping that wouldn't be an issue—parents looking all over for their kids. Dan, you poor thing! You're soaked through!"

Dan grinned. "Best day ever!"

"I'll get you some dry clothes," Mac said, starting up the stairs.

Leah shifted the baby. "Danny, hon, would you mind getting his little bed from the car? And the crockpot, please."

He nodded. "Sure. Susan, can I walk you home on my way to the car?"

"Thank you, yes!"

Mari rose too, accompanying Mrs. Gordon to the door. "I'm glad it worked out for you to be here today. And I'm glad Dr. Grant's boys got to play kickball."

Mrs. Gordon smiled. "Yes, hon. That's quite a crew you have!"

"I know! Isn't it? But hey—would it be okay if I stopped by some afternoon? Just to chat. Maybe after visiting my grandfather and before watching Aubrey—?" Leah's story had stirred up a tiny envy in her to have a mentor too. She knew Mrs. Gordon. Why not ask? Plus she would welcome an opportunity to tell *her* version of what happened with the dogs.

"I'd be delighted!" the woman replied. "Anytime! But I *do* still have my cleaning business, so I'm gone a lot. And then Thursday afternoons I have Bible study at the church. And I also meet with a few young gals some afternoons. Hmm. It'd have to be before three o'clock, right? We could probably fit you in somewhere."

She was too busy. Mari shook her head. "It's nothing urgent. It's just to chat. Maybe sometime."

"Okay. Well, we'll see. Maybe some Monday."

"Yeah. We'll see." It figured.

"Marissa—hang on! Don't leave yet!" Mac called down the stairs. "I need to talk to you!"

"I'll wait!" Mari called back. She smiled at Mrs. Gordon, who glanced up the stairs and back at her.

"Have a lovely evening, Mari. Enjoy your date with Will."

"Thank you. Good night."

A minute later Mac came downstairs dressed in jeans and a T-shirt with an armful of clothes. He handed off a dry T-shirt to Leah, who had tucked the sleeping baby on the couch to use the bathroom. He offered one to Mari too, but she declined because she was leaving soon. She was a little surprised to see him in casual clothes since she was familiar with only his work attire.

He dumped the extra shirts in a corner and found his slippers on the mat. "Hey—so I asked around at the nursing home this morning, and it appears that our Miss Ariel Marquette has officially quit her job."

Mari gave a disappointed sigh. "That's what I was afraid of. I just hope she doesn't do something she regrets."

"Well, if she's too sick to work, maybe she's still considering her options."

"Good point. But how do I get in touch with her?"

"There's got to be a way to find her. Anyway, I wanted to tell you that. And you have some news for me?"

"Yes. Our banana bread hotshot Ty West showed up at the field this afternoon. He never even acknowledged Aubrey."

"Oh, brother. How'd she take that?"

"Not so well. But get this—while we were getting started, his brother came strutting across the field to beat on him. Trey, the one who stopped me at Whitmore the other night!"

"No!"

"Yes! From the sound of it, Ty stole some stuff from him, and he was mad at him. I don't think he recognized me, but boy, was I ever glad to have Coach Dan there!"

"He's a good guy, isn't he?"

"Totally. He was able to talk him down and send him on his way— thank God. But that's not all. Later while we were playing kickball, Ty's *mother* came to drag him out by his ear!"

"Goodness! You're getting to know the whole family!"

"Yeah, well, guess what else? I *work* with her at the Taiton Coffee Break!"

"No way!"

"Way! She's the meanest, crabbiest lady I've ever met! I couldn't even believe it!"

Mac looked at her without speaking, his mouth drawing into a smile. She frowned. "What's so funny?"

He shrugged. "What an amazing 'coincidence'! Why do you think God allowed that to happen?"

"You think this is from God? To me it only confirms there's a *devil*! I'm already walking on eggshells at work. Now I'm gonna have to be even *more* careful around her!"

He laughed. "Oh, I think you can handle it! She's probably terrified of *you*, with all your spunk!"

"Yeah, right! All my spunk!" She laughed with him. "Anyway, before I go I wanted to ask if I could have this." She slid the banana bread that Connor had brought for Aubrey out from the cubby under the stairs. "It's the weekend, so it wouldn't be totally fresh for Hailey's mom on Monday, and if *you* kept it, I think it'd only remind Aubrey of how things went awry at school. I was thinking of leaving it on Roger Eden's doorstep as a peace offering for all the issues we've had with his dogs. Plus I need to thank him for accommodating us this afternoon. I asked him to hold off on walking them, and he did."

"That's a great idea!"

"I'll take it over on my way out. Can I borrow another notecard?"

"Help yourself."

"Thanks."

He laughed again, shaking his head.

"What?"

"You are something else, you know. You and Roger Eden, you and the West family, you with all those kids—"

"No kidding! I'm becoming my own reality show! What am I going to do with all of them, Mac? I'm outnumbered! Your buddy Dan says I need to use my influence! Where do I start with that?"

"Yeah? What a *great* problem!"

She huffed. "That's no answer! I could use your help, you know."

"Well, count me in."

Mari heard the bathroom door open. Leah was returning to the living room.

"And them. They'd help." Mac tipped his head, indicating the DeSotos. "Dan's the bomb with kids, and Leah is Aubrey's Sunday school teacher. They'd have lots of ideas for you."

"But they have their lives."

"Of course. Everybody does. But I think they had a blast being connected to yours today!" He motioned to the door. "I'll let you go. Have a great night, Marissa."

"Thanks. Good night."

Chapter Seventeen

Mari drove straight from Mac's house to Will's apartment, finding him, as the last time she had been there, slouched across the couch playing video games. He sat up quickly when she came in, his eyes darting to the wall clock.

"Whoa—you're early! I didn't expect you for another hour at least!"

She left her shoes by the door, coming to stand beside the couch. "Hi. It rained. Plus Mac came home a little early." Then she noticed the Chinese takeout containers on the table. "Did you eat already?"

He set the controller aside. "Yeah—you weren't supposed to see that. I was hungry on my way home from work, so I picked something up. I didn't know you'd be here *this* early. I figured it would be a couple hours before we ate. But we could go somewhere if you're ready."

"Well, not if you just ate."

"No—I was planning to eat again. I just know you don't like Chinese."

She paused. "Okay. I'm not in a hurry, I guess. What was your plan?"

"Plan for what?"

"For dinner. Were you taking me somewhere?"

Will sat back. "Okay, I can tell you're upset—"

"I'm not upset."

"Yes, you are! You're upset because I got Chinese."

"No, I'm not! I'm only asking what the plan is."

Will spread his hands. "What plan? Do we need to have a plan? Why can't we just let things happen? Or hang out here?"

"Fine! I'm okay with that! I'm not upset."

"Well, you're charging in here demanding to know the plan like you've got better things to do with your time than chill on a Friday night with your boyfriend!"

Mari blinked. No doubt his apologies would kick in soon.

But Will simply eyed her back.

She let out a sigh. "Actually, do you have any leftover spaghetti from the other day? I wouldn't mind that, and staying in sounds perfectly fine to me. I've had one *crazy* day. I'm tired, and my knee aches."

"I'll get it for you." He pulled himself off the couch, gathering up his takeout trash.

"No, Will, I'll get it."

"No, *I'll* do it! It's the least I can do, since I wrecked our dinner plans."

"Well, leave it to you to wreck nonexistent dinner plans!" she teased, at which he failed to crack a smile.

She followed him to the kitchen, hovering nearby as he loaded a paper plate and popped it into the microwave. "How was your day?" she asked, waiting for it to chime.

"It was okay," he replied.

"Well, mine was a circus! Want to hear about it?"

He folded his arms. "Uh—not if it's going to make me frustrated. I have a hard time with whiny, bratty kids."

"It might."

"Then let's talk about something else."

The microwave dinged, and he handed her the warm plate.

She took it, staring at him. "What's going on, Will?"

He shrugged, returning to the couch. "Did you think more about that job offer?"

Mari bit her lip, following him. So *that's* what it was. She put her water on the table and sat beside him. "Yes, I've thought about it and decided to stay put where I'm at for now. I know you're disappointed, but like I said yesterday, it's not about you."

He gave a heavy sigh. "I wish you'd change your mind."

"I know." She looked up at him. "Do you have any of that garlic bread left?"

He jerked his head toward the kitchen. "Beside the toaster."

She fetched it, then started in on her meal. "This is really good—again. What game are you playing?"

"Same as the other night—the new one."

"Fun. I'll join you when I'm done, if you don't mind getting your butt whipped."

He sniffed. "You're still in your work uniform."

"Yeah. My other clothes got totally soaked."

"I also noticed you're still not wearing my ring."

Mari groaned, holding out her hand. "I know! Sorry. I'll have time to fix it this weekend. Tomorrow, I promise." She turned to him, brow raised. "Any other complaints?"

He hesitated a moment, then shrugged. "That probably covers it."

"Okay. Well, I'm going to finish my spaghetti now, so you'll have to sit in your funk by yourself for a bit. Let me know when you're back so that we can relax and have fun. So far this has been *anything* but fun." She turned back to her plate.

Still sulking, he watched her eat. Finally he sighed. "Okay, I guess I'm back."

"No, you're not." She scraped up her last bite and set the empty plate on the end table, tossing her wadded napkin onto it. She held out her hand. "Controller, please."

He set one in her palm.

"You're going down!"

He finally broke a smile. "You're on!"

"*Now* you're back," she stated, settling in beside him.

After a couple of hours they took a break.

"Want to go out for ice cream?" Will asked, stretching his arms.

"I want to, but I probably shouldn't. I've already had a few too many cookies this afternoon."

"Oh, what's a few cookies?"

"Right. *You'd* never know because you're tall. Tall people like you and Shannon have ample space to hide a few pounds, but not so for short folks like me. Everything shows!" She slapped her thigh.

Will grinned. "I'll eat yours!"

She smiled. "Fine."

"Then I get to pick where we go!"

"I guess you do."

Once they were settled in a booth at Will's favorite ice cream shop, Mari asked the question that had been nagging her all evening.

"Will, what's your story with God?"

He shrugged. "I believe in God, Mars. What's there to tell?"

"No—like how did you get here? How did you come to believe in God?"

"I don't get the question."

"Well, did you grow up going to church? Did someone in college talk to you about Jesus? What's your, er—faith story?"

Will paused with his plastic spoon over his cup. "I didn't grow up with religion. Honestly, I've never thought about God much. Only since going out with you. But I'm cool with it and everything. I know it's important to you and your mom."

"So what do you think about Pastor Keith's sermons?"

He shrugged. "They're cool. I mean—I agree with most of the stuff. I do want to be a better person."

"But what about Jesus?"

"Yeah—and that too. I'm down with all that stuff. I get that he died on the cross to forgive my sins."

Mari nodded. "Okay, good. So do you ever think about your purpose in life? Like why you're here on the earth?"

His lip curled. "Marzipan, you're getting weird on me! Where's this going?"

"I'm just asking."

"How do you define 'purpose in life'? Are you asking what *I* want to do? Or what I think *God* wants me to do?"

"Shouldn't they be the same?"

He cocked an eyebrow. "I'm not that spiritual! Look—I'm all for the 'life, liberty, and pursuit of happiness' thing. I think God's okay with whatever we choose to do. He's there for us, you know. He's got my back. What about you? You've obviously been thinking about this if you're asking the question!"

"I have been." She scooped a spoonful of ice cream from his cup. "I guess I'm not quite sure what I'm called to do, but I don't want to miss it."

Will shook his head. "That's way too much pressure if you ask me. How could you ever know anyway?"

"I'm not sure." She took another bite. "I think maybe God might lead us by our inner desires—by what makes us feel fulfilled in serving him. But I don't know."

"Uh-huh. Well, speaking of inner desires, let's finish up and get back to the apartment. I've got a few ideas of what we could do next." He raised his eyebrows playfully.

She set the spoon down, shaking her head. "We shouldn't, Will."

He frowned. "Why not? What's going on?"

"It's not right."

"Says who? We're getting married."

"It's—it's not right."

He made a little sound, setting his ice cream aside. "Well, aren't you full of all sorts of joy tonight! What's going on? Is this because of the Chinese takeout deal? Is this some kind of power play?"

"No, Will. I just think—"

"You're almost twenty-three, Mari. It isn't like you need your mother's permission to have sex! And we're responsible."

"Will, I want to do right before God."

He nodded. "Okay. So move in with me."

"What?" She laughed. "Didn't you hear what I just said?"

"It shows we're committed. At least *I'm* committed. Are *you*?"

She shook her head. "I'm not moving in with you, Will. My mother would freak, and my father would be home from wherever he is in a flash. No, from now on, we're not having sex until we're officially married. Period. If you don't like it, break up with me."

"Come on—you can't be serious!" He stared at her, then sat back shaking his head. "Way to freakin' ruin a date, Maribelle!"

Mari slid out of her seat. "I guess that's my answer."

"No, sit down! We're *not* breaking up. I just gotta deal." He let out a long breath. "You are the most old-fashioned chick I've ever dated! You're like—you're like black-and-white movies old-fashioned. Sheesh!"

"I'm fine with that. And I thought you only dated one other girl."

"Even so, it's still true. All right—truce. We'll do things *your* way. I don't like it, but—"

"It's *God's* way. I want to do right by God, so it's the way it's going to be."

"Fine."

"Plus, we've got to *do* things on our dates, Will. Something besides video games. And we can't just be in your apartment. That's a recipe for trouble right there."

He spread his hands. "Oh, great! I'm glad you think so highly of me! Fine. We'll go bowling or something. But just so you know—I can't afford to be taking you to expensive places all the time."

"How much did you spend on me tonight?"

He rolled his eyes. "Mean-o."

"I'm saying I'm easily pleased. I can't go bowling with my knee anyway, and walks are free. Okay, by your expression I can see that hanging out with you the rest of the evening is not going to be fun. We should call it a night. Then tomorrow you can text me if you still want to go out with me."

"I told you I'm *not* breaking up with you! But yeah—let's go." He grabbed his half-finished ice cream and walked it to the trash.

The drive back to his apartment was quiet. Time would tell, Mari thought as Will dropped her off at her car. She drove home alone in the dark. It would be disappointing if Will dumped her, but it was a boundary she had to set.

Colton had just brought Shannon home at the same time, and the two girls met in the elevator.

"Did you have a nice evening with Will?" she asked, pushing the button to their floor.

"Yep," Mari answered. "You?"

Shannon smiled dreamily. "I can hardly *wait* until he doesn't have to bring me home! One hundred and five days!"

Mari sighed, bugged that she'd had to drive herself home. "Shannon, do you ever feel like two different people? Like when you're with Colton, you don't quite know yourself?"

Shannon turned in surprise. "Quite the opposite! With Colt I feel like I'm truly free to be myself. Do you feel that way with Will?"

"Sometimes. We're still figuring things out."

"I remember that phase. Well, hang in there. The two of you will find your groove."

"Yeah. Thanks."

The next morning Mari reached for her phone to check for a text from Will, but there was nothing. Perhaps he wasn't up yet. She rolled onto her side, anxiously hugging her pillow. Her chances for a breakup were fifty-fifty. She only hoped that if he were going to do it, he would get it over with quickly.

While lying there, Mari found her thoughts drifting to Mac and Aubrey. She wondered what Saturday mornings were like at their house. She imagined Aubrey sleepily padding to her dad's bedroom in her girly unicorn pajamas with her hair all frizzed out, asking if she could watch television. On the other hand, Mac was an early riser. He would likely be downstairs in his jeans and T-shirt before Aubrey got up—maybe having coffee at his dining room table. Or perhaps in the kitchen making breakfast for the two of them. If Mari were there, she would make pancakes. No, she would have Aubrey making pancakes *with* her. With sausage for her daddy.

Mac. She did admire him. He was a good dad, a good physical therapist, a good friend to his friends, a gracious neighbor. Plus godly—to the extent that he would pray for reconciliation with his ex. That was hard core. His was a life changed. Mari knew only glimpses of his wild high school days. Certainly nothing from his past with Elena, his ex-wife. She wondered what had happened between them. Where was she now? Why wasn't she in Aubrey's life? What was she like? One of these days she wanted to get the full scoop from Mac. She sighed. She would miss being over there today. She had grown attached to that girl.

Half an hour later Mari was in the kitchen standing over a hot griddle when her mother moseyed in to pour herself a cup of coffee.

"Well, look at you this morning—dressed already and making pancakes! Is that sausage? Will must be coming over! We haven't had pancakes in ages!" She opened the refrigerator for the creamer.

Mari waved the spatula at the cakes accumulating on the plate. "It seemed like a pancake morning. And no, I haven't heard from Will. These are for us." Crazy—she hadn't even thought to invite Will. Was it too late? If she texted him and woke him, would he be irritated? Plus how long would it take him to drive to their condo? They might be waiting for a while if she invited him. She eyed the hot pancakes. She wasn't even sure she still had a boyfriend.

Her mother dropped her spoon into the sink and set her mug on the counter. "What a treat! Shall I wake Shannon?"

But Shannon appeared from around the corner. "I'm up. Wow—what's the occasion? Is Dad home?" She glanced toward her parents' bedroom.

"That's *next* weekend," their mom said, lifting the plates from the cupboard.

"No occasion," Mari said. "Just felt like making pancakes. Dad's coming home?"

"Yes, Friday—and just for the weekend, which is good timing because I need his wisdom. We need to decide whether Poppy stays in nursing care or goes back to assisted living. They won't hold his room past the first." She separated the plates and reached for a handful of silverware.

Shannon slid onto the stool at the counter. "What's your opinion, Mom?"

"Well, the doctor says he might be maxed out in his recovery. This could be as far as he'll go."

Mari handed her mother the tray of sausage patties. "What does Mac say?"

"Mac says there's no way to predict how far he'll go, but he's hopeful. He says the human brain and the power of God are amazing. We never expected him to come as far as he has."

"I'd go with Mac," Mari said simply. She removed the last pancake from the griddle and turned it off.

Shannon snitched a piece of sausage. "Go with Mac, definitely! Or Option *C*—pay Mac to live with him! That'd be my vote!"

Their mother nodded. "Mac's a blessing, but at this stage we need to figure out if Poppy will be able to live on his own again. That's the question. It's hard to tell."

"Option *C*—I'm tellin' you! Mac's the goods. Mari, grab the maple syrup from the fridge, would you? Mom—a coffee please?" She popped another chunk of sausage into her mouth. "Mmm, yum! I seriously don't know why that man isn't married! You'd think he'd be snatched up in a second. I mean—what a great guy! I wonder if he's dating anyone."

Mari set the syrup onto the counter. "I'd guess not, since he's praying for his marriage to be restored."

Her mother turned in surprise. "I didn't know Mac was married!"

"*Was*—key word. He's not wearing a ring, but I saw in his, um—I came across a note that said he was praying for reconciliation with his ex and for restoration of their marriage. But don't say anything. I'd be embarrassed if he found out I read his stuff."

"Snoop!" Shannon smiled mischievously as she divvied out napkins. "That makes me respect him even more, but she better be worth the effort. I'd hate to see a good guy like that get strung along. Come on—sit down, you two! Let's eat!"

Mrs. Coleman slid onto her stool. "Huh. I did not know that."

Mari's phone chirped as she took her place next to her mother. Will. *Finally.* She opened the text. "Good morning. Sooo how do we work this now? Want to go to a movie tonight? Does this mean I have to stay away from you all day? This sucks!"

With a breath of relief, she texted back. "You goofball! Eating breakfast. Call you soon." She set her phone aside. Whew! Their relationship had survived the night.

It chirped again as her mother blessed the food. She raised her brow when she finished. "Everything all right?"

"Yeah. It's Will. We're planning our day." Mari glanced at her phone and straightened, seeing that it was *Mac* who had texted the second time. Curiously she tapped the text.

"Morning. What's Ariel's house number? Dan and I are going over there after racquetball."

Surprised, Mari typed a rapid reply. "Thx! Not sure, but her front door is red."

He returned a thumbs up. "Helpful. Thanks. How's the knee?"

"I'll survive. Be careful! You're not bringing Aubrey, are you?"

"No. She slept over at the DeSotos with the Grant bros. She's helping Leah with the baby."

"Nice. Well, keep me posted."

Another thumbs-up.

Mari set her phone down and plopped a short stack of cakes on her plate. So Mac and Dan were scoping out Ariel's house! That confirmed it—Mac was totally a great guy! And Aubrey was with Leah. Leah DeSoto wasn't so bad either.

"So what are you and Will doing today?" her mother asked, eyeing Mari's phone.

"I'm not sure. We haven't talked yet. That was Mac."

Shannon's head swung over. "Mac? You and Mac are texting?"

"Yeah, Shannon, I watch his kid. He had a question."

"That's so weird!" She shook her head.

"What's so weird about it?"

Mari's mother smoothed a pat of butter across her pancakes and said, "I'm checking out the Farmer's Market before I visit Poppy. I hope to be home by two. You're both welcome to join me."

"I work at eleven," Shannon said, taking a bite. "Going to Colt's after."

"I'd do the Farmer's Market if we go early enough," Mari answered. "But I'll drive separately. I'm thinking of going to Leah DeSoto's Bible study later this morning."

Her mother flashed her a look. "Wow! Good choice, Mari!"

"She's super nice," Shannon affirmed. "I did her hair for her wedding."

Mari shrugged. "I thought I'd try it. And I was thinking of having Will over for dinner before we go to a movie. You can join us, Mom."

"For dinner, yes. Not the movie."

Shannon snickered. "I should *hope* you wouldn't join them at the movies!"

Mrs. Coleman offered Mari the sausage plate. "After breakfast you should tend to those roses in the living room. They're starting to smell."

"They're disgusting!" Shannon chimed.

Mari glanced over her shoulder. "I feel like I didn't even get to enjoy them. I've been so busy."

"Pull out the good ones and make a smaller bouquet," Mrs. Coleman suggested. Then she turned to ask Shannon if she had had any progress with selling her car.

After breakfast Mari called Will. Waiting for him to answer, she wandered to the corner of the living room and stood looking out over Taiton Green, where she had initially proposed to meet Dr. Grant. She would have to ask Shannon about her schedule. Would it be awkward talking to him with Shannon present?

Will answered on the seventh ring. "I was in the shower. What are you doing?"

Mari let out a happy breath, leaning her head against the window. "Looking out over the Green. Know what—? They hold an Arts Fair on the Green every spring. That'd be a fun thing to do together, wouldn't it? It's free! It's in a couple of weeks."

"For what—to buy matching tie-dyed T-shirts and look at old grandpa wood carvings?"

"Knock it off! I like to look at things! Some people are super creative."

"Who has money for that?"

"Never mind. Anyway, I'm trying out that Bible study at Leah DeSoto's this morning. Want to come over after lunch?"

"It'll be at least mid- to late-afternoon 'til I can get there. My dad called. I have to help my parents move. Just across town."

"Your parents live in New Hampton?"

"You didn't know that?"

"No, you've never mentioned them. I'd like to meet them!"

"Well, today's not the day for that, but sure, we can arrange that sometime. Are we still doing the movie tonight?"

"Yep. And I'm making dinner before. Any special requests?"

"Nope. Just no spaghetti, and go light on the veggies. And I don't like anything with that yellow sauce."

"Yellow sauce?"

"Curry or whatever it is. I don't like unusual flavors. And don't make Chinese. If we're doing Chinese, order from The Wok. Otherwise, no."

Mari rolled her eyes. "Well, I'm glad you're not picky!"

"Thanks. Oh, now my dad's trying to call. Hey, Mars, I should go."

"Okay, see you this afternoon, Mac." She cringed. "*Will.* Sorry!"

He huffed. "Geez, would you quit doing that? If I had five bucks for every time you've called me Mac—"

"Sorry! See you this afternoon!"

She drew her hand over her mouth as she hung up. Why did she always call him that?

She turned to heft the enormous bouquet of wilted roses to the kitchen, where she found a smaller vase for the handful of salvageable blooms. The water was gaggy nasty, but she worked quickly, and with the help of her kitchen shears, she soon finished. As she dumped the discarded roses and stems on top of the greasy paper towels in the trash, she smiled to herself thinking of the BLTs she planned for dinner. Facetiously she imagined presenting Will's sandwich to him with a side of curried vegetables. She could never do it for real. First, it would be a waste of good vegetables. Second, what if he didn't get that she was joking? But she enjoyed the thought of it.

She was washing out the stinky vase when her phone rang. It was Mac. Part of her hoped he needed her for something.

"Hey, Mari. Sorry to interrupt your day off, but it was quicker to call than text. It's about Ariel."

"Yes?" She shut the water off.

"Dan and I just got back. We found her house—red door, as you said—but no one was home. However, the next-door neighbor was out having a smoke, and he was very talkative. Apparently she hasn't been around for days. Ariel's mother has been looking for her. He says she's quite worried."

"*What?* Has she gone to the police?"

"I don't know. She wasn't there to ask. I guess her mother works nights somewhere."

"Mac! Oh, my goodness! Something's happened to Ariel! What if she's been murdered or something?"

"Murdered?" He laughed. "Rein it in, Marissa! Given the circumstances, it's more likely she left on her own."

"But where would she go?"

"That's the question, isn't it? I suspect she's tucked away somewhere with her secret boyfriend. I think her mother might be clueless as to what's going on."

Mari nodded to herself. "You might be right about that. Oh, Ariel! What are we going to do, Mac?"

"She's not a minor."

"I know, but it's *Ariel*. She could be in danger! We should go to the police!"

"I doubt that she's in danger, but it wouldn't hurt to let them know what we know, just in case—especially if Ariel's mother has gone to them too. I can't see there's much they could do, but at least they'd be looking for her."

"We'd have to go together so we can each tell our part."

"Right." He paused, as if thinking. "I could pick you up at one."

"One o'clock works for me."

"Okay. See you then."

As Mari set down her phone, she was aware of a movement behind her. She turned to see her mother eyeing her curiously from across the dining room table.

"You're going somewhere with Mac?"

"To the police. Ariel's gone missing."

Her mother blinked in confusion. "Ariel's *missing*? What's happened?"

"We don't know. Mac and Dan DeSoto went to her house this morning and talked to a neighbor who said she hasn't been around for days. We thought we'd report it."

"Is this related to you going over there the other night? I assume you've talked to her mother—?"

"Yes. And no, I haven't talked to her. But the neighbor said her mom was looking for her."

She frowned. "Don't you think you should talk to her mother first? Maybe she knows something you don't know."

More likely the other way around, Mari thought. "Uh, you're right. Do you have her number?"

"No, but Susan might."

"Okay, I'll text Mrs. Gordon for it."

"What's going on, Mari? Why your sudden interest in Ariel?"

Mari shifted uncomfortably. Everything in her wanted to spill all, but the way Ariel had begged her not to tell anyone—she just couldn't say anything. "Well, she was really sick the day I gave her a ride home from Riverview. I'm just checking up on her."

"Could she be in the hospital? Honestly, Mari, call her mother!"

The hospital! She hadn't thought of that. She would text that to Mac. "You're right! I'll call her mother. Are you waiting for me? I'm ready. I just need to finish wiping the countertops."

Chapter Eighteen

For the entire jaunt across New Hampton, Mari argued with herself about what she was doing. It wasn't so much going to a Bible study that was the problem. She was actually looking forward to the "study" part. Rather, it was knowing that JoyAnne would likely be in attendance that took things out of her comfort zone—far, far, *far* out of her comfort zone. So why, oh, why was she doing this? What on earth was she thinking?

The DeSotos, she answered herself simply as her car proceeded up Richmond Road. They were why. She liked Leah, and Dan was friends with Mac. But were they worth the risk of having to deal with JoyAnne? That was still in debate, but she had better decide, for she was almost there. *Just do it*, she commanded herself, passing Brother Warren's house and reaching the turn to the DeSotos'.

Mari saw Leah coming out of her house with the baby in her arms right as she pulled off the highway to creep up her driveway. She waved as Leah strained to see who was driving the unfamiliar car. Parking, Mari grabbed her handbag from the passenger's seat. Her stomach was in knots. Was she really doing this? But she was committed now. She was here. She got out of the car.

"Why, Mari!" Leah exclaimed. "Hello!"

"Hi. I'm, uh—here for the Bible study." There, she said it. The point of no return.

Leah's mouth dropped open. "Oh—I'm *so* sorry! We cancelled this morning because Kyla couldn't make it! I would have texted you, but I didn't know you were coming!"

"No, I—I only decided this morning."

"Oh, I'm so glad! We'll be on next week for sure, but I'm sorry you drove all the way over here!"

Inside, Mari was practically hyperventilating with relief. "No worries. It's totally fine!"

Leah smiled. "Hey, that was so fun hanging out with you yesterday! Aubrey's here—did you know that? She slept over. The kids are out back playing in my climbing tree. I was just going next door to visit Jackie. Why don't you come with me?"

"Oh, I wouldn't want to impose."

"No, no! It's just for a visit. She would love it! She loves this kind of thing! Please—come!" She beckoned, and compelled, Mari followed.

"How was your night?" Mari asked, glancing at the fair-haired baby contentedly sucking on his pacifier. His miniature athletic pants matched his smart zippered jacket.

Leah threw a look over the baby's head. "Oh, let's just say I've had better nights! He was definitely missing his mama! But that's all right. She'll be back tonight, and we'll *all* sleep again!"

When they knocked next door, Jackie's lap dog exploded into a yapping fit, making little Kenny jump. His face puckered as he wound up to produce a frightened wail.

"Aww, sorry, Kenny! Shhh—it's okay!" Leah murmured, pushing open the door.

"Angel! Angel, *shush*!" Jackie scolded, hurrying to meet them. "I'm *so* sorry!"

Leah repositioned the baby, cooing to comfort him as she attempted to replant his pacifier. "Jackie, you remember Mari—from the shower? We're just stopping over."

"Oh, of course! Yes! Come in, come in—we're thrilled to have you! Come join us in the kitchen! We are about to enjoy some fresh scones! *Angel!* My goodness, that's *enough*! You're scaring the poor baby!" She shook her head apologetically as the little dog slunk back. "So sorry, Kenny! Aww! Come now, ladies. I have coffee already made!"

As Jackie led, the little dog trotted alongside them through the tidy living room toward the sunny kitchen and source of the tantalizing aroma hanging in the air. Ahead Mari noticed two other ladies at the kitchen island.

"Ladies, we have guests!" Jackie announced as the women turned. "Mari, you know JoyAnne, don't you? Of course, you do—you were at the shower! And this is our friend Ariel—Ariel Marquette! She's been staying with us for a few days."

Mari halted, speechless.

"Hello," JoyAnne said politely. "Nice to see you again."

Ariel dropped her eyes, her cheeks rosy red against her jet-black hair. She had a different nose ring in today.

Jackie began pulling down mugs from the cupboard, asking if Mari took her coffee black or with creamer. "Or plain milk, if you prefer," she said. "I have that too!"

Mari swallowed, still looking at Ariel. "Are you all right? I've—been looking for you!"

JoyAnne shifted protectively. "She's all right."

"Oh, are you two friends?" Leah asked, swaying the baby.

Mari couldn't even answer.

At the long silence, Jackie turned. "Is there a problem, girls?"

Mari made a sound. "I've been texting and calling you, and you've never answered! And you've been staying *here*?"

Leah gently touched Mari's arm. "What's going on, Mari? Are you two in a disagreement?"

Mari shot her a look. "No, I've been trying to *help* her!" She frowned at Ariel, who was now tearing up. "Are you okay? Why wouldn't you answer my texts?"

JoyAnne slid closer, patting Ariel's leg. "It's all right, hon." She looked up at Mari. "Ladies, Ariel's had some recent difficulties. She reached out to Susan, my future mother-in-law, who brought her here for a while."

"To *Susan*? She reached out to Susan?"

"Yes. She knows Ariel. She's been bringing her to church with her for years."

Mari's mouth opened. "I—I didn't know that."

"Yes. Anyway, it was necessary for Ariel to go somewhere safe for a while, so we brought her here."

Leah's face crinkled into a frown. "Somewhere *safe*? I thought she was just staying here as a friend!"

Jackie set the mugs down. "She's getting help through the Sunlight Center. JoyAnne's been over every day spending time with her, walking alongside her." She smiled at Ariel. "You're going to make it, darling."

JoyAnne squeezed Ariel's leg again.

Ariel raised her eyes to Mari, mumbling breathily, "I don't have my phone anymore."

"Yeah, she left it behind," JoyAnne blurted. "The poor girl ran to Susan's in the night!"

Leah gasped. "You did *what*?"

"What happened?" Mari asked. In her mind flashed the defiant tattooed thug, pounding his fist on her window. "Ariel, did someone hurt you?"

JoyAnne immediately looked guilty, as though she realized she had said too much. "I'm sorry. We need to honor Ariel's privacy. It's best for her not to say."

"Oh, brother," Leah moaned. "I'm sorry for coming over! I didn't know! I thought we'd just have coffee together. I had no idea all this stuff was going on!"

"No, hon, of course, you didn't!" Jackie exclaimed. "But it's okay. We're all adults. We'll just make the necessary adjustments. You two know, of course, that you can't let anyone know that Ariel is here."

"Absolutely!" Leah said.

Mari nodded, glancing at JoyAnne. "Okay. All I want to know is— Ariel, did you find out—I mean, are you—do you know if you're—" She raised her brow in question.

Ariel's eyes flicked from Mari to the floor. "I'm pregnant—yes."

Everything in Mari wanted to ask about the father. Was he the buff young man on Ariel's front step downing those beers? But she remained silent.

"You made the right choice to get help, sweetie," Jackie affirmed. "We're going to help you *and* your baby."

Mari let out a long breath. "Yes, Jackie's right. You made the right choice. And I'm glad you're here. But I didn't know, so I've been trying to contact you. In fact, Mac Sinclair and Dan, Leah's husband, drove over to your house looking for you this morning."

Leah turned in surprise. "*My* Dan?"

"Mac said a neighbor told him your mom is quite concerned. She's been looking for you."

"My mom can't know," Ariel said hastily. "She wouldn't like this. She'd make me get rid of it."

"But shouldn't she at least know where you are?"

Ariel's eyes darted to JoyAnne, who cleared her throat and said, "Okay, thanks for letting us know. Was there anything else?"

"No. Except that if you two need to go to the authorities, you should."

"We've already taken that step," JoyAnne stated crisply. "It's our protocol. The authorities are actively involved."

"Oh."

The room fell silent. Ariel sniffed, raising her tattooed arm to fiddle with her hair.

"I suppose Danny had no way of knowing," Leah mused quietly. "I never told him you were here. I thought you were just staying here as a friend."

"She *is* my friend," Jackie said warmly.

Mari glanced toward the door. "Well, I should probably go then."

Leah swung her head. "Why?"

"No, hon!" Jackie exclaimed. "No, we've covered all the awkward stuff, and now it's time to sit. Ariel is going to need some support!"

Mari's eyes flicked to JoyAnne, who waved a capitulating hand. "She's right, I guess. Welcome to Team Ariel! Pull up a chair."

"And I'll get your coffees," Jackie said sweetly.

Unbelievable, Mari thought as she and Leah slid onto their seats at the island. Making room, JoyAnne quickly slid aside a few booklets that Mari recognized as Sunlight Center resources. And a Bible. Mari closed her eyes. How could this be happening?

She turned to JoyAnne. "Um, I might have been a little rude when we arrived. I was so shocked to see Ariel—I couldn't even think." Her dad would score her a *D minus* for the apology, she knew, but it was all she could currently manage.

JoyAnne nodded. "I understand. However, I *would* like—"

"Here you go, hon!" Jackie said, handing Mari a hot mug of coffee. "Creamer?"

"Thanks. No, black is fine," she replied.

JoyAnne started again, "As I was saying, I *would* like to get together with you sometime. If it works out with your schedule. I know you're very busy."

Mari kept her expression pleasant. "Oh, um—sure. Maybe this week. I'll, um—I'll get back to you." Shoot. It didn't look as though she was going to get out of it.

Right as Jackie lowered the plate of fancy scones onto the island, the patio door rumbled open, and in burst two chattering Grant brothers with Aubrey in tow. Recognizing them, baby Kenny squealed and flapped his arms, making everyone laugh.

When Aubrey saw Mari, she rushed to her side. "Mari! I didn't know you were here! Guess what? I got to sleep over with Howie and Hank last night! I helped Miss Leah with the baby!"

"She helped a lot!" Leah proclaimed with a wink.

"Can I have one of those?" Hank asked, eyeing the scones.

"Me too!" Howie chimed eagerly.

"Here," Jackie said. "I'll make you kids your own plate for the deck!"

Leah glanced at the clock. "Help me out, ladies. I've got to keep track of the time. I want to be sure to take Aubrey home before Kenny's nap."

"I could take her," Mari offered. "I'm meeting Mac at one—" She stopped, realizing their appointment was no longer necessary.

"Really? Thank you!" Leah smiled gratefully, then turned to Ariel. "So how are you feeling, Ariel? Have you been sick at all?"

It was almost dinnertime when Will showed up—all freshly showered and in new jeans and a nice shirt. Thankfully, Mari had just finished her ring-sizing finagling in her bedroom and had slipped it firmly onto her finger when he knocked, although she decided not to bring attention to it.

"You've cleaned up nicely!" she told him. "And you smell good too!"

He sniffed his shoulder. "I broke out the soap-on-a-rope my grandparents gave me for Christmas! But I'm surprised you could smell anything over the bacon haze in here! Sheesh! Let me guess—BLTs tonight?"

"Yes—"

"I told you I only eat *turkey* bacon, right?"

Mari drew back in surprise.

He bumped her arm. "I'm kidding! Dang, you're gullible!"

"Hello, Will!" Mari's mother called from the other end of the house.

"Hello, Mrs. Coleman," he replied. He threw Mari a look and motioned her to walk ahead of him.

Maybe it was because of their new boundary, or perhaps because he had noticed her finally wearing his ring—whatever it was, Will was on his best behavior. He offered to help Mari finish their dinner prep, and he was especially attentive to her mother, telling her all about his parents' move across town.

"Of course, they weren't ready," he said, his tone indicating his annoyance with that. "Mom was still packing boxes. But my dad and I *did* get some of the bigger stuff moved."

Then Mari's mother asked about his work, and he was more than eager to describe his dramatic problem-solving exploits at his company, the topic taking most of their mealtime. Mari didn't mind. She had had a good cry and a nap after getting home from Jackie Burke's, but she was still subdued, not feeling too talkative. Ariel had gone to Mrs. Gordon for help. Something about that stung, but she didn't know why. She toyed with her sandwich, mentally reviewing JoyAnne's protectiveness over the shy girl.

After dinner, Will had his heart set on a particular new release he wanted to see, and Mari went along with his choice since she wasn't really in a movie mood anyway.

"All right, what's going on? Are you mad at me again?" he asked as they waited in their seats for the show to start. He positioned the extra-large popcorn between them.

"Why would I be mad at you?" she asked, declining the snack.

"You're quiet. I've been trying super-hard to be nice."

"You're doing good, Will," she said. "I'm just overtired." He *was* really trying, she observed.

Later when he drove her home, he asked again, "Are you sure you're okay?"

"I'm all right. Just dealing with some stuff. It's not you."

His chin rose. "Ah, I get it. Girl stuff." He made a face.

She let it pass. "Will I see you in church tomorrow?"

"Yeah, sure. I'll pick you up. Then let's do lunch after again. I promise not to beg for Chinese."

She smiled. "Sounds good. I'll be ready."

Will arrived ten minutes early the next morning, right as she was starting her makeup.

"Take your time," he told her. "I'll wait in the living room."

But in her rush to get ready she was so distracted that she left the condominium without her jewelry. Then, fingering her naked earlobes, she also discovered she had forgotten Will's ring.

She groaned, facing him in dismay. "Shoot! Your ring's on my dresser with my earrings!" They were already halfway to the church.

"Maribelle!" He bounced his hands on the steering wheel. "You and that ring! I still have my sharpie marker—do I need to draw one on your finger?" He threw her a playful smile. "I'm kidding, of course! I trust you."

"Thanks. Oh, man, I feel like I'm not completely dressed! Those earrings matched my outfit."

He snatched the marker and held it out.

Dan and Leah DeSoto met them in the church foyer, clad with greeter lanyards.

Leah gave Mari a friendly hug. "Good morning! Nice to see you again—for the third day in a row!"

Mari smiled. "Yes! Have you met my boyfriend? Will, Leah and Dan DeSoto. They were at Mac's Friday night. And Dan and Leah, this is Will. William Wallace."

Dan nodded as Will shook his hand. "Hello."

Mari turned to Leah. "I see you're baby-less. Looks like you survived the weekend."

Leah spread her arms. "More like *he* survived! He was so glad to see his mama!"

They both laughed.

"But I *do* miss him. He's sure a sweetie!" She glanced at her husband, who met her eyes and smiled. "Anyway, glad you're here. Go on in. We'll talk later." She waved them toward the seats and turned to greet another family entering the church.

"He was *clueless* about my name," Will remarked as they moved along. "And what was that about Friday night?"

"They were watching the Watkins' baby and Professor Grant's boys on Friday. They came over to Mac's for dinner."

He frowned. "Why were *you* there? You had a big hangout with people I don't know, and you never told me—?"

"We overlapped. They came before Mac was home, and then when he got there, I left—to be with *you*—remember? I got to your apartment early." It was a barebones explanation, but it seemed sufficient.

"Okay," he said, giving a confused shrug. "It'd be nice to know some things."

Aubrey appeared at her side the moment they found a spot. "Can I sit with you? *Please*?"

Mari located Mac two rows behind them, sitting with the Gordons— Mr. Gordon, Susan, JoyAnne, and Douglas. He nodded hello, and when she pointed questioningly to his daughter, he shrugged, as if to say, "Sure, why not?"

"Okay," she whispered to Aubrey, "but we're not going to talk."

The girl slid up tightly against her.

On the other side of her, Will let out an impatient breath. "*One* day. Can't you have just *one* day off?"

"It's fine," Mari whispered.

Aubrey clutched her hand, and Mari smiled down, suddenly noticing the girl's hair was braided on only one side of her head. The unbraided side sported a plain ponytail. Oh, Mac! Really?

"Fancy hairstyle there, girl," she said quietly.

248

Aubrey's face fell, as if suddenly remembering it. "My dad said we didn't have time to finish."

Mari checked the time, then surveyed the gathering crowd preparing for worship. They had three minutes. She nudged Aubrey. "Come on."

Turning to Will, she added, "Be right back."

"Wait—where are you going?" he asked.

"I'm taking Aubrey to the ladies' room."

The two of them slipped back into their places during the middle of the first song. Aubrey, of course, sought her father's attention by dramatically flipping her braids and looking back multiple times. When Mari peeked back at him, Mac flashed her a covert thumbs-up.

As with the previous week, Will was ready to leave directly after the service. However, Leah's husband snagged him in the lobby, introducing him to Peter Watkins. As the three of them visited, Mari excused herself to use the restroom. She was coming out when she ran into Mac—or he ran into her, for he paused on his way down the hallway.

"I've been looking for you," he said. He shot a brief glance up and down the hallway, adding, "Susan called me last night. About Ariel."

"Yeah." Mari nodded. "Sorry. You were busy yesterday when I brought Aubrey home. Plus I was asked not to say anything, and I didn't know if that meant to you too or what. Anyway—"

"Anyway—" he said at the same time, and he smiled. "Anyway, I wanted to tell you that I know. How are you doing with it all? I know it must have been a surprise with—you know—everything. And JoyAnne."

"It was."

"Yeah, unexpected."

"I'll be okay. But thanks for asking. And I'm glad she's getting help."

He nodded. "Good. And your knee?"

"The same. Sensitive, but improving, I think. I hope. Thanks."

"Good." He held up a finger. "Hey, good move on the banana bread. Roger Eden came by yesterday morning to say thank you."

"Did he? That's great! Good thing Aubrey wasn't there!"

"Yes, good thing. Especially since he invited himself in! We were talking at the door, and he noticed our houses were identical inside—mostly, you know. Anyway, he walked right in, so I gave him a tour, mess and all!"

"Cool."

"Yeah." They stood quietly for a moment. "Well, I was on my way to pick up Aubrey—"

Then, as if she was cued, Aubrey cried his name from the end of the hall. They turned to see her break into a run, leaving Leah DeSoto behind.

"You forgot me at class, Dad!"

Mac received his daughter's hug. "Sorry, little flower. I got talking to Miss Mari." He turned to Leah. "Sorry to keep you waiting."

"Nope," she said cheerfully, walking up. "She's my last kid, so I decided to deliver. How's everyone?"

"Good!" Mac said. "How was class?"

"Great!" Leah answered. "Did you think so, Aubrey?"

Aubrey had sidled up to Mari, taking her fingers. "It was *so* fun! We walked on water like Jesus—for real!"

Mari squeezed her hand. "That's great! Well, I should get back to Will." She nodded in the other direction.

"Let's walk up together!" Leah suggested. "So what's everyone doing today? Any big plans for the afternoon? Dan and I are going to Wynnbury for lunch."

"Wynnbury?"

"Oh—Peter and Kyla's. Sorry. We want to hear how it's going with her father. He's dying—did you hear? It's so sad."

"Who's dying?" Aubrey wanted to know.

"Miss Kyla's birth father is sick," Mac said. "And no big plans for us. Maybe a park or something."

"Can Mari come with us?" Aubrey asked excitedly. "Please?"

"Mari's probably got her own plans," Mac said as they re-entered the foyer. "She'll be over tomorrow after school."

"I'm hanging out with my boyfriend today," Mari told her, gesturing to Will, who was approaching. "But I'll see you tomorrow for sure."

The girl groaned. "Why can't you come *today*?"

Will joined them, frowning at Mari. "Where were you? I've been looking all over for you!" He gave Mac and Leah a courteous nod.

"We were just talking about you," Mari said. "I was telling them we're hanging out this afternoon."

Will glanced at the others a little confused. "Okay—?"

"Just chatting about plans for the day," Mari clarified.

"I should check in with Danny," Leah said. "Nice to meet you, Will! And have a great week, Mari. Maybe I'll stop by after my visit with Susan this week."

"Yes, I'd like that," Mari replied.

"I should keep moving too," Mac said. "I need to connect with a few people before we leave. 'Til tomorrow, Marissa. Will." He nodded, then poked Aubrey in the belly. "Stick around, squirt." He strode off toward a pair of men visiting beside the coffee bar.

"See you tomorrow," Mari said after him, but Aubrey remained fixed at her side.

Will's eyes flicked from the girl to Mari. He spread his hands. "What the heck? She's a barnacle!"

Mari shook her head. "It's fine, Will. Did you enjoy your visit with Dan?"

He shrugged. "I guess. He's an okay guy. And the tall fellow—"

"Peter Watkins."

"Yeah—did you know he was in that Watkins Nursery ordeal some years back? Remember that? *He* was the guy who assaulted that nursery employee! That's him! And now he leads the men's Bible study Wednesday nights!" He shook his head in disbelief.

"Really? Well, I'm ready to go. Are you?"

"Yes."

But right then Susan Gordon happened by, pausing beside Mari. "So this must be the boyfriend I've been hearing about!"

"Yes! This is Will—William Wallace," she answered. "And Will, this is my former neighbor, Susan Gordon. The Sinclair family lived on one side of us and the Gordons on the other."

He shook her hand. "Hello."

"Pleased to meet you, William Wallace," she said. "I pray you live up to your namesake—bringing many to freedom!" She smiled.

His head drew back. "What? Oh—right!" He laughed. "Excuse me. I'll let you two visit while I use the restroom." He motioned down the hall and walked away.

"Seems like a nice fellow," Mrs. Gordon mused, her eyes following him.

That stinker! Slinking away from Mrs. G! Embarrassed, Mari smiled. "He is. We met at the church Christmas party."

"Nice!" She turned back to her. "So how's it going since you've been back from school? Are you adjusting?"

"Yes. I'm finally coming to terms with the disappointment. This knee thing threw me for a loop, but if it's healed, I can repeat the semester next fall. That's what I'm hoping anyway. So meanwhile I'm helping out with Poppy and working Shannon's old job at the Coffee Break. Plus helping Mac." She smiled down at Aubrey, swinging their hands. "This has been a great distraction!"

"Yes, you're really good with her." Mrs. Gordon also smiled at the girl. "You know, sweetheart, I think Howie and Hank were hoping to play with you today! They're here. Have you seen them?"

Aubrey immediately looked around. "Where are they?"

"I think they're in the Fellowship Hall with Miss Kyla and baby Kenny."

The girl turned an eager face to Mari. "Can I go?"

"Ask your dad," she said, pointing across the lobby. "He's right there!"

As she left, Mari looked questioningly at Mrs. Gordon. Had she deliberately sent Aubrey off?

"You care about that girl, don't you?"

Mari let out a breath. "I—yes. I'm surprised at how much I do! I can't explain it—it's like our hearts have bonded. I want to help them—Mac and her. My heart goes out to them."

Mrs. Gordon raised her chin in a nod.

Mari waited. Something was coming.

"Honey, have you ever gone through Pastor Keith's Soul Wash group?"

"Never heard of it."

"Ah." Mrs. Gordon said. "It's a class he runs once a year. I've led it a few times. We talk about lots of things—forgiveness, breaking bondage— you know, those kinds of things. Anyway, one of the topics is soul ties. Have you ever had any teaching on that? I have it on my heart to warn you about soul ties, dear."

Mari felt her face turn red. Here she had thought they would be talking about Aubrey. "Yes, I remember you teaching about that before, and, well, we've struggled some physically, but we're not doing that anymore. I set my boundaries, and Will seems okay with that. I told him it was that or we had to break up."

She nodded slowly. "Oh. All right, that's good. Now let's talk about the Sinclairs."

"With *Mac*? There's no need to talk about that—I assure you!" She glanced at him across the foyer.

"With Aubrey."

"Aubrey?"

"Mari, be careful with her heart! I can see the mutual bond between you two."

"What's wrong with that? I love her!"

"I know you do, hon! But have you ever considered that she's starting to view you like a mother—a wannabe mother? She's attached herself to you."

Mari stared.

"You have a boyfriend. You're planning to go back to Boston in the fall. You're going to leave her high and dry. If this continues, she's going to get her heart all wrapped up in a soul tie and be devastated. Think of where she's coming from. She already struggles with abandonment issues from her own mother. She doesn't need it reinforced from someone else who doesn't understand emotional boundaries."

Mari's stomach twisted. "I'm—only babysitting her," she sputtered. "Don't girls *need* love? I'm not trying to hurt her!"

Mrs. Gordon nodded gently. "I know, sweetheart. Of course, you wouldn't want to hurt her! That's why I'm saying something right away—to protect you both! You can't play 'mom' and not experience some emotional repercussions. Life isn't a Hallmark movie, my dear. You've got to keep yourself in reality."

Mari couldn't speak.

"Mari, it's not wrong to love Aubrey, but you need to be up front with her. You need to define your role in an honest way—that you're her *caregiver*. Tell her your plans to go away for school—and often—so she'll be equipped to deal with it. *And* your plans with Will."

"I thought I *was* being honest with her."

"And perhaps you have been," Mrs. Gordon added. "I may be wrong. It's only an outside observation. I care about both of you. There's wisdom in God's boundaries, hon. You can't just go making emotional promises to people that you can't follow through on. You're not her mother. Don't pretend to be."

"I—I wasn't trying to be her mother." Her throat felt like cotton.

"I'm sure it wasn't intentional." The woman gave Mari a quick hug. "Aww, it's okay, hon. We all need to grow. I know it stings to hear this, but it's truly the best for you both."

Numbly, Mari bobbed her head again.

Then across the room someone hailed Mrs. Gordon. She waved and turned back to Mari. "Listen—you asked to get together sometime. I'm not sure when I'd be free for that, but if it's all right, I think I'll just walk over to see you at Mac's whenever it works out. Would that be okay? To just play it by ear?"

What could she say? She nodded as the woman hugged her again and then left to visit with her beckoning friend.

Someone who doesn't understand emotional boundaries.

Will came sauntering down the hall. "Okay, now I'm ready. Let's get out of—" He frowned. "What's wrong with you? Are you *crying*?"

"I'm okay," she said, brushing her cheeks.

"You're *not* okay! What happened?"

What could she tell him? Given the subject, he would only be thrilled that Mrs. Gordon had talked to her. She shook her head, trying to pull herself together. "You know, Will, sometimes you just like people a lot and you can't help it. Do you know what I mean?"

"Yeah. Sort of. I think." His brow rose questioningly.

"I've just had one of those moments."

"Okay." He looked around. "Seriously, what happened? Is this about—wait—is this related to your womanly stuff?"

"Maybe," Mari replied simply. Enduring the annoying comment was easier than explaining. "We should go."

"Then let's scram, Marzipan!"

The two of them settled for a low-key afternoon hanging out at the condominium playing competitive board games with Shannon, Colton, and her mom. For hours Mari kept up her smiling façade, enjoying appetizers and sipping her ginger ale with the crew. Outside, however, the drizzly weather supplied a more appropriate backdrop for Mari's gloomy mood. But she couldn't talk about anything.

Afterward, they moved to the living room, where Will and Colton switched to video games while she and Shannon stared into their laptops, by preference. Shannon was wedding shopping, but Mari simply poked around online trying to distract herself from Mrs. Gordon's stinging words still swirling in her head. The woman had clearly indicated that Mari didn't understand emotional boundaries, which made her feel like a clueless fifteen-year-old. She had thought things with Aubrey were great. Hadn't people praised her for doing a good job with her? Did others share Mrs. G's opinion? Did Leah and Dan? Or *Mac*? She was mortified at the thought!

On a whim, she typed "healthy emotional boundaries" into her search bar, cocking her laptop away from Will, lest he see it and think it was about him. Things were already fragile enough. She scrolled through various articles until Will and Colton took a break, then quickly closed out her browser.

Later, when Colton and Shannon decided to run out to a sports equipment store, Will suggested that he and Mari tag along. "I want to get you some mace or pepper spray for those dogs," he said.

"Really?" Shannon responded. "Are they aggressive?"

Will flayed his hands. "Duh! Anyone who names their Rottweilers Loki and Thor is only begging for a confrontation!"

"Sounds like a Marvel comics fan to me," Colton observed.

"Right. I know that, but two Rottweilers—? I mean—come on!"

"He controls his dogs," Mari said in Mac's neighbor's defense. "But it's actually not a bad idea. It might give Aubrey some peace of mind to have something like that around. Plus then Mac wouldn't—" She stopped herself in the nick of time, having almost shared that Mac wouldn't be tempted to get out his handgun again. "Uh, then Mac would have it available to use too," she finished. Yikes—how would Will have responded to that?

"Do they even sell pepper spray at sports shops?" Shannon asked.

"Maybe. But let's just order online," Mari told Will. "It's still raining, and I'd rather stay home."

"Suit yourself," Shannon said as the two left.

Then while Will was back to gaming, Mari did an online search on Roger Eden. "Pest exterminator," it came up, with his address on Frost. Her eyes lingered on her old address as she thought about the middle-aged fellow living there with no family and two dogs. Two intimidating dogs. Was that normal? It felt so strange. She closed her laptop.

"I think I need to lie down, Will."

He turned in surprise. "Are you sick?"

"Just super tired."

He gave a knowing nod. "Oh, I get it. Okay, I'll go."

After creating a few tentative plans for the week, Will left, and Mari retreated to her room where she sat propped on her bed staring into nothing. Had Mrs. Gordon been referring to anything in particular? She frowned, reviewing the Friday rainstorm adventure at Mac's, mentally sifting through each scene and interaction. Yet all she could think about was how much she cared for Aubrey, even with all the girl's childish immaturities. She shook her head. What a crazy weekend! First everything with Ariel and JoyAnne, then a scolding from Mrs. Gordon. At least she and Will hadn't broken up, and for that she was grateful. She yawned, rolling onto her side, wishing it were bedtime.

Chapter Nineteen

First on Mari's agenda at work Monday morning was to check Tatum's timecard. Tatum *West.* Sure enough, Tatum was Ty's mother. Trey's too, apparently. Mari wondered how their brief encounter at Frost Park over the weekend would affect their work relationship. Perhaps it would build a bridge to the angry woman. She hoped so. It would be nice to talk about Ty. On the other hand, the event might only provide more ammunition for Tatum to fire her way.

She didn't have to wait too long to find out, for while she and Boris were back in the kitchen perfecting their slick sandwich-making operation, Tatum came back and sent Boris up front. Now apprehensive, Mari kept her nose down, working in the frosty silence for a few minutes as she waited for Tatum to initiate. Yikes—that woman could teach a master class on the art of intimidation.

Finally, Tatum spoke. "How old is your baby?" Civil question, gruff tone.

Mari's eyes flicked up in confusion. "Baby Kenny? Oh, he's a friend's baby. And six months—maybe seven. I grew up on Frost and go there after school to watch a former neighbor's daughter—Aubrey Sinclair. She's eight and might be in Ty's class in school. I think. She knows him anyway." She kept her response nonchalant, lest she be perceived a threat for knowing everything.

When Tatum didn't reply, she added, "I got Aubrey playing kickball after school, and it's turned into a neighborhood thing. Ty is welcome to play. It's just a casual game with kids of all ages."

Her chin rose in acknowledgement, and they again worked in silence. When they finished, Mari offered to stay and put the food away.

Tatum lifted the tub of sandwiches and paused. "Can we get one thing straight?"

Mari met her eyes.

"You stick to your kid games and keep out of Ty and my's business. And I'll stay out of yours."

"It's just kickball, Tatum. I *like* Ty. He's a good kid." Frankly, Ty was a *rascal*, but stretching the truth seemed appropriate at this moment. Then, assuming Tatum's statement indicated he was allowed to play, she added, "You're welcome to come watch if you want. I'll give you my phone number too, in case you ever need me to send him home early or anything."

Uttering something unintelligible, the woman nodded and disappeared around the corner.

Mari's shoulders dropped in adrenalized relief. Restacking the sandwich fixings in the refrigerator, she wondered what business Tatum wanted her to stay out of. How could she possibly be a threat to Tatum? Unless it referred to whatever shady activity the manager had corrected her for that day Mari had walked in on them. Maybe it was a warning not to probe in that direction. At any rate, Ty could play kickball. She had gained a victory there. Now she would work on winning his trust. Scrounging the counter for a pen, she jotted her phone number onto a napkin and propped it on Tatum's jacket.

Dr. Grant was engrossed in study when Mari made her regular rounds bussing the dining room.

"Good morning, Dr. Grant," she said, pausing beside his table.

The professor straightened, pulling off his reading glasses. "Miss Coleman, how are you on this fine day? My boys tell me they had the 'funnest day of their lives' at your house last Friday!"

Mari broke into a smile. "It *was* pretty fun! Did they tell you we got soaked? Although it wasn't at *my* house. It was at Mac Sinclair's, who lives two doors down from Susan Gordon, who I heard cleans for you. I watch his daughter. I'm learning we have a lot of the same friends—the Gordons, the DeSotos, Brother Warren, Jackie Burke—"

"Yes—isn't that amazing!"

"It is! I grew up next door to the Gordons. Mac lived on the other side of me."

"I see! He's the physical therapist, correct? And the Watkinses—Peter and Kyla. Mutual friends as well."

"Acquaintances, yes," Mari clarified. "Although I've become a solid baby Kenny fan. Leah had him over the weekend."

"My boys adore him!"

She sighed, skipping right to her point. "Dr. Grant, Shannon isn't available afternoons when you and I were going to try to talk. It's her busiest time of day. You wouldn't by chance make an exception for me, would you? We could talk out in the open like this right here, like we usually do. I wouldn't mind. I could really use someone to talk with. And for more than five minutes." She flashed a winsome smile. Sometimes a little extra charm worked with her dad. It was worth a try for Dr. Grant.

He shifted in his chair. "I'm honored that you'd ask, Mari, but I'm not taking exceptions. Talking like this is one thing, but sitting down at a table together to *talk* is quite another. I want to protect my marriage and my name. But find a partner to join us, and I'll make time for you."

"I was hoping for *today*. I did my homework and everything!"

"Good for you! Well, I'm good for an hour after lunch if you find someone. Otherwise, maybe Shannon would take a longer lunch for you this week."

"Yeah. Maybe." She held up her dishcloth. "Well, I have to keep moving. I'm sure I'll be by again later."

"It's always a pleasure, Miss Coleman."

Disappointed, Mari finished loading the bin with dirty dishes and lugged it to the kitchen to load the dishwasher. Who else could she ask? Definitely not JoyAnne or Kyla. But perhaps Leah. The more she thought about it, the more attractive the idea became. Maybe Leah would be impartial. Then again, Leah knew so many of the people she wanted to talk about. Plus she worked days, so she would have to arrange a special time with Dr. Grant for that to work—and if she was going to do that, she might as well work things out with Shannon anyway, and who knew when that would be? She gave a defeated sigh. Maybe she should just talk to Mac. He was easy to talk to. And maybe he would be honest about her relationship with Aubrey.

When the 9:52 rush hit, Mari moved up behind the counter to help process orders. To her surprise, Candace switched places with another coworker to work alongside her.

"How was your weekend?" she asked over the whirring of the steamer. When it stopped, she poured the hot milk over the coffee she was preparing.

"Not that great, to be perfectly honest," Mari answered.

"What—did you break up with your boyfriend or something?"

Mari chuckled, spritzing whipped cream onto her blended coffee creation. "Funny you should say that! That's the one thing that *didn't* happen! But it was close."

"Then what happened?"

Mari popped a dome lid onto the finished cup and snatched a straw. "Let's suffice to say that I felt misunderstood every time I turned around." She set the cup on the opposite counter and started her next order.

"Well, my partner and I are in a good place for once. We get each other."

"Nice. Enjoy it." Mari frowned at the code written on the next cup. "Can you decipher this?"

Candace rolled her eyes. "Mark's handwriting is the *worst*. I think that's a *C* for caramel."

"Okay, I'm going with that. And I'm glad things are good with you and yours."

"Yeah. We had a great weekend."

Then, as they clipped through the orders, the next two hours rushed by, and Mari's shift was over. Grabbing her bag, she went to change her clothes in the restroom, revisiting again her disappointment that it hadn't worked out with Dr. Grant, for she had selected her Bourdette hoodie especially for the occasion. Perhaps this afternoon she would talk to Mac. Or her mom. There was *that* option too. Or maybe just no one.

Candace was in the parking lot leaning against her car having a smoke.

"See you tomorrow," Mari said unlocking her dad's vehicle.

"See you tomorrow," she echoed.

As she prepared to back out, Mari caught Candace's fuchsia hair in her rear-view mirror. She paused with her foot on the brake, eyeing her. After a moment's hesitation, she put the car in park and opened her door to lean out.

"Candace! Are you on break or are you getting off right now?"

"I'm done for the day." She finished the cigarette, dropping it to twist it underfoot.

Mari's mind was racing. "What are you doing right now?" Her idea was a huge risk.

Candace straightened, pushing off her car. "Why? Wanna go somewhere?"

"Well, I'd like to do something, but I need another person to do it with. Can I hire you for one hour? I'll pay you, um"—she pulled the loose cash from her jeans pocket—"twenty-three dollars if you will give me an hour of your time."

She laughed. "To do what?"

"To do nothing but sit in on a conversation and remain quiet. Seriously! I want to ask Dr. Grant some personal questions, and he won't meet with me unless there's a third party present. You don't have to say anything. In fact, I'd prefer you didn't. I simply need you to sit there while I talk to him. I'd even buy you lunch."

Candace surveyed her with a puckered brow. "That's bizarre! Why would he require that?"

Mari shrugged. "It's an integrity thing. He wants to live above reproach."

"Strange."

"All you'd have to do is sit there. You don't even have to listen, really."

"Yeah, but it's *him*."

"Just one hour. Aren't you curious? Wouldn't you want to hear what we talk about?"

Candace eyed her warily. "I don't know. Is this some kind of setup? This is crazy weird!"

"No. And if you're willing, let me know, 'cause he only has an hour, and I'd like to get in there."

She stared. "And I don't have to do anything?"

Mari shook her head. "Nope. All I ask is that you keep my private stuff private."

"Can I leave if it goes longer than an hour?"

"Yes."

She shrugged. "Oh, what the heck—I'll do it."

Mari handed Candace the cash on their way back into the coffee shop.

"This is totally crazy," Candace murmured, shoving it into her pocket.

The professor looked both surprised and pleased when Mari showed up beside his table with Candace.

"Do you still have an hour to talk?" she asked.

"You are one determined lass, aren't you?" He nodded cordially to Candace. "Hello. All right, where would you like to meet?"

"Right here is fine," Mari said, pulling out the chair across from him.

Candace shot an intimidated glance toward the front counter. "Heck no, not *here*! I'm the impartial third party, but if it's all the same, I'd prefer not to have people gawking at me."

"Fine—go find us a spot," Dr. Grant told her as he packed up his laptop.

"Yes, that's fine with me," Mari agreed, following the girl to the lounge side of the shop.

When the three of them were settled on armchairs in a cozy corner, Mari started in. "First, thank you for your time. I've been thinking a lot about some stuff, and I need to talk it through."

Dr. Grant nodded. "What's on your heart, young lady?"

Mari noticed his eyes dropped to her Bourdette sweatshirt, but it didn't seem the time to talk about it. She let out a long sigh. "Well, I had sort of a crappy weekend. For the last week I've been looking for this friend of mine—a neighbor, sort of—" She met his eyes. "I'm sorry. First, I need to ask you a question: can you keep a confidence? And if this involves people you know, are you able to listen impartially?"

"Yes, on both accounts. Unless it involves your or someone else's safety. You'll have to trust my discretion on that."

"Okay. Because it involves JoyAnne Strang and Susan Gordon." She ignored his raised brow to plunge on. "Anyway, I've been looking for this friend of mine who I thought was in trouble. Then on Saturday I showed up at Leah DeSoto's for a Bible study not knowing it was cancelled, so we went next door to her neighbor's instead—Jackie's—just for a visit. And who was there, but the friend I'd been looking for! She was staying there! I was right—she *was* in trouble, and she'd gone to Susan, who connected her to JoyAnne, who brought her to stay with Jackie. All of it was the right thing to do. She needs what Sunlight has to offer. But I'm having a tough time with it.

"I guess what bothers me is that I thought *I* was the one who could really help this girl. I was on a mission, and it was because I *cared* about her. I thought about her in the night even! So it was a blow that she went to someone else. It made me feel so unimportant, so what-the-heck-am-I-thinking that I could help someone? I don't know." She paused. "And JoyAnne—honestly, she was doing good with her. Great, actually, and that's part of the problem too."

"Why is that part of the problem?"

"'Cause I don't *want* her to do great! Look—can I be really honest here?"

"I hope you will!"

"I struggle with her."

"I think you've made that clear."

"No, it's—it's more than the childhood nemesis stuff. I don't know why, but I can't get past it. I was floored to hear she was marrying Dougie Gordon. She was such a—such a—" She bit her lip, not allowing herself to speak what she wanted to say. "Anyway, since I've been back, I can see that she's changed. She's apparently saved now, attending Bible studies, counseling with Susan and Kyla, and everything but—" She shook her head. "I don't know."

He pressed his fingertips together, waiting.

"It's like everything in me is mad at her. I'm *not* happy she's saved. I *don't want* her to be saved! I *don't want* her to do good at her job. I want her to fail. I want her to struggle. I want her to still be the slut that I'm mad at." She scrunched her face, ashamed of herself. "I know that sounds awful, but it's true.

"Remember when we talked about that prodigal son stuff? Well, I didn't see it at first, but I am *definitely* like the older brother in the story. JoyAnne's life was messed up, and you'd think I should be happy she's gotten straightened out, but I'm bugged! I'm mad at her, and I'm mad at God! I know it's wrong, and I don't want to be like this—but I don't want to change either. All I want is for her to go away!"

He nodded thoughtfully. "When did this start with her? Have you two ever talked?"

Mari threw her head back. "Oh, please. Yes, we've talked! And when it started? JoyAnne has had it out for me for as long as I've known her!"

"Had it out for *you*—?"

"Yes! We have an ugly history that I'd rather not go into. And *yes*, we've talked. My parents made us sit down to try and work things out in high school. It was the worst night of my life! She was a master manipulator, and my dad totally sympathized with her. For some reason the fact that she was being raised by her grandmother nullified any of the crap she was pulling on me. But we talked and talked and talked some more—and in the end it was still all *my* fault. It was a nightmare!"

"Your dad didn't defend you?"

She jerked her shoulder. "He listened and *said* he understood, but he told me he was 'calling me up to a better way.' He wanted *me* to apologize to *her*—but for what? *She* was the bully! But I did it for him anyway. It about killed me."

"Uh-huh. Have you ever forgiven your dad for that?"

Mari raised a hand, shaking her head. "Listen—I have a great dad. He was manipulated. He didn't understand."

"Is that a yes or a no?"

"It's a 'not applicable.'" She cast a quick glance at Candace, who stared stone-faced at the coffee table. "My dad didn't know what she was really like."

Dr. Grant sat quietly before he responded. "So help me understand. JoyAnne was a first-class jerk to you in high school, but God has changed her life. However, you're still mad at her for what she did to you back then."

"Well, yeah, but it's so much *more* than that!"

"Explain."

Mari fidgeted in the chair. "She was always trying to outdo me. If I did anything good, she found a way to do it better. In every class. She was *fixated* on me, like she had this need to exert her power over me or something. It's like she was always smarter, always prettier, always more popular, more talented—more *everything*! There was nowhere to escape it!"

His eyes narrowed. "And now she's a believer. And outdoing you *again*."

Mari couldn't stop the tears that suddenly erupted. Her throat was tight.

"That's what hurts, isn't it? And then *she* got the Sunlight job. And your friend went to *her* for help."

She nodded, brushing her cheeks. "Basically, yes. I mean—I went to school in Boston to get *away* from her, and now—" She trailed off.

"Interesting. Why do you think God brought you back to New Hampton right now, right in the middle of a semester?"

"Well—my knee."

"Yes, of course. But I'm wondering if God's got something greater in mind. Do you think he wants you to live all toxic like this?"

"Dr. Grant, don't guilt me, like this is somehow *my* choice! I get what you're asking, but I don't really see a way out of this, apart from avoiding her for the rest of my life."

"You can't work this out?"

Mari shook her head. "I don't know. I mean—this weekend JoyAnne said she'd like to talk, but I can't do that again. I just can't."

"Maybe it'll be different this time."

Mari gave him a knowing look. "You know what they say—insanity is doing the same thing over and over again, expecting different results."

Dr. Grant remained silent, thoughtfully rubbing his chin.

Eventually she sniffed. "That was only *part* of my sucky weekend. After church on Sunday, Mrs. Gordon took me aside to scold me for having inappropriate emotional boundaries with Mac's daughter. She said I'm pretending to be her mother, and I swear I'm not! She has totally misunderstood, and I feel like I can't do anything right! But I respect her. I respect her so much. Mrs. G is like, she's—I don't know—my hero. She's an expert when it comes to helping people. I've always revered her, so it really cut when she said that." Another batch of tears slid down her cheeks.

"I'm sorry that happened," he said.

"Sorry," she squeaked, fumbling in her pocket for a tissue.

He shook his head. "It's all right." He too cast a glance at Candace, but she did not look up.

Mari blew her nose.

"I just want someone to acknowledge me for what *I* can do. I love Aubrey and helping her, but suddenly it's wrong. I want to help my friend Ariel, but I'm not good enough for the position. Plus she chose to go to someone else anyway. It's like I'm the perpetual loser—like I'm defective or something! Is it wrong to want someone to just say, 'Good job, Mari!'?"

"My boys fell in love with you. They were thrilled to be with you."

She snorted. "They were thrilled with Dan DeSoto and all the craziness of being rained on! And honestly, Dr. Grant, it's *kickball*, for heaven's sake. How much of a college education does it take to organize a kickball game?" She dropped her head in her hands. "Anyway, that's beside the point. Back to JoyAnne." She wiped her nose again.

"I know it's wrong for me to wish ill on someone and hate them, but I *do*. And I admit that part is *my* problem, not JoyAnne's, but I don't know how to get past it. I know I need to forgive her, but it seems so overwhelming. For years my parents went on and on and on about forgiving her until I couldn't talk to them about anything anymore. I've lived under a constant barrage of crap from her—and now she's back again. I'm *stuck*!"

She set the wadded tissue beside her leg. "And you know what else? It hit me that at least the prodigal son had a solution. He was an idiot for messing up his life, but there was a point where he knew home was his only option. The other brother—" She shrugged, flaying her hands. "It doesn't even say what happened to him. He was already home. Where else was there to go? He just had to figure it out, I guess."

"Oh, I don't know," Dr. Grant said. "Maybe those boys had the same problem. Neither of them really knew their father's heart for them, did they? There's a solution for that." He straightened in his seat. "So how has this issue affected your spiritual life with God?"

"Oh, I'm good in that department."

"Are you?"

"Yes. I mean—I know God loves me and that Jesus died for my sins.

I've been trying to read my Bible more now that you and Mac have urged me to. I'm working at it. I think I'm okay."

"Uh-huh. Let me ask you another question: Do you think God knows what's happened between you and JoyAnne?"

She let out a breath. "Yes."

"Do I detect a hesitancy?"

"Okay, there's a difference between knowing something and how you feel about it. I *know* God knows what's happened between us, but I *feel* like he's on vacation! I don't know why he hasn't answered my prayers about this, and sometimes it feels like he's siding with her. So yeah, I guess there's some distance there."

"Like with your dad."

She made a sound. "Maybe."

"And how do you think God views you? What does God think when he looks at Mari Coleman?"

"How could someone possibly know that?"

"You're right. But still—take a stab at the question."

She pursed her lips, shaking her head. "That's tough. I know he loves me, but I'm so far from where I should be. I'm a screw-up. I would guess he's disappointed in me." She looked away. "Maybe I shouldn't have told you all this. I guess I was hoping you could give me some direction or something, but now I'm just embarrassed."

"Don't be embarrassed! I admire your honesty! Isn't that the first step in getting help?"

"I'm not that optimistic. Sorry. I'm just weary of dealing with this."

"I can tell it's been difficult." He leaned forward in his chair, resting his arms on his legs. "I wish I had an easy solution for you, Mari, but I don't. God can help you, though, and you're not alone. Everyone has struggles. And if the Spirit of God abides in you, he's probably already been nudging you in a certain direction. What's he saying to you?"

"I don't know. I mostly feel guilty."

"What do you feel guilty about?"

She paused, struggling to say it. "I know I've reacted in some really bad ways, and like the saying goes, 'Two wrongs don't make a right.' JoyAnne's issues aren't an excuse for *me* to sin. Plus, I know I'm supposed to forgive her. It's not fair, you know. Why isn't JoyAnne distraught? Why doesn't she have to deal with her part in all this?"

"How do you know she's not? And yes, of course it's hard. But on the other side of where you don't want to go is where you truly want to be.

It's worth the work."

"I'm not so sure about that!"

"Understandable. And it *is* your choice, of course. That's the dilemma, isn't it? Do you want to get over this, or do you want to stay miserable? The first is hard work, and it'll cost you. The second will cost you too—in a different way. God's not going to stop loving you, whichever path you choose, but there's gain with pressing through and loss with circumventing God's process. Either choice involves pain."

He paused. "Listen, Mari—you have God's heart and utmost sympathy for what you're going through. He's a tender and compassionate father, patient with our immaturities and such, but he won't coddle your sin. We all have the tendency to minimize our sin and think it's no big deal, but sin is his enemy and yours. It creates a barrier between you and God. It's not fun to hear, but sin will only make things worse, never better. Never. If you want to get over this, you're going to have to come to terms with that."

They sat again without talking.

She sniffed. "Well, I *do* want to get over this. I just can't handle another talk with her."

He nodded. "Then maybe have a talk with God first. Look—could I offer a suggestion?"

"That's why I'm here!"

Ti-ti-dit. Ti-ti-dit. Ti-ti-dit—

Both of them turned as Candace scrambled to silence the alarm on her watch. She dropped her eyes. "Sorry!"

That hour had flown by, Mari thought. "Thanks, Candace," she said. "You can go."

But she shook her head. "No, go ahead and finish."

Dr. Grant, too, checked the time. "As I was saying," he continued, "maybe I could offer some pre-forgiveness suggestions. What if you asked God to help you see things differently? What if you asked him to show you how *he* sees this situation? What if you asked him to show you any barren spots in your heart that are screaming to be filled with his love?"

His questions alone struck a chord, making her throat grow tight again.

"Will you do that?" he asked.

She nodded.

"Ask God to show you your value in his eyes. He loves you, Mari Coleman. He's not on vacation. He sees you and knows you—every part of you. Right now you're like a ship in a storm, tossed mercilessly at sea. You could stay in this place indefinitely. But if you choose freedom, there's a way out. There's direction and a destination. Choose freedom and you'll get through this storm. It's attainable. Just keep moving forward."

She nodded again, suddenly noticing Candace discreetly brush away a tear.

"Well, thank you for your time," she said. "It's given me a lot to think about."

Dr. Grant pulled himself out of the armchair. "You're welcome. But promise me you'll do more than think about this. I want you to *pray.* Be honest with God and ask him for help. He will. And now I need to head to my class. We're covering the Roman Empire today. Such a fascinating era!"

Mari gave a twisted smile. "That's a little subjective!"

"If you took my class, you'd find out how very fascinating it is!" He turned. "Candace, thank you for joining us. I apologize if anything I said made you feel uncomfortable. And you too can pray any of those prayers. God will hear you. Ladies, it's been a pleasure. See you tomorrow."

"See you tomorrow," Mari echoed, watching him go. She turned to Candace. "Well, now you know what I'm really like! I'm sure that was *way* more than you ever cared to hear, but thanks for sticking it out. At least you made twenty bucks."

Candace rose to her feet. "It—went fast."

"Yeah, too fast. Let's go."

They cut through the Coffee Break toward the doors that led to the parking lot, trekking to their cars without conversation. What was there to say? Mari was exhausted, and Candace was probably regretting having donated an hour of her life she couldn't get back.

"Well, thanks again," Mari said as they separated. She got into her car and buckled in, then dropped her head back on the headrest. That wasn't exactly how she had envisioned her conversation with Dr. Grant unfolding, but what a relief to finally have someone to talk to! Saying it all out loud, however—wow—what a hurl of verbal vomit! She closed her eyes, feeling stupid and ashamed.

"I need help, God," she breathed. "Show me your perspec—"

Tap, tap, tap—

Mari jumped at Candace rapping her knuckles on her window. She lowered the glass. "Dang—you scared me!"

"Sorry," she said, leaning in. "Hey—I can't talk right now, but I wanted to tell you that we'd like to do it—my partner and I. The Bible thing you offered—reading and talking about it. If the offer is still open." Her voice was rushed and husky, like she was nervous. Or fighting back tears.

Mari blinked. "Oh—yes! Okay. Um—*we?*"

"My partner and I, if that's okay."

She nodded. Oh, she was absolutely going to need Mac! "Uh—great! Yeah, we can do that! What's your boyfriend's name?"

Candace smiled. "Her name is Quinn. Does that make a difference?"

Partner. Duh. "Uh, no—of course not!"

"Okay. Thanks." She dropped Mari's twenty-three dollars through the window. "See you tomorrow."

Chapter Twenty

Mari choked back tears all the way to the nursing home. There was so much to think about, and Dr. Grant's words kept echoing through her mind: *Do you want to get over this, or do you want to stay miserable?* She knew she needed to change. Her admission to him regarding her animosity toward JoyAnne had been frightening. What kind of believer in Jesus lived with that kind of muck inside? She knew it was so wrong, yet she didn't know how to fix it. Although she *did* know. She just didn't want to do it. It was hard.

It'll cost you.

She glanced at the time on the console. It almost didn't pay to go visit her grandfather today. She would barely get there and then it would be time to leave for Mac's. Part of her wanted to go sit in a park somewhere and have it out with God, but she wasn't quite sure what "it" was. All she knew was that she didn't like the way she was. Following the professor's advice, she shot off a silent prayer for God to help her see her situation in a different way. The way *he* saw it. *I need your help, God.*

Dr. Grant's voice wisped in: *Your choice. Hard work. Pain.*

Words like that made her want to bolt, but she had done that already, and what had running away solved? Her hatred had simply gone dormant in Boston, only to spring to life again when she returned home. It was time to face herself, which was difficult and confusing. JoyAnne had hurt her repeatedly. Was it a sin to be hurt? How could Mari be faulted for that? She had *tried* to forgive JoyAnne—hundreds of times! Why wouldn't all those hurts just go away? Or was there something deeper going on in her that she wasn't getting? *God, are there barren spots in me screaming for love?* Why had Dr. Grant mentioned that? Is that how he saw her? As emotionally needy?

And now she had Candace looking to *her* for spiritual guidance.

How absurd! What a fine candidate *she* was—offering to help someone understand the Bible when she barely read it herself! She shook her head, completely overwhelmed and disgusted with herself. And there came Dr. Grant's voice again: *Sin makes things worse, never better. You're going to have to come to terms with that.* Man, everyone was kicking her butt lately!

Then why did you talk to him? she chided herself.

Now at the nursing home parking lot, she checked her phone, noting she had two texts.

The first was from Mac: "Warning! Crazy weekend. House still a wreck from Friday."

She smiled, quickly texting, "Do I have to do everything for you?" Then she sent a laughing icon, adding, "No worries!"

The other text was from Shannon. "Call me ASAP."

Doing so, Mari learned that a prospective buyer was taking Shannon's car to his mechanic, leaving her without a vehicle. However, if Mari swung by her salon to get her on the way to Mac's, Shannon would drop her off and pick her up later. The car shuffle again.

"Sounds good. I'll text you when I'm on my way," Mari told her. "And maybe Will can bring me home."

Now she had even less time with her grandfather. Hurrying through the hallway to his room, she was reminded of the day she had driven terribly sick Ariel home. Hearing a tad bit more of her story was intriguing. Mari wondered what could have happened at Whitmore that would make Ariel need to run through Frost field in the dark to get to Susan's. Did Trey West and his group of no-goods have anything to do with it? Well, Ariel was out of her hands and into JoyAnne's now, she told herself—which was good, right? *Right.* It smarted like crazy! She sighed. Oh, for a magic wand to wave away her troubles.

She found her grandfather at a table in the dining room with jumbo-sized picture cards laid out before him. He brightened. "Hi, Marree!"

The aide smiled. "He's been asking for you!"

Mari kissed him on his head. "Sorry I'm late, Poppy. What are you doing?"

"Worrk," he said. He pointed to a card, speaking slowly, "Cat in tttree."

"Wow! Nice!" she praised.

He moved his finger to the next card. "Car on road. Cake with fffork."

"It's pretty impressive," the aide said, patting the old man's shoulder. "It just started bubbling out of him today. I'll leave you two for a bit."

Mari thanked her and turned back to her grandfather in amazement. "Poppy, that's wonderful! Do this one—" She pointed to a random card.

"Purrple currr—" He paused, struggling.

"Curtains," she offered. "Almost there!"

He leaned back, smiling. "And Mac in pocket."

Her cheeks grew warm. She had been secretly hoping for something to be in that plaid shirt pocket for her. "May I have it, Poppy?"

He tugged it out. "From Mac to Marree!"

Another small envelope. "Thank you. Let's see what it is!"

Inside was another little card of intricately cut paper, a "paper quilt" pieced together in a mosaic of colors and textures, creating the image of an old-fashioned clipper ship on a peaceful sea. It was a lovely seascape, so artfully constructed, she thought, examining it in appreciation. Then noting a small protruding tab on one side, she gently gave it a tug, gasping in surprise as billowy gray clouds slid over the sky and lacy white-capped waves rose out of long vertical slits, "tossing" the ship as the delicate art changed from still to stormy. Delighted, she pushed the tab inward, transforming the tempest back to calm.

"Look, Poppy!" she exclaimed, showing her grandfather. "Isn't this amazing!"

Strangely, something about it made her want to cry. It wasn't a magic wand, but the card spoke to her of change—that she would not always be hurled about if she kept moving toward freedom, as Dr. Grant had encouraged. It was a tangible image of hope. On the reverse side, Mac had written her name—"Marissa: of the sea." Her name and its meaning.

She looked at her grandfather, pressing the card against her chest. "Poppy, Mac Sinclair is one great guy. I needed this today. This card—this comforts me."

"Arrre you sad?" he asked.

She nodded. "A little. But it's okay. I need to make some hard changes in my life. I'd appreciate your prayers."

"Yesss." He nodded. "I will prray."

It suddenly occurred to her that she was having a conversation with her grandfather. She stared at him in wonder. "You're talking!"

"Yesss!" He grinned. "I'm working hard."

Aubrey's school bus was grinding to a halt on the curb across from Mr. Dixie's little store right as Mari and Shannon entered the Frost neighborhood in their dad's vehicle.

"Good timing," Mari said. "Just drop me off here. I'll call if I need a ride later."

She stepped onto the boulevard right as Aubrey stormed off the bus in one of her mad-at-the-world moods. Accompanying her on the sidewalk, Mari shortly learned that her book report had been missing from her folder at school, and she was convinced that Ty West had taken it.

"Why would he do that?" Mari asked.

"'Cause he's mean! I'm *not* playing kickball if he's there!" She broke into a power walk, ditching Mari as she stomped home.

This again? Mari sighed.

Breathing in the scent of freshly cut grass, she observed up ahead that the field had been mowed. Not all of it, just the kickball part. By Mac, no doubt. It was super nice of him to think of it. The first handful of her after-school crew was already there, waiting for the others to trickle in. She wondered if Ty would join them today. Or Trey.

Passing the Gordons, Mari was reminded of Susan's corrective words to her after church the day before. Mentally she rehearsed the changes she would make to emotionally prepare Aubrey for her return to college. A sit-down talk would be too much, she decided. No, simple, strategically placed comments to the girl would have to do. Nevertheless, she struggled with what those might be. "I wonder who your new caregiver will be when I go back to school in the fall" seemed a little harsh.

The tulips in front of her old house had finally opened, Mari noticed. The bright red ones. At the same time, a metallic bluish teal car parked at the curb caught her attention, where two men sat with the windows down, presumably waiting for Roger Eden to arrive home. The gentleman closest to the boulevard transferred his gaze from following Mac's red-faced, clomping daughter to Mari as she trailed behind, offering her a curt nod. Mari nodded back, no doubt pegged as the pouty child's mother. See? It was a natural assumption, she thought, making her point to an invisible Mrs. Gordon. How could she be blamed for it?

As it turned out, Aubrey's book report was on the dining room table.

Mari raised her brow, handing it to her. "Now don't you feel bad for accusing Ty?"

The girl shrugged, stuffing it in her folder. "I *still* don't want him to play."

"But all the other kids want to play with *you*, so come on." She jerked her head toward the porch.

"What's for snack? I'm hungry. Did you make cookies again?"

"Nope. Sorry." She had had such a blue weekend that she hadn't planned ahead. "I don't have any treats for today. But if you hold out, I'll make you a smoothie later."

"What about the other kids? My dad has a package of cookies in the pantry. I snuck one yesterday!"

"Oh, did you? Just one, huh? Well, those wouldn't go very far. If you want, I'll make you a snack now, but that means everyone else has to wait."

Aubrey threw her head back, huffing, "*Fine then!*" and marched for the door.

Mari shook her head, following. Why would anybody think she would *want* to be that girl's mother?

Perhaps they needed a new game, she mused, toting the ball to the field. Red Rover? Freeze tag? She tried to imagine keeping order with either. Plus the bigger kids might be rough on the younger ones. No, it was kickball for today.

From the pitcher's mound, Connor Haddington pointed out a sizeable food container in the area where the kids dumped their belongings. "That's from my mom." It was a bin of washed grapes with a nest of string cheese stacked to one side. Mari closed her eyes, breathing out her gratefulness.

"Tell her thanks," she said. Then she announced to the group that they were having snacks first. Holding the container while all the eager hands grabbed for the food, Mari gazed over the children's heads toward the distant Whitmore apartments, hoping to see a familiar figure trotting in.

But Ty didn't come that day. Neither did a few others. However, managing a slightly smaller group was a welcomed reprieve for Mari—especially since without Ty present, Aubrey quickly abandoned her foul attitude, and their afternoon unfolded drama free. At quitting time Mari gathered everyone in and had them clap to thank Connor for the snacks.

"Listen up! I want everyone to point to the sky!" she said. It was time for her to wield her influence, as encouraged by Dan DeSoto.

All hands flew upward, and it grew quiet.

"Remember—God always sees you and hears you when you pray. You can talk to him about anything! Now everyone point to the ground."

With a burst of giggles, all hands dropped.

"Look around! I don't want to see any wrappers in the grass! Pick up before you go! See you all tomorrow!"

She lingered as the children gathered their belongings and scattered for their homes.

Aubrey hugged her waist. "You're so fun!" Then she jerked back, pointing. "Hey, look—it's Miss Leah! Hi! Did you bring the baby?" She broke away to meet Leah DeSoto, just walking up.

Leah waved. "Hi! No, Kenny's with his mama. Sorry I missed your game! I was going to come assist you, but I'm too late. Hope it went okay." She looked in question at Mari, who raised her hands in victory.

"One day and incident free!"

They both laughed.

"Come inside with us! Aubrey and I are about to make banana bread."

"Aww, do we have to?" Aubrey grumbled. "I don't want to take it to school again!"

Mari looked at her in surprise. "Hey, it won't be like last time—I promise! And think of how special it will be to Hailey's mom. Plus, Leah's here!"

"Can you stay?" Aubrey asked Leah, who nodded, and the three strolled up to the house together.

Mac's warning text about his house being a mess came into bearing when they entered from the porch.

"Oh, my," Leah said, eyeing the disarray. "Maybe I should have helped him clean up before we went home the other night. I feel bad! We spent the whole evening talking in the kitchen."

"He warned me earlier today," Mari admitted. "I think he was embarrassed. I was planning to pick up a little for him."

"Let's do it together," Leah urged, starting to collect empty water bottles. "I'll straighten the living room. Is there a vacuum nearby?"

After Aubrey fetched it for her, Mari sent her to complete her own chores while she and Leah tidied the front part of the house. The towels mounded under the arch between the foyer and the living room were still damp, Mari discovered. She scooped them up, making a face at their mustiness as she turned for the laundry room. Leah called out, tossing her a few more from across the room. When she returned, she slid aside Aubrey's pink backpack and another camouflaged one, presumably Mac's, from under the stairs. Then she pulled all the shoes off the mat, shook it out, swept and mopped the area, and then fitted the backpacks into separate cubbies.

"Yikes, what's in here—rocks?" she commented, muscling in the larger, camo one.

By that time, Leah was ready for her to help move the furniture back in place and fix the rug.

"There—doesn't that feel better?" Mari asked Aubrey, and the three went to start their project in the kitchen, chatting and having fun while they baked.

Later, when the bread was in the oven, Aubrey relocated to the dining room to do her homework, and Mari and Leah had a moment alone.

"That's so wild that Ariel's home is nearby," Leah mused, gazing out the window at the apartments in the far distance.

"Yeah, right across the field. I confess I'm bursting with curiosity to know what happened to her."

"Me too! But I'm glad she's getting help from JoyAnne. She's really good with her."

Mari nodded, though she preferred not to linger on the subject. "And speaking of help—" Then she shared with Leah her encounters with Candace at the Coffee Break. "So she wants to meet with me to learn about the Bible, and I don't even know where to start!"

"Invite them to my house on Saturday mornings! That's exactly what we do—read the Bible and talk about it. Kyla's really good at that."

"Right. But it's a matter of trust. Candace knows *me*. I don't think she'd be ready for Kyla yet."

"Oh, sure. Well, you could learn what to do from Kyla and repeat it with Candace. She'd definitely help you."

"I was thinking Mac might have some ideas."

"Yeah, him too. And maybe eventually she'd want to come. But anyway, way to go! That's really great!"

By the time Mac got home, Leah had already left, and Mari and Aubrey were heating up leftovers for supper. There was something gratifying about seeing him happy, Mari thought, as he came in through the kitchen door and hugged his daughter, commenting on how wonderful the house smelled.

"Don't tell me you made banana bread a second time and it's still not for me!" he said playfully aghast to Aubrey, who rolled her eyes.

"Dad, you already *know* who it's for!"

He threw Mari a wink. "And how was kickball today, squirt?"

"Super fun! Ty wasn't there. And Miss Leah came at the end!"

"Oh? Nice!"

"Yes, she came in for a while," Mari reported. "We hung out and talked."

"And *cleaned*," Aubrey said. "A lot!"

"Oh, *great!*" he groaned, looking toward the front of the house. "I'm going to go broke if I have to pay you for everything you're doing around here!"

"You don't. And it was fun," Mari said. "We all worked together, and it didn't take long at all."

"Well, thanks." He began his routine of rolling up his sleeves to wash his hands. "I'm sure Aubrey showed you her new bedroom. We spent most of Saturday afternoon making that change."

Indeed, Aubrey had revealed to her that her dad had switched her bedroom with the one across the hall, which entailed minor painting and moving all her furniture, including disassembling and reassembling her bed. But her windows no longer overlooked the neighbor's yard or his dogs.

Mari dipped her head. "She showed me, and I like it! Smart move!"

He turned and they exchanged a look.

"Well, that's where my time went, and that's why the house looked like it did."

"No judgment! And hey—thanks for mowing the field."

He nodded. "You're welcome! That was another Saturday project. There was a lull where it had dried out enough to do it. I filled in the hole too."

"Hole?"

"Beyond third base. How could you miss it? Someone was obviously digging out there, but for what, who knows! It was probably a foot across and two feet deep. A kid could have broken a leg in it. I'm glad the mower went over top."

"Crazy! I never noticed it."

"*I* seen it," Aubrey piped up.

"*Saw* it," Mari corrected lightly.

"Well, if you find something like that again, let me know," Mac said, turning off the water.

"I reheated some of Leah's chicken-and-rice dish, if you'd like," Mari offered.

"Sounds wonderful! Aubrey, my little flower, is your homework done?" He dried his hands and straddled a stool at the counter.

"Yep. *And* chores."

"Excellent! Tonight feels like a night for a school science project!"

"Oh, *yes*! My volcano!" Aubrey pumped her fist, turning to Mari. "Can you stay?"

"Stay for dinner at least," Mac urged. "Since you prepared it."

"Reheating food hardly counts. But"—she grinned, not budging from her chair—"you don't have to twist my arm. It looks delicious!"

Over dinner Mac gathered a report on Aubrey's day, firing off questions about the best and worst parts of it and probing her about various classes and teachers and assignments. Mari studied the girl's expressions while she talked, searching for Mac's features in her face. When they had finished discussing school, Mari inquired about Hailey.

"She's fine. They might move in with her grandma now 'cause her mom can't go to work. It's somewhere in the country."

"Hmm. Maybe I'll write her mom a little note to send with the banana bread tomorrow."

Aubrey grunted. "Ty better not wreck it again!"

"He won't," Mari assured. She noticed Mac looking at her and added, "His mom grounded him after the first time, and she and I talked today. We have an understanding."

"Do you?" he asked.

"Well, sort of. She indicated he could play kickball if I stay out of her business, and I'm like—fine! But now *he's* the one I want to go check on in Whitmore! I think his brother beats on him. It makes me sad to see a kid struggling like that. You can see he wants love and attention, but his behavior is awful. I told Tatum I *want* him to come play with us. He wasn't there today, but hopefully he'll come tomorrow."

Aubrey frowned. "Why do you want him?"

"Well—he's struggling. Maybe it would do him good to have *one* kind person in his life. Maybe it would help him if he knew there was someone he could talk to if things were bad." She tipped her chin. "But if he hurts you, he's in *big* trouble, just so you know."

"I still don't want him there."

Mari nodded. "I know. But remember how mean Connor was to you until he had to join your reading group? Sometimes kids don't know how to process their emotions. Like you—remember how you thought you hated everything but you were just sad and disappointed? That's how a lot of people are. It *feels* like one thing, but it's really another."

"He never even said sorry when he hit me in the face with the ball."

"Yeah. I wish he would have. Maybe he was afraid of you."

"Afraid of *me*?" She snorted.

"Yeah. You started the game. You and I together. Maybe he's afraid you'll kick him out."

"I *want* to kick him out." She ate quietly for a minute, then added, "Well, if he's mean again, can you make him go home?"

"I'll give him a chance to change first. But if he's hurting people, he has to go."

Aubrey gave a thumbs-up. "Deal. Dad, can we have ice cream for dessert?"

Mac's brow rose. "Yes. I think ice cream is in order after that."

"*Yes!*" The girl scraped up her last bite, murmuring through a full mouth, "After what?"

Mari smiled at him. "I got your card. Thanks. It was amazing. Same artist?"

Mac brightened. "Yes—she's good, isn't she? I liked it."

"I also noticed you looked up my name. You're the only one who calls me Marissa, you know. Not even my parents do."

"Do you mind? It's my way of reminding myself that you're not a kid."

"I don't mind. It reminds me that I'm an adult."

They both laughed.

"Anyway, the card really spoke to me," Mari said. "I won't go into it, but I didn't have the greatest weekend. It was good to remember that God can calm a stormy sea."

"That was in my Sunday school lesson," Aubrey piped up.

"That's cool," Mari said.

Mac pushed his plate in, leaning his elbows on the table. "I take it you're referring to the thing with Ariel—? Your weekend."

Mari nodded. "Yes. Though mostly the JoyAnne end of it, if you know what I mean. And some other things too."

"Well, maybe it *feels* like one thing, but it's really another."

She looked up in surprise. "What do you mean by that?"

He shrugged. "Oh, I don't know. We're not much different than those kids." He turned to his daughter. "Aubrey, little flower, go get us the ice cream."

Aubrey jumped excitedly from her stool. "Yes! Big bowls or the little ones?"

"Little bowls!" Mari answered automatically.

Mac swung toward her. "Says who? It's my house!"

"*Little,*" she repeated.

"Well, that's the last time I invite *you* to stay!" he muttered teasingly.

After dinner Mari asked if she could have a card on which to write a note to Hailey's mom to be sent along with the banana bread. Of course, she already knew where Mac's notecards were, but it felt awkward to poke around in his stuff with him there. He showed her and threw her a pen from beside his journal, then left her at the dining room table while he returned to the sink, where he and Aubrey did dishes together.

Sitting, Mari quickly scrawled out an encouragement as personal as possible for coming from a stranger. She was about to add that she would be happy to take Hailey for a weekend, but then remembering what Aubrey had shared of their family history, she decided to offer her rides to her medical appointments instead.

"I'm available afternoons or evenings all summer," she wrote before signing her name. She was about to seal the envelope when she paused. Heaving a sigh, she made herself remove the card to add a postscript: "Sunlight Women's Center has some helpful resources too." She set the pen down. Why was making that recommendation so difficult?

Returning Mac's pen to his end of the table, Mari noticed a napkin protruding from his journal, likely marking his place. She eyed it for a moment, then glanced toward the kitchen, where father and daughter cheerfully worked. Quickly flipping the book open, she peeked at the upper right corner under the "daily prayer" heading. Yes, there it was again: Elena—reconciliation and healing of marriage. But then she blinked in surprise. Written below it was an added name: Marissa Coleman. Instantly she replaced the napkin and dropped the book shut. Goodness—he was praying for *her*? She didn't quite know what to think.

"I should go," she said, returning to the kitchen. She placed the folded note beside the banana bread.

The two had finished, and Mac was hanging up Aubrey's dishtowel. "I'll walk you out," he said. Then eyeing her note, he added. "Her name's Nora Cross. I have her address if you want to hand-deliver that. She doesn't live too far away."

Mari nodded. "Thanks. I think for Aubrey's sake we'll stick to Plan *A*. She needs a win here."

"Yeah. Good call."

On the porch, Mari glanced around for her vehicle a second before remembering she was supposed to call Shannon for a ride.

"Oh, we'll take you home," Mac said. "It's no problem. I'll get Aubrey."

"No, I'll call Will," she said, but Mac insisted it was no trouble.

They waited back in the foyer for Aubrey, who had run up to her room.

"Oh, by the way—here," Mac said, pulling the camouflaged backpack out of the cubby. "Is this yours? It's been here over the weekend. It's a little dirty."

Mari groaned. "That's not yours? Oh, brother! That means some kid has been missing their backpack since Friday after school! No one's called you about it?"

"No," Mac said. "I just assumed it belonged to you. It's kind of big for a kid's backpack."

"And heavy. Is it Dan's? Here, let's check—" She knelt to unzip it. But when she pulled open the flap, she gasped, her hands flying back. "*Mac!* Oh, my word! Look—there's *money* in here! Lots of—" She squeaked, her jaw falling slack at the bundles upon bundles of hundred-dollar bills packed tightly in the bag.

Mac too gave an incredulous cry, ripping the zipper further open. "Holy buckets! This is all—this is all cash!" He stared at her. "Whose bag is this?"

Wide-eyed, she shook her head. "I have *no* idea! I can't believe this! How much do you think is in here?"

He let out a breath. "A lot. A *lot!*"

Both gaped at the bag.

Then Mari began a search for some mark of identification. "It was right here—sitting against the wall. I thought it was yours, and I put it in the cubby!"

"It was buried under a pile of towels all weekend. I set it there thinking it was *yours*. And you have no idea whose this might be?" He unzipped the small pocket on the front, swiping his hand through the empty cavity.

"It had to have come in from the field. When it poured on us, everyone just grabbed stuff and ran. Dan DeSoto and I stayed behind and gathered up everything else. This couldn't be his, could it?"

"Why in the world would Dan carry around money like this?"

"Well, it can't be one of the kids'!"

"Well, it's not Dan's!"

Above them the stairs creaked as Aubrey descended. Mac zipped the bag shut. "I'm taking this to the police. Can you stay here with her?"

Mari huffed indignantly. "Absolutely not! I'm coming with you!"

He looked at her a moment, then nodded. "I'm calling Susan."

"What are you guys doing?" Aubrey asked, turning at the bottom step.

Mari tapped the bag. "Aubrey, do you know whose this is? Do you recognize it?"

"Hmm, no. Ty has one kinda like it. But his is more brownish."

"Were any of the kids missing their backpacks today?"

Aubrey shrugged. "I don't know."

Mac pointed toward the kitchen. "Aubrey, would you go check if I left my phone by the back door?" As she left, he pulled it out of his pocket and dialed Susan's number, turning to Mari as he held the phone to his ear. "Can you get a laundry basket and some towels or sheets or something?"

"For what?" She glanced at his daughter and back at him.

"I guarantee you *someone* is looking for this! We're not walking out of the house with this bag in sight." Then he disappeared into the dining room for the call.

In a minute the three returned to the foyer. Mari noticed the lump of Mac's handgun tucked in his belt.

He turned to Aubrey. "Ready, squirt? I'm walking you over to the Gordons'."

Aubrey looked around in confusion. "What? What are we doing?"

"I'm taking Mari home and making a few stops. You get to hang out with Miss Susan until I get back."

"Why can't I come?"

Mari gave her a quick hug and a kiss. "You'll have fun with Mrs. G. See you tomorrow, sweetie."

Mac turned to Mari. "Be right back."

Chapter Twenty-One

Mari sat beside Mac in the very same examination room where she had been the previous week. Across from them a police officer diligently recorded their statements on his laptop, while nearby two officers in latex gloves swabbed the camouflage backpack on the table and photographed it from all angles. The transcribing officer slanted the computer toward them, producing a small aerial map of Frost Park.

"Can you show us where you found this?" he asked.

"We're not exactly sure *where* it was," Mari said and then reiterated her story of the sudden downpour last Friday. "We were shoving stuff in the stroller so fast that we didn't stop to look at any of it. But that's how and when we suspect it came into the house."

He nodded. "Okay. I'll need the contact information of the gentleman you were with."

Mac tapped his finger on the screen. "I discovered a freshly dug hole right around here on Saturday. It could have been dug for the backpack, but we don't know. I *did* notice the bag looks new, even though it's dirty."

"And your reason for being in the field?" the officer asked, glancing at the backpack.

"Mowing the grass. For the kids' games after school."

The officer marked the map. "All right. We'll need a list of the names of everyone who was there and anyone else you can think of who uses the park." He slid Mari a legal pad. "Indicate which are adults, please."

Mari took the pen. "There's something else. One of my kickball kids is from the Whitmore development, and there was an incident that day during our game that you should know about." Then she explained in detail what had transpired on the field between Ty and his brother, Trey, and his pack of friends. "Trey was adamant that Ty had stolen something from him. He specifically said *money,* and if he didn't get it back someone named Burne would kill him. I heard it clearly. I know who that is—he's the scruffy, bald guy with all the skulls and flames tattooed all over. Maybe this is it! Maybe it's drug money or something!"

With an acknowledging grunt, the officer rotated the laptop to type additional notes. "Put them on your list."

"Their mother showed up at the field that day too," Mari added. "Tatum West. Just to pick up Ty. But I happen to work with her at the Taiton Coffee Break, and there's something strange going on with her. The other day I walked in on the manager reprimanding her. He said it was her last warning, that next time he'd call the police. She might have been stealing from the till."

Mac made a sound. "That's not cash register money!"

But the officer only nodded and typed more notes, murmuring, "Taiton Coffee Break."

Turning to the legal pad, Mari began listing out as many of the adults that she could think of: the DeSotos, Susan Gordon, Tess Haddington, Kyla Watkins, JoyAnne Strang—

"Carl Fordunger," Mac offered, watching her write. "Roger Eden. And all the other neighbors."

She scrawled several names, then looked up at Mac. "I don't know the last names of the kickball children."

"We'll take whatever you can give us," the officer commented. "And we'll send an investigator to look over the park."

"Thank you," Mac said. He turned to Mari. "How about watching Aubrey at your place tomorrow?"

She frowned. "What about all the other kids? They'll be waiting there! And wouldn't that just send a signal to whoever might be looking for the money that we found it? I think things should go on as usual."

The officer nodded. "If you're willing, we'd prefer to keep things as normal as possible. Your little Frost Park was likely the rendezvous for something illegal, and someone's out a lot of money. With some armed surveillance we may find out who's looking for it."

Mac raised his brow. "But these are *kids*! Isn't that a bit risky? I don't want my daughter caught in the middle of something. Or *any* of them!"

"We're only out there an hour at max," Mari interjected. "And in broad daylight. Whoever's looking wouldn't be out there when we are. Not unless they're totally stupid."

Mac looked at the officer. "And you can guarantee surveillance? For how long?"

"We'll keep you informed. No doubt whoever we're looking for has already discovered the money's missing, so he, she, or they have probably moved on to trying to find out where it went. Now walk me through this list of names. Is anyone here new or out of the ordinary?"

Thus proceeded a discussion of each person on their list.

Later, Mari sat contemplatively beside Mac as he drove her home.

"I'm sorry, Mac," she said finally. "I feel like this whole thing is my fault. If we hadn't been playing kickball out in the field—"

"If you hadn't been playing kickball, whatever was supposed to happen with that cash would have still happened. It's not your fault, Marissa. This only exposed what was already in progress. I'm just glad one of the kids didn't stumble upon it. Can you imagine?"

She nodded. "But maybe that's what *did* happen. Maybe Ty stumbled upon it at home and hid it from his brother."

Mac moved into the exit lane for Kingswood. "If that's the case, Trey West is up to his eyeballs in drug trafficking. That was a significant trade." He whistled.

"Or Tatum," she mused. "But I don't know. As rough as that lady is, she *did* ground Ty for wrecking Aubrey's banana bread. That's a good mom move if you ask me. And she was willing to let him play if I stayed out of her business—whatever that might mean. It's like she's trying."

"Let's hope her business doesn't involve a camouflaged backpack!"

"No kidding!"

Kingswood came into view as they rounded the last curve of Juniper Street.

"It could be entirely someone else, you know," Mac said.

"Yeah, but who? Even the infamous Roger Eden doesn't look like a druggie." She grinned. "Maybe it's JoyAnne!"

He laughed. "Let it out, Marissa! Come on—let's have a full-fledged animosity dump!"

"You know I'm kidding!" And she was. Mostly.

Turning into the circular drop-off area of the condominium, he pulled alongside the curb and put the vehicle in park. He turned in his seat. "Thus ends another Marissa Coleman adventure."

"Another?"

He shrugged. "Well, you can't say that being at the police station twice in a week isn't a little adventurous. And then there's the volleyball to the knee and the meatball thing and the banana bread fiasco—you're a magnet for it!"

"And the rainstorm."

He waved his hand. "See?"

His eyes. The look in his eyes and his smile.

She slipped her hand for the door handle. "Either that or a magnet for *trouble*! But I should go. Thanks for the ride."

He popped his seatbelt. "Let me walk you up."

"No—no, Mac! That's not necessary! The ride is enough—thanks." Quickly she hopped out. "Will you let me know what's going on—if the police call you?"

"You'll be the first to know. Good night, Marissa. See you tomorrow."

"See you tomorrow."

Alone in the elevator, Mari closed her eyes, cupping a hand over her mouth. What on earth was happening? She had no business feeling what she was feeling toward Mac. No business whatsoever. But the way he had looked at her. She blew out her breath. What on earth was happening?

Shannon was starting laundry when Mari walked in, the hall spread with piles of sorted colors.

"Want to throw your uniform in?" she asked, pushing the settings on the machine.

Mari shook her head. "No, I washed it at Mac's."

Shannon threw her a look. "At Mac's?"

Mari waggled her head. "Don't read into it! I taught Aubrey how to do her own laundry so I could wash it there. Then it's clean and done. Is Mom home?"

"She's at a meeting. How's Will?"

"Uh—fine, I think. We're getting together tomorrow."

"Then where were you?"

"At the police station with Mac."

Shannon straightened, her eyes round. "What's going on?"

So Mari gave her a streamlined version of what had happened and how it was connected to Friday afternoon.

Shannon shook her head. "Whoa! But why would you think Tatum would have anything to do with that?"

"Well, she might not, but I heard her reprimanded at work by the manager last week. He told her that what she was doing was wrong and that this was her last warning. Next time he was calling the police."

"Tatum?" Shannon frowned. "Mari, Tatum's growly but she's loyal to a fault. There's not a harder worker at the Coffee Break. I highly doubt she'd steal money from there. In fact, if someone was pocketing money from the till and Tatum found out—oh, would they hear it from her, and it wouldn't be pretty! I can't see what he'd be referring to."

"Well, it was something. But you could be right." She shrugged. "I only thought that with the connection to Trey and everything—you know. Plus she's always mad!"

Shannon folded her arms. "Well, she's been betrayed enough times! She picks these loser guys! And now apparently one of her ex-boyfriends is back and messing with her boys. He's bad news. Maybe that's what's going on. Maybe Trey is mixed up in something stupid. But I guess that whole neighborhood is bad news! Just be careful, Mari. It's scary that this is so close to our house. Our *old* house."

"I know," Mari agreed. It had been Will's concern all along.

Mari had a hard time settling down that night. In the shower she found herself poring over every detail of the Friday rainstorm that she could recall, thinking through her list of those who had made their mad dash for her house. *Mac's* house, she corrected herself. Drying off, she stood with her towel in her hands thinking of him. Don't go there—you can't go there, she told herself, meeting her own gaze in the mirror. You *must not* go there. And then came the flood of guilt. She had a *boyfriend*, for heaven's sake! Plus Mac was praying for his marriage to be healed and restored. But then—but then why was her name written in his journal? And the way he had looked at her!

Stop it, she commanded herself. Maybe he was only praying for her because she was immature.

As she pulled her pajamas out of her dresser, her eyes came to rest on the little collection of notes he had left her in her grandfather's pocket. She paused, opening the tiny floral bouquet card to study its beautiful, intricate blooms. *No more boyfriend jabs, I promise.* There—he had acknowledged her boyfriend. Still, he could have used an index card for the same message. But he hadn't. She closed her eyes. Oh, boy. If Mrs. Gordon had scolded her for inappropriate emotional boundaries with Aubrey, what would she think of *this*? Even her own mother had warned her. She shook her head, setting the card back onto the dresser with the others—right next to Will's ring.

Will.

She swallowed. She hadn't even thought to text him today. She hadn't thought of him at all. How in the world had she gotten here? She cared deeply for Will; he was a great guy, but—but now in comparison to

Mac—*Mac*. She threw a hand to her forehead. Mac, who was praying for the *restoration of his marriage.*

"You idiot!" she whispered to herself. "Knock it off right now!" Hadn't she told Will a short while ago that he could trust her?

Donning her pajamas, she slid into bed, arranging her pillows to lean against the headboard. Already she was behind in her one-chapter-a-day commitment. It was time to catch up—and hopefully get her mind on something other than Mac.

Thankfully it helped, for as she pulled her Bible onto her lap, all her prodigal son conversations with Dr. Grant trickled back, as well as her most recent talk with him about JoyAnne. As she paged to the parable in the Bible, his voice swirled through her mind: *You have God's utmost sympathy. He's a tender, patient father, but he's not going to coddle sin. It's his enemy and yours. What's God saying? He's already been nudging you.* Her horrible attitude toward JoyAnne gave one enormous tug of guilt.

Sin. Why did it suddenly seem so menacing?

She had never denied her sinfulness as a human being before a holy God. Having been taught her need for a Savior as a young child, she was grateful that Jesus had come to earth to die in her place to pay for her sins. She knew she was forgiven, and thus sin had never been that big of a deal to her—until now, when she felt trapped in it!

So much crap had happened in her relationship with JoyAnne. They had experienced such a dark history together. Yet those hurts had happened *to* her. Now Mari was starting to see the yuck that she had allowed to accumulate *in* her—a whole garbage heap of sin by her own choosing. Yes, it was *sin*. JoyAnne was a prodigal come home, but she—Mari—was an "older brother" living in her own form of squalor: hatred, bitterness, and pride. *Sin only makes things worse, never better. If you want to get over this, you're going to have to come to terms with that.* Certainly she had her own version of "coming home" to do.

She laid her hand on the page, reading the prodigal son's words: *"Father, I have sinned against heaven and against you. I am no longer worthy to be called your son."* Here was the first step in the prodigal's return: humbling himself and admitting his sin. She closed her eyes, baring herself before God as the young man's prayer resonated in her own heart. She knew she had to start there. There would be many more layers to come, and it would cost her, yes, but as Dr. Grant had said, now she had a destination: home.

Yet coming home was far more than dealing with her JoyAnne issue, she realized. As a good girl in her youth, Mari had prayed to receive Christ, but she had never *walked* with Christ. She hadn't needed him—that's what she had thought anyway. Nor had she wanted him, honestly, for she had been offended that God hadn't helped her in the matter of JoyAnne. Her "faith story" had stalled out in chapter one. But now that she was getting to know Mac and the DeSotos and Dr. Grant, she saw her lack. Their faith in God was vibrant. They were growing. They related to God in a way that was *real*, and she wanted that.

She said it out loud: "I want that, God. I want *you* like that. Would you help me get there?"

Shannon suddenly knocked on her door and stuck her head in the doorway. "Yeah? Did you need me?"

Mari shook her head. "No."

"You were talking. I thought you were calling me."

"No. Just—praying."

"Oh. Sorry." She lifted an apologetic hand and went out.

Mari's gaze lingered on her bathrobe hanging behind the door. She sighed. Her conscience was bugging her about Mrs. Gordon too. Whether the woman was right or wrong, Mari did want to have proper boundaries with Aubrey. And the same for Mac. She bit her lip. To be liking a man who was praying for his marriage to be healed didn't seem right, whether he had initiated those feelings or not. But she *did* like him. Was that a sin? Technically he wasn't married. But what if she were to be the stumbling block for what God wanted to do in his life?

"I'm going to need your help with this too, God," she whispered.

She returned her attention to the Bible, unable to read it now with new thoughts spinning in her brain. At the forefront was lanky Will Wallace. The crazy admission of how she was starting to feel about Mac had brought a secondary revelation: As great a guy as Will was, she couldn't see herself with him long term. She shook her head. No, she couldn't. She would try her best to let him down in a kind way. But then there would be no one. No boyfriend. She would be back to being single until Mr. Right came along, and that was dang depressing. On that sour note, she plopped the Bible onto the nightstand and turned out the light.

But then in the dark, her brain still wouldn't shut off. For hours Mari tossed and turned as her mind skipped from person to person. Was Trey West connected to that backpack of money? Was he serious about someone killing him, or was it a figure of speech? Had Ty hidden that money from his brother? It was a lot of cash. Were either of them in danger? And what did "armed surveillance" look like? She imagined suit-clad men in sunglasses and earpieces concealed in an inconspicuous van decked out with high-tech cameras and sound equipment.

And Tatum—what was going on with her? Shannon's estimation of the woman hadn't matched her own, which then bunny-trailed her thoughts to Candace sitting in on her conversation with Dr. Grant. Pursuing Mari had been a big step for Candace—and to include her partner too. Yikes! How in the world would she navigate that? She had meant to talk to Mac about it. Was there anything wrong with her talking to him about that? What would Mrs. Gordon think?

Mac. He was such a wonderful guy. The way he had turned in his seat to look at her made her stomach flutter still. Would there be another note in Poppy's pocket for her tomorrow? She hoped so. And, oh—that reminded her that she had meant to say something to Mac about her grandfather talking so well. She rolled over, hugging her pillow, entreating her mind to go to sleep.

Poppy. He was able to follow conversations and communicate a little now. Maybe Poppy would be a good ear for her. He loved God. Maybe he could give her advice on everything going on—or at least comfort her. She remembered how wonderful it had been to nap against his back that first weekend back from Boston. That was after her fight with Will. Right before she had happened upon Ariel so very sick in the hallway restroom.

Ariel.

Mari sat up in bed with a sudden thought. She reached for her phone.

Mac answered groggily. "Hey—it's Mac."

"Yeah, hi. Sorry to wake you."

"Marissa? What's going on?"

It was two in the morning, she just realized. But still. "I thought of something, and I had to call you. Could it be Ariel? What about *her*?"

A pause. "Ariel?"

"She was in the field! Saturday at Jackie's, JoyAnne let slip that Ariel had run to Susan's in the night—across the field."

He cleared his throat, as if moving around. "Why would Ariel have a pile of money like that?"

"I'm just saying—maybe it wasn't Ty that took the money. Maybe it was Ariel! Maybe she was running across the field and dropped it."

"Yeah, I suppose that's possible. We could call the station with that tomorrow."

"Right. But JoyAnne and Jackie asked me not to talk about it to anybody."

"Then talk to them first."

"Yeah, I suppose I'll have to."

He chuckled. "So you're not sleeping either, huh?"

She smiled. "How can you tell? Have you been awake this whole time?"

"I'd just fallen asleep when you called."

"Oh. Sorry."

"I'm not complaining. Okay, listen—I was thinking about this earlier too. If it was Ty—or Ariel, as you suggested—then why was that hole dug? If they took off running with someone's backpack of cash—and that was *heavy*—how would they know to put it right there? Unless one of them dug it, which is pretty unlikely. That hole would have been the perfect size for that backpack—and I can't even show the police because I filled it in! I wish I knew which kid grabbed that bag from wherever it was when you all scrambled for the house. I'll bet anything it was in that cavity, which says to me that it was put there on purpose. And you don't remember who?"

"Mac, I was holding baby Kenny, and everyone was screaming and running. Maybe it was Dan—or maybe he'd remember who took it. He was coaching for me, thanks to you."

"It wasn't him, and he doesn't know. I called him." He let out a breath. "I guess it's possible the bag had nothing to do with the hole. I wish we had some evidence. Were any of the ladies taking photos by chance?"

"I don't think so. But hey—Roger Eden has cameras all over his house. Could they have picked up activity as far away as the field? It's possible."

"Yeah, it's possible. That's not a bad idea. In fact, the police should know that too. There may very well be some useful footage there!"

"Do I want the police to see that? What if he shows them the meatball clip, and I get my name in the police records again!"

"Right—for the *third* time in a week!"

They laughed.

She leaned back against the headrest, staring into her dark room. "What about Roger Eden?"

"Yeah, he crossed my mind too—he and all his security cameras, which are somewhat excessive, to be honest. And he's in the park every day. And those dogs." He let out a breath. "Golly, what if Aubrey was right all along? What if he really did—you know."

Mari shuddered. "That's so creepy, Mac! Don't even say it! Delivering banana bread and polite boulevard talk is as far as I'll go with him. Have the *police* request his camera footage, not you. I'm keeping clear of him. I don't want to risk being buried in the yard of the house I grew up in!"

"Oh, look—we've become like Aubrey! Next we'll be gawking out our windows at him!"

Mari laughed. "On a serious note, why would a pest exterminator have a truckload of money like that? I don't know, Mac. As weird as Roger Eden is, to me he seems less of a possibility than Ty or Ariel. What if he's just a quirky bachelor into his dogs, with cameras to keep an eye on them when he's not there? I mean—the guy is all about those animals! Have you ever seen him carry a backpack or any sort of bag to the park? He's got his hands full with their leashes."

"You're right. I haven't."

"Which may or may not mean anything." She sighed. "All these years Frost has been such a nice, quiet little haven. No through traffic and safely tucked behind the cemetery. It's depressing to see something like this in our neighborhood. I never thought I'd see this day."

"That's my concern too." He let out a breath. "I wish you'd take Aubrey to your place this week."

"I know, but what about the other kids? I can't take Aubrey and not the rest."

"You're not being paid to watch the rest. But yeah, I get it. Maybe I'll take some time off—just for the week."

"Let's see how tomorrow goes, okay? Maybe we'll hear from the police. And at least they said they'll be there keeping an eye on us. That's something at least." She adjusted the blanket over her legs. "Anyway, there was something else I wanted to tell you. I had a conversation with Poppy today—er, yesterday now, I guess. An actual two-way conversation. It was beautiful. Thank you, Mac."

"Ah, that's great! I'm so encouraged by how he's doing. He's the one doing the work, Mari. He and the Lord God."

"Well, thank you to both you and God."

"You're welcome."

A little silence passed.

"And another thing—I had a good talk with Dr. Grant at the Coffee Break after work. About JoyAnne. I want to change, Mac. Pray for me. I want to forgive her and get free of this icky stuff between us. I'm really trying."

"Good for you. I will. I'll pray."

"Thanks. I've started to face that it's just plain sin. And it's ugly. I don't know why I've been so afraid to let everything go. But I don't want to be like I am anymore. I've asked God to forgive me and help me. But I'm scared."

"I'm proud of you."

"Thanks. So another thing. Today Dr. Grant wouldn't talk to me unless I had someone with me, so I asked one of my coworkers—Candace—and she sat in with us. She's not a believer, but afterward she said she'd be open to meeting with me to learn more about the Bible. She and her partner, Quinn."

"That's wonderful!"

"Did you hear what I just said?"

"I did. Looks like you've got two for one! It's okay. It all starts with the gospel. That's the starting point for everyone."

"I'm going to need some help with this."

"I already said I would. Plus I've heard Kyla Watkins is good at that. Maybe she could help you too."

Mari nodded. "Yeah, I've—heard that too. So what did Mrs. G say when you picked up Aubrey? Did you tell her what happened?"

"No. I didn't want to alarm her. But yeah, Susan's great! She and Aubrey made up these little snack bags of trail mix for your kids tomorrow. Peanuts and raisins—that sort of thing. Aubrey can hardly wait to show you!"

"Aww! How sweet! See? All the more reason for us to be there!"

"I know you love it. And so do those kids. It means a lot to them."

"I do. I do love it. And Aubrey. She's pretty special too." She let out a happy breath. "Okay, I think I'm starting to get tired."

"Are you? Whew, *finally*! I was trying to come up with a creative way to hang up on you!"

"Mac!" She laughed at the teasing in his voice. "I suppose if I want you to visit Poppy in the morning, I should let you go."

"I'm not making any threats, but yes, both of us should get some rest."

And then neither spoke.

"Good night, Marissa," he said finally.

"Good night, Mac."

Chapter Twenty-Two

"I'm leaving!" Shannon yelled from the front hall. "Mari, are you coming or not?"

"Give me *one* minute!" Mari hollered back. "Bye, Mom! See you tonight!" She blew her a kiss.

Her mother raised her brow. "Bye, hon. You'd better hurry."

In record time Mari was hopping to the door, pulling on her shoes, her pockets stuffed with her makeup. "Sorry. I overslept."

Shannon's face displayed her irritation with having to wait. "You need to get your *own* car."

"Well, you shouldn't have sold *yours*," Mari flung back, checking her shirt to make sure she had secured every button. She patted her phone, hoping she hadn't forgotten anything.

"Maybe if you and Will weren't talking all night you wouldn't have slept through your alarm. You two have the strangest relationship!"

Mari shot her a look. "I didn't sleep through it. I forgot to set it."

"Well, he shouldn't be calling you in the middle of the night. That's being clingy and weird. You should have better boundaries!"

Clingy and weird? Mari followed her onto the elevator. Was it clingy and weird to call Mac? She hadn't thought so. As they neared the garage level, she asked, "Are you dropping me off?"

Shannon tossed her head. "We don't have time for that now. You'll have to drop *me* off, which means I'm left without a vehicle. *Again*."

Mari spread her hands. "Sor-rry! Geez, why are you so crabby?"

"Maybe because of all your talking last night! You weren't exactly quiet!"

"I'm *sorry*! Should I pick you up again? You can drop me off at Mac's."

"No, I'll call Colt."

When Mari arrived at the Coffee Break, she headed directly to the kitchen to construct sandwiches, lugging the tote up front to fill the case when she was finished. Candace was in a quiet mood, and for a moment Mari wondered if she had jumped ship on the idea of getting together, but as Mari was cleaning one of the machines, the girl happened by to inform Mari that Wednesday evenings or Saturdays were the only times that worked for her and her partner.

"She's not that excited about it," Candace told her. "But she said she'd try it once."

Oh—well, no pressure there, Mari thought sarcastically. No pressure at all. "I'm not an expert or anything," she warned Candace. "We'll see how it goes."

"See how *what* goes?" Mark asked, slipping past them.

"Nothing that concerns *you*," Candace replied crisply. She turned back to Mari. "Thanks for trusting me to listen to you yesterday."

Mari wiped down a metal tray and snapped it back into place on the machine. "I'm still living down the embarrassment. And I'm leaning toward Saturdays, but I'll get back to you."

Tatum suddenly appeared, dropping a box of paper cups onto the counter to replenish their supply. "Those tables won't bus themselves," she barked.

"I'm gettin' there," Mari said lightly.

Rinsing out her cloth, she candidly observed Tatum roughly shove the new cups into position. She lived hard. And she was so perpetually angry. But was she a thief? Shannon insisted not. And as Mac had said, a bag snugly packed with hundred-dollar bills wasn't exactly cash register money. Turning off the water, Mari wrung out the rag and turned, speaking to Tatum as she brushed by. "Is Ty sick? We missed him yesterday. Tell him I hope he feels better soon." Without waiting for her reply, she continued into the dining room.

Dr. Grant was in a new spot. When he spied Mari nearing his table, he sat up, pushing his materials aside. "How are you today, Miss Coleman?" His tone entreated her to skip frivolities and supply an honest answer.

"Well, I heard what you said yesterday, and I'm ashamed of myself. I want to change, and I'm willing to take the necessary steps. Or at least the *first* step. That's my choice. But I'm scared."

He dipped his head. "Good girl. That's what I was hoping to hear."

She sighed. "Last night it hit me that the older brother has his own version of pig slop to leave behind. I don't want to be that kind of person anymore, having that kind of attitude toward people. Granted, I'm not exactly eager for what needs to happen, but if I'm at least willing—" She shrugged.

"That's huge—being willing."

"Yeah." She gave a wry smile. "I'm trying not to think about it too much, cause when I do I get mad at her again. Why can't things be fair? Why do I always get the short end of the stick? But there I go again."

"Didn't we already talk about 'fairness'?" He pivoted in his chair, regarding her. "So of all the people in your life, why did you ask to talk to me? Why did you pursue that conversation yesterday?"

Mari glanced back at the counter. "I don't know. I guess you've initiated spiritual conversations with me, and I trusted you."

He nodded. "Thank you. Do you trust me today?"

"Today?"

"Yes. Do you trust me?"

She hesitated. "What do you mean?"

"What if I had an idea that could help you?"

"What's your idea?"

"That's where I need you to trust me."

She eyed him. "It depends on what you're asking me to do."

"I'm asking you to trust. And keep in mind, Mari, that when that prodigal son came home, his father hurried to meet him. God's going to help you with this."

"Help me with what?"

He lifted his chin. "Go to Susan's before Mac's today. As early as you can get there."

"Why?"

"*Trust* me. You opened yourself to me yesterday. Surely that was a risk. Would you do it again?"

She blinked. "Are *you* going to be there?"

"No. But your Father will."

"You're scaring me." She knew he meant God.

"Yes. But you were already scared, weren't you? This is being scared in the realm of *help*. Will you do it?"

"You're not pulling a 'dad' on me and making me meet with JoyAnne, are you? I can't do that." She shook her head.

Dr. Grant's eyes narrowed. "Maybe it's time you forgave your father for what happened back then. Even good dads fail, you know. Maybe it's time you trust that your heavenly Father knows what's really going on and won't leave you out to dry. Maybe your heavenly Father knows how to defend you even when others get it wrong. Maybe—just maybe—he's got *good* in store for you. Have you ever thought of that?" He paused. "And on the other hand, you are completely free to say no to any of this. That is your prerogative."

Mari sniffed. "Well, we'll see."

Mari's stomach churned for the remainder of her Coffee Break shift. Dr. Grant hadn't specifically spelled it out, but she knew what was ahead: JoyAnne Strang would be at Mrs. Gordon's, and there would be another talk. The thought of it made her want to puke. She would rather endure another painful knee injury than subject herself to what was about to happen, but she didn't have a choice.

Well, technically she *did* have a choice, she admitted. No one was forcing her to do anything. *You are completely free to say no. That is your prerogative,* Dr. Grant had said. But having declared with her own lips that she was willing to take the necessary steps to press through, she was determined to hold herself to it. Plus Mac. She had told him she wanted to work things out with JoyAnne. How could she turn back now? Nevertheless, her walk through the Taiton parking lot was like navigating a mental war zone:

You can still back out.

You're not *backing out!*

You know what it's going to be like.

Doesn't matter. You're doing this!

You're just going to sit there and let her dump on you again—? Didn't you learn anything last time?

Dr. Grant's voice rose to her defense. *Maybe your heavenly Father knows what's really going on and knows how to defend you even when others get it wrong.*

But Mrs. G has it out for you. She's going to side with JoyAnne.

Keep in mind, Mari, that when that prodigal came home, his father hurried to meet him. God's going to help you with this. Trust me.

Trust.

Mari shut the car door and blasted the radio to drown out her thoughts as she headed for Riverview. There she joined her grandfather in the courtyard, where he shuffled behind his walker in the warm afternoon sunshine, his attending staff nearby. She accompanied him for a single lap around the broad oval path, explaining that she couldn't stay that day. She was stopping by only to say hello.

He turned to her with bright, inquiring eyes. "Don't you want—my pocket?"

She had been trying not to appear too eager, but there was that stir in her belly again. "I do," she said.

It was a little sprig of lilac—slightly crushed but fragrant and beautiful. No doubt from the bushes beside Mac's garage. Mari held the sweet blossom to her nose, then offered the stem to her grandfather. He closed his eyes, relishing its scent.

"It's no"—he struggled to express the word—"sssecret."

Mari blushed, shaking her head. "No, it's not. I like him. But I want to do the right thing. Pray for me, Poppy. I have a lot going on."

He nodded. "I pray."

When she got to Frost, she parked in front of Mac's. Visually sweeping the neighborhood, she spied two unfamiliar gentlemen across the street, enjoying their beers on the porch of Mac's elderly snowbird neighbors, who for as long as she had known them, resided in Texas until May. Her armed surveillance, no doubt. Check. With that in place, she resolutely faced the Gordons' house. She was plenty early. In some ways she wished she had stalled to cut the anticipated torture short. But here she was. *You got this, Coleman,* she told herself. With lead feet she climbed the porch steps to knock on Susan's door.

But no one answered.

Peering through the glass, she knocked again, then glanced around in relief. No lights on inside, no cars in the driveway. They weren't there yet, a delay to work in her favor, affording a comforting retreat to the safety of her home—er, Mac's home, she corrected herself as she topped his porch steps to let herself in. It felt like hers, having grown up in such a similar layout. She would wait there for Mrs. Gordon and JoyAnne to arrive. She could see their driveway from his sitting room window.

Meanwhile, since she was alone, she cut straight to the dining room to check Mac's journal again. She needed to know his exact wording: *Elena—reconciliation and healing of marriage.* She flopped the pages shut. Well, how much clearer could it be? So then why was Mac pursuing *her*? It didn't seem right. Neither did crushing on him knowing it. Especially with Will. It stirred up a multi-faceted guilt. Maybe it was better she *did* have a boyfriend, a protective barrier for misplaced emotions all around.

Impulsively she pulled out her phone, texting, "Hi, Will. Looking forward to seeing you tonight!" She added a smiley face and pushed send, hearing the resulting swoosh. Then she kicked herself. Now how did that help anything? She felt so mixed up.

Next door one of the dogs was going crazy. They were so annoying, she thought, eyeing Roger Eden's fence through the dining room sheers. That lovely, boarded fence. How absolutely inconsiderate of him to put that in. Wouldn't a chain link fence have been sufficient? Then at least Mac could look at something besides those vertical planks. Why a privacy fence? Why not simply put—

Mari cocked her head at a sudden thought. Indeed, *why* a privacy fence? It wasn't as though he was protecting his kids—he didn't have any. Did Roger Eden have something to hide? She frowned, considering the clean-cut gentleman next door. Everything about him was neat. His tidy front lawn, flawless boarded fence, sleek, muscular dogs. Without pause, her mind jumped to the crisply cut hole in Frost Park. And the nearly new camouflaged backpack. Could—could Roger Eden be connected to that money somehow?

She turned to glance at the foyer. Mac said Mr. Eden had stopped in on Saturday morning to thank him for the banana bread—and had invited himself in for a tour. A tour? Why would he need a tour of a house that was laid out practically the same as his? Could he have been looking for the backpack? It would have been buried under those damp towels at that point. She returned her gaze to the fence. Was he their backpack guy? Could Roger Eden have placed that bag of money in the field for someone? Or had someone perhaps placed it there for him?

She leaned toward the window to peek out toward the Gordons' driveway. No vehicles yet. Good. Turning for the stairs, she climbed hastily to enter Aubrey's former bedroom to survey the neighbor's yard from above, though hanging back so as not to be caught on his security cameras, which, she observed, were pointed outward beyond his yard, not simply downward. Why? What was he concerned about? Especially with that fence. Furthermore, he had told Mac that Aubrey had a habit of making faces at him, but how would he have seen her do that if he hadn't been looking up at her? Why had he been observing Aubrey in the first place? She shuddered. Her imagination was getting creepy.

His dog wouldn't stop barking. She could see only one of the animals below, straining at its chain, worked up in a frenzy about something farther back in the yard—a rabbit or squirrel perhaps. In her downward gaze she examined the lawn again for suspicious patchy spots, but nothing had changed from the scabby area she had previously noticed. Had Roger Eden been putting in an asparagus patch? Not a chance—even if it was right next to the fence. There was no garden in sight. Something wasn't right.

You're sleep deprived, she reminded herself. *You could be totally off.* Perhaps she was viewing everything through Aubrey's filter now. And as she and Mac had discussed in the night, what would a guy like that be doing with that amount of cash? But on the other hand, what if her gut feelings were correct? Should she tell the police? And say what—that she had bad vibes about Roger Eden because he had built a security fence and had cameras and Rottweilers? She had only suspicions, which could sound very foolish. Or her information could be important. It could go either way.

She decided she would let the police determine if Roger Eden was worth investigating, but her phone was downstairs on the table where she had set it after texting Will. Turning to go, she paused in the upstairs foyer, craning her head for a glance through Mac's partially open door, spying a few clothes on his bed, a sports water bottle on the end table, socks on the floor. *Mari Coleman, knock it off,* she commanded, directing her body toward the stairs.

Automatically her eyes dropped to the photo of Elena on the skinny table beside the door at the bottom. Shannon had voiced it once, but Mari couldn't agree more. "You had better be worth it," she muttered, reaching for the baluster as she rounded the bottom of the stairs. Then crossing the foyer, she looked up—right into the face of Roger Eden, who had unexpectedly appeared from the kitchen hallway. Instantly Mari lurched, belting out a shriek.

"Hey—hey, hey!" His hands flew upward. "Sorry—I'm sorry! I was looking for Mac, and your door was open! I thought he was here—I'm sorry!"

Looking for Mac. Right.

He was already waggling his phone in the air. "Let me call him! Truly, Margaret, I didn't mean to scare you! I called out when I came in, but you must not have heard me. I'm so sorry!"

"It's *Mari,*" she sputtered, trying to catch her breath. "Mac's not home. He doesn't get off work 'til later." Crud. Why had she told him that?

"Yeah—shoot, I should have known that. I apologize! I saw the door standing open and thought—anyway, I'm having some trouble over there and was looking for a hand." He jerked his head in the direction of his house.

"I'm working," she said.

"Not asking!" he returned. "Nope! It's nothing urgent. It can wait until he gets home." He met her eyes, not moving from his place in the foyer.

Mari swallowed, her heart racing. The way he was looking at her—she didn't like it. Was he sizing her up or something? Considering his options? He was searching for it, she bet. He had to be. Perhaps he had already checked his camera footage and had watched the bulging backpack rushed into Mac's house in the pouring rain. It was possible. Why else would he be there in the middle of the day?

In the split second of holding his gaze, she too weighed out her options, whether to suddenly make a fuss and demand that he leave or to keep up the polite façade until he left on his own—*if* he left. Or to simply take a mad dash for the street, which could look really stupid if she were wrong. Each of her choices carried risk. What would happen if—

Suddenly Mari heard a commotion behind her—voices and the shuffling of someone on the porch. Turning, she spied Leah DeSoto step up to tap on the screen door with a sober-looking JoyAnne Strang at her side—JoyAnne, who twisted her hands together in front of her, doubtless experiencing the same degree of anxiety for their impending conversation as Mari was. Nevertheless, their timing was impeccable. Mari had never been so glad to see the pair in her life.

"Come in!" she called eagerly to Leah, gesturing as she turned to explain. "I'm meeting some friends."

Once more, he flashed his hands. "I'll get out of your hair. Again, my apologies."

"I'll tell Mac you stopped." She motioned to Leah. "Hi! Come in! This is our neighbor, Roger Eden. And these are my friends, Leah DeSoto and JoyAnne Strang."

"Yes, I believe we've met. Hello, ladies. I was just leaving." He nodded curtly, passing them on his way out.

As the screen door closed, Leah threw Mari a strange look. "What was *he* doing here?"

Mari waggled her head. "Looking for Mac, he said. The door was open, and he walked right in! I didn't invite him!" At her first chance she needed to call the police.

"That's bold of him!"

"No kidding! Honestly, I'm glad you arrived when you did. He scares me." She wished she could say more, but this wasn't the time. Her eyes flicked to JoyAnne in her modest T-shirt and jeans. "Uh—hi. Where's

Susan?"

JoyAnne's brow rose questioningly. "Susan? Um, cleaning somewhere, I think. I'm not sure."

"I thought we were meeting with her."

"Oh. No, I asked Leah to come. I asked Susan if we could use her house, but we can meet here if that's okay with you. It's all the same to me." She glanced toward the living room.

"Uh—sure." Mari waved them to the couch. "Um, I'll get us some water." She veered through the dining room for her phone on her way to the kitchen. Guests or not, she was calling Mac.

But he didn't answer. Of course not. He was at work.

Filling the glasses at the refrigerator, she debated taking a minute to call the police right then, but she knew it wouldn't be quick. She would have to give them a thorough explanation of why she had suspicions about Roger Eden, and that would mean putting off JoyAnne. Though an attractive out, Mari knew it wouldn't be right to delay their talk. Roger Eden's trespassing needed to be communicated, but there didn't appear to be any outright emergency. Calling the police would have to wait, as would Mac. She lifted the waters in a cluster to carry them out. It was time to get this over with.

Chapter Twenty-Three

After delivering three glasses of water to their respective coasters on Mac's coffee table, Mari took her place on an armchair across from Leah and JoyAnne, awkwardly folding her hands in her lap to hide their shaking. It had been a beast of an afternoon so far, and it wasn't over. Next door Roger Eden's dog was still going at it.

Leah drew her water up for a sip.

JoyAnne stared at hers, rubbing her hands on her lap. She cleared her throat. "Um, I guess I'll start. I was visiting my friend Kyla last night, and while we were out on her patio, Dr. Grant stopped by to chat. She's their nanny, and she and Peter live in their upstairs apartment." She sniffed. "But, um—it turned into this sort of counseling session, and he recommended that I talk to you as soon as I could. I know we mentioned getting together sometime down the road, but he said he'd try to help make it happen sooner. I understand that this is hard for you, so, um—thanks for being open to this. It's hard for me too. I apologize if it feels like I'm charging you."

"It's fine," Mari responded politely, glancing up at Leah, who gave a reassuring smile.

JoyAnne blew out a long breath. "Well, I'm not quite sure how to frame this conversation, but it might be helpful for you to know some things. Last summer I was invited by some friends to a neighborhood picnic out on Richmond Road, where Kyla Watkins spoke for a few minutes. I was blown away by how similar her story was to mine, with her father leaving her when she was a kid, except that *both* of my parents left. Anyway, we were introduced, and she gave me her phone number. Then a few weeks later I came across her card and decided to call to ask if we could talk. I was curious at how she'd learned to cope with"—she shrugged—"you know—all that stuff. That night changed my life. She introduced me to Christ, and my whole world is different."

"I was at the same party," Leah interjected. "But I left before Kyla spoke."

Mari shifted in her chair. Where was this going?

"So since then, I've been meeting with Kyla and Doug's mom, Susan. We study the Bible and talk. Lots of talking. I know that you know what my life was like before, and I'm *not* proud of it. The more I learn about God the more ashamed of myself I become." She dropped her eyes. "But I'm—I'm growing."

"And you're *forgiven*," Leah added.

She nodded meekly, taking a sip of water. "Anyway, Kyla has this way of asking questions about what we read in the Bible so that we think about it and put it into practice. A couple weeks ago we were going through a chapter in Matthew. There was this verse that says that if you know someone has something against you, that you should go and be reconciled to that person before bringing your offering to God. Kyla asked me if there's anyone I needed to—" Her voice cracked, and she put her head in her hands, unable to continue.

They sat in uncomfortable silence as JoyAnne's tears dropped to her lap.

"Do you have any tissues?" Leah whispered.

Mari fetched a box from the dining room and set it on the coffee table. JoyAnne grabbed a few and blew her nose.

"Sorry," she squeaked, then dissolved into tears once more, holding her hand over her face.

Finally she blew her nose again and yawned to pop her ears. "I fooled myself into thinking I didn't have to deal with this because you weren't around, but that next weekend was my bridal shower—and there you were! I couldn't even believe it! I've, um—I've made a commitment to God not to lie or manipulate people anymore and to do what the Bible says, so I knew I had to talk to you." Her gaze lingered on the wad of Kleenex in her lap. Taking a breath, she looked up.

"Mari, where do I even start? I'm sorry for everything in our past. Will you please forgive me for the hateful way I've treated you?" Her mouth quivered as her eyes again brimmed with tears. "I've been mean beyond belief, and I wish I could say I didn't mean any of it, but it wouldn't be true. I've been cruel to you—unbelievably so—and I'm *so* sorry." She wiped her cheeks, throwing her a rueful glance.

Mari's mind was whirling. Was this really happening? "Uh—um," she murmured hesitantly as JoyAnne continued.

"For a long time now I've been eaten up with guilt for how I've hated you. I kept telling myself that it was because of *you* and the way you were, but I know that's not true. It was because of *me*. I think I obsessed on you as a diversion from how much I hated myself. Last night when Dr. Grant sat down with us, everything started to become clear. He started asking me about my family history and stuff. Just asking me questions. And he kept going down this road where all of a sudden, I could see some things about myself. Terrible, awful things. But also *why* I behaved like I did. All my fixation with my body; my boy-crazy, promiscuous behavior; all my competitiveness—and everything towards you." She sniffed, wiping her nose.

"Mari, I was—I *am* the queen of insecurity. All my self-esteem has been based on a desperate attempt to get attention and approval from anyone who would notice me and in whatever way I could get it. It was one never-ending performance. When you came along, you were the threat that blocked that goal, and I had to prove myself even more. All I wanted was to get you out of the way—to destroy you because you had what I wanted. I'm sorry I bullied you, Mari. I spread terrible lies about you. I did everything I could to tear you down in the eyes of others, and it was wrong. So wrong. I wish I could ask you to beat me up or something, but I know it doesn't work that way. It seems so lame, but all I can ask is for you to forgive me. Please."

Mari huffed, spreading her hands. "What could I have *possibly* had that you wanted so badly?"

JoyAnne shrugged. "Everything! You were smart and athletic and fun. All the teachers liked you. Plus, you had parents and a house. And nice clothes. Friends."

"I wasn't the only one with parents, JoyAnne. There was a whole class of us! And *you* had nice clothes and friends—a lot of friends!"

"I know. But not that I trusted. I never felt they liked me. All the girls were afraid of me, and the boys—well, you know what they wanted. And I'd see you come to school with your principal mom who'd kiss you goodbye—" She let out a breath. "Man, I was *so* irked with your lovey-dovey, picture-perfect life—but only 'cause I'd never had a mother to say anything positive to me ever. And then your dad—" She lifted a hand, sighing heavily. "Anyway, it was all *so* irrational, but I wanted to destroy you. The point is—the way I treated you was *wrong*, Mari, and I'm sorry! My envy soured into hatred, and I just got crazy—evil crazy."

Mari frowned. "My dad—? What *about* him?"

"Well, you *had* one, for one thing. I never had a father at all, much less one who affirmed me. Your dad was so nice. He would always say kind things to me and wouldn't stare at my chest and look at me in that—that lusty way, you know, which is ironic, 'cause that's how I *wanted* guys to look at me. But not him."

"When would my dad have talked to *you*?"

JoyAnne jerked her shoulder. "Oh, just random times—like parent-teacher conferences or after our school concerts. And at the gas station where I worked. All in passing. It was all just little things—like he'd tell me I did a good job, or I had a good voice, or I looked confident—little stuff like that. He probably wasn't even aware of it.

"Mari, look—I'm not here to grind anything in. None of this excuses my behavior, so don't think I'm trying to make you feel sorry for me. I only know I can't live with myself knowing how awful I was to you, so I'm pleading with you to forgive me. I don't want to be like that ever again. Talking to you scares the daylights out of me, but if I want to change, I have to face myself, and that means facing you."

Mari sat there stiffly, knowing she needed to respond. But it was hard. And having been repeatedly manipulated by JoyAnne didn't help things. She was nagged with suspicion. Was it happening again? How many years had she put up with JoyAnne's crap? How many years had she endured her condescending, devious smile? Not to mention Mari's own dad sympathizing with her! She never would have believed she would see the day JoyAnne would beg her forgiveness, and now what was she supposed to do? Just let her go? Boom—and done? Conflicting voices sparred within. Of course, she knew she needed to forgive, but she couldn't pretend it didn't matter. For once she was justified! For once! Everything in her wanted to twist the knife and twist it hard! But—

But.

The word loomed like a fork in the road. Mari stared at the coffee table as the image of the tiny seascape card from Mac popped into her head—the one with the little tab on its side. As Dr. Grant had said, right now she was at the mercy of the sea—a ship tossed in the tempest. And it was suddenly becoming clear to her that she didn't want to stay as *she* was either. But in order to forgive JoyAnne, in order to truly let anything go, and in order to see the change she desired, she needed to face *herself* too. Like the tab on the ornate card, here was the intersection of change.

Dr. Grant said that if she chose freedom, she would at least have a direction and a destination. *Just keep moving forward.* He knew the two of them were meeting right now, and she could imagine him rooting for her, along with Poppy and Mac. The professor was right: it *was* a choice. In her mind she saw Poppy nodding, as if encouraging her that she could do it.

Mari lifted her head, facing JoyAnne. "With all honesty, JoyAnne, you *did* treat me terribly—"

"I'm not defending myself, Mari. I *know* I did! That's why I'm here apologizing!"

"Hold on—let me finish!" She paused, steeling herself for what she needed to say. "*You* treated me wrongly, but I had choices too. I could have walked out of this conflict a million times, but I chose to hate you right back and let it steep inside of me. That was equally as wrong. And not only that—I certainly took my opportunities to jab you as often as I could. You're not the only one in need of forgiveness, JoyAnne."

JoyAnne's breath caught. "But it's *my* fault! I don't deserve—" Her words became all jumbled and muffled as she drew her hands over her face.

Leah straightened, looking anxiously between them.

In direct opposition to what she was inclined to do, Mari rose and slid onto the couch beside the crying girl, her heart pounding as she put her arm around her. JoyAnne shrank down, crying harder.

"JoyAnne, listen to me. We've had a horrible past. We've *both* been horrible to each other. And you saying all this today—I agree, it's time for it to end. So I'm cleaning the slate. I'm wiping it clean. You don't owe me anymore, JoyAnne. I *forgive* you. I forgive you for everything. Will you forgive *me*?"

In another burst of unintelligible words, JoyAnne turned to hug Mari tightly, and the two wept loudly together.

Somewhere during their crying, Mari heard shouting outside. Then came the tromping of hurried footsteps across the porch. Aubrey burst through the front door, yelling over her shoulder, "I am *not*! *You* are!" The screen door banged shut as she dropped her backpack onto the floor, calling, "Mari! Connor Haddington won't stop calling me a chicken-face!" She stopped short, staring into the living room. "What happened?"

Leah had already risen from her chair. "You girls take your time. I'll manage this. Hello, Aubrey! How was school today?"

Aubrey frowned. "What's wrong? Did something happen? Why are *you* here?"

"Nothing's wrong, sweetie. Something's *right*. Let's go outside, shall we?"

"But what *happened*?"

"I'll tell you outside." Leah turned Aubrey in the direction of the porch. "Do you know where the ball is? We could be the first ones to the field!"

"Connor's already there, and I need to get my snacks. Did someone die?"

"No. And yes, go get your snacks."

Reluctantly Aubrey disappeared into the kitchen, returning in a moment with a reusable tote bag. She peered curiously at Mari sitting so tightly beside JoyAnne on the couch. "Are you crying?"

Mari snatched a couple of tissues to blow her nose. "Yes. Don't worry. I'm all right."

Aubrey's eyes flicked to JoyAnne and back. "I gave Hailey the banana bread. She's taking it home to her mom."

"That's wonderful! It's all right, Aubrey. We're just talking. Nothing bad happened."

"Come on, hon," Leah urged, guiding her out. "Let's get the ball."

And then it was quiet.

Mari took a deep breath, sliding a little away from JoyAnne. "Well, I certainly didn't envision *this* happening today! But I'm glad it did."

JoyAnne gave a teary smile. "Me too. I'm so ashamed of who I was, Mari. I don't want to be like that anymore. I'm so sorry."

"I know—me too. But we're forgiven, right?"

She nodded, wiping her face. "Yes, thank God. But you have no idea how much regret I live with. So much regret. It's a constant battle. And not just with us. I've wrecked my whole life and my reputation."

"That can be restored."

"Right. But now I have two little girls who need me."

"It's not their fault. Your daughters are a blessing!"

"Yes, they are. But navigating visits with two separate fathers isn't easy. I wouldn't trade them for the world, and Douglas is wonderful, but it's been very difficult. I wish I would have done things right—like you."

Mari shook her head. "JoyAnne, stop. Don't you dare compare yourself to me. I've been the model of critically judging others. This right here shows you have far more courage than I—I would have never initiated this conversation! I haven't done things as right as you think."

"Well, I think we both owe Dr. Grant a huge debt of thanks."

"I second that!"

JoyAnne let out a breath. "But, um—there was something else I wanted to tell you." She paused. "I, uh—I heard that you had applied for the Sunlight job too."

Mari waved her hand. "It's okay."

"Well, I talked to the board about it, and I wanted to let you know I submitted my resignation for the position. I think you should have it."

"*What!*" Mari leaned away, stunned. "No!"

"You have more experience with the center and way more education in that field. I don't know how I got the job to begin with."

Mari shook her head. "*No!* You're not doing that!"

"I already did it."

Now it was Mari's turn to break into tears, as she was suddenly engulfed in a landslide of shame.

"JoyAnne, that was extremely thoughtful," she said when she could finally speak, "but if I get a call, I'll refuse the job. It can go to someone else—I don't care who—but I'm not taking it. The way you were with Ariel the other day—JoyAnne, you were *good*. I was impressed. The position belongs to *you*."

She shook her head. "I don't know. I don't know what I'm good at. Of course, all I've heard from Douglas' mom is how gifted you are with kids."

Mari snorted. "Seriously? Well, *that's* encouraging! The other day she rebuked me for not having proper emotional boundaries with Aubrey!"

"What? I'm sure she was only being cautious. She'd never hurt anyone on purpose!"

"I know. I guess I *have* gotten super-attached to the girl. Susan may be right. It's hard. I really love her. But anyway, I think you're the one for that Sunlight position."

JoyAnne nodded a meek thanks, and the two sat quietly.

"I'm glad it didn't work out to talk until today," JoyAnne said. "I really needed to have that conversation with Dr. Grant last night."

"He's a good listener. I just had one with him too."

"Yes. We talked a lot about how comparison breeds envy and jealousy and how self-destructive that can be—how it keeps you petty and immature. Honestly, I was so self-righteous and full of pride, so full of my own opinions. I just wanted to feel important. I wanted to *be* someone and have people like me. It gave me a sense of power—of feeling good about myself. But if anyone challenged that, I would twist things around to make it all about *them* so that I could be the victim. My attitudes and behavior stunk.

"Dr. Grant said I needed to expand my view of God." She smiled.

"He said I was like a dog who wanted another dog's bone, and I couldn't even see that my master has a whole storehouse full of them. He said I need to learn how much my Father loves me, that he's got enough love to go around to fill up everyone, and that he's big enough and wise enough to unfold his plan for *my* life if I trust him. I don't have to live my life grasping for significance."

"Oh, brother. That sounds totally like *me!*"

"The hardest thing was hearing him say that my jealousy had caused me to make a judgement against a gal who might have been a great friend, but now I'd never know."

Mari made a little sound. "Never say never. Hello, new friend."

JoyAnne shook her head. "Why would you ever want to be my friend? I've given you no reason to like me, much less trust me."

"I'm asking you the exact same question. But I'm in if you are." She extended her hand.

JoyAnne met her eyes. "Mari, I solemnly promise that I will do my best to be the kind of friend Jesus would approve of." She shook her hand. "I'm in."

The two looked at each other for a moment. Then JoyAnne let out a monstrous breath. "I am *exhausted!*"

Mari flopped back onto the cushion. "Me too!" And they both laughed.

JoyAnne motioned toward the door. "All right. I've kept you long enough. You have your after-school thing."

"I think Leah can handle it for a while."

"I'm sure she can. She's the best."

"I like her a lot." Mari rose to peek out toward the kickball crew, checking on how things were going. She turned back, sharing candidly, "Leah and Dan were here Friday afternoon. We got rained on in the field, and everybody scrambled for the house. Then last night we found an extra backpack in the foyer here." She gestured. "I thought it was Mac's, and he thought it was mine, so we opened it, figuring it belonged to a kid. It was packed full of money. *Lots* of it."

JoyAnne's jaw dropped. "What did you do?"

"Took it to the police, of course. But that got me thinking about Ariel, who you said ran across the field in the night." She paused. "You don't have to tell me anything, but I wanted you to know what happened. And I think the police need to know about that part too."

JoyAnne shook her head. "She didn't say anything about a backpack or money. She had nothing but the pajamas she was wearing." She paused, adding, "I probably shouldn't say anything, but she told me a crazy lady showed up at her house that night looking for her mom's boyfriend. His ex, apparently. The woman unleashed on him, and things got out of hand. Ariel walked in on him beating her, and then he threatened *her*, and that's when she ran to Susan's."

"Oh, boy! I hope he was arrested!"

"Not yet. That's part of the problem. It's like a mini-mafia over there. No one will rat him out. That's why it's not safe for her to go back there, especially now that she's pregnant. She says his name is Burne Batson, but everyone calls him Bats. And supposedly he carries one."

Mari gasped. "*No!* I know who that is! I saw him at Whitmore one night!" She shared with JoyAnne what had happened the night she had been looking for Ariel. "He's bad! They were chanting something, and *that's* what it was—his name, Bats! Someone brought him his baseball bat, but right then the police came, and everybody scattered. It's true—no one knew anything about it! JoyAnne, please tell me he's not the baby's father—is he?"

JoyAnne shook her head. "No, thank heavens! No, Ariel's got her heart all wrapped up in some lusty young buck over there who goes by the nickname of Cobra."

Mari's chin rose. "Ah. That explains—"

"Correct." Their eyes met. "She's so convinced he loves her, but I'm not so sure about that."

"Poor Ariel. And yikes—what is her mom thinking to have a violent guy like Burne Batson live there? That's nuts!"

"Right—so that's the thing. People are controlled by this guy. He's got a way of schmoozing people so that they do his dirty work. They want in, but then they can't get out. Even last week—that Whitmore funeral shindig—who do you think forks out money for a beer bash drug party like that? Everyone loves the guy at first, but there's a price to pay. Toxicology reported the guy died of a drug overdose, but there's plenty who wonder if he wasn't—you know—'disposed of' by this Batson fellow. It's scary. Ariel said the woman who came to her house was furious for Bats messing with her boys."

Mari shivered. "I hate to think of kids growing up in that environment! Right over there!" She pointed toward the field. "And Ariel! I always thought she was this shy, good girl from some nice, quiet family." She shrugged. "I mean—she came to my youth group!"

JoyAnne nodded soberly. "Well, she kind of was—until her mom got in with Bats. Things might have been a lot worse for her if it hadn't been for Susan's influence. She's the one who has brought her to church for years."

"Susan Gordon is a saint."

"Yes, she is."

They stood silently together.

"Well, thanks, JoyAnne. You didn't have to tell me all that. Nor do you have to share anything else."

"I don't know anything else—except that the police are still trying to find him. He's so slippery, and I wouldn't be surprised if that money you found was somehow tied to him. In fact, it's highly likely it is. I'm only glad Ariel got out of there."

Mari let out a breath. "Me too! At first I was devastated that she went to Susan instead of me, but know what—? That was about *me* trying to feel significant, exactly as you said just now. Why should I care who helped her, as long as she was getting help?"

"So I'm not the only pathetic creature in the room—? I'm still the winner, though!" JoyAnne grinned.

Mari laughed. "JoyAnne, you're *always* the winner! Come on—let's go help Leah."

"Wait!" JoyAnne caught her arm. "Can we pray? Let's thank the Lord for what just happened."

"Oh. Sure," Mari replied, a little embarrassed she hadn't thought to suggest it.

JoyAnne gripped Mari's hands. "Lord Jesus, thank you for shedding your blood to forgive us for our sins. And thank you for helping us to forgive each other. By faith we shut the door to the past and ask you to help us build from here. In Jesus' name we pray. Amen."

"Amen," Mari echoed, hugging her again.

As they exited the porch, JoyAnne motioned down the street. "What about that little convenience store by the bus stop? Could it have been robbed? Maybe that money was hidden to be picked up later."

Mari followed her gaze. "Dixie's? I haven't heard of any break-ins. Plus, I can't imagine Mr. Fordunger having that much money in the store. It was a lot. *I'm* wondering about our neighbor Roger Eden here. The way he showed up today—" She shuddered again. "I don't trust him at all!"

"The dog guy? Isn't he a pest exterminator? How would *he* get a load of money like that?"

"Maybe he stole it from someone's house."

JoyAnne raised an eyebrow. "Was he working at Burne Batson's by chance?" She nudged Mari. "Hey—looks like Leah needs help on the field. We should go."

As they started away, Mari glanced back at Roger Eden's. Now privy to Ariel's experience with Burne Batson, Mari had to agree with JoyAnne: Burne and his Whitmore gang were far more likely to be connected to that pile of money—and any associated illegal activity—than Mr. Eden. She supposed it was possible her imagination had slipped into hyperdrive, especially with wanting to validate Aubrey's interactions with him. Which made her a little glad she hadn't called the police earlier in her panic. For certain, Roger Eden was creepy and had zero social skills, but she had encountered Burne Batson firsthand, and comparatively, that guy was frightening. Nevertheless, she still didn't trust Roger Eden. Not at all. She would definitely be talking to Mac about his "visit." And notifying the police about him wouldn't hurt either.

Chapter Twenty-Four

Mari and JoyAnne arrived at the field to a stalled-out game with Aubrey facing Leah in an animated tizzy at the pitcher's mound. As Mari approached, Aubrey was pointing her finger at the ground, demanding that Ty be kicked out of the game.

"You *have* to send him home!" she insisted.

"Aubrey, settle down! It was an *accident*!" Leah responded calmly. "He didn't mean to knock you down! I saw it!"

"But Mari said that if he hurt anybody—"

"What's going on here?" Mari asked, breaking in.

Aubrey turned in relief. "Tell Miss Leah that Ty has to go home! He pushed me!"

Leah faced Mari, her brow rising. "Ty and Aubrey accidentally collided. Miss Bossy Boots here says he needs to leave. Please advise."

Aubrey dug her hand into her hip. "You *said*!"

"Did Ty really mean to hurt you?" Mari asked. Their conflict was becoming a wearying theme.

"Yes! It was the *way* he bumped into me. He shoved me with his shoulder!"

Mari glanced around for Ty, who was currently roughhousing with another player in the outfield. She sighed. "Be right back."

But when Ty spied her coming, he automatically started for home. "This game sucks," he said. "I don't want to play anyway!"

His tough-kid façade couldn't hide his rejection. Mari pictured his little heart like an electrical cord, searching for a place to plug in.

"Ty, wait!" she called, trotting to catch up. She touched his arm. "Hey, I didn't see what happened, so I was going to let you stay. If you have to leave, though, it's all right. But listen—if you ever need someone to talk to, you can come to me, Ty. I'll listen. I'm safe. And I'll help you, okay?

You know where I live. I mean—I'm always at Aubrey's after school." She gestured toward the house.

Ty glanced briefly at her, then tugged his arm away and took off across the field.

"You *never* listen to me," Aubrey accused when she returned.

Mari spread her hands. "He went home!"

"But you shouldn't have talked to him!"

"My work is done here," Leah said sweetly, meeting Mari's eyes. "I'll turn this over to you."

Mari scooped up the ball. "Aubrey, relax. It's going to be okay." She looked up, calling to the rest of the children. "Okay, everyone—sorry I'm late today! Thank you, Miss Leah, for getting things started! Now let's finish this game!"

Aubrey folded her arms. "See! You don't care about me!"

Mari blinked, then bent to whisper in her ear. "Young lady, I care about you more than any kid here! Now take your position before I make you sit out!"

As the pouty girl dragged herself to first base, Mari was suddenly blown away by a new perspective. Was this what it was like years ago for her dad with JoyAnne and her? Her dad, Mr. Kindhearted to the outcast. She shook her head in enlightened wonder.

The play resumed, and before long their game came to a close. Mari waved everybody in, announcing that Aubrey had supplied the treats. It was then that she noticed *three* people on the sidelines—Leah, JoyAnne, and Mac—who raised his hand to her in acknowledgment. A swirl of happiness shot through her.

Aubrey, too, beamed when she saw him. "That's my dad!" she told every peer as she doled out her snack bags. "My dad is here!"

When they were nearly finished, Mari pointed to the sky. "Everybody—arms up! Who can tell me what this means?"

"God always hears us when we pray!" a child called out.

"What else?"

A few blank expressions. And then someone piped up: "You can pray about anything?"

"Yes! Now how about this?" She pointed to the ground, producing a collective groan.

"We *know*. Pick up our trash!"

"See you tomorrow!"

"Impressive!" Mac said when she joined the cluster on the sidelines.

"Nice job!"

His smile was so warm. "Thanks. You're home early!"

"Yeah. It just—I felt like I should come home." He glanced over his shoulder toward the men still on the porch across the street. "And I saw that you called."

Mari's brow rose. "Right. I need to talk to you about something important as soon as possible."

"I've been telling Mac about our little pow-wow this afternoon," JoyAnne commented.

Mac nodded approvingly, giving Mari a thumbs-up. "Pretty amazing! Way to go, both of you!"

"I want to tell you about that too!" Mari said. She smiled at JoyAnne.

"Sorry. We need to get going," Leah broke in regretfully. "I'm supposed to meet Danny at school in ten minutes."

"Okay," Mari said. "Thanks for your help and support today. And for hanging out."

"You're quite welcome, friend," Leah said, kissing her cheek. "By the way, I left a bag on your front seat. It's an extra Bible, in case you need it for the girl you're meeting up with."

"Thank you."

"I'll probably see you tomorrow," JoyAnne said, hugging Mari goodbye. "Kyla and I walk on Wednesdays." She motioned to the field.

"I look forward to seeing you," she said, waving them off as they left. Then noticing that the kickball had wandered, she went to retrieve it while Aubrey chattered on to her father about her day.

"—and she was *crying*! I seen her!" she was telling her father as Mari returned.

"*Saw* her," Mari corrected.

"Talk about an amazing turn of events!" Mac exclaimed.

"I know! It was a *miracle*," Mari said simply. "I can't wait to tell you about it."

"I can't wait to hear about it," he said.

Those eyes. There went that wonderful rush again.

Aubrey looked between them. "What was a miracle? What are you talking about?"

Mac suddenly frowned, turning toward the street. "Looks like you've got some more company today!"

Mari gave a cry of surprise. It was Will! What was *he* doing here? She lifted her hand in a wave as he pulled his lime-colored Jeep alongside the curb.

"Hi! This is unexpected!" she called as he got out of his vehicle.

As they met on the boulevard, Will strode up to greet Mari with a big kiss. "I just got off," he declared, slipping his arm around her waist. "Thought I'd stop by and join the action here. Gotta see what my girl is up to!" He tipped his head, meeting Mac's eyes.

"Mr. Wallace," Mac returned quietly.

"Wow, um—crazy timing," Mari stammered, her pulse racing. "Mac just got here too! He's, um—home early, and we just finished our game. Of kickball." She patted the ball and gestured as Will surveyed the field and the few lingering children still playing there. He looked back at Mac and Aubrey.

Mac cleared his throat. "Well, since I'm home, there's no sense in you hanging around, Marissa. I got it from here. You're free to go!"

Aubrey gave a cry. "What? She can't go! I didn't tell her about school yet! Or Hailey. Plus, my homework—she has to help me! And I need to make my volcano!"

"I've got it, Aubs," Mac said.

"I'm not *Aubs*, Dad!"

Mari handed Aubrey the ball. "You can tell me first thing tomorrow—I promise."

"We never even got to talk!"

Mac spread his hands. "What am I—chopped liver?"

"You'll have a special night with your daddy," Mari told her. She looked at Mac. "But I *do* need to talk to you about a few things." He absolutely needed to know about Roger Eden.

He nodded dismissively. "Right. We can discuss those things tomorrow too. You two have a good night. Come on, squirt."

Aubrey huffed in protest, stomping off and muttering that she *never* got to talk to Mari.

"I can't believe you *like* this job," Will murmured through his teeth as the father and daughter reached the porch steps.

She and Will were so different, Mari thought, turning to him. So different. "Do you want to get dinner somewhere?" she asked.

"It's kinda early, but sure. Where do you want to go?"

"Anywhere casual enough to put my leg up. I overdid myself, and my knee aches."

He raised an eyebrow. "The Wok?"

Mari sighed. "Fine. Meet you there."

Starting her vehicle, she paused to look over at Mac's house, her mind an emotional tumbler. It stung that Mac had so abruptly dismissed her. He had *intentionally* quit the conversation—just dumped her onto Will and walked off. But then—but then why wouldn't he, with Will, her *boyfriend*, right there, walking up to kiss her like that! She groaned, rubbing her forehead. The way those two had looked at each other—Will glaring at Mac, as though challenging him to a duel. Oh, brother! She and Will needed to talk, but how would that go over now? Everything was getting so complicated.

Her eyes dropped to the package from Leah on the passenger seat. She pulled the plastic off a purple embossed Bible and rubbed her thumb over the nubby design. That's right. She still had the thing with Candace to figure out. Bummer. She could probably rule out Mac's help now.

At the Wok Mari picked a sunny booth by a west window because she was cold. Will talked about his work for a while, which was fine with Mari, since she had a lot on her mind. But eventually he changed the subject.

"Do you think God would judge someone if they did something wrong but had good intentions?"

Mari had given up on her chopsticks and was scraping together her fried rice with her fork. She looked up at him. "What do you mean?"

"Like if people mean well, do you think it's still sin?" He popped a piece of sauced chicken in his mouth, talking as he chewed. "Think about all the people in the world who just want to live good lives and be good people. How could a loving God condemn them to hell? I mean, I *get* that evil people deserve hell, but what about the nice ones? There's plenty of good people out there."

She studied him a moment. "Where's the line between right and wrong then? Who determines that?"

"I'm not sure there is a line. Maybe it's about our *intentions*."

"Then who defines sin?"

Will pointed with his chopsticks. "Exactly! That's what I mean! Who's to say what sin is? Maybe something is sin to *you*, but it's not to *me*. It's not black and white."

Mari frowned. "But how does that play out? What if I think it's right to steal your bike? Then which is it—right or wrong?"

He huffed impatiently. "But that's universal. Everyone knows stealing is wrong! I'm talking about ambiguous things."

"Okay. I'm Robin Hood—I steal from the rich to give to the poor. Good intentions, right? I steal your bike to give it to a poor kid. Is that wrong? I steal your car and give it to my cousin who doesn't have one."

"You know what I'm trying to say!"

"I do, but I don't agree. That makes sin a moving target. I think there *are* absolutes, and *God* determines what they are. Stealing is one of them."

"Right, but doesn't the Bible say that God sees our hearts? Wouldn't he know if you had good intentions or not?"

"Well, that *is* true, yes, but it's only *part* of the Bible. The Ten Commandments spell out pretty clearly what's right and wrong."

Will held up a finger. "Those were *Jewish* rules. And that's another thing. There's a big difference between saying the Bible is the Word of God versus a collection of words *about* God."

"What do *you* think it is?"

Will shrugged. "I don't know. I mean—who's to say? Plus the 'one way to heaven' thing." He loaded his chopsticks with another chunk of sushi. "I don't know. Maybe God weighs our good deeds against our bad deeds whether we believe in Jesus or not."

"Where's the good news in that, Will? Isn't the gospel the 'good news of salvation through Christ'? We could never be good enough. It'd be like trying to jump to the moon!"

"Well, there are good people in all religions, aren't there? Why are Christians suddenly the exclusive club?"

Mari blinked. "I thought you believed in God, Will."

"I *do*! But aren't there other valid belief systems in the world too? Who's to say Jesus is the only way? Peter Watkins acts pretty confident about everything, but I have a lot of questions."

"Peter Watkins? What does this have to do with him?"

"He invited me for coffee last night, and we talked."

She dropped her arm. "You didn't tell me that!"

He snorted. "I have a life, you know! He called, and I decided to go. What were *you* doing last night—washing your hair? Anyway, it just got me thinking about what I really believe."

Mari stared at him, debating whether to tell him about visiting the police station with the camouflaged backpack. So much had happened lately. Right now she felt worlds apart from him. "So are you going to his group tomorrow? I'm going to the women's study." And JoyAnne. She hadn't told him about JoyAnne either.

"Yeah, I'll go. He's an interesting guy. And it sounds like he wants me to come even if I have questions. He's pretty excited about the Bible study."

"Good. So, hey—remember that girl, JoyAnne Strang? I had a conversation with her today. She's the—"

"Isn't she that floozy marrying your old neighbor? The nasty girl from the bridal shower?"

Mari nodded. "Yes. She came to apologize for the way she treated me in high school. It blew me away."

Will cocked his head. "No way! Are you kidding me? Hmm, I smell a rat! What does she want?"

"She wanted my forgiveness. We reconciled."

He choked into his hand. "Whoa! Who are you, and what have you done with Mari Coleman?"

She smiled. "It was pretty wild!"

"Are you sure she's not manipulating you for something? I'd be careful!"

Mari took a drink of water and stared at her ice. They needed to break up, but was now the time? If she gave him the axe tonight, would he still go to the Bible study? She wanted him to go. But *why?* she asked herself. How had Will's spiritual life become her problem to solve?

"What are we doing tonight?" she asked.

Will shrugged. "I don't know. I have a headache. I didn't sleep well after having coffee so late."

"I had a short night too," she mused, recalling her middle-of-the-night conversation with Mac. Should she tell Will what happened with Roger Eden walking into Mac's house? She absolutely needed to call Mac about it. "Maybe we should take a raincheck."

"I'm down with that," Will said, tossing his napkin onto his plate. "Let's talk tomorrow—after the group thing."

The moment Mari was in her car after leaving The Wok, she immediately called Mac, but he didn't pick up. She called him again on her drive home and once more in the Kingswood parking garage, but each time the call went to his recording. The last time she left a message.

"Hey, Mac—it's Mari. Hey, I wanted to let you know that Roger Eden came into the house while I was upstairs this afternoon, and I didn't have a good feeling about it. He said he was looking for you, but he might have been looking for that bag. Plus a few other things didn't feel quite right. Um, can you call me back? If you want. Or we can talk tomorrow. Bye."

She sat unmoving in the driver's seat, staring at her phone. Why wouldn't he answer? She had hoped to talk all the Roger Eden stuff through with him before calling the police. Although now, in light of her talk with JoyAnne about Burne Batson and all the gang activity in Whitmore, did it even matter? Still, she wanted to tell Mac about it. She sighed. He could be busy. Maybe he had company. Or maybe he was doing something with Aubrey—her volcano project perhaps. She would give him another hour, she decided. Maybe when Aubrey was in bed he would call her.

Shannon and Colton were addressing wedding invitations at the dining room table. Mari joined them for a while, but her phone remained silent.

"Weren't you and Will getting together tonight?" her mom said, passing through.

"We had dinner and called it an early night."

She frowned. "Are you all right?"

"Yeah. Just tired," Mari replied.

"I wonder why!" Shannon remarked, throwing her a look.

Mari simply rose. "I'm going to bed."

But she tossed and turned between the sheets. Mac. Why wouldn't he call her? But she knew the answer: because of Will. Something had changed when Will had showed up at his house and kissed her like that. She had felt it—as though Mac had taken a giant step back from her. She rolled over, reaching for her phone one last time, eyeing his number. Everything in her wanted to try again, but she sent a combined text to Leah and JoyAnne instead.

"Hi. I'm struggling with something tonight. Asking for prayer." She added a second text. "It's unrelated to you, JoyAnne."

JoyAnne texted back immediately. "On it!"

Leah's text followed shortly: "Praying for you, friend. Call if you need to talk."

In the morning when Mari went to the kitchen, her mother was eating cereal at the island, scrolling through her phone. "You're up early."

"Trying to read my Bible more," Mari responded. She dropped a bagel into the toaster and went to pour her coffee.

"Good for you! I have to say—I have mixed feelings about you going to work today. There was a murder in Whitmore last night! A man was shot!"

Mari whirled. "What? *Who?*" Oh, please, not one of the Wests. She hurried to the table as her mom tapped to enlarge the picture.

"No one we know," she said, holding it out. "He's not even from

New Hampton. He's from out west—Seattle. They're still searching for the suspect."

"What happened?" Mari studied the photo, not recognizing the victim, although something about him did look vaguely familiar.

"Doesn't say. Maybe drug-related. Or a burglary. Who knows?"

"Crazy!"

"Yes! With Ariel gone missing and now *this* happening—it makes me nervous! That's way too close to Frost! You better be careful over there!"

"I'm careful. And Ariel showed up. She was, um—staying with some friends." Mari wondered how long she would need to keep Ariel's information in confidence.

"Did she? Well, that's a relief! Thank God for that! Still, keep your eyes open and be *smart*."

"Always, Mom. Can you send me a screenshot of that? I'd like to show Mac."

"Of course." She completed the task and set her phone aside. "Come sit. Seems like we haven't talked for a while. How are things at the coffee shop?"

"Good!" Mari set her mug on the counter. "One of the girls there—Candace—is interested in learning about the Bible."

"That's great! And at Mac's—?"

Mari looked down at her cup, wishing she could divulge everything to her, yet in light of the murder now, her mom would freak if she learned about that backpack of money. That brought crime into Mac's very house! Plus, what would she think about her sudden feelings for him? She opted to stay shallow. "Well, there's some stuff going on, but I like what I'm doing. It's a good fit."

"Good. I'm glad."

Chapter Twenty-Five

Mari arrived at the Coffee Break early that morning, even before Tatum arrived. As usual, it took some time for her to fulfill her regular responsibilities, but at her first opportunity Mari went to give Dr. Grant a brief report of what had happened the previous day with JoyAnne.

He slapped her a high five. "Fantastic! I'm so proud of you!"

"I was scared to death, but thanks for setting up the meeting."

"Well, now, I couldn't exactly have two women crying on me about the same issue and not do anything about it! I'm relieved it worked out as it did."

"I'm still pinching myself! The craziest thing is that I think we might actually become friends. I know that's not a requirement for forgiveness, but the way she was—well, her humility totally surprised me, and it makes me want to know her for who she is. I guess once I got out of self-protection mode, my perspective changed."

"Bingo!" He lifted his hands in a quiet applause. "I have to say—I'm extremely impressed with both of you ladies! Nine out of ten people would have made up some excuse not to go there. Truly! It's rare to see people work out an issue like this."

"It wasn't easy! There was a lot a pride to swallow. But I think what you said about forgiving my dad really helped me be more open to talking again. There's no way parents can fully understand their kids. He was doing his best back then, but he didn't know everything. He isn't God. Like you said, even good dads fail."

"That's true. Only God is a perfect father."

"I'm learning that, yes. Plus, there's no way I could fully understand everything my parents did back then either. I didn't have the full picture. Anyway, thanks again for your part in this, and if you think of it, would you pray for me? I've got a few other things going on."

"More opportunities to trust God?"

"I guess so."

When the 9:52 rush started pouring in, Mari took her station behind the counter.

"Where's Tatum?" Candace called over the hiss of the steamer. "Did she leave?"

Mari glanced around. "She's here somewhere."

"Well, who's checking the front case?"

"Got it!" Alyssa said and swung around the counter. "Almost out of fruit cups!" she announced.

"I'll get them," Mari offered, quickly turning for the kitchen. But as she rounded the corner, she discovered Tatum West and the manager in a heated discussion next to the work counter. Both turned to look at her.

Mari motioned toward the fridge. "I'm—here for fruit cups."

The manager jerked his head, and Mari went to gather an armload in uncomfortable silence. With a brief smile, she scooted out of the kitchen.

"What's going on between the manager and Tatum?" she whispered to Candace when she had returned to her station.

Candace craned her head in surprise. "What? A love tryst in the kitchen?"

"No! It was something serious!"

Candace shrugged, handing her a finished order. "Beats me! A manager meeting?"

A few minutes later, Tatum was back to work in her typical brisk and silent manner. Mari eyed her covertly, imagining what her life might be like at Whitmore. As if sensing it, Tatum turned to glance toward her, and Mari quickly returned her attention to finishing her current order.

Eventually Mari needed to bus tables again. She zipped efficiently through the lounge side to finish in the main dining area. Setting aside the bin of dirty dishes, she paused to talk to Dr. Grant.

"I've been thinking about something you mentioned the other day," she said. "We were talking about the prodigal son story and how there was no resolution in the story for the older brother. You said you thought those boys had the same problem—that they didn't know their father's heart for them and that there was a solution for that."

Dr. Grant leaned back, folding his arms.

"So what's the solution?" she asked. "That's *me*. I mean, I've always known God loves me, but I don't feel it, and I'm obviously missing something because look at how I was behaving—just like the older brother. What does it mean to know the Father's heart for me? How do I find that?"

He smiled. "Great question! It's what I'm pursuing now."

"And—? Help me out here!"

"Are you sure you want to go there?"

"What do you mean? Why wouldn't I?"

"It might not be what you expect."

She eyed him thoughtfully. "Okay, I hear you. But here's the deal. When I was with JoyAnne yesterday, she—" Mari shook her head. "The way she was and the way she talked about God—about *Jesus*—it was different. There was a light in her eyes, and I don't have that. I don't have that excitement in my life. That humility. And gratefulness."

He sat up. "If you want God, you have to pursue him. Seek him. He's drawing you, isn't he?"

She nodded.

"He wants to be found. Ask the Holy Spirit to reveal the Father's heart to you. He will, if you truly want him. Ask him to show you who Jesus is and how he reflects the Father."

"Okay, I will."

"The other thing is that God expresses his love through people. Kyla's dad, Kendall, was key in my life. He helped me get established as a new believer. And our parents are super important too. How's your relationship with your dad? Our parents represent God to us when we're young. Sometimes our view of God gets locked onto what our earthly dads were like. The most freeing thing is to forgive your dad for his faults and failures and acknowledge that only God is infinitely perfect, as you said earlier. I believe it opens us up to receive more of God's love."

"Huh. Our relationship is good," she responded. "Although I'm seeing how critical I was of him when I was young. He wasn't perfect, and I forgive him, of course, but he didn't deserve the way I judged him. I'm starting to see things in a new way."

"That's good. Well, I'm a staunch advocate of people getting to know their fathers. It's kind of a soapbox thing of mine. I squandered my relationship with mine."

Mari smiled. "My dad is coming home this weekend."

"Nice! I hope you have some quality time together."

"Thanks."

"And now I have a question for *you,* unrelated to this subject." He shifted in his chair. "Have you ever noticed those tight long-sleeved shirts

Tatum wears under her uniform? Not all the time. But often."

She followed his gaze to where Tatum worked behind the counter.

He stared thoughtfully for a few seconds before turning back to Mari. "Why does she wear those? It's warming up outside. She can't be cold."

Mari glanced again toward Tatum. "I don't know. Style? Comfort? Personal preference? Why?"

"I don't know," he said.

"I've never thought about it."

"Nor I, until today. It just struck me as peculiar a minute ago. No matter. Perhaps she has eczema or something." He shrugged, pulling a stack of papers to him. "Mari Coleman, it's been a pleasure."

"Same. See you tomorrow."

As she went about cleaning a few machines, Mari furtively studied Tatum, pondering his question—until they were interrupted a short minute later by a herd of baby-faced high schoolers entering the dining room. Dang. Another rush. And right before her shift was over too. She watched the prospective students line up en masse to stare at the menu. Dutifully she took her position in the narrow corridor, staying to fill orders until the noisy youngsters were settled in the seating area.

When she finally finished, Mari changed her clothes in the restroom and headed for the parking lot. All day long Poppy's pocket had been in the back of her mind, and now it was all she could think about. As she hit the doors, however, she found Tatum on the steps having a smoke. Mari passed her, then on a whim paused at the bottom to address her.

"Is there anything I can do for you, Tatum?"

Tatum jerked back. "What the heck kinda question is that? What do you want?"

"Nothing! Sorry. Just asking." When there was no reply, she nodded. "All right then. See you tomorrow."

But as she started for her car, Tatum spoke up behind her. "Ty didn't come home last night."

Mari pivoted in surprise.

The woman exhaled a puff of smoke. "Do you know where he is?"

Mari shook her head. "No. He was with me after school, but he took off early. Have you called the police?"

"Oh, he's around."

"Do you need help finding him?"

"I expect he'll come home. He's gotta eat." She took another draw on her cigarette, looking away.

Recalling the Whitmore news on her mother's phone, Mari couldn't let it go. She took a step toward her. "Tatum, he's a child. If he's missing, you should go to the police. I'd be willing to take you if you'd like. Let me go with you."

"It's okay. He'll show up."

Why won't she look at me? Mari wondered. She always looked away. Her eyes dropped to Tatum's spandex undershirt. *Eczema.* Or something else. Her pulse quickened.

"Tatum, is there something going on at home? Do you need help?"

She straightened defensively. "Do I look like a charity case?"

"No. You look like someone who's afraid."

Tatum met her eyes. "I can take care of myself."

"I won't argue with that. You're incredibly strong. But I suspect you need help."

"Did John tell you?"

John, the manager. Was that what they had been talking about? "No. No one's told me anything."

She pointed the cigarette. "Well, you just mind your own business."

"Tatum, if you're being abused, it *is* my business. There are places you and Ty could go to be protected. I know of legal assistance, counseling help, child advocacy workers, and—"

"Stay out of it!"

"I know some of these people personally. They would help you. Come with me, Tatum. Let's go to the police."

Tatum's eyes narrowed. "You're so clueless! You obviously don't know what it's like to have your kids in danger. There's a time to leave well enough alone so things don't get worse. I'm handling this."

"And there's a time to *not* leave well enough alone so that things can get *better*! Listen to me—"

Tatum threw the burning stub to the pavement. "I'm *not* going to the police, so you can get out of my face!"

"Tatum, you can trust me. I'm on your side."

"I trust *no one*."

Mari regarded her for a moment. "All right. What would you like me to tell Ty if he shows up?"

"Tell him to come home."

Mari tipped her head. "Done. Mind if I take a look at your cigarettes?"

Tatum huffed. "You don't smoke."

Mari beckoned the woman to hand them over, then scribbled her phone number on the bottom of the pack before returning them. "If you call me, I will answer."

Mari's head was spinning as she left Tatum and headed to her car in the student center parking lot. Well, well, well! She had heard it from Tatum's own lips: *you obviously don't know what it's like to have your kids in danger.* How much clearer could it be? Mari certainly wasn't going to mess around with that kind of information drop; she was going directly to the police. And *kids*—plural. She wasn't sure how old Trey was, but Ty was unquestionably a minor, which called for action on his behalf.

Mari uttered a helpless groan at Tatum's impossible attitude. Had she guessed correctly about that ornery woman? Was that spandex undershirt hiding bruises? If so, from whom? From some jerk boyfriend? Or an acquaintance of Trey's? That thug Burne Batson perhaps? Bats. She pictured him again smashing his fist on her window with the hellish images crawling up his inked arms.

And now Ty was missing. What was going on there? Was he really missing, as in "missing child" missing, or had he run away? Did Ty have a habit of disappearing, or was he in danger? Did this have anything to do with the stuff he had supposedly stolen from Trey or—or with the murder over there last night? Heavens—she hoped not! Regardless of the reason, why wouldn't Tatum go to the police? But *Mari* was going to the police, she determined—right now before going to the nursing home! And her list of what she needed to tell them was getting rather long.

Now almost at her car, she checked the time. When she looked up, she was surprised to spy Candace leaning against the passenger door of the car next to hers, obviously waiting for her.

"Candace! What's up?"

The girl smiled amiably, fingering a cigarette. "Nothing. Just chilling." She drew a strand of pink hair behind her ear. "Where are you off to now?"

Mari smiled politely. Dang, this had to be the hundredth time the police had been put on hold. She gestured to her car. "I visit my grandfather before my childcare job. I watch an eight-year-old after school."

"Ah. Sounds fun."

With effort Mari hit the brakes to take a moment with her. "It *is* fun. Mostly. So what's going on? You don't usually wait around after work."

"Just wanted to say hi."

Influence. Dan DeSoto's words dropped from out of the blue. *God has given you influence. What's your message? It would be a shame to waste an opportunity like this.* Candace was looking to her for something. Friendship probably. And yet Mari's time was limited. She couldn't simply hang out today. Rather than rolling with the conversation, she decided to take control of it.

"Well, I'm glad you're here. I have something for you," she said, opening her car door to snatch from her passenger seat the Bible Leah had given her. "Here. My friend gave it to me to give to you."

Candace stared at it in surprise.

"I'll be honest, Candace. This plan of getting together is all new to me. I grew up going to church, but I never really invested myself in knowing God. I'm not bailing on you, but would you mind if the two of us met with someone else? I know someone who might be better at leading this than me. Then you and I could attend as friends."

"What about Quinn?"

"Her too—the three, well, four of us. And I'll find a Bible for her too."

She nodded. "Yeah. That'd be okay."

"Good. And hey, I wanted to tell you—remember the girl I was talking about to the professor the other day? The one I had the conflict with? Well, we met up yesterday and talked!" Mari then revealed to Candace what had happened with JoyAnne.

Candace's mouth dropped open. "There is *no way* that happened!"

"I was floored too! I wish you could have seen it!"

She waggled her head in awe. "I have *never* heard of people working things out like that. In fact, I don't think I've ever had *one* person apologize to me for anything in my entire life!"

"Oh, I'm sorry to hear that."

Candace snickered. "I guess that makes you the first!"

Mari laughed. "Right! Look, Candace—I need to get going. I'll see you tomorrow, okay?" She gave her a quick hug.

As Mari got on her way to the police station, she made a mental note to get in touch with Kyla Watkins.

Unfortunately, the officer who had taken her and Mac's previous statements was off duty, and Mari ended up relaying all her information to someone unfamiliar with the backpack case. Worried that she would forget important details, she let everything tumble out at once, a jumble of concerns about Ty, Tatum, Roger Eden, and Ariel.

"Take your time, Miss Coleman!" the officer said, motioning her to a chair opposite his desk. He pulled a form from a shelf behind him and handed it to her. "First, you'll need to fill out a missing person's report. We'll need a full name and description and any other details you can share, like what he was wearing—shirt color, hat style, the like. Plus any recent pictures—"

"No, not me." Mari shook her head. "*I'm* not filing the report. I only heard from his mother less than an hour ago that he's missing. I encouraged *her* to come in, but she wouldn't. I'm just letting you know about it. I'm concerned for his safety."

The officer looked at her a moment, then set the paper aside, turning to his laptop. "All right, let's start again."

"All I'm saying is that I believe Tatum West may be a victim of domestic abuse, and there's a child in her home who may be in danger. He's gone missing. I would like to recommend an investigation."

Tap, tap, tapping of keys.

"Has Ms. West told you of any such encounters with her or her son?"

"No."

"Have you witnessed any altercations, abuse, or signs of abuse—bruises and so on?"

"With Tatum—no, but the clothing she wears and her demeanor make me suspicious." She shared with the officer the conversation she had just had with Tatum in the Coffee Break parking lot, as well as Ty and Trey's interactions, and Ty's black eye.

"And when did these events occur?"

"Um, last Wednesday and Friday."

"Would you consider Tatum to be a vulnerable adult?"

"No. But Ty's a child, and I'm pretty sure he's got some kind of alphabet letters going on."

"And to your knowledge, how long has he been missing?"

"Well, he was at kickball yesterday after school, but his mom said he didn't come home last night."

"So less than twenty-four hours."

"Yes."

"And kickball?"

"I have an afterschool kickball club at Frost Park that Ty comes to. An informal neighborhood thing for children."

"And your relationship to Ms. West?"

"Coworker."

"And she didn't act concerned about her son—?" His eyes rose questioningly to hers.

"No, but look, officer—I think she's *afraid* to report this! She's a tough lady, but she is tight-lipped and terrified right now. That's the vibes I'm getting anyway. I don't know—maybe I'm wrong. Maybe it's something with her other son, Trey. He's definitely going down the wrong path. In fact, I wouldn't be surprised if he or someone in Whitmore were somehow involved with that backpack of money! But we reported that before."

"Uh-huh. Any evidence of substance abuse with Ms. West?"

"No evidence. But those long-sleeved shirts—" She shrugged. "Who knows? And I'd guess it's likely with Trey."

"All right." He frowned, making a few edits. "And again, how is this business with the Wests related to your neighbor, Mac Eden?"

"*Roger* Eden. And he's Mac Sinclair's neighbor, not mine. Mac's my employer. And I don't think the two are related at all."

He looked up. "So you're saying—"

"I'm saying I *also* have suspicions about Roger Eden regarding the backpack of money that was found. He's got security cameras on all sides of his house and two Rottweiler dogs. And yesterday he walked into Mac's house uninvited while I was there. I think he was looking for it! He told me he called out, but I didn't hear him."

He looked at her a moment. "Did Mr. Eden ask about the backpack?"

"No, but why would he?"

The officer raised his brow. "Just taking the facts, ma'am. Was he looking around? Was he armed?"

"He said he was looking for Mac. I didn't see if he was armed."

"Did he threaten you?"

"No. He was apologetic, but it seemed odd. Phoney-like."

More tapping of the keyboard.

Mari jiggled her leg, waiting for him to catch up. "There's just a few things about him that don't seem right. His fence, for one. It's way overkill for our little neighborhood. Those cameras and his dogs. The way he stood there just seemed creepy, and Mac's daughter said one time she saw him—" She paused. Dare she tell him Aubrey's claim about burying a body?

He stroked the keys, murmuring, "—daughter said she saw him—?"

"Bury something in his yard," she finished. "She thinks."

"—in his yard. And this was yesterday?"

She shook her head. "No—no, that part happened a while ago."

"Days ago? Weeks? Months?"

"Weeks, I think. I'm not sure."

"And what was buried?"

"Uh—we're not sure."

"Did you witness this personally?"

"No."

More typing. "And you said he dug a hole in Frost Park. Was he burying something in the park?"

Mari brought her hand to her forehead. This was going all wrong. "No. We're *speculating* that it could have been him that dug it, but we didn't *see* him do it. But the hole was the perfect size for that backpack of cash that was found. That part is in our previous statement."

"You keep saying 'we' and 'our.'"

"I was with Mac Sinclair when we found it. We brought it to the station together Monday evening."

"Ah." He furled his brow, making a few additional notes. He looked up. "And do you speculate Tatum West is somehow connected to that backpack too?"

"No." Mari sighed. "I mean—she could be, but I highly doubt it. But maybe her son, Trey. Maybe. But we talked about this before. It may have to do with some people he's involved with in the Whitmore neighborhood. He's in with a bad crowd." Honestly, she was confused. Her suspicions kept bouncing all over the place—from Burne Batson back to Roger Eden and on to the kid, Trey. Each seemed convincingly guilty.

The officer continued taking notes. "Have you ever seen Tatum West in Frost Park?"

"Only to pick up Ty."

"Have you ever observed Trey or Tatum West interacting with Roger Eden?"

"No."

"And your employer. Have you ever observed Mac Sinclair interacting with Roger Eden or the Wests?"

Mari blinked. "No—well, yes, with Roger. As neighbors. He's helped Roger with minor household things. Chatting in the yard. That's all, to my knowledge."

"And how often does Mr. Sinclair frequent Frost Park?"

"Um—I don't know. He mowed it for me on Saturday. That's how he found the hole out there."

"Has there been any evidence of substance abuse in the Sinclair household?"

Mari frowned. "No! Absolutely not!"

He typed again. "And have you ever noticed vehicles in front of the Sinclairs' that show up at random times and stay for only a short time—late at night or in the middle of the afternoon?"

"Are you insinuating that Mac had anything to do with that backpack of cash?"

"I'm not insinuating anything. Just asking questions."

"The answer is no!"

"How about the Eden residence? Any vehicles that show up at random times and leave soon?"

"No."

"Any unusual visitors in the neighborhood?"

"No. We gave you a list of everyone who was at Mac's over the weekend."

"Uh-huh. Has Mr. Sinclair been away recently? Any trips or nights out?"

"Not that I know of."

"How about Mr. Eden?"

"I—don't know."

"Has Mr. Sinclair and his daughter had any relatives show up recently?"

"No—I can tell you right now that this has *nothing* to do with him!"

"There's no accusation, ma'am. I'm only gathering facts. One last question: To your knowledge, does Mr. Sinclair have a firearm in his home?"

"Having a registered firearm is not illegal! He keeps it in a gun safe, out of reach."

"Thank you. I'll print this up and have you sign it, and you can be on your way."

Chapter Twenty-Six

Mari drove away from the police station livid. For one thing, it appeared Ty West wasn't even on the radar of their concern, for all she had heard were vague suggestions of officers "keeping their eyes open" for him. For anything beyond that, Tatum herself would need to make a report. And second, all those questions about Mac irked her, especially with him totally unaware of it! *Does Mr. Sinclair have a firearm in his home?* Right—like somehow *he* was connected to the murder in Whitmore now! He didn't even have an opportunity to defend himself! She wished she hadn't even gone to the police. She wished she had talked to Mac first, although she had tried to.

She bit her lip, still bugged that he hadn't called her back. And now once again her allotted time for visiting Poppy was eaten up. This was crazy. She shot a frustrated glance at the clock. She shouldn't even go. Even if she didn't stay, she was still cutting it way too close to beat Aubrey's bus to the Frost drop-off, and the last thing she needed was an Aubrey meltdown because she wasn't there. But what if Mac had left her a note in her grandfather's pocket? What if it was an apology or an explanation for why he hadn't called her back? So she threw her car in park and hustled toward the Riverview entrance.

Mac. It wasn't like him to blow her off. And now her imagination was running wild. What if—what if some gangster had showed up at his house for that money? She felt a stab of fear. What if it was that Bats guy? What if Mac had been murdered last night too and Aubrey with him, and they hadn't found their bodies yet? *Stop it right now,* she scolded herself, reining in her dark thoughts. If that were the case, she needn't worry about hurrying to collect a note from Poppy's pocket. She shook her head at the irony.

Her grandfather was hobbling down the hallway with his walker, returning to his room from the courtyard. "Hello!" he called happily.

"Sorry I'm so late, Poppy. I had to make a stop before I got here, and now I can't stay. I came by to see if Mac left me a note." She smiled sheepishly. "Since my secret's out, I'll be direct."

Her grandfather tapped his chest. "No pocket today. Couldn't come."

She tipped her head. "He didn't come?"

"Tomorrow."

"But—but doesn't he stop in every morning?"

He nodded. "But not today."

She swallowed. Maybe he *was* dead. "Well, I've got to go," she told him, giving him a quick kiss. "I *promise* tomorrow we'll spend more time together!"

Arriving to Frost Street in record time, Mari scraped her tires along Mac's curb right as Aubrey reached her porch steps. She honked and waved, then hurried to join her in the house.

"Here," Aubrey said, shoving a note card in her hand. "From Hailey's mom. Did Mr. Eden find his dog?"

Mari glanced from the card to the girl. "Did Mr. Eden lose his dog?"

"It ran away. I'm not playing outside if it's still loose."

Mari snatched her pepper spray from the top of the coat cubbies. "I've got this. This would protect us."

Aubrey eyed it skeptically. "Are you sure?"

"It's what it's made for. How was school today?"

"Good. Ty wasn't there again."

Mari's head perked up. "Again? Was he gone yesterday too?"

"Yeah. It was *so* nice. What's for snack?"

"Fig bars and string cheese."

Aubrey nodded agreeably. "Okay. Can you read that to me?" She gestured to the notecard. "It's in cursive."

Mari opened the note. "'Aubrey, Your banana bread was a bright spot on a bleak day. Thank you for your thoughtfulness! Love, Nora and Hailey. P.S. Please tell your mom thanks for the encouraging note.'" Mari looked at the girl. "I'm your caregiver, you know. Not your mother."

Aubrey shrugged. "I know. But you're *like* a mom." She sighed. "I *wish* you were my mom. And I wish I didn't have to go to Grandma's next week. I won't even get to see you!"

Mari blinked. "You're going to your grandma's?"

"Yeah. Dad says I have to." She sniffed, peeking out the door. "There's kids out there now. Can I go?"

"Yeah. I'll catch up," Mari said.

The screen door banged as Aubrey disappeared, the threat of the rogue Rottweiler momentarily forgotten. But Mari couldn't move. She stood paralyzed in the foyer, staring into the silent living room. Mac had made other childcare arrangements for his daughter. She could hardly believe it.

Her phone buzzed. A text from JoyAnne. "Want to walk with Kyla and me in an hour?"

"Sorry. Watching Aubrey," she texted in reply.

"We'll stop by anyway," came JoyAnne's reply, which Mari acknowledged with a thumbs-up. Then, pulling herself together, she returned her phone to her pocket and went to join the gang.

Apparently their afternoon kickball fun was routine enough to run on autopilot, for by the time Mari arrived at the field, Aubrey and Connor had already designated themselves as captains and had chosen teams. The game was underway, with Aubrey's team up to kick. Mari folded her arms, observing their cooperative, happy play. Admittedly, everything *did* seem more peaceful without Ty. And yet she preferred the troubled boy there. But no one loped across the field to join them today. She was beginning to resign herself to the idea that if he wasn't in grave danger and had simply run away, he would likely show up again soon. Eventually. She wondered if he would return once she was no longer there.

She glanced back at the house, feeling a wisp of shame. How had everything gone so awry? She certainly hadn't intended for anything weird to happen between her and Mac. Or her and Aubrey. She was only being herself—and enjoying it. She had felt so comfortable with Mac. So comfortable. Until last night.

A commotion at third base snapped her attention back to the game. One of the little girls had gotten a nosebleed, which turned dramatic when a few of the children who had never seen one before became overly alarmed. Mari sent Aubrey home at a run to fetch a Kleenex box while keeping the flow at bay with a tissue she had in her back pocket. Then she tended to the lass while the rest of the kids resumed their play. Before long it was time to gather up for snacks, after which Mari closed their time together in her regular way.

"I like it when we point up like that," the nosebleed girl said in a nasally voice, the wad of Kleenex still in hand. "I prayed to God last night."

Mari turned in surprise. "Did you? What did you pray?"

She leaned closer, whispering, "I prayed my daddy would come home soon."

"That's good!" Mari affirmed, her mind zinging off to Hailey's mom's family scenario and Tatum and Ty's. "I'll pray for that too."

"He's an army guy."

"Oh," Mari said, her mental picture suddenly altered. "That's cool! Well, God hears your prayers, sweetie."

On their stroll back to the house, Aubrey asked if Mari could braid her hair again like before.

"Do you have any homework?

"A little."

"Okay. Homework, then shower, then hair."

As Aubrey cheered and took off running, Mari noticed two cars pull up down the block in front of the Gordons'. Dressed in athletic attire and walking shoes, JoyAnne Strang and Kyla Watkins met on the sidewalk and hailed her as they started her way. Mari lingered until they joined her at the foot of Mac's porch steps, where JoyAnne greeted her with a hug.

Kyla gave a little wave. "Nice to see you again!" Her ponytail flopped to the side as she bent to tie her shoe.

"Sorry to hear about your dad," Mari offered. "I hear things are hard."

"My birth father. Yes, thanks. It's hard. He's not doing well."

JoyAnne turned to Mari. "Hey, I have a question for you. Today at the Center we got a call from a lady who said she was referred to us by her daughter's classmate's mom. Some story about a note being delivered with some banana bread. Was that you and Aubrey?"

Mari felt her cheeks grow warm. "I'm not her mom, and I keep telling her that!"

Kyla laughed. "Oh, she'll get over that! But way to go reaching out to her friend's mom!"

"Yes!" JoyAnne affirmed. "She was so touched she cried telling me about it! The Center will certainly help her. Thanks for referring her." She smiled. "Aside from that, how are you doing with *us*? I know it takes a while to process, so if you're still angry with me, it's okay. I'm willing to talk or apologize again if needed. I want to get it right. Kyla here has agreed to keep me accountable for working this out."

Kyla smiled proudly at JoyAnne.

Mari nodded. "You've been very generous, JoyAnne. I won't deny I've had a few suspicious thoughts, but then I remember our talk, and they melt away. You *have* apologized, so it's *my* problem if I hold on to anything. I want this worked out too."

"There were *a lot* of offenses, so it's okay. You can be real with me. I'm open to talking about anything."

"Thank you. Same."

"Other than that, how are you doing? I've been praying for you since you texted me last night."

"It's been hard," Mari replied, choosing to be honest despite its moping effect. "I have a few things going on right now, but the biggest, I guess, is that I've made some naive relational choices that have come back to bite me. Plus, I need to break up with my boyfriend."

JoyAnne groaned sympathetically. "Oh, I've only been *there* a hundred times in my life! No fun! Hang in there. My new motto is 'No compromise.' It helps if I decide ahead of time that I'm going to obey God!"

"Sometimes it's not so clear what that is. But I *want* to do the right thing."

"Just keep your heart open and pure before God," Kyla encouraged. "He'll guide you."

Mari shifted her feet. "Well, if we're going for openness, there's something I need to say to you, Kyla. I've made some pretty harsh judgments against you too. I was so mad that you got Peter Watkins, and I decided not to like you because of it. That sounds terribly childish when I say it out loud. There was no reason for me to dislike you because of that. I'm sorry."

Kyla smiled. "It's okay. You're not the only one whose hopes were dashed."

Mari smiled back. "I suppose not. He's a great guy."

"He is!"

JoyAnne bumped Mari's arm. "But God's got a whole storehouse of bones, right?"

They both laughed.

JoyAnne shook her head. "Take it from me, the expert: envy and jealousy keep up such a nice front, but everything about them is dark, nasty, and divisive. They judge, gossip, lie, plot, and hate—but all in a slippery, disguised way! I used to live critical of people every single day. I didn't know my value from God, so every day I cut people down to feel better about myself. All without thinking about it! But it never worked!"

Mari gave an embarrassed shrug. "But you were an unbeliever! What about me? There's something really wrong with a *Christian* who has a critical spirit like that. And I thought it was a *good* quality!"

"I think we can all relate to that," Kyla said. "You're forgiven, Mari. And truth be told—even married to the great and wonderful Peter Watkins, I still need Jesus to meet my needs."

Mari nodded. "I guess. And thanks. So I have a favor to ask. I sort of bit off more than I can chew with a coworker of mine. I offered to meet with her to talk about the Bible, but I don't know where to start. I'm embarrassed I don't know the Bible better, but I hear you're good at asking people questions about what they read. Care for a few more students? It's my coworker, her friend, and me."

"She is!" JoyAnne interjected.

Kyla shifted modestly. "Sure, I'd be open to that. How about Saturday after our morning study? Peter will have Kenny."

Mari gave a breath of relief. "Perfect—thank you! And speaking of Kenny—your baby is adorable!"

Kyla beamed. "Oh, isn't he? I'm so smitten!"

After a little more chitchat, JoyAnne and Kyla commenced their powerwalk, and Mari went to check on Aubrey's progress.

Mac came home much later than usual. Mari had just finished Aubrey's braids where the two of them sat in the living room watching a show.

Aubrey flew to him with her customary hug. "Daddy! Look how Mari did my hair!"

"It's beautiful!" he affirmed. He gave Mari a curt nod. "Sorry I'm late."

Mari stood, admiring how good he looked in his dress shirt and slacks. "It's no problem. But I didn't make any food." The last part was a nervous add-on.

"No need. Wednesdays are our night out."

"Yes. Before your groups. You told me."

"Yeah, we're meeting the DeSotos' tonight." He glanced at the time. "In a few minutes, actually."

Aubrey clapped her hands. "Goodie! Can Mari come with us?"

"Honey, Mari has—"

"I have plans," Mari said hastily. "I have—other plans."

Aubrey groaned. "You never get to do anything with us!"

"Go on!" Mac said, nudging her toward the stairs. "Run up and get ready. We need to go."

As Aubrey ascended, Mac turned back to Mari. "You're not obligated to cook for us, you know."

"Right—I know. You've told me that. It's only an activity that works well with Aubrey. Tonight we did hair."

"Okay."

They looked at each other.

"You didn't call me," Mari said.

Mac spread his hands. "Yeah, sorry. We said we'd talk today, so I—"

"It was *important*, Mac!" she cut in. "Roger Eden came into your house unannounced yesterday!"

He made a sound. "Yeah, I got your message, and that's not exactly true. I talked to him. Roger came over right away to tell me what happened. He said he called out when he came in, and he was very sorry that he had spooked you."

"So what did he want?"

"Nothing. He came over to apologize."

"He didn't ask for help with anything?"

"Oh—yeah, he needed help moving a table. He's refinishing part of his dining room floor. And he wanted to let me know that Loki ran away. He dug under the fence again—by the Gordons' this time."

"Aubrey told me." Refinishing his floor—for real?

"I offered to help him set some planks in the hole so the other dog doesn't get out. He was also wondering why the police were walking the field yesterday morning. He didn't want to alarm you by asking you about it."

"What did you tell him?"

He lifted a shoulder. "I told him it looked like a kid from Whitmore stole some stuff. He doesn't know any of those kids, and I didn't get into it."

Mari raised her brow. "Why would he be curious about that?"

"Why wouldn't he? Wouldn't *you* be curious if you lived here?"

Mari shook her head. "Mac, there's something up with that guy! I don't doubt the dog stuff, but I think moving the table because of his floor was a convenient story to save face. What if he was here looking for that camouflaged backpack? Everything about him—those dogs, the fence, those cameras. You said it yourself the other night—everything is just—just—anyway, I went to the police and made a report this afternoon. I told them what happened."

"Okay. Yeah, we discussed doing that. So—good. It's done. Great. Thank you."

"Yes, but aren't you concerned? It feels like you're defending him!"

"I'm not defending him!" He spread his hands. "I'm being *cautious*! He came over, and I talked to him! I'm not going to shut the door in his face! Haven't we talked about this?"

"Well, I don't trust him, and I think we need to be careful. There was a murder near here last night—did you know that? I have a picture of the victim on my phone." She moved to show it to him, but he waved his hand.

"It was in Whitmore, not here, and yes, I saw it. And I agree, we need to be careful! Which brings up another subject. We need to talk about next week."

"Yeah, so what's the deal, Mac? Am I being fired?"

He drew back. "*Fired?*"

"Aubrey said you're having her go to your mom's next week. You could have told me!"

He blinked. "My mom's having carpal tunnel surgery Monday morning. Since there's no school Monday through Wednesday, I'll need someone all day for Aubrey, and Mom asked if Aubrey could stay and help her."

"Oh." Mari shifted awkwardly. "I didn't know that."

"The no-school thing snuck up on me too, but I'm telling you now so you have two days to tell your kickball kids of the change—unless you want to come here anyway. That's an option too, since it means a lot to you."

"Okay. Thanks. But—but I asked you to call me."

Aubrey skipped noisily down the stairs. "I'm ready, Dad!"

He patted her shoulder. "Go get in the car, squirt. I'll be right out."

But Aubrey smiled, lingering with them.

Mac looked back at Mari. "We're running late. I'm sorry. Are you okay locking up?"

"I can let myself out," she answered. Was he brushing her off?

"Okay, let's go." He nodded, motioning for Aubrey to walk ahead of him. "See you tomorrow, Marissa."

He *was*. He was brushing her off! Before she could stop herself, she spurted, "I know what you're doing, Mac, and it doesn't feel very nice."

Mac turned, giving her a long look in return. "And what about *you*? What are *you* doing, Mari Coleman? Come on, Aubrey—let's go."

Mac's words stung, as did the close of the door behind him as he and his daughter left. Through the living room window Mari watched his vehicle drive away. *And what about you? What are* you *doing, Mari Coleman?* No, it wasn't her imagination. Mac had developed feelings for her too. And now it looked as though she were toying with him, flirting while she had a boyfriend, like some kind of clueless, two-timing ditz. She dropped her head. Crud. Why did Will have to show up at the ball field yesterday when he had? And why hadn't she broken up with him over the weekend when she had the chance to?

She stood there in the center of Mac's living room feeling hollow. Her gaze swept over his chair and his books on the end table. His shoes on the mat below the stairs. How crazy that she could feel such an ache—a physical ache in her chest, especially after only being around him for less than two weeks. But she liked him. She liked everything about him. She turned, looking across Aubrey's science project mess to survey Mac's spot on the far side of the dining room table, where his journal lay beside his Bible. Had he written her name in his journal because he was praying *about* her, not just *for* her?

She sighed. It was time to go. In the foyer, however, she glanced up the stairs, betting anything that Aubrey had left the lights on.

Sure enough, both her bedroom light and the bathroom lights were on. Mari flicked them off and paused in the hallway, peering into Mac's room. *You shouldn't,* she told herself, but stepping in, she tugged one of his shirts from a pile of clothes on his chair and pressed it to her face. The smell reminded her of the night he had picked her up from the airport and had offered her his coat. She closed her eyes against the fabric. Technically, he wasn't married. In that regard, it wasn't wrong to like him. But that wasn't the full picture.

JoyAnne's voice echoed through her mind: *My new motto is 'No compromise.' It helps if I decide ahead of time that I'm going to obey God.*

Mari draped the shirt back onto the arm of the chair. What did "No compromise" mean in this situation? She glanced around his room, struggling. Any normal girl would just go after him, and she was tempted to. Yet it wasn't as though she didn't know about Elena, the phantom ex-wife. She groaned to herself. Why in the world had she snooped in Mac's journal? It would have been so much easier not to have known about her. Then at least she wouldn't be accountable for the guilt she now carried.

No compromise.

She knew what she needed to do. She needed to quit this job. Staying on to care for Aubrey would only be cruel—both to Aubrey and to herself. How could she keep coming here and not be totally overwhelmed by her feelings for Mac? How long could that go on?

Just keep your heart open and pure before God. He'll guide you.

It sounded so simple, but it was so complicated.

She moved to the window, numbly looking down on intimidating Thor panting in her old yard, his sleek, dark coat shiny in the sunshine. She would have to untangle herself from all this drama too—all of Aubrey's anxieties about her "evil" neighbor and his supposed wiles. How could she just let that all go? Especially since discovering that backpack of money with Mac. How did she just walk away from it all?

And the kickball group.

She moseyed across the hall into Aubrey's new room to gaze glumly out over Frost field. But really—had she thought it would last forever? Wasn't it remarkable it had kept the kids' interest thus far? In a few weeks school would be out, and those same kids would be on to swimming lessons and summer sports activities anyway. It had had a good run.

But how would she tell Mac? And Aubrey? Her eyes lingered on the row of Mac's lilac bushes dotted with blossoms, reminding her of the sprig he had left for her in Poppy's pocket. She sighed. She used to want JoyAnne to go away. Now it was Elena. But Elena wasn't just some old love interest of Mac's. She was Aubrey's mother. Mari knew that wishing her out of Aubrey's life would be completely selfish.

As she stood by the window, a little movement below suddenly caught her attention. Tilting her head for a better angle, she peered downward to see—her eyes bugged out as a cry escaped her lips—why, it was Ty West! Ty West, crossing Mac's driveway! Where had he come from so suddenly? And what did he have there? She frowned, studying the bulky cloth bag he was lugging toward the front of the house. Well, she was about to find out.

Turning, Mari hurried down the stairs as fast as her knee would allow, bursting out of the house right as Ty reached the bottom of the porch. Flinching at her sudden presence, he let go of the cloth bag and started to run.

"No, Ty—Ty, stop!" she called. When he paid no mind, she blurted, "Ty, *wait*! I have some fig bars and string cheese for you!"

The words were magic. Ty paused, looking warily over his shoulder. She, too, glanced around, searching for their armed surveillance. Where in the world were they? She could use some police assistance right now!

"Come—wait on the porch," she urged firmly. "I'll be right back!"

Breathing a prayer, she turned away, heading to the kitchen. Scrambling through the refrigerator, Mari grabbed every cheese stick she could find, plus some of Mac's beef sticks, stuffing them into a purple reusable bag with a sleeve of fig bars, two apples, and some soda crackers. Ty was waiting at the edge of the steps when she returned.

"Good—you're still here," she said breathlessly. "We missed you today. How are you?" Fearing he would snatch the bag and bolt, she momentarily kept it in a tight grip.

The boy eyed it, shifting nervously. "Good."

"Good!" She nodded, gesturing to the lumpy cloth bag beside the porch steps. A pillowcase knapsack, she noted, beige and dirty, both from sleep drool and from being dragged across the ground. "What did you bring me?"

He shrank back, as if guilty.

"Never mind. I'll look later," she said hastily. "But know what? I work with your mom. She said she'd like you to come home."

His face. Mari noted the way he squirmed and shifted about. He cared, but he was obviously scared—and hungry too, she observed, as he waited patiently for her to hand over the food.

"Ty," she said gently, "remember what I said? You're safe here—I promise. Do you need to tell me anything?" She paused. "Is someone hurting you or your mom at home?"

He cast a look over his shoulder and back at Mari.

"*Who,* Ty? It's important that you tell me. Is it Trey? Is your brother hurting you and your mother?"

He shook his head. "I can't say."

"They always tell you not to say anything. But the way to get help is to tell someone you trust."

He looked at the food and back up at Mari.

"That's how they control you—by threatening to hurt you or someone you love."

"Trey is in trouble," he said quietly.

"What does that mean? What kind of trouble?"

He hesitated, as if weighing out what might happen if he told. "A guy is super-mad at him."

"Who, Ty? Who's mad at him? Is it that Bats guy—the one who was pounding on my car window the other night?"

His eyes answered her question.

"Why is he mad? What's going on with him and Trey?"

Another glance behind him. "He thinks Trey stole his stuff."

"Is he threatening him? Is he hurting him?"

He nodded, turning away as he wiped a dirty cheek. "And my mom. She's standing up for Trey, and he's mad."

Mari eyed him. "But Trey didn't steal anything, did he?"

Ty dropped his gaze.

"You took something, didn't you? Ty, do you need to give it back?"

He looked up. "I ain't going to."

"What did you steal? Was it money? Did you find a lot of money?"

He didn't answer.

The food bag was getting heavy. "Ty, listen. You need to stay away from that guy. Does he come to your house?"

He nodded. "He's my mom's old boyfriend. He comes to our apartment to make Trey do bad stuff."

Mari straightened. "Bad stuff like what? Does Trey do what he wants?"

"He has to. He has to, or else—" He looked behind him again, and this time she could see he had reached his limit. Any second he was going to run.

She handed off the bag of food. "Here's this, but would you like to come to McDonald's with me? I'm going there right now, and I'd buy you whatever you want. Even ice cream." If she could get him in the car, she would take him right to the police station. "A cheeseburger would be so good right now, wouldn't it? And hot, salty fries. Mmm. Whatever you're hungry for."

Ty wound his hand through the cloth handles, clearly torn. Starting to back away, he kicked his foot toward the pillowcase. "Don't tell nobody I gave you that."

"Okay," she said. "Your mama wants you home, Ty. But I'll put a blanket on my porch for you, just in case."

Mac's porch, she corrected herself, patting her pocket for her phone as she watched him jog across the field. She was calling the police immediately. Dang—where had she left her phone? She started into the house, then stopped, looking back at the bulky bag on the grass near the front steps. What had he brought her? She supposed she should check. She grabbed the top flaps to lift it to the sidewalk, finding it heavy.

Spreading the opening, she peered in—and instantly froze, staring horrified at a mishmash assortment of drug paraphernalia. Bags of pot, colorful glass pipes, various little scales atop an assortment of small plastic bags filled with white powder. Wads of cash. And then, as if suddenly coming into focus, she noticed a black metal handgun lying right smack in the center of it all.

"Oh, my word—Ty!" she cried, closing the fabric flaps to look around her.

Had anyone seen this? She needed to take this whole pillowcase to the police right now! She grabbed the mouth to heft it to her car but stopped again, having another quick thought. In a flash, she ran up the porch steps to fetch her phone, returning to take multiple photographs of the bag in front of the house lest she be stopped with it on her way. Then she lugged the bundle down to the boulevard to stuff it into the back of her car. Locking her car doors, she hurried back into the house to run upstairs. Locating Mac's linen closet, she snatched an old, blue, buffalo-plaid comforter and pillow to tuck in the corner of the porch.

Then locking up the house, she hurried for her car, punching in Mac's number on the way. *Oh, please answer!* she silently begged.

Chapter Twenty-Seven

A million scenarios whipped through Mari's mind as she fidgeted in the hard chair, gnawing on her knuckles as she waited for the police officer to pull up the appropriate file on his laptop. What in the world was a nine-year-old doing with a cache of drugs like that? Ty was a child! And Aubrey—why, anything could have happened with Ty dragging that up to their house! *Mac's* house. And where was Mac anyway? He should have been here by now! He hadn't answered his phone, but she had called Leah, who had agreed to pass on the message that she needed him at the police station ASAP.

"Someone needs to get a hold of Ty's mother," she told the officer. "I don't have her phone number, but she needs to know about this right away."

"Uh-huh." He frowned into his screen, making a few clicks.

"Her name is Tatum West. She needs to know what's going on."

"Okay."

Was he even listening? Frustrated, she dropped her fist on the table. "Have someone call her! What are you waiting for?"

"Miss Coleman—"

"And the armed surveillance you promised—where *were* they? How does it happen that a *kid* walks around with that much dope? And out in the open, for heaven's sake!"

The officer held up a hand, speaking calmly. "Miss Coleman, I assure you that our department is actively pursuing this case."

"Actively—*right*! I was here just five hours ago telling another officer that Ty West and his mother need help! Why weren't they out looking for him? What were they *doing* this whole time?" Spying a movement out of the corner of her eye, she suddenly noticed Mac rushing into the room, his face marked with concern.

She shot to her feet. *Finally.*

"What's going on?" he asked.

"Mac—thank God you're here!" she said, fighting back tears.

"Are you all right? What's going on?"

"It's Ty—Ty West—" she choked. She couldn't get any further.

"What's happening here?" Mac looked questioningly at the officer, who waved for them both to take a seat.

The officer's eyes moved from Mari to Mac. "We've had a sizeable drug recovery go down on Frost this evening at the hands of Miss Coleman and Tyler West, the latter who apparently dragged the stash to your doorstep in a pillowcase."

Mac looked at Mari in astonishment. "Is Ty all right? Are *you* all right?"

She sniffed, dabbing her eyes, trying to pull herself together. "I'm okay. He brought it to me and then ran away. Mac, there was a *gun* in there! It could be the murder weapon from last night!"

Mac turned to the officer. "What happened?"

"We're about to go over that," he replied. "Miss Coleman, I'm ready for your statement." He beckoned another officer, who set a box of tissues and two cold water bottles on the table.

Mari blew her nose and started in, relaying all that had happened since Mac had left his house.

When she finished, she looked at Mac and the officer. "I'll bet you anything the stuff in that pillowcase belongs to that Bats fellow! Burne Batson. Ty told me he's his mom's ex-boyfriend and he comes over to 'make Trey do bad stuff.'" She held her fingers up in quotes. "I can't imagine what that might entail!"

"Buying and selling his drugs," the officer said quietly. "Among other things."

"Well, he's like—he's like the *devil*! Whatever threat he made must be serious, because both Tatum and Ty are terrified of him. My friend JoyAnne says he controls people. They want in, but then they're stuck, and they can't get out."

She tapped her fingers anxiously on the table, adding, "I bet Ty stole that stuff from Trey not realizing it was tied up with Bats. He probably thought he was doing a good thing for his brother. Just getting it out of their house. Maybe he collected it little by little over time—who knows? But regardless of what is going on, that kid needs to get out of there. He needs to get out of Whitmore and away from that man!"

The officer nodded. "Do you know where Ty went?"

"Running toward Whitmore is all I know."

"And have you seen Trey today?"

"No. Not since Friday—and that's when Trey told Ty that Burne was going to kill him if he didn't get his stuff back." She rubbed her forehead. "Oh, man! This is so crazy. Officer, how old is Trey West? Is he a minor?"

"Trey is eighteen."

Mac held up his hand. "Wait—can we back up? Who is this man 'Burne'?"

"Burne Batson," Mari clarified. "He's called Bats because he carries one to use it on people!"

Mac shot out a breath, and the officer raised his brow. "She's right. He's a Whitmore ganger with a lot of influence."

"Influence! More like intimidation! A slippery fellow whom the police can't seem to catch," Mari added somewhat snidely.

The officer's eyes flicked up to hers.

Mari waggled her head. "Well, I heard someone say that."

"We're doing our job, ma'am. Update your sources." He rose from his computer. "Be right back."

Mac swung to Mari in question.

She dropped her face in her hands. "My word, Mac—this keeps getting crazier! Burne Batson is Ariel's mom's boyfriend. He lives with them. But he's also Tatum's ex!"

Mac straightened in surprise. "Is that right?" He shifted, removing his arm from the back of her chair.

"I'm connecting the dots. JoyAnne told me Ariel had to flee when her mom's boyfriend threatened her. One of Bat's previous girlfriends had come to see him, and they had a big, violent fight. That would have been *Tatum*. She was mad at him—probably for the way he was using Trey. Ariel witnessed it, and that's when Bats threatened *her*." She looked up at him. "Mac, everything in that pillowcase implicates *Trey*, not Bats. Trey could be in huge trouble! What a slimy and conniving creep that guy is! Oh, man! I can't believe this is what Tatum deals with!"

The officer returned to the room. "All right. That's been dispatched. We currently have units on the way to Whitmore."

Mari stood. "Officer, you've got to find Ty! And you've got to get his mother and him out of there!"

"Miss Coleman, I assure you we have every intention of doing that. Our best-case scenario is that he shows up at home tonight, but if he doesn't, we will be looking for him. Now if you'd please take your seat, we'll finish up on your statement."

Mari slid in beside Mac. "I don't have anything else to share."

"Mr. Sinclair?"

Mac shook his head. "No. I have nothing either. But, officer, is it safe to say we know that cash from the field is related to what Ty dragged in? Is it all drug money?"

"Right," Mari cut in. "Now we got their cash *and* their stash! All we need are the culprits. Please let it end tonight!"

The officer inclined his head. "We can hope for that, yes. However, the backpack case is still under investigation." He typed a few more notes, then with a few clicks, closed out of his laptop. He rose, extending his hand. "Mr. Sinclair, you have my card."

Rising, Mac returned the handshake.

"Will you please let us know when you find Ty?" Mari asked.

"We'll do our best," the officer replied, shaking her hand too. "Do you know your way out?"

"Oh, she knows her way out," Mac said dryly.

Mac motioned for her to go ahead, and the two of them walked the long hall in silence. As they neared the exit, Mari finally spoke.

"Thanks for coming, Mac. I'm sorry that I pulled you away from your meeting and—and I'm sorry for everything else!"

He held the door. "Stop apologizing, Mari. You know this isn't your fault."

"I know. But if I hadn't told Ty he could come to me with anything, he wouldn't have brought all that stuff right to your house. I put Aubrey in danger, and I'm so sorry. And if anything happens to Ty—oh, I won't be able to live with myself!"

"No, you did the right thing. He needed help. Except you should have *called* 911 and had them come to *you*! What were you doing—putting that in your car?"

"Yeah, sorry. I didn't think of that. I'm only glad Aubrey wasn't there." She paused on the steps. "Mac, I left a blanket on your porch for Ty. In case he comes back."

"Okay." He nodded. "Let's hope they find him and he doesn't need it."

"Yes. And I'll watch Aubrey at my house tomorrow. I'll pick her up from the bus stop and tell the other kids we can't play."

"Okay. Thank you. At least until we know."

"Yes, until we know."

They looked at each other, and he chuckled, waving at the building. "Well, here we are again!"

She smiled. "Could be worse. Could be the hospital!"

"True!" He paused, letting out a long breath. "Mari, I owe you an apology. When I was leaving the house tonight—hey, I'm sorry for what I said."

"No, I get it. You were right. I've been—I—I shouldn't have—"

"No, it's on *me*," he cut in. "I should have taken responsibility for not—you know—for not letting things get—"

"Mac, I know," she said hastily. She wanted to say more. So much more. She wanted to tell him how she felt about him, but Will and Elena loomed invisibly between them. *It helps to make up my mind ahead of time to do what's right.* How ironic that the words were JoyAnne's. She shifted uncomfortably, adding, "But, um—I don't think I can work for you anymore. I'll finish out the week—or longer, if you need me. But I think you'll need to find someone else to watch Aubrey."

He nodded. "I understand. You've been the greatest, but I wish you and Will the best."

"Yeah, thanks. And same. I wish you the best too."

Another pause.

"Well—" He turned toward the parking lot. "Is your car nearby?"

"Over there." She gestured, continuing down the steps. "I hope you can still catch some of your meeting if it's not already over."

"I already asked Dan to bring Aubrey home. I was thinking of heading over to look for Ty."

She gave a cry, pausing on a step. "That's what *I* was going to do!"

His brow went up. "Okay, then! I guess we'll look for him together!"

She laughed.

He paused when they had reached her car. "By the way, the police called to ask about you today. Did you know that?"

"Me? Mac! Are you kidding?"

"I know! They wanted to know if you had traveled anywhere recently. I'm just telling you so you know."

"Funny. Well, guess what? They were asking about *you* too! Same thing. And if you've had any friends or relatives show up lately. And if you had a firearm in the house. It kinda made me mad!"

They looked at each other, bewildered.

She dug her hand on her hip. "Mac, if you turn out to be the bad guy here, I will be *very* disappointed in you!"

He grinned. "See you at the house!"

As he strode off, Mari got into her car, sighing as she watched him cross the parking lot. *Mac.*

When they got to Frost, Mari discovered that she and Mac weren't the only ones searching for Ty West. A half dozen police officers were spread out, combing Frost Park in the dusky light for the missing boy, and another couple walked the perimeter of the cemetery, aiming their flashlights at the bottom of the wrought iron fence. Mac revealed that he had had the same thought and wanted to search inside the cemetery, so the two of them walked the several blocks to the tall iron gates and spent the next hour or so peeking around granite gravestones and stately oaks. Eventually Mari reminded him of Aubrey, and they returned to the house.

Seeing them walk up, Roger Eden joined them from his porch. "Good evening. Do you two know what's going on here tonight?" he asked, indicating the police presence in the neighborhood.

Mari regarded him with caution, but Mac shook his hand freely.

"A boy from Whitmore has gone missing," he explained.

Mr. Eden's shoulders slumped in relief. "Ah—I was so afraid it was your *daughter*! When you walked up without her, I felt sick! Although it's too bad for the other kid and his family."

"Now *that* would be terrible!" Mac agreed soberly. "No, they're looking for a nine-year-old named Ty West."

"One of my after-school kickball kids," Mari added quietly, surprised at Mac's neighbor's response. The evil Mr. Eden cared about Aubrey Sinclair?

Mr. Eden gave a sympathetic grunt. "That's too bad. Well, I'll keep a lookout. And I'll let the police know I have camera footage." He glanced toward his house. "They might find it helpful."

"Thanks," she said. His offer was unexpected and, well, genuinely kind. She met his eyes and looked away.

He cleared his throat. "Miss Margaret, I want to apologize again for scaring you yesterday. I'm truly sorry. I can promise you it *won't* happen again!"

"Oh, thanks. Yeah, it was a shock, but, um—it's okay." On a whim she added, "How is your floor project coming?"

"Well, slow. I'm not as limber as I used to be. It's a little more work getting up and down!"

His response seemed natural, she thought, studying him.

Mac jerked his chin at an approaching car. "Ah, here we go—here's my Aubrey!"

Mari glanced over to see Dan DeSoto driving up. That meant the men's group at church was over. She wondered how it had gone for Will. He would no doubt be calling soon, and she would find out.

Roger Eden shook Mac's hand again. "Well, I'll let you go. You two have a good night." He nodded. "Margaret."

The two stood quietly for a moment as Mr. Eden left. Then Mari looked at Mac, who broke into a grin.

"Come on, Margaret. I'll walk you to your car before Aubrey sees you and we have yet another meltdown when you can't stay."

Once in the driver's seat, she lowered her window. "All right, Mac. I'll admit it—I *may* have been wrong about Roger Eden. He was actually quite nice right there. Sensitive, even. It's possible I might have misjudged him. *Might* have. He still shouldn't have come into your house. But now with everything with Ty and the drama in Whitmore, well, it changes things."

He opened his hands. "I know—see? The guy is odd, but—" He shrugged. "Once you get to know him, he's not so bad. He's an interesting fellow."

She smiled, shifting the car into gear. "Good night, Mac. Go put your little treasure to bed."

Closing the window, she sighed. It was going to be super-hard to let him go.

Her eyes scanned the neighborhood as she made her way out to the highway. Somewhere out in that chilly night was a nine-year-old who needed help in a myriad of ways. She hoped the police wouldn't give up searching for him. And now with the authorities involved, maybe Tatum would kick it up a notch too. Mari imagined the woman's prior reluctance to go to the police had something to do with one intimidating thug of an ex-boyfriend, who would hopefully be behind bars this very night. What an enormously stressful life! No wonder Tatum was mad all the time.

Mari was in the kitchen fixing a snack of veggies when Will called.

"Well, what do you know—you answered!" he blurted.

"What's that supposed to mean?" She returned the ranch dressing to the refrigerator and closed the door.

"You're the only one I know who *never* answers their phone!" he replied.

Her brow shot up. "Oh, really? Well, I'm here. How was the group tonight?" On the drive home she had rehearsed a few different scripts for breaking up with him, but it seemed only courteous to let him tell his news first.

He laughed. "It was amazing! Incredible! Life-changing!"

"Do I detect a little sarcasm?" She dipped a broccoli spear and popped it into her mouth.

"No, I'm serious, Marzipan! I got born—you know, that born thing. I prayed that prayer to give my life to Jesus Christ tonight."

Mari stopped chewing. "Are you serious?"

"Did you know all this already?"

"Know what?"

"About sin and the consequences and stuff—all that."

"Uh—"

"I can't believe you've gone to Eagle Bluff Church all your life, and you never knew this!"

She grabbed her plate, heading to her room. "Of course I knew about sin, Will!"

"Well, you never once told me! I can't even *believe* how blind I was! It was all right under my nose, but I couldn't see it! Everything Pastor Keith says on Sundays—it was all in there, but I didn't get it until tonight!"

"And what—Peter Watkins explained everything to you?" Sheesh, what was so magic about the way *he* told it?

"Yes. Peter and all the guys—Dan, Doug, and a few others. Mac was there, but he had to leave right away."

She set her plate on the nightstand and sat on the bed. "Well, that's—that's great news, Will!"

Will let out a breath. "It's just so weird. All that stuff we talked about at The Wok last night—all those questions I had—I wish you would have just *told* me the answers if you already knew! You should have told me what was true, Marzipan! Peter just laid it out so plainly that by the time we were done, all those questions just seemed stupid."

She hardly knew what to say. "Huh. Well, I'm—glad! And sorry, I guess."

"It's okay. I just thought it was funny that I've heard you talk about God so much, but your life—I mean, you aren't exactly—well, anyway, I get it now! Hell is a real place, and that was the whole point of why Jesus came—to save us from going there. There *is* only one way to heaven, and it's through Jesus. He's, like, a *real* person!"

Chapter Twenty-Seven

She felt the jab. "Right. That's right."

"They gave me an extra Bible. I'll probably try to read it tonight. It was an amazing time!"

"That's great, Will."

He paused. "So that leads me to something else I wanted to talk about."

Minor key. She could hear it in his voice. "About *us*?"

"Yes. I was just thinking that—I mean—we have fun and all. We like each other. But I'm wondering if it might be smart to mature a little for a dating relationship. Spiritually, you know. And not just *me*. I think we *both* have room to grow."

Mari swallowed. This was miles away from how she had envisioned things unfolding. "Um, okay. Are—you—?"

"I don't want to hurt your feelings, Mars, but I think it might be best if we broke up. Then we can both focus on growing in the Lord. Plus, Dan suggested it might be important for me to work on my relationship with my parents right now. You and I are both kind of moving in separate directions anyway, with you being all about your kickball job and stuff. So I thought it might be—you know—time to do it."

"Yeah, maybe it is."

"Yeah. So—"

There was a long pause.

"I guess this is it then. Do you want your ring back?" She glanced toward the dresser.

"Uh—probably. You'd never wear it anyway. I should have asked your size first."

She nodded. "I'll bring it Sunday. I hope we can still be friends."

"Yeah, that's what I want—to be friends."

"Well, I think we're doing the right thing, Will. And I'm excited for you."

"Good. And thanks. So, uh—bye, Mari."

"Goodbye, Will."

Before she even brought her phone down, Will had hung up. She held it awkwardly in her hand, noting he had finally used her correct name—Mari. To break up.

So it had happened—and so quickly. It was what she had wanted, but now it felt weird that *Will* had initiated it. Sort of like being dumped. A *lot* like being dumped. Yet what stung the most was what he had said and insinuated about her need to mature. Ouch. Deflated, she dropped her arms into her lap, her colorful veggie plate untouched on the bedside table.

Okay, Mari conceded, he did say they *both* needed to mature, but she had always prided herself as being spiritually ahead of Will, and now their conversation had made her feel like a loser again, as if he were all buddy-buddy with Jesus now and she were yesterday's news. Good grief! She had *wanted* to end the relationship to begin with. Where were all these feelings coming from? Why did this bug her so much?

Probably because she was immature, she admitted glumly. Those competitive stirrings were all too familiar. The same thing that had plagued her relationship with JoyAnne was popping up again! Same issue, different form. What was this thing in her that had to outdo others and be on top? What was this thing that made her feel like the loser if she wasn't the winner?

JoyAnne's words flitted through her mind: *Honestly, I was so self-righteous and full of pride, so full of my own opinions. I wanted to feel important—to be someone and have people like me. It gave me a sense of power.* Yes, that about summed it up, Mari concurred. The need for power and approval to feel significant. Admitting it made her squirm. Maybe this was what Dr. Grant meant when he referred to her heart "screaming for love." Was it also why she struggled to be happy for Will in his newfound faith? It seemed her sour, older brother-ish attitude was a default.

Again JoyAnne's voice echoed back: *He said I needed to expand my view of God.*

Well, maybe she did too, she confessed. With a sigh Mari checked the time, then set her phone onto her bedside table. Her day had been physically and emotionally exhausting, but it was time to address those ugly, critical feelings. Pulling her Bible from the nightstand, she got comfortable and settled it atop a pillow on her lap.

"Okay, God. Expand my view of who you are and what you're like," she murmured to herself.

She *did* love Jesus; she was grateful for what He had done for her, grateful for her salvation, though she had significant room to grow in every facet of her relationship with him. But she intended to. She wanted to pursue God, as Dr. Grant had encouraged. She wanted to seek him. She wanted to see how Jesus reflected the Father. *He's drawing you, isn't he?* Yes, he was.

He wants to be found, Dr. Grant had said. It reminded her of his commentary on the older brother in the prodigal son story. *Neither of those boys really knew their father's heart for them, did they? There's a solution for that.*

She opened her Bible. "God, however this is supposed to happen, fill in my missing gaps. Help me know your heart for me."

Then, as she started reading, she had an idea. Sliding everything aside, she scooted off the bed to find her journal, which was still in her backpack from her flight home from Boston. She decided that as she studied through the book of Matthew, she would record a list of every quality she could see that described Jesus. Then she would cross-examine those traits to see which also described God, the Father.

Flipping the journal open, she immediately happened upon Marilee Montayne's autograph. She had almost forgotten about it! She smiled at the memory of their chance meeting in the airport restroom—and of sitting beside her husband, Dr. Grant, on their flight. A God-coincidence. Who would have ever thought she would end up friends with that actress' husband? Someday she hoped to meet her again, and not just because she was famous. She eyed the woman's words again.

Mari, Sometimes surrender is the only way to win. God bless. Marilee Montayne.

What an upside-down concept, but the sentiment rang true, she mused. This was what God had been showing her through her reconciliation with JoyAnne. Surrender. Complete surrender to God. To face herself squarely without defending herself. To deal with her own shortcomings, as cringeworthy or embarrassing as they were, and to look to God for help in those same weaknesses. JoyAnne had done it. So could she.

Returning to her nest, she flayed her journal open to a fresh page and began taking notes, skipping back and forth between her Bible and the notebook for quite a while until she needed to rest. Wiggling off the bed, she returned her plate to the kitchen and got a drink.

On her way back she tapped on Shannon's door. "What are you doing? Mind if I come in?"

Shannon was cross-legged against her headboard with papers flayed out in a semicircle. "Finalizing our menu. Man, Dad's gonna freak! Food is so expensive!" She slid a pile of clothes over with her foot. "What's up?"

Mari sat on the edge of the bed. "Not a lot. Just popping in to tell you what a great sister you are."

Shannon lowered her clipboard. "All right, what happened?"

Mari smiled. "Well, a few things. I thought I'd tell you that JoyAnne and I had a talk. She apologized to me for all our high school crap—like, sincerely apologized! It blew me away. Believe it or not, we're working things out."

Shannon sat back in amazement. "Seriously? That's like—a *miracle*!"

"That's exactly what *I* said! She even submitted her resignation for the Sunlight job to give it to me."

"*No way!* Mari—"

"I'm not taking it, but that's what she was like—so *broken*. And honest."

Still wide-eyed, Shannon simply shook her head.

"She shared with me some things she had learned about envy and jealousy—how looking down on people was one of the ways she coped with feeling insecure about herself. That I'd been a threat to her happiness because 'being the best' was how she perceived her worth. But know what? I'm so much the same. She was *my* threat to happiness for the same reason. No one could be better than me. I had to be on top. Which leads me to you."

"Me?"

"I've always compared myself to you, Shannon. I always felt you were prettier, smarter, and funnier than me."

"Oh, stop!"

"No, it's true. And taller."

"Well, I can't help *that*!"

"Exactly! What did I gain by being envious of you? It did nothing to help me feel better about myself. It only put a barrier in our relationship. But you were a lot nicer to me than I was to you."

"I'm not so sure about that! But I have always admired you. You're my big sister!"

"Well, I can't fathom why, but I want you to know that I'm sorry for my sucky attitudes. I love you, Shannon. And you're free to be exactly yourself."

Shannon shook her head in amazement. "Wow, Mari! What's going on with you?"

She gave a sober smile. "Well, I'm starting to see that God values me for who I am. I've always known in my head that God loves me, but I've been so consumed with propping myself up that it never mattered. I never took the time to open myself to him—to let him see me as I really am, which I know he already does, but it's starting to get personal. I'm seeing that Jesus loves *me*. He loves me just as I am—even as an insecure, self-obsessed sinner, without me having to perform for him. That kind of love and forgiveness makes me truly grateful. I don't deserve it."

Shannon nodded thoughtfully. "Well, I love you too, Mari. And for the record, you are totally cute and smart and funny! Plus, *I* was always jealous because *you* were Dad's favorite!"

"Oh, right! All I ever heard was how neat and organized you were! And how pretty your hair was."

"And all *I* ever heard was what a smart and capable athlete you were. I wish you could have seen how concerned Dad was when you injured your knee!" She laughed. "Case in point, huh?"

Mari nodded. "Exactly. I know Dad's not perfect, but I think he's been pretty good at loving us both. We just get sidetracked with comparison and don't always see it. But like God—there's no shortage of his love."

Shannon threw Mari a pillow. "Did he ever do that money illustration with you—the thing about knowing your worth?"

Mari stretched out her legs, wedging the pillow behind her back. "Only a dozen times!"

"Well, remind yourself of it! I had to this week. One of my coworkers is such a snob. She goes around the salon dropping snide remarks about me to the other employees—and I can hear her doing it!"

"So annoying! I bet she's jealous."

"All I think about is Dad holding up that fifty-dollar bill."

"Huh. He always used hundreds for me." Mari tossed her head and grinned.

Shannon gave her a playful kick. "Oh, man—I'm *so* relieved, Mari! Honestly, when you came in here, I thought you were going to tell me that you and Will broke up!"

Mari raised her brow.

"You *didn't*!" Shannon dropped her hand.

Mari nodded. "Just a bit ago. I was going to tell you that next."

Shannon scrambled to give her a hug. "Oh, that's the worst! I'm so sorry!"

"It's okay. It was the right thing."

Shannon patted her quilt. "Come sleep with me tonight."

"I might. But I'm going to read for a while in my room first. I'm trying to focus my thoughts."

"What are you reading?"

"The Bible. I'm on a mission to define my faith. To get back to the basics, sort of. I want to know who Jesus is and why he deserves my love and worship. And how he's like God the Father. I want to know more than 'about him.' I want to know him here." She tapped her chest.

Shannon let out a breath. "Wow—you inspire me! I'm glad you're home, Mari."

"Me too."

Chapter Twenty-Eight

Mari's heart gave a little leap as she pulled into the Student Center parking lot the next morning, for there stood Tatum West on the side doorsteps, doubtless waiting for her. Maybe she had some positive news about Ty! Quickly she parked, but as she headed for the entrance, she noticed that Tatum was now on her feet, agitatedly pacing while looking in her direction. Mari swallowed. Crud. There wasn't one thing remotely positive about Tatum's expression. This did not look good.

"Morning, Tatum," she said, approaching slowly. She hadn't even considered Tatum's reaction to last night's presumed show of police at her apartment.

With a steely gaze, Tatum marched directly for her. Mari straightened, prepared to face a verbal barrage—oblivious of the stiff fist punch Tatum promptly wielded right smack in her face. Mari recoiled, grabbing her mouth.

"*Tatum!*" John, the Coffee Break manager, hollered, having stepped outside right that moment to witness the incident from behind them. He rushed down the steps to pull Tatum away. "What's going on here?"

Tatum stuck her finger in Mari's face, ignoring his presence. "What the hell do you think it means to stay out of my business?"

"Tatum!" Mari sputtered, her hands raised. "It was because of Ty! He showed up at my house with drugs! I had no choice! I had to call the police!"

"You don't know what you've done! You don't know what you're getting us into! And yourself too!"

"No, I don't! But I know it's not safe for you to be there!"

"Yeah? And where do you expect me to go?"

"I'll help you find a place. You and Ty."

Tatum huffed. "You're so freakin' clueless!"

369

Mari tasted blood. She wiped a smear off her mouth.

The manager looked nervously between them. "Do you want to call the police?"

Mari scrunched her forehead. "No!" She turned back to Tatum. "Tatum, I know your ex is threatening Trey. I know he's bad news."

Tatum swung her head back and forth. "You don't get it. I can't leave. Not if I value my sons. No one just leaves."

"Someone's got to stand up to him! He can't hurt you if he's behind bars."

"That's not the way it works over there. In Whitmore, you cut off the head of the snake and it grows back two."

Mari wiped her hand on her slacks. "Well, we'll see about that! Ty turned in a truckload of evidence against him. Plus, we found the money he hid in Frost Park. His days are numbered. The police are on to him."

Tatum's head shot up. "What money? What are you talking about—money in the park?"

"Bats hid some money, didn't he? In Frost Park. We know about it."

The manager looked around and motioned toward the steps. "Look—do you two want to go inside?"

Tatum ignored him. "No, he didn't!"

"Then did Trey steal some money and hide it? Or did Bats have Trey hide it?"

She shook her head, her brow puckered. "I don't know what this money thing is about. There was a fellow that came looking for Trey at the apartment the other day, badgering him about money he'd supposedly stolen from the field. Trey swore he didn't know anything about it, but the guy kept after him and after him. It was getting so bad I needed to call Bats for help."

Mari frowned. "Really? Who was he?"

"Don't know. Never seen him before. He wasn't from Whitmore." Tatum hesitated, adding, "He's the one that ended up dead."

"What?" Mari blinked in surprise. "Did Bats kill him? Or—or did—" Oh, man. She drew her hand over her mouth. Had Trey just made a big mistake?

As if reading her mind, Tatum jutted out her chin. "My boy, Trey, is in a heap of trouble, but I'll tell you one thing—he ain't no murderer! And Bats didn't do it neither. He was with me. I don't know who this guy was, and we don't know nothing about that money!"

Mari waggled her head. "Tatum, you need to take this information to the police!" She gestured to the manager. "Both of us can give testimony to what we've heard you say. This is important!"

Tatum looked away. "I don't know anything."

Mari sighed at her obstinance. "Did Ty show up last night? I told him you wanted him home, like you asked."

"Not when I was there. I left to spend the night in my car."

"Your car!" Mari huffed. "Tatum, *please* let me help you!"

Dropping her arms, the woman turned to the manager. "I'll be in tomorrow," she said, then strode off across the parking lot.

Mari gave a cry of protest, motioning after her. "She just left! She just walked away!"

The manager spread his hands. "What can I do? She came in earlier to ask for the day off."

She faced him. "How long have you known what she's dealing with?"

He shifted uncomfortably. "I confronted her on some bruises a few weeks ago. I've been trying to convince her to get help, but she's one stubborn cuss of a lady."

Mari bit her lip, now understanding those mysterious kitchen clashes. "Well, that's commendable, John, but don't wait next time. You know I'm going to have to report all this."

"Yes. I was thinking that one of us needs to. I suppose you'll want the morning off now too."

"No, I'll work my shift. I want to give her time to maybe go to the police herself. I'll swing by the station when I'm done." She dabbed her lip, now swollen and pulsing. "I'll need to wash up a little."

"Yes, you will." He took the stairs to open the door, noticing her wince on a step. "Are you limping?"

"I twisted my knee when she punched me. I might need to park myself on a chair this morning."

"Oh, for heaven's sake!" he murmured, shaking his head.

The usual morning staff eyed Mari and the manager with curiosity as they slipped into the Coffee Break bustle together. Mari simply performed a fancy bow.

"Sorry I'm late. I hurt my knee and split my lip open in the parking lot, but I'm okay. Ask me what other tricks I can do!"

Her explanation produced a mixture of laughter and concern, as well as a natural acceptance of the stool the manager delivered for her. Promptly she propped herself in front of the blender and began her contribution to beverage production while Alyssa and Mark assembled sandwiches and

Boris bussed tables in her place. The task was perfect for her, as her mind was occupied with more important matters, namely the current whereabouts of Ty and Trey West, and one Mr. Burne Batson, not to mention the thought of Tatum spending the night in her car.

Midmorning, Candace sidled up to her. "How are you doing?"

Mari smiled. "Fine—thanks. It helps to sit. How are you?"

She nodded. "Good. Hey, Tatum isn't here, you know."

Mari flashed her a look. Did Candace know something about Tatum? Or was she expecting an inside scoop on what had happened that morning or about anything else that was going on with Tatum?

But Candace smiled demurely. "Which means no one's going to yell at you if you go talk to your friend. Maybe do it now before the rush." She winked and walked away.

Mari let out a breath of relief and then took her up on the suggestion, hobbling out to find Professor Grant.

When he saw her, he grimaced. "Oy, what happened to you?"

With a quick glance behind her, Mari boldly pulled out a chair. "I got my nose in someone else's business. And I'm breaking your policy, Dr. Grant. It's my knee. I have to sit."

"No fun. Live and learn, huh?" He waved to the seat. "Make yourself at home."

"I won't stay long. And honestly, it was Tatum's business. I probed her with some questions after our shift yesterday. Without going into it, her family is in crisis right now. She could really use your prayers. But you probably already knew that."

"Yes, she's a troubled lady."

"Yes. The girl I watch is friends with her son. Believe it or not, Tatum's growing on me. I'd like to help her. In fact, I'd like to help a lot of people."

"Yeah?" He tipped his head, his fingers tapping his coffee.

"With everything that's been happening lately, I've been rethinking my life. So much of my past has been lived trying to outdo someone else. Now that I'm learning to find my approval in God, I'd like to do something that truly helps people. I know there's no shortage of ways to serve him, but I'm at a crossroads with my degree right now, and I want to be wise in what I choose. I want God's will for me."

"Good for you, Mari Coleman."

"This disappointment with my knee has been a blessing in disguise. What God's done in me since I've been back in New Hampton is—" She shook her head. "It's been so good. I've learned so much about myself—mostly the hard way. I've had to face some ugliness, but in it, it's like he's taken my drive for achievement and put compassion there instead."

He gave a pleased nod, leaning forward on the table.

"And now it's *your* turn to talk," she said with a smile.

He chuckled. "And I will! Mari, God's will for you first and foremost is that *you* have him, and *he* has you. The world is filled with zealous people doing remarkable things, but if God's not at the center, you're missing it. Your true calling comes from God himself working through you with *his* heart, *his* compassion, like you said. You keep seeking him, and he'll guide you. God uses college degrees, but he's also far beyond that. He's all about the process of getting there. He's about everyday life."

"I've seen that. I simply agreed to watch a little girl after school, and amazing things just opened up from there."

"Exactly. God's about loving a child as much as holding some position somewhere. Trust his leading. He's making you a tool, Mari—*his* tool, to do *his* work."

She nodded thoughtfully. "Thanks. Someday I'd like to hear your faith story, Dr. Grant. And how you got so wise."

"I'd be happy to share it someday. But regarding wisdom, I too have learned the hard and ugly way." He glanced over at the counter. "You seem more at ease today. No one's chasing you off?"

She followed his gaze. "Nope. Tatum's gone. And Candace is—changing. With all that's happened lately, I see there's a lot more important things in life than what people think about me talking to you. Let them bark! I don't care!"

"Good for you!" Dr. Grant said. "So, hey—I need to keep working here, but before you go, I have a question for you. Just a few things we haven't talked about."

"Oh?"

"When the prodigal son came home, the father fetched his best robe, a ring, and some sandals."

Mari pointed her finger at him. "Yes—what do you make of that? You think about that tonight, and I'll ask you for your answer tomorrow!"

The professor burst out in a laugh. "Mari, Mari! I'm praying for your situation with Tatum. See you tomorrow."

When Mari returned behind the counter, Alyssa had moved her stool to a new position.

"I thought you might need a change. Top these off, would you?" She set a few blended drinks before her, nodding to the caramel and whipped cream.

"Thanks," Mari replied, sliding onto her perch.

After the whir of the blender, Alyssa filled another plastic cup, saying, "It's too bad about him, isn't it?"

"Too bad about whom?"

"Professor Grant." She motioned with her head.

Mari glanced behind her. "What's going on?"

"You didn't hear? There's a big bruhaha about him bringing his Bible here and talking to students."

"I knew that a few students took issue with him."

"Well, it's gone to the administration now. Apparently he's being reviewed by the Board of Regents. He could lose his job." With a noisy clatter she scooped fresh ice into her container. "I don't get why he'd do that, why he'd put his job in jeopardy. Yes, he has a right to have a Bible, but he certainly doesn't need to ruin his career because of it. He's a totally nice guy, but what's he trying to do? What does he gain?"

Mark paused on his way by, catching the tail end of her comments. "Who's trying to gain? My friend blended extra nut butter into his protein drink and that helped him. He gained ten pounds in two weeks. Said with the chocolate it wasn't too bad, but with the piña colada it was nasty."

Alyssa blinked. "We're not talking about that, Mark."

"Oh, he's trying to *lose* weight? I saw an ad on my phone for a new fat-burning pill—one of those specials where if you order two, you get one bottle free."

"Nope, we're good, Mark." Alyssa wiggled the ice-filled container onto the blender and the machine roared to life.

At the police station the attending officer greeted Mari with amusement. "Back already, Miss Coleman? What do we have going on today?"

His questions embarrassed her, as though she were some middle-aged busybody stirring up drama for kicks.

"I've learned a few things that might be important," she said, taking her usual spot at the table.

"Okay." He pulled open his laptop and typed in his code. "What's up with your lip?"

"I walked into a door."

He grunted, staring at the screen.

"Has Burne Batson been arrested yet?" Mari asked.

He glanced up. "I'm not at liberty to share."

"Have you found Ty West?"

He eyed her, then cast a quick glance around. "No. And that's all you get."

She sighed, waiting.

"All right, Miss Coleman, what do you have for me?"

She leaned forward. "Okay. I saw Tatum West this morning at work. At the Coffee Break. She told me that someone came harassing Trey about some money hidden in Frost Park and wouldn't let up about it. Then she found out later that this was the same guy who'd been murdered over there. She insists Trey had nothing to do with it. Or her ex, Burne Batson, who was with her that night. They'd never seen the guy before, and she said they didn't know anything about the money—which may or may not be true, but *I* believe her."

His fingers clicked at his keyboard. "And this was where? At Tatum's residence?"

"Her apartment, yes."

"And she said Trey talked to this guy personally?"

"Yes."

"And Tatum witnessed this? What day?"

Mari frowned. "Yes, and the Bats guy too. And I'm not sure when. Tuesday, I think."

"Time of day?"

"No idea."

"Okay. And have you or Mac had any inquiries about that money?"

"No." She shook her head. "No one knows about it except Dan DeSoto, whom you talked to as well. And I told my sister, Shannon. And my friend, JoyAnne."

He nodded. "Good. Anything else?"

"No."

"Thank you, Miss Coleman." He clicked out of his file, closed his laptop, and rose to his feet. "Thank you for coming in with this."

Mari was happy that her stop at the police station had been quick, but nevertheless, it pushed back her visit at Riverview once again. Checking both her grandfather's room and the courtyard, she finally found him in the dining room practicing his picture cards, his flip-top water bottle nearby. Immediately he noticed her swollen lip, but the briefest explanation was sufficient, and thankfully, the subject passed without fuss.

"Your grandfather has a lot of energy this afternoon," the aide stated, spreading out a new row of cards for him. "He had a little nap after lunch, and he's raring to go!"

Slowly her grandfather tapped the pictures. "Go to the zzzoo. Go to the ffffarm. Go to the park." He looked up proudly at Mari, who patted his arm through his plaid flannel sleeve.

"Wow, look at you go! And I'd *love* to take you to a park or the zoo!"

He pointed to another. "Go in the car."

"That's right!" Mari smiled at the aide. "Wow—he's keeping you busy!"

"He sure is!" the aide returned. "It's like he's flipped a switch. His language skills have really accelerated this week!"

"Go for a ride," Mari's grandfather said, pointing to a card. He looked up with a grin. "In Marree's car!"

Mari laughed. "Now wouldn't *that* be a blast! We should do that some time!" She turned to the aide. "Do they allow that? That would be so fun!"

The staffer nodded. "Yes, of course! You'd just need to sign him out. I wouldn't advise being gone very long initially, but an outing would do him good. He'd love that!"

"Even today?" she asked, her mind spinning a sudden plan. What if she took her grandfather to pick up Aubrey and came right back? The jaunt would be short, but at least he would have a change of scenery.

"Sure—why not?"

Mari smiled questioningly at her grandfather. "What do you think, Poppy? Would you be up for that today? Would you like to go to Mac's with me?"

"Yesss! I'd like that verrry m-m-m—" He began scraping together his cards.

"You'd like that very much."

"Yesss!" As her eyes dropped to his pocket, he added, "Mac says, 'Hello.'"

She smiled, a little embarrassed. But only a little, for it was Poppy.

As it turned out, getting out the door was a drawn-out affair, as permission needed to be granted by her mother first. After they got a hold of her and he was finally cleared to go, her grandfather had to be toileted and given his afternoon medication before they left, as well as fitted with the proper walking shoes and a jacket. Then there was signing him out and the slow walk through the parking lot, getting him situated in the car, and belting him in. Then instructions on stowing his walker and re-opening it for use later.

Even so, Mari didn't mind. It was still time spent together. Plus while she was waiting, the thought occurred to her that having Poppy would be a great diversion for Aubrey, given that Mac wanted them elsewhere in the afternoon. Mari would need to return him to the nursing home shortly, a fitting excuse to cancel kickball for both Aubrey and the pack, though doubtless they would be disappointed.

They parked in front of Dixie's, across the street from the bus stop so that Poppy could see the colorfully dressed school children disembark from the bus and scatter noisily to their homes. Mari honked to get Aubrey's attention, letting her know they would meet her at home, then drove ahead to park at Mac's curb. She left Poppy in the passenger's seat but came around and opened his door, visiting with him while they waited for Aubrey to arrive. In front of Roger Eden's, she noted the same metallic teal car that had been there earlier that week, although no one was in it.

"I met two new friends who want to play kickball!" Aubrey announced as she arrived, her cheeks rosy. Then spying who was along, she exclaimed, "Hey, it's your Grandpa Poppy! Hello! Did you bring me a lollipop?"

Poppy, of course, was thrilled. He turned in his seat. "Hello, Bree! Not today."

"Aww! Did you come to watch us?" She turned to Mari. "Two girls moved into that blue-and-gray house by the bus. They said they'd ask their mom if they can come. And Parker's mom gave me these at the bus stop." She whipped off her backpack, producing an extra-large package of sandwich cookies. "He's coming later. What happened to your mouth?"

"I cut my lip. Hey—I'm not sure it's going to work out to play kickball today, Aubrey," Mari told her. "This is Poppy's first outing. It's kind of an experiment. I'll need to take him back soon."

Aubrey's head swung toward him and back at her. "We can't play?"

"Well, he's—old. He gets tired quickly."

"But—but everyone is coming!"

Indeed, Mari was aware of the kids currently congregating on the field. "Aubrey, I'm sorry—"

"Just got here," her grandfather spoke suddenly from the car. "Can't go now."

"Can't he watch us?" Aubrey asked.

Poppy raised his gnarled hand toward the field. "Yesss! Let them play."

Mari shook her head in protest. Just getting him this far had been an ordeal, and now she was supposed to walk him over uneven ground to sit on his walker at the field—? "I think that might be a difficult walk for you," she told him gently.

"I stay here." He tapped the dash, as if indicating he would observe from the car.

Mari sighed. "Okay—here's what we'll do. Aubrey, go get the ball. I'll move the car so that Poppy's closer. And then when kickball is over, I'll need to take him right home."

Both Aubrey and Poppy grinned in triumph. Handing off the cookies, Aubrey scurried for the house while Mari got in to move the car.

"You certainly know how to get your own way, don't you?" she told him on the tiny drive to the edge of the field. "You're like a teenager again."

Poppy laughed with delight, and Mari's heart felt full. And now that Plan *B* was in operation, she could admit that she was overjoyed to have him watch her on the job. She felt like one of the kids. Secondarily, he kept her attention off Ty, who, as she had expected, was absent again.

After the game Aubrey begged to have their cookie snacks over beside the car so that the other kids could meet Mari's Grandpa Poppy. Rallying everyone, she led the way, only to find him sound asleep in his seat. Awakened by the giggling children, he brought his muffed head up in surprise.

"Aubrey wants to introduce you to her friends," Mari told him.

He smiled broadly at the amused and staring crew, raising his hand to wave. "Hello! Nice kids. Nice kids."

Mari passed around the treats, sharing a cookie with her grandfather too, who was thoroughly enjoying himself. But after allowing a healthy space of time, she clapped her hands. "All right, kiddos! It's time to call it quits today. Aubrey and I are going to take my grandfather back to his home."

Charging in, Aubrey pointed skyward. "Hands up, everyone!" She looked to Mari to finish.

Mari smiled. "How 'bout we say it together. Ready? Nice and loud—"

It was a collective shout: "God hears you when you pray!"

"That's right! Now this!"

And with a grumble all hands and heads dropped to scout for trash.

"See you tomorrow, everyone!" Then with a jolt, she corrected herself. "Wait! I'm not going to be here tomorrow or next week! So no kickball!"

All heads snapped up.

"Sorry! There's no school, and Aubrey's going to be at her grandma's."

More groans and protests. Aubrey, of course, let everyone know that the decision was clearly not her choice.

Mari turned to the girl. "Ready? You get to come with me to take Poppy back."

Aubrey cocked her head. "What about my school project? Will I have time to do it after?"

"You'll have to bring it."

"What? I have to do it *there*?"

"No. We'll stop at my place for a little bit."

Aubrey looked utterly confused. "We're going there too? Why?"

"Uh, your dad thought it would be a fun change."

She frowned. "Okay. Weird. Well, you're going to have to help me bring it to the car. It's my volcano. Dad and I stayed up late making it, but I couldn't paint it 'cause it wasn't dry. I'm supposed to bring it to school tomorrow."

"Nice. I can't wait to see it."

"It's so cool! We made it *so* huge! He's going to have to drive me. Can I show Grandpa Poppy?"

"Well, I expect he'll see it when we bring it to the car."

But in the miniscule drive back to Mac's curb, Aubrey invited Grandpa Poppy inside to see her and her dad's creation, and flattered by her attention, Poppy insisted on doing that very thing. Mari quickly nixed the idea, but Aubrey pressed it, and during their deliberation, Poppy happened to open the car door and slide off his seat to a standing position. Quickly Mari hurried around the car to clarify why they needed to get back, but Poppy simply closed his eyes and inhaled the fresh afternoon air.

"Sun is so nice," he said. "So nice."

She conceded, but only partially. "All right, Pop Pop. Here's what we'll do: I'll let you sit here until we get her volcano to the car. Aubrey, no more questions! That is my *final* answer!"

Disappointed but agreeable, Aubrey ran ahead into the house, and after setting up her grandfather on the sidewalk with his walker, Mari followed.

When she was halfway to the porch, her phone rang. It was Mac.

"Hi. This is one of those stereotypical good-news-bad-news calls," he said.

"What?" she asked, bracing herself.

"I just got a call from the NHPD. Trey West and Burne Batson have been taken into custody. Not sure on what charges. Possession maybe."

Mari huffed. "Now why do *you* get that call and not me? So what about Ty? Did they say anything about him?"

"That's the bad news part."

"No! What happened?"

"Just that they haven't found him yet—that's all."

Mari's eyes scanned the field for the thousandth time. "Okay. Well, I suppose that's good—about Trey and Bats. Although, Mac, I had a confrontation with Tatum this morning in the Taiton parking lot, and guess what? You know that murder in Whitmore the other night? Well, turns out the victim had been over there in Trey's face about *our* money! The field money. Then he ends up *dead*! It's so creepy! She swears Trey knew nothing about it."

"Interesting."

"I stopped to report it. I think they're sick of seeing me in there! Anyway, something's going on. I'm sure curious about that gun in Trey's pillowcase. Maybe it's *not* the murder weapon."

"You didn't touch that, did you?"

She made a sound. "Are you kidding? Absolutely not! Anyway, I'm currently in a dilemma, Mac. My afternoon isn't going according to plan. I brought Poppy with me from the nursing home on a whim, and we ended up staying for kickball. And now if we go back, Aubrey needs to bring her volcano, which I haven't seen yet, but—"

He chuckled. "Oh, golly, I'll bet he's loving that! Leave the volcano. We'll finish it tonight."

"That's what I was thinking, but I wasn't sure."

"No, it's a beast. I'd prefer you didn't move it."

"Thank you. Although she's begging for Poppy to see it. Do you mind if he takes a peek? Then we'll leave—I promise."

"Fine. I'll see you at Kingswood when I get off work."

Mari hung up to hear Roger Eden hailing her from next door where he was out treating weeds with a spray bottle. Dogless. He took a few steps in her direction.

"Hello there! Did they find the missing boy?"

She shook her head. "No, but I hear they have a couple of fellows from Whitmore in custody." She gestured across the field.

He tipped his head in alarm. "Goodness! They're not suspecting foul play, are they?"

"With Ty? No. I sure hope not! No, it was in connection to some other stuff that was found."

"Oh? What'd they find?"

"Oh, you know what it's like over there," she said evasively. She refused to divulge anything about the backpack. Nor did she particularly care to have Roger Eden know that a pillowcase of hard drugs was dragged next door to his home. "But I suspect Ty will show up now. How about you, Mr. Eden? Have you found Loki yet?"

"Still gone. I thought by now he'd find his way back, but—" He trailed off with a shrug. He motioned to her grandfather, who Mari noticed had been slowly making his way toward the house with his walker. "I see you have an extra hand today."

"Yes. This is my grandfather, Delbert Jones, who's a little more active than I anticipated!" She smiled, giving Mr. Eden a knowing look. "Poppy, this is Mac's neighbor, Roger Eden. He lives in our old house."

Her grandfather raised his head to smile.

Mr. Eden nodded. "Sir. Need a hand on those steps?" Swiftly he crossed his yard to help them.

"You're a saint," Mari replied, having not yet considered that challenge. "This excursion was *not* thought out! And I split my lip open before work, in case you're wondering."

He chuckled. "Didn't want to ask."

After Roger Eden assisted her grandfather onto the porch, he delivered his walker and said goodbye. Mari thanked him for his help but was grateful he was gone before Aubrey spied him there. But perhaps that was why he left, she mused.

Aubrey met them at the door, her brow all furled. "Wait—we're staying now?"

"Your dad says to leave the volcano. I'm going to let Poppy look at it."

"Yes!" She opened the door wider for him to pass. "But when will I paint it?"

"Tonight, he said."

"Aww, I wish I could paint it now. Wait until you see it!"

Mari motioned to the girl's backpack in the middle of the floor, and Aubrey moved it to her cubby, then stood back as Poppy entered the house.

"Mac's girrrl!" he chirped happily, making them both giggle.

"Over here, Poppy," Mari said, guiding him into the living room within sight of the hefty paper mâché creation on the plastic-and-newspaper-covered table. She picked a spot. "Let's park you here." She noticed her grandfather seemed winded. He was not accustomed to stairs.

"All right, girl. Show us what you've got!" Mari said, coming to stand near her.

In classic TV game show style, the girl's arms glided smoothly and dramatically around the paper mâché mountain, beside which a partial bag of flour sat near a pile of papers and an old bucket of leftover pasty goop. In detail she described how her dad had constructed the wood-and-wire frame for their sloppy project. As she listened, Mari's eyes were drawn to one of the newspaper pages protecting the table: the article her mother had shown her about the Whitmore murder, only in print. She regarded the photo of the victim, now having Tatum's new information mingled with the disturbing sense that she had seen that man somewhere. At the nursing home? Or on the Taiton campus maybe?

"Like it?" Aubrey asked proudly, flicking the dry paint brushes over the volcano's sides. "I can't wait to paint it!"

"Love it!" she replied, stooping for a handful of sticky masking tape debris on the floor. "But you two sure made a mess!"

"Yeah, we were up *so* late! It was like midnight—or ten o'clock or something! Dad said we'll clean up when it's done."

"Well, hey—Grandpa Poppy needs a few minutes to rest. Let's do your chores. Then we'll take him home and go to my house."

"Could we watch a show? He could rest while we watch it!"

"Sorry. We're not staying that long."

As Aubrey skulked out of the room, Mari deposited her trash into the kitchen bin that had been brought into the dining room for the volcano construction. As she pushed the wad of tape down, she suddenly noticed something colorful below. Carefully she pulled out a stiff card, discovering a greeting card print of a Van Gogh-ish style seascape, now quite bent up and spotted with crusty, dried goop from last evening's creative endeavor. She opened it to Mac's handwriting: "Marissa—"

Her breath caught, and she pivoted so her grandfather wouldn't see. Her name and nothing more. There came that familiar flutter inside. Mac Sinclair had been starting to write her a note! Why had he stopped? But then she thought that perhaps it was from before Will had showed up at the field, before she had told him she couldn't work for him anymore. She stared at the empty card, somewhat indignant, as though he had thrown *her* in the trash! Determinedly she picked off the dried chunks, rubbing the paper clean against her shirt. Then after bending out the creases, she slipped the card into Mac's Bible on the little desk behind the table.

And then afterwards while washing her hands in the kitchen, her conscience pricked her. *No compromise.* What was Mac supposed to think when he found it? He would get her message—basically telling him not to give up on her. And wasn't that her point? She sighed, drying her hands, staring out the kitchen window in a mental tug-o-war. No, she couldn't leave it there. She would take it with her instead, she decided. But right then her eyes fell on a little movement on the far side of Mac's driveway, right at the front corner of his garage. She blinked in surprise as whatever it was instantly disappeared into the lilac bushes. Was that—was that an animal? It had looked like fur. Almost like it could have been the hind end of a dog!

Immediately she reached for her phone. Pulling up Roger Eden's name, she sent him a text. "Hey, I think Loki might be in our driveway." As the text sent, she corrected herself. *Mac's* driveway.

Then glancing out the window again, she frowned, spotting something else lying in the underbrush. Quickly she set her phone on the counter, pushing up with her arms to see better. Sure enough, she spied a small purple bag on the ground under the lilac. A reusable purple bag. It looked like—oh, my, could that be—was that Ty's snack bag? Her heart began racing.

She glanced back toward the living room. "Aubrey?"

"Almost done!" she called.

Mari grabbed a large pack of sandwich meat from the refrigerator. "Okay. Hey, I'm running outside for a minute. I changed my mind. You can start a show with Poppy, okay? Pick one that he would like!" At the moment she was fine with anything that would keep Aubrey from spying that dog.

Aubrey gave a cheer. "Thank you!"

Chapter Twenty-Nine

After sneaking the pepper spray from the top of the foyer cubbies, Mari hurried out the back door. As she crossed the driveway, her first mission was to get a closer look at that reusable bag—and, yes, she confirmed, it was the one she had given to Ty. She recognized the bank logo. And it was empty. She straightened, casting a quick look around before facing the thick lilacs beside the garage. She shouldn't be out here. She should let Roger Eden come and look for his dog and *then* figure out how that bag ended up there. But what if Ty was nearby? What if he had returned it and that was as close as he could bring it?

On the other hand, Loki might have found it and dragged it there. Certainly the cloth would have absorbed the scent of meat sticks.

She fingered the sandwich meat. Days ago when she had pacified those dogs with meatballs, there had been a fence between them. If they came face to face today, there was no guarantee that Loki would be interested in smoked turkey. Nor was Mari confident she wouldn't miss if she had to use the pepper spray, *if* the dog was even there. He may have long disappeared already.

Deciding to take a peek, she cautiously approached the corner of the garage, softly calling the dog's name so as not to surprise him if he was indeed resting under the bushes. However, when she moved aside the lilac limbs and poked her head around the corner, she gaped in astonishment at the makeshift camp before her—a jumbo cardboard appliance box wedged tightly between the bushes and the garage, its opening facing away from her. Scattered in the underbrush were apple cores, string cheese wrappers, ketchup packets, empty plastic water bottles, and candy wrappers. *Tons* of candy wrappers. Under any other circumstances she might have regarded the spot as a play fort of Aubrey's; however, protruding from the far side of the box she spied a small patch of the blue buffalo plaid comforter she had left for Ty on Mac's porch.

So this was where that little rascal had been hiding! Right under their noses. Mari shook her head in wonder at how protected from view the little hideout was. Had Ty been sleeping in that box? Why, he might have even watched them play kickball less than an hour ago! Leaning down, she could see their homemade diamond through the newly leafed branches. But where was Ty?

Sucking in her belly, she nimbly slid alongside his box to check out the inside. Swinging her head down to look into the opening, she unwittingly loomed over a hidden and mutually startled Loki, who sprang to his feet in a snarl, baring his teeth. Mari screamed, jarring her knee as she flinched, bumbling the pepper spray, which bounced into the bushes.

"Whoa—hey, hey, Loki," she croaked, frozen with her hands up. "Hey, boy!"

The dog uttered a low, warning growl, watching her with his black eyes. And then he was still, panting heavily as he stood on the comforter, which Ty had folded and spread out in the box like a bedroll. Mari observed the dog for a moment, then cautiously brought down the package of sandwich meat.

"Easy, boy," she said softly, slowly peeling a wad of meat from the crinkly package. She held it up for the dog to see. "Hey, Loki! Here you go!" Gingerly she tossed it to the blanket.

After a brief exploratory sniff, the dog gulped it down. But as he raised his head, he gave a sudden agonizing yelp. Mari stiffened, watching the dog hobble awkwardly in a circle to flop onto the blanket, from where he turned his imploring eyes back to Mari. Clearly, Loki was hurt. Or very sick. The dog needed a vet.

"You poor thing!" she breathed, craning her head to see where he might be injured. Carefully she lobbed him another slab of meat, which was promptly gobbled up. She continued until the package was empty, then held up her hands. "All gone, Loki."

With a pathetic whine the dog lowered its head to rest his muzzle on the blanket.

"Your master's coming," she murmured. Had Ty fed him chocolate, perhaps?

Behind her she heard the slam of the back door.

"Maaarrrri!" Aubrey called at top volume.

Quickly Mari scooted back alongside the box to dart around the corner. "I'm right here!"

Aubrey crossed the driveway in her stocking feet with Mari's phone. "Here. Someone called. Your phone rang and rang and rang in the kitchen."

"Oh, thanks." Mari took it, observing that Mac had left a message.

"What are you doing?" Aubrey asked.

"Checking some plants," she answered ambiguously. "How's it going in there with Poppy?" Yikes—the nursing home was probably wondering where they were.

Aubrey gave a thumbs-up. "We're good. We're watching a funny *Tom and Jerry.* But I have to go!" Not wanting to miss a moment, she disappeared inside.

Mari pulled up Mac's message and was about to listen to it on her way back to Loki, but as she parted the lilac bushes at the corner of the garage, she glanced up to see Ty simultaneously arrive there from the back of the yard. Her hand flew to her chest as their eyes met over the top of the cardboard box.

"Ty, don't run!" she exclaimed, and the two simply gawked at each other. "Are you—are you all right? Are you hungry?" She tucked the phone under her arm to hold up the empty meat package.

He shook his head, wide-eyed. "What happened?"

Her mouth. "Oh, I split my lip open. It's okay."

He sniffed, gesturing inside the box. "Teacher, I found a dog."

"I see that! It's our neighbor's missing dog, Loki. He's hurt, isn't he?" Quickly she slid between the shrubbery and the box to join him, where he gazed down at the panting creature.

He pointed. "It's his back leg. He's hurt real bad. Real bad."

Mari silently agreed, now observing blood on the blanket. "I already texted Mr. Eden that his dog is at our house. He'll be along soon to help him."

Ty didn't reply.

She studied him—dirty face, filthy arms and shirt, grass-stained knees caked with dirt. His jeans were shot. "Are you sure you're not hungry, Ty? I could get you something." But he said no. Given the quantity of candy wrappers strewn about, she was tempted to ask if his lunch had been courtesy of Dixie's. Images of her childhood wisped through her mind. But stealing was a subject she didn't want to broach right now.

Instead, she jerked her head toward his box tent. "Quite the camp you have here! Nice job!" Then she regretted saying it, as if she were insinuating that he had built it for fun instead of survival. His small shoulders carried a weight far beyond his age.

Gently she touched his arm. "Ty, you did the right thing yesterday—bringing me those drugs. That was a super-smart thing to do. I took them to the police, and they took Bats away. They're going to help you and your mom have a home that's safe." She thought it best not to mention Trey.

He nodded, though his creased brow showed no relief.

Her phone chirped. She checked it in case it was Mac again. But it was Roger Eden, replying to her text about the dog: "Thanks. Be there in a few minutes."

Good. Now they could get that dog taken care of.

"There—that was Mr. Eden," she told Ty, shoving the phone into her back pocket. "He's coming for his dog. He'll make sure Loki gets help." She kicked the edge of the blue checked blanket. "Were you warm enough last ni—" She stopped, her jaw dropping as her foot uncovered a stiff bundle of hundred-dollar bills. Ty shrank back as she cast him a stunned look.

"Ty! Where did you get this money?"

His face was plastered with guilt.

"Ty—"

"I didn't steal it!" he spurted defensively. "I *found* it!"

"You found it? Where?" She lifted the comforter to see if there was more.

No answer.

"Where, Ty? You have to tell me! Is there more than this?"

He regarded her a moment before his hand twitched. "Over there. In Aubrey's backyard."

"Aubrey's backyard?" She snorted. "Right! Why would it be there?"

"Um—I think her dad was hiding it."

She stared as his words slowly sank in. Then she turned her face incredulously in the direction of Mac's house, her thoughts reeling as her eyes rested on the garage siding. No way!

"It was in a bag with some other stuff," Ty added.

Her hand went to her head. There was no way! Could it—could it be? Had that backpack been his all along? Had Mac been dishonest the whole time about that money? She felt sick. "Ty, can you show me exactly where you found this?"

His expression—his eyes—and the way his shoulders tensed. Mari could tell he was struggling. She shook her head. "Don't run! You're not in trouble, Ty. Just show me what you found. Please."

To her surprise, he turned without a word, signaling her to follow. Hastily he slipped back the way he had come, leading her around the back of Mac's garage and across the yard to the base of a large spreading tree in the far corner beside Roger Eden's fence. Mac's lawn was patchy in the shade there, but nevertheless, she could see the ground had been dug up, mostly beside the fence, doubtless an indication of Loki's shenanigans sometime in the past. Yet the yard was sealed, Mari ascertained with relief, as there was no gap between the ground and the fence where a hundred-pound hound might have wiggled through.

"I found it hidden back here," Ty said. Motioning for her to stop, he continued to a cluster of scraggly buckthorn bushes at the yard's edge, where he crouched to disappear for a second, then reappeared, carrying a dirty carry-on-style suitcase, small and black.

"This is part of it," he said, rolling it to her across the dirt and crouching in the moist underbrush to unzip it.

She hovered curiously, wondering if he were telling the truth. Was the bag *his*? Had he packed a little overnight bag to run away and stashed in some of Trey's money? If so, it was both endearing and awfully cunning for a boy like Ty. But as he raised the top, her presumptions scattered, for all its contents were wrapped in a layer of thick plastic sheeting. It crinkled as Ty spread it apart, revealing neatly folded medical scrubs. Surgical blues.

Mari gave a cry. "Scrubs!"

"It's hospital stuff," he said, snatching up the top layer to expose what appeared to be a lab coat underneath, plus medical goggles, surgical head and shoe coverings, face masks, and a box of latex gloves, all nested tightly together.

Bewildered, she bent down for a closer look. Were these some college surplus of Mac's perhaps? Why were they in his yard? Was he hiding them?

"Plus there's this," Ty said, moving the medical garb aside to pull out a tan button-down shirt.

Mari held it up, observing its delicate piping and a logoed cloth patch sewn on the arm. A security company uniform. Men's size large. Its coordinating brown slacks lay on the layer of plastic at the bottom of the suitcase. She turned to him, her brow furled. "Ty, what is this? And where's the money?"

He waved toward the buckthorn. "It's in the other bag."

"Go get it," she urged, draping the shirt over her arm. Good heavens—what was Mac doing with money and medical garb in his yard? And a security company uniform—? It made no sense.

But then as Ty scrambled back toward the bushes, something else occurred to her. Had Ty fabricated this whole story? Was this Trey's suitcase perhaps? Or Bats'? Had Ty whisked this suitcase away from Whitmore along with that pillowcase of drugs and hidden it here? But why such odd contents, she wondered, watching as Ty produced a dirty and somewhat tattered garbage bag from back in the bushes. A *black* garbage bag, she noted as he dragged it to her under the tree. She shot a brief glance over her shoulder toward Aubrey's old window, hoping it wasn't a misplaced body bag of Roger Eden's.

Squatting, Ty rustled open the bag. "Here," he said, handing up a hairy, pelt-like object.

"Eww!" She cringed, drawing back. "What is it?"

"It's a hair thing—like a wig, I think."

Sure enough. Pinching it by the edge, she took it, identifying a men's medium-brown hairpiece.

"And these," Ty added, showing her a shallow box of mustaches the same shade.

Mari let out a breath. "What in the world? What is this, Ty?" A men's toupee and boxed mustaches? Plus medical garb and—

"And Teacher, here—" he whispered, bringing up a flat bundle of cash. "There's tons of these in here! See?" He spread the bag open to uncover dozens of neatly bound bundles. "It's *real* too! I bought stuff with it at Dixie's."

Mari's stomach twisted. "Ty, look at me."

He met her eyes and immediately looked away.

"I need you to tell me the truth. Where did you find these? Where did you find this bag and this suitcase? Who do they belong to?"

He squirmed.

"I need to know. It's important. Did you find these hidden in those bushes or somewhere else? Are they Trey's? Did *you* hide them here?"

He hesitated, then reluctantly pointed to the fence. "There. I heard the dog making sad noises, and I came over to see."

Mari turned to look where he indicated. "Sad noises?"

"Crying-like. From its bloody leg, I think. It was trying to dig under the fence—maybe to get home—but it was too hurt. I used your sausage to get him to my camp. But that's when I saw that suitcase in the dirt. Only part of it showed. So I came back and dug it out, and this bag was under it, pushed flat." He motioned back to the bushes. "I hid them in there 'cause of the money. Then I pushed all the dirt back under so the other dog wouldn't get out. It was hard work."

Indeed, Mari observed what might have been a dark blood smear low on the lumber. She moved her gaze to Ty. "Did this happen today?"

He nodded.

Her eyes grazed his dirty shirt. "And were these bags buried on *this* side of the fence or the *other*?"

"The other side, but close. Kinda under it—like right by the edge. Maybe they're that dog guy's Halloween clothes."

"Yeah, maybe," she said dryly with a sudden shudder. She cast an anxious glance along the fence toward the street. Roger Eden. She had known something wasn't right with him all along. And now at any minute he could show up for his dog. Hastily she threw the hairpiece into the bag. Another pile of money, a security uniform, and medical scrubs—she couldn't fathom what they were all about, but the combination had creepiness written all over it. She and Ty needed to scram.

"Ty, we need to go." Wadding the shirt, she tossed it into the suitcase and roughly tucked the loose plastic around the medical garb. Flopping the lid, she brushed off a chunk of mud, fumbling for the zipper. "Thanks for showing me this, but we need to get out of here." Righting the little carry-on, she turned the handle toward him. "Here—go put it back. Quickly! Both of these."

But Ty hadn't moved.

She wiped her hands on her jeans, nudging the garbage bag with her foot. "Ty—go on! Hurry! Put these back so we can leave! I'm calling the police." She pulled out her phone, casting another nervous glance behind her.

"Will I have to go to jail?"

Her head whipped back at him. "What?"

"For taking his stuff."

She blinked. "No! No, Ty. You didn't do anything wrong."

He looked guiltily at the fence.

It occurred to her then that maybe Ty felt more than guilty. Maybe he had thought he had hit the jackpot with his find. Perhaps he had intended to help his brother settle his debt with that Burne Batson thug, and Mari's intrusion had foiled his plans. Was he disappointed? But what could she do?

"Ty, you're not in trouble, but this stuff is important. The police need to know about it. But, um—maybe I could take you home first. If you want." No, she wouldn't, of course. She would take him straight to the station. But he couldn't know that.

She fingered the phone, glancing again to the front of the yard. If she called 911, she risked having him flee, but convincing the nervous lad to deliver his booty to the police station with her seemed near to impossible.

The boy's eyes darted back to her. "Is Bats for real gone?"

She nodded. "I—yes, he's in custody. He's at the police station." She shot another look toward the street. *Come on, Ty.*

"'Cause he says if I call the police for *anything,* he'll kill my mom."

Mari swung her head side to side. "He won't know about it, and he's not going to find out!"

"He might *sometime.*"

"I'll do my very best to see that you're protected," she said. "But I'm sorry, Ty—we have to call the police."

As she eyed him, she suddenly remembered Aubrey in the house—and Poppy—the situation growing more complicated as she tried to determine how she would handle Ty, Aubrey, and her grandfather all at the same time when the police arrived. Ty needed her full attention, period. Yet the combination of Aubrey and Ty was volatile. And Poppy—he needed to go back to the nursing home, pronto. Plain and simple, she needed Mac. She needed Mac *now.* She was mortified that she had even momentarily suspected him.

She held up her phone. "Okay, I'm calling Aubrey's dad, all right? I'm calling him first. Then the police."

But Mac didn't answer his phone. Dang. She was afraid of that. Debating what to do, she sighed, pushing the icon and bringing the phone to her ear to listen to his message:

"Hey, Marissa—thank God you're out of there! My appointment is starting, and I can't talk, but real quick—you've *got* to hear this! The police called just now to make sure you weren't at the house. The officer said they traced that backpack money to a bank robbed at gunpoint a few months ago! A bank robbery—can you stinkin' believe it? In Seattle! They're pretty sure the Whitmore murder is connected, but the pillowcase gun was *not* the murder weapon. Thank God.

"Anyway, they're questioning both Bats and Ty's brother about the incident now. Sounds like they're hot on their suspect and moving in. Stranger than fiction, I tell you! Anyway, glad you're out of there—and don't go back, okay? There's a lot more, but I'll tell you at Kingswood. I'll try to leave here as soon as I can."

Mari suddenly felt cold. She stared at Ty as she brought her phone down. But before she could even process Mac's news, Ty gestured behind her.

"Teacher—"

Mari followed his gaze toward the street—this time spying Roger Eden crossing Mac's lawn at the front of the house, doubtless heading for the driveway. Crud. With a jolt of panic, she turned to Ty, still sitting with the trash bag between his knees.

"Ty, get up! We've got to hide these now! Right now! *Quick!*" She snatched the suitcase, dragging it toward the buckthorn bushes. "Roger Eden's on his way, and—"

Ty looked stricken. "Are you going to tell on me?"

"No, I'm not telling him anything, but hurry up!" Urgently she motioned him to follow.

He hefted the bag, lugging it over in what seemed like slow motion.

"Go on—hide them where they were before! Hurry!" She nudged him into the bushes, handing in the suitcase after him. When he reappeared, she caught him by the front of his shirt. "Listen, Ty—I need your help! I need you to run like the wind—either to Dixie's or back home to your mom. Tell her I'm in trouble and she needs to send the police, okay? To the last house before Frost Park."

Ty stared, his face puckered. "Trouble?"

"Because Mr. Eden is coming!"

"Isn't he—I thought he was getting his dog!"

"Ty, Roger Eden is—"

But right then Mari spotted Roger Eden on the driveway between the house and the garage. Crud. There he was. Instantly she dropped Ty, guiding him away from the bushes.

Spying them, Mr. Eden raised his hand, turning to cross the lawn. "Hey there! I got your message! So that Loki rascal finally showed up, eh? Is he still around?"

"Hello!" Mari called, waving back, continuing to sidle out from under the tree. Oh, crud. He was coming straight for them. She hoped he hadn't observed them dump those bags. With a smile locked on her face, she turned to Ty, speaking quietly through her teeth, "Ty, go do what I said. Right now! *Run!*"

Ty threw a shocked and confused look at the approaching man. Then with another wild glance at Mari, he bolted away through the side yard along the fence to the street.

Chapter Thirty

"*Hey!*" Mari shouted after Ty as he sprinted away through Mac's side yard. "Hey!"

Feigning indignance, Mari disregarded Roger Eden to trot feebly after the kid, making protesting sounds as though calling him back—though she dared not actually do it, lest she confuse him and make him stop. At the edge of Mac's house she halted, dramatically dropping her arms in fake defeat as she turned back to Mr. Eden, who had paused to observe her from the center of the yard.

"*Dang it!* That was *him*—the missing child!" she cried, trying to sound breathless. "I almost had him! I *almost* had him! I'm calling the police!" She patted her back pocket for her phone, alarmed to find it gone. Crud. She had probably dropped it shoving that black carry-on into the bushes, and now she dare not go back for it. Crud, crud, crud. Why hadn't she called the police right away? She slapped her thigh. "Rats! My phone's in the house. Can I use yours?"

"I don't have mine either," Roger Eden said coolly, sending a long glance toward the fence in the corner where she and Ty had been.

"Maybe I'll run in and get it," she said, starting for the driveway.

But he shook his head, raising a hand to stop her. "Naw, don't bother. That kid is long gone. They're never going to find him now."

"Oh, right," Mari said, pausing to glance at the grassy corridor through which Ty had escaped. "Probably not, huh? Man, I can't believe it—he was *right here*! I saw what I thought was your dog on our driveway, and then when I came out, there was *Ty*—hanging out by the garage! He took off back here, and I was able to talk to him a little. I almost had him convinced to come with me—almost—until you showed up!"

Now he was looking at the tree. *Oh, God, let him not investigate.* She was still in disbelief at Mac's call. Had she heard him correctly? How was a bank robbery even possible this day and age with the high-tech security equipment banks used? But it sure explained a lot. A lot. Her heart was racing.

"But um, hey—Loki's over here—" she continued loudly, beckoning for him to follow. "You better come quick! He looks hurt. I think you'll want to get him to a vet." She strode off briskly for the back of the garage, pivoting at the edge to find him following. But slowly. He was walking too slowly.

"Over here," she babbled, waving him on. "Right between the lilacs and the far side of the garage. The kid built a fort. He's been sleeping here—can you believe it? And someone else is using it too." As she rounded the corner, she motioned to the dog now panting on his side on the blanket.

At the sight of his master, Loki's tail flicked, and he raised his head. Laboriously he pulled himself up, hobbling forward with a yowl of pain. It was then that Mari noticed the mangled flesh of the dog's back leg. She grimaced, covering her mouth. It looked as though the poor thing had been hit by a car or caught in barbed wire or something sharp. Or—or as though he had been shot. The thought gave her the willies, and she backed a step as Roger Eden impassively studied the animal.

"Loki, heel!" he commanded, and the dog halted. He glanced at Mari. "Look away."

"What?"

Reaching back, Roger Eden drew out a handgun, took aim, and fired on his dog.

Mari screamed as the dog dropped. "Oh, my God!" she cried, stumbling backwards. "You shot your dog!"

Calmly he returned the gun to its hidden holster. "I told you to look away."

She stared at him horrified, her hand on her chest.

"He wasn't going to make it," he said, observing the lifeless animal, now twitching as it bled out in the grass. He gave a sigh, motioning toward the house. "Let's go inside."

"You shot him! You could have taken him to the vet!"

His lip curled into a smile. "I know what I'm doing. It was too late. Trust me."

Trust him? She had zero trust for Roger Eden. None. But now Aubrey was outside, calling her from the opposite side of the garage.

"Coming!" she yelled back, then dazedly made herself walk. The last thing she wanted was for Aubrey to come searching for her and find the dead dog. Its plight made her sick to her stomach.

As they neared the driveway, Mari spied Aubrey on the back step hanging out the door. "Did you hear that loud noise? What *was* that? Why did you scream?" She suddenly noticed Roger Eden and tensed. "Why is *he* here?"

"We heard it too!" Mr. Eden declared, his brow creased with concern. "It sounded like a gunshot or something—from over there!" He pointed to the field. "I was looking for my dog, but we'd better get inside!" He waved Mari toward the door.

"We're all right, Aubrey," Mari said, not budging from where they had paused on the driveway.

"What happened?" Aubrey repeated, peering anxiously where Mr. Eden had indicated. "Is there a bad guy?"

"There might be!" Mr. Eden said, casting another worried glance over his shoulder. He waved Mari toward the house.

Mari jerked her head, urging Aubrey in. "You go on, sweetie. I'll be in soon. Go make sure Poppy's not afraid!" All she wanted was to get that girl and her grandfather in the car and speed away.

Aubrey hesitated, then with a dubious look, disappeared inside.

When the door closed, Mari drew herself up, thrusting out her chin. "Mr. Eden, you are *not* going into Mac's house! What do you want?" Her heart was pounding out of her chest.

He regarded her with amusement. "You honestly need to ask? Don't play the fool with me, Miss Coleman. You know exactly what I want, and you're going to give it to me. Go on—"

She shook her head. "I don't know what you're talking about, but you are absolutely *not* going in there! Anything we need to talk about can happen right here."

He made a sound, reaching up to scratch his neck. "Look, Margaret, we can do this the hard way or the easy way. Your choice."

"There's a *child* in there! What do you want?"

"All right," he said with resignation. In one smooth motion he reached back for his handgun and brought it up to cock it. "The hard way it is. Now move it!"

Mari looked him directly in the eye. "Okay, whatever it is you want, I'll give it to you. But don't you *dare* traumatize that child! If you so much as—" She was cut off by the sudden violent smack of his pistol across her face, the force sending her reeling. She cried out, catching herself with her arms as she landed on her bottom, the fall delivering an excruciating jar to her knee.

"*I'll* call the shots, thank you!" Mr. Eden said. He motioned with the gun. "Now, get up! Next time I'll use the other end."

Submissively she rolled, but in her attempt to rise, the pain was agonizing. "My—knee—" she moaned. "I can't—I can't get up."

Silently he offered her a hand, pulling her upright, where Mari caught her balance. She sniffed, brushing a tear from her cheek. Her jaw throbbed, as did her wrists and knee.

Mr. Eden waved to the door. "*Please*— after you!"

This time Mari complied, slowly and painfully limping her way up the back entrance. Once in, he shut the door behind them, snapping the locks.

"Please don't hurt her," she whispered, stepping into the kitchen. "Or scare her. I'll do what you want. Just put the gun away."

"Get me the money," he said simply.

She knew it. But which—the backpack money or Ty's find? She waggled her head. "What money?"

"Don't act stupid. You know what I'm talking about. Go get it."

Having heard the back door, Aubrey popped her head in the kitchen. "Is Mr. Eden gone yet? I'm still hungry—" She stopped, eyeing her neighbor warily, who had repositioned the gun discreetly against Mari's back.

"It's okay, Aubrey," Mari said hastily. "I invited him in for a short visit." She twisted a banana from a bunch on the island and handed it to her.

Aubrey's face wrinkled with concern. "Your mouth is bleeding! Bad! And your cheek! What happened?"

"Is it?" She touched her face. "I must have bumped my lip again."

The girl didn't move.

"Is Poppy still okay?"

Aubrey gave a guarded nod. "Our show is over. When are we leaving? Can we take Grandpa Poppy back now?" Her eyes flicked up to Mr. Eden standing closely behind her.

Mari dabbed her mouth with a napkin. "Not quite yet. We've had a change of plans."

"Again? *Now* what are we doing?"

"Just a few things."

"Can I call my dad?"

"That's an excellent idea!" Mr. Eden said smoothly over Mari's shoulder. "Go get your phone, Miss Coleman."

Mari squirmed. "Aubrey, will you check if my phone is on the table in there?"

Aubrey scrunched her brow. "You have it already! I brought it to you outside—remember?"

"Oh, right," Mari said, frowning. "Huh, I must have lost it somewhere."

"We'll look for it in a bit," Roger Eden asserted. "Don't worry, Miss Aubrey. You go on and play."

"It's okay, hon," Mari said, trying to be reassuring. "We're going to have a short talk. Then we'll take Poppy to the nursing home."

Without responding, Aubrey backed a few steps, then turned for the living room.

Mari leaned to the side, flashing a look back at Mr. Eden. "Please stop this! She's a kid, and my grandfather is an old man. They don't deserve this! I'll do what you say—just please don't hurt them."

"Where's your phone?" he asked.

She shook her head. "I—I'm not sure. I might have dropped it when I found Ty's camp. Or when I was trying to talk to him in the yard."

"You're lying to me," he stated, running his hands over her jeans to pat her pockets. "What are you hiding?"

She shook her head, skirting away from him. "Nothing."

"Why did the kid run away like that?"

"He's afraid of you! He's afraid of *me*—of everybody! It was a miracle he even talked to me! And if *you* hadn't shown up when you had, he might have let me take him somewhere safe!"

"Like hell. What were you doing over there?"

"He was showing me where he found Loki. There's a blood smear on the fence where he was trying to dig under—go see for yourself! I'm telling the truth!" She motioned to the other room, adding, "Look—may I please check on my grandfather? This is his first outing from the nursing home, and I'm worried about him! He's been gone for *way* longer than he should."

He stared at her for a moment, then gave an accommodating nod, following her down the hall toward the living room. As they slipped through the foyer, it pained Mari to think that not only was her phone outside, but also the pepper spray, which might have been useful. She could only hope Ty ran fast and that Tatum would be home when he got there. Meanwhile, what was she to do? She tried to think of some way to sneak Aubrey out the front door to make a dash for the Gordons'. But what if it didn't work? What would Roger Eden do to the girl? And if it *did* work, what would Roger Eden do to *her*?

Her grandfather had relocated himself to an upholstered chair to watch television with Aubrey, his walker parked within arm's reach. Mari sat on the edge of the coffee table, plucking a tissue from a nearby box and dabbing her wounded lip in a conspicuous manner as she faced him. He was powerless, she knew, but perhaps he would understand that something was wrong.

"How are you doing, Poppy?" she asked.

He inclined his head. "Nice day. Mac's girrrl."

"Yes, it's nice to hang out with Aubrey! We're not going back to the nursing home quite yet because Roger Eden is here—the neighbor who helped you up the stairs. Remember? We're going to stay put and watch another show." She squeezed his hands, leaning in closer and lowering her voice. "Poppy, please pray." It was debatable if he even heard her, given his age, much less understood. Yet perhaps he would read her expression.

Behind them, Mr. Eden watched from the archway.

"Would it be all right if I started Aubrey on a project?" Mari asked him. "She could be painting her volcano to stay busy."

Roger Eden scowled. "What is this—a daycare?"

"Technically, watching her *is* my job," Mari fired back. "Aubrey, you can start. Be careful not to get paint on the floor."

Aubrey looked nervously between them. "Can you help me?"

Mari shook her head. "Not right now. But you can do it, hon! I'm going to talk to Mr. Eden."

With a pink and puckered countenance, Aubrey shuffled stiffly to the dining room table, blinking back tears.

Roger Eden was gruff when Mari joined him in the foyer. "What did you tell the old man?"

"That we're not going to the nursing home now," she answered quietly.

His eyes narrowed. "You told him something! What did you say?"

"That we're not going back yet—because of your visit."

His head twitched, and he took a step toward her.

"Okay, *fine*," she huffed. "I asked him to try to hold his bowels! I'm not prepared to deal with that, and I think he deserves a little dignity in his old age—don't you? And I'm sorry, Mr. Eden. I don't have any money for you. I don't know what you're talking about."

His brow shot up. "Oh, but you *do*, don't you? I know you do!"

"I *don't*. Nor does Mac."

The man regarded her a moment before looming in her face. "I'm not here to play games. I watched that backpack enter this house, and I've pored over every second of video footage to see that it never left! So don't lie to me, Margaret. I know it's here. You and Mac hid it, didn't you? You're a couple of opportunists. Well, the game is over. Go get it."

His nose was practically touching hers. Mari pressed herself tightly against the wall. "We took it to the police—assuming you're referring to the money you hid for someone in the field last week. That was an epic fail, wasn't it? Did your guy not show up or something?"

"You've got two minutes!"

"The police have it!" she stated firmly. "We took it out in a laundry basket Monday night! Go check your fancy security cameras—you'll see!"

He brought up the gun. "You're lying! Last chance before I shoot the old man in front of the little brat."

"No—stop!" Mari cried. "I'll help you search any room—we can search the whole house—I'll do it! But you'll see that I'm telling the truth!"

In the dining room Aubrey suddenly erupted into a frightened wail. "I want to call my da-a-ad!"

Roger Eden lurched back in irritation.

"No, I'll stop her!" Mari declared. "Please—I'll make her stop!"

At his release Mari hustled around the corner to embrace the sobbing child, who stood awkwardly beside the volcano, having heard everything.

"Can you make him go away? I want my daddy!"

"Shh, Aubrey!" she whispered, stroking her hair while the girl gulped air, straining to control herself. "It's so important to not cry right now—so, so important! It's time to pray. Pray and help Poppy. Shh!" She squeezed her, crooning into her ear, "I'm not leaving you. Shh!"

Time to pray. Yes, it was. Indeed, Mari already had been praying, now so strangely assured that she wasn't on her own. God hadn't left her to figure things out by herself while he was somewhere far away on vacation or away at work tending to everyone else's important business. He was right there with her at Mac's house, a very present help in their trouble. She didn't have to perform the exact right way for him to help her. She didn't have to achieve anything or be good enough to be worthy of his attention. She knew God loved her and was with her. *With* her. It was as though her heavenly Father were whispering it to her too: *I'm not leaving you. Shh!*

"I want my dad!" Aubrey murmured.

"I know, Aubrey. But God is with us."

As she held the girl, her eyes happened to graze the newsprint affixed to the dining room table, coming to rest on the photo of the Whitmore murder victim. From Seattle, the caption read, the words popping off the page at her. Seattle, where Mac reported some bank had been robbed at gunpoint.

The two were doubtless connected, she mused. The thief Roger Eden and the mysterious Seattle man. Wow—how in the world had a shrewd crook like Roger Eden come to live on little old Frost Street in her modest town? She could now easily imagine him disguising himself in medical scrubs or a security uniform with a fake mustache and toupee to rob a bank. The man was both brilliant and stupid at the same time. But he hadn't been acting alone.

The Seattle man. She stared at the picture, suddenly recalling where she had seen him. Yes—it was that same man who had nodded politely to her after school from the metallic teal car parked in front of Roger Eden's house. She was sure of it! Was that man Roger Eden's accomplice? Or his enemy? Bits of hazy information were starting to come into focus. The Seattle man had come to see Mr. Eden. And the Seattle man had gone to rough up Trey in search of the same money Roger Eden had been looking for—to the extent that Tatum had had to call on Bats for help. Then the Seattle man had been murdered. But there had been *two* men in that car that day. Where was the third guy?

Roger Eden appeared in the dining room, motioning with his weapon. "Enough. Go sit."

At the sight of the handgun, Aubrey whinnied, clutching Mari's waist more tightly, but Mari coaxed her along, guiding her to the corner of the couch near her grandfather, who gravely met her eyes. He understood. He absolutely understood.

"Come, sweetheart," she urged. "Let's sit by Poppy and be very quiet."

But Mr. Eden jerked his head at Mari. "No, *you're* coming upstairs with me." He held the gun out menacingly toward Aubrey. "See this, kid? You sit there nice and quiet. If I come down to find you've moved an *inch* from that spot, I will shoot your Miss Margaret *and* your Poppy dead—do you hear me?"

Aubrey quivered. "Y-yes. Her name's M-Mari, not Margaret."

Mr. Eden huffed, looking at Mari. Then he waved the gun. "Upstairs."

Obediently Mari mounted the creaking staircase with Roger Eden at her heels. What would they do when they got upstairs? They'd be searching for money that wasn't there! But he would think she was holding out on him. She wished there was some way she could convince him they didn't have it. Or some way to at least distract him.

She blurted, "You weren't totally convinced that your backpack was here, were you? Probably because of the downpour and the rain on your cameras. You couldn't see it clearly. You had to probe around for it—asking questions and showing up here for a tour of Mac's house. *Right,* like you needed a tour! You thought it might possibly have gone to Whitmore. And so you went to visit Trey West. You and your friend from Seattle."

He halted on the landing, framed from behind by the bright stained-glass window, his eyes boring into her.

She appraised him from the stair above. "But it didn't go to Whitmore. It went to the police station in a laundry basket, as I already said. And I'll tell you what's going to happen—we're going to look all over up there"— she nodded up the stairs—" and you're not going to find it because it's *not there!*"

His eyes narrowed. "What do you know about my friend from Seattle?"

Mari swallowed, noting the flush creeping up his neck. "I—nothing. Except that I recognized his picture in the newspaper. He was waiting in a car in front of your house earlier this week. The paper said he was from Seattle."

"And how do you know about my visit to Trey West?"

She met his eyes. "I work with his mother. Did you kill that man? Your Seattle friend—did you kill him?"

The seconds ticked by in an eternity as she stood paralyzed under Roger Eden's fixed glare. Then a feeling of dread washed over her as his hand slowly raised the gun. All she could think about was the way poor Loki had dropped to the ground at the sudden blast of his pistol. She closed her eyes, her shoulders taut as she held her breath. *Oh God—be with Aubrey!*

Suddenly a squeal arose from downstairs. "It's the police!" Aubrey piped up excitedly. "The police are here!"

Roger Eden gave a startled twist, bending to look downward through the spindled rail. Relief flooded Mari, though only for a moment, for he grabbed her roughly by the shirt to redirect her down the stairs.

"Ouch—no—hey, my knee!" she cried, the pain unbearable in their rush.

"Shut up and get in there!" he snarled, shoving her into the dining room. Quickly he snapped off the lights and crouched low beside the window next to Mac's fireplace, inching his head up to peer out.

Knee pulsing, Mari sidled up to the colonnade, craning her head to see outside too, though sharing only a sliver of Mr. Eden's view of the boulevard in front of his house. A second police car had arrived, she noted—and now a third, coming up behind it. She chewed her thumb, begging them to hurry.

And then a cluster of officers formed, standing in the street behind their vehicles, speaking into their radios while surveying Roger Eden's house. *Roger Eden's house,* Mari observed, crestfallen. They had the wrong house!

"What the hell!" Mr. Eden muttered, watching curiously as several more vehicles arrived, parking in front of the Gordons' and further down. Next door his dog began barking.

Behind him Aubrey twisted on the couch to look anxiously at Mari, but Mari pressed a finger over her lips, pointing skyward with her other hand. Nodding, Aubrey turned back. Poppy reached a wrinkled hand across the end table toward the girl, his eyes darting toward Mari.

Something big was going on outside, but try as she might, Mari could see only a narrow slice of the activity. She wished there were some way to get the attention of the police. She scoured Mac's dining room buffet, searching for a flashlight or a mirror to aim out the window—anything that would either give or reflect light. Her eyes fell to the glass doors under the colonnade and Mac's handgun case in the corner of the top shelf. She glanced back at Roger, intently focused on the action outside.

She had never fired a handgun before. She had never even held one in her life, so the idea of going for Mac's pistol was crazy. What would she do with it? Threaten Roger Eden? She wouldn't even know if it were loaded, and even on chance that it was, it wouldn't be a fair contest, surely. Yet something stirred in her to try to get it, even if it was just to fire it to get the authorities' attention. She eyed the latch on the cabinet, aware the glass door would rattle when opened. Plus the electronic code on the safe—how could she possibly guess it? Closing her eyes, she breathed a prayer, then cleared her throat.

"Excuse me, Mr. Eden. I think Aubrey needs to use the restroom."

While Aubrey flashed her a look, Roger Eden simultaneously threw a glance behind him.

"We're not doing that now," he said.

Mari sniffed. "Okay. Just FYI, she gets squirmy when she has to go."

He was silent, craning to see out the window from another angle.

"Can she at least stand by me?" Mari asked. "She might get scared if something—you know—happens out there."

He cast another irritated look over his shoulder. "Okay, go!" he ordered Aubrey.

While the girl scurried over, Mari took the opportunity to yank open the cabinet door. At the noisy shake of the glass, Aubrey froze, while Roger Eden whirled.

Immediately Mari threw up her hands. "Ouch—that was me! Sorry! I crashed my knee into the cabinet! I was trying to see."

He straightened, commanding in a low voice, "Get the hell away from there! Both of you—on the floor!" He was coming to join them.

Leaving the glass door slightly ajar, Mari meekly stepped back, drawing her arm around Aubrey.

"On your knees," he directed.

Trembling, Aubrey dropped down at once, but Mari shook her head.

"Please, Mr. Eden—I can't! I can't kneel! I've had a knee injury. Please!" She waved to a dining room chair Mac had set beside the buffet. "Please! I promise I'll sit and not move!"

"Sit! And you'd better not!" he spat. He glanced around. Then going to the window, he ripped the tiebacks off the curtains and tugged the sheers to cover the glass. Returning, he bound Mari's wrists with one of the ties, but the fabric was too short for both of her feet. Instead, he bound one of her ankles securely to the leg of the chair.

"One peep and you're dead!" he threatened before hurrying back to his fireplace window lookout.

His breathing. He was jumpy and his breathing was erratic. Plus the way he lurched side to side to see out the window. Mr. Eden was stressed, and Mari knew it.

She eyed Aubrey, glued worriedly at her knees. The bathroom diversion hadn't gone how she had hoped, but at least she had the girl near her. Twisting her wrists, Mari felt the silky curtain tie easily loosen. Swiftly she wiggled her hands free, stuffing the strip in her lap in case she needed it again. Then snatching a pen from the table, she scrawled a note to Aubrey on a scrap of newspaper: "You're so brave! When is your birthday?"

Aubrey looked up questioningly, then took the pen, writing shakily: "Febary 7."

Mari wrote, "Mine is in March. What's your favorite color?"

February seventh, Mari mused, handing off the pen. She subtracted the girl's age to determine her year of birth. Okay, the girl's birth date would be her first code attempt at the gun safe when she had a chance. Now for the next distraction so that she could get to it.

But in the living room her grandfather suddenly let out a strange moan. Peeking over at him, Mari was stabbed with alarm to see his body making little twitches. Was he having a seizure? Or another stroke?

"Hey!" she exclaimed, rising, still tethered to her chair. "Something's wrong with my grandfather! He needs help!"

"Sit down and shut up!" Roger Eden warned sternly.

"Poppy!" she cried at the old man's spasms.

Then at the very same moment, she stiffened, spying a motion through the dining room sheers. Police officers! Half a dozen uniformed officers were spread out, crouching low along Roger Eden's fence, as if preparing to blast over or through it somehow. She gawked in disbelief at their helmets, body armor, weapons, and belts packed with critical equipment. But their *backs* were to her! Some kind of SWAT team was preparing to descend on *Roger Eden's* house—with Roger Eden looking on! Mari watched him crawl to squat at a front window with a better view of the street.

Across the room her grandfather uttered another moan. Then another. And again—each one increasing in volume as his body shuddered.

"What the hell is wrong with you?" Mr. Eden snapped. "Shut the heck up!"

"*Please*—we need an ambulance!" Mari implored, though asking was futile, she knew. Her eyes darted to the plethora of help outside that was completely unaware of their plight. If only there were some way to alert them! She wanted to jump and shout and wave her arms. If only they would turn around!

Another moan.

"I said *shut it!*" Mr. Eden growled menacingly to the old man. "I'd put you out of your misery, but a death by natural causes would be one fantastic stroke of luck!"

"What's wrong with Grandpa Poppy?" Aubrey whispered urgently.

Mari put her finger over her lips.

"Is he dying?"

Outside in the street one of the police officers broadcast his voice through an electronic megaphone, demanding that Roger Eden come out of his house with his hands up. Looking on, Mr. Eden snorted, muttering under his breath.

The dining room window, Mari thought desperately. If she could throw something at it—something like a book—maybe she could get their attention. No—something hard or significant. Something that wouldn't just bounce off. Something that might break it or make a loud crash—like Mac's gun safe, maybe. But it was too big to throw, and there wasn't time to try to open it. Maybe a potted plant or a picture frame. But how would that help? Jittery Mr. Eden would only freak out—and maybe even do something crazy.

Anxiously she bit her lip. At this point it was almost worth the risk of trying to run away. Then she slowly straightened at the thought. He *was* distracted. Perhaps if she and Aubrey crept super stealthily, they could make it to the back door. She could write a note to Aubrey right now and send her out there first. Help would be waiting for them outside. They would just have to make it through the kitchen and unlock the back door. Mari's pulse quickened. They could do it.

Then across the room her grandfather let out another groan.

Mari's stomach churned. But Poppy. An attempt to flee would leave Poppy at Mr. Eden's mercy—or lack thereof. No, she couldn't leave him.

She let out a defeated breath, returning to the idea of throwing something at the window. Maybe a dish from Mac's credenza. Twisting to glance behind her—she jerked in surprise, then froze, gawking at the figure of a police officer standing right there in the kitchen doorway, a weapon fully extended in one hand, his other hand at his lips, commanding her silence. He pointed to Aubrey, who hadn't yet seen him, inclining his head for them to move to the kitchen. Likewise, three other police officers stood poised for imminent action behind him in the hall.

Immediately Mari took Aubrey's chin in her hand, signaling the urgency to remain quiet before indicating the officers' presence. Even so, the girl gave a startled squeak when she turned. Mari half prodded, half shoved her in their direction, then scrambled to untie her leg from the chair, not daring to lift her eyes lest Roger Eden smell her fear. She hoped those officers saw Poppy. He should be warned! She wasn't sure he could take the shock of an ambush. Then as the curtain tieback gave way, she scurried soundlessly out of the kitchen, where one of the officers propelled her to Aubrey in the kitchen.

Poppy! She turned back in a panic—

"Police—freeze!" Loud shouts cut the air before she could finish her thought. *"Drop your weapon and get your hands up!"*

Beside her, Aubrey uttered a deafening shriek, rushing to clutch Mari.

The mission was over in a matter of seconds. Through all the shouting and rough-sounding commotion, Mari heard the snap of handcuffs, and an officer's voice rose: "August Borwich, you're under arrest for suspicion of armed robbery and murder. You have the right to remain silent. Anything you say can and will be used against you in—"

"Wait—no!" With a cry, Mari broke from Aubrey, dragging her with to the dining room. "This man is *Roger Eden*! His name is Roger Eden! That's his house next door!"

One of the arresting officers stepped in her direction. "We've got it, ma'am," he assured in a calming voice. "We know who this is. Is there anyone else in the house?"

She met Roger's steely glare from across the room. "No. But there's another man involved. I'm sure of it. Someone who knew the fellow who was killed at Whitmore."

"Yes, ma'am, we're aware of that. Is there anyone else in *this* residence?"

"No." She shook her head.

"Anyone upstairs or down?"

"No."

Then she and Aubrey watched as two police officers escorted Roger Eden out the door.

One of the remaining officers began tending to her grandfather. With an enormous sigh of relief, Mari pulled Aubrey into her arms.

"We made it, girl! Thank God we're safe!"

Promptly Aubrey burst into tears, bawling for her dad. Mari just held her and stroked her hair. Her own hands were shaking.

"We need to call an ambulance for my grandfather," she told the police over her head.

The officer beckoned. "Come! Are you or the girl hurt? Come on—come sit down." He ushered the two of them to the couch, speaking gently, "Way to hang on, ladies! You've done good! Come, have a seat! Let's take a look at you, Miss Aubrey, you brave girl! You're safe now! Your daddy is on his way!"

"Please—my grandfather needs an ambulance," Mari repeated, taking the edge of the couch nearest the old man, who now sat slouched in his chair, quiet but alert. She reached for his hand.

"Yes, the paramedics will be right in."

"He needs help! He's been sitting in the same position for way too long, and he started having seizures or something! Maybe a stroke—I don't know." Her voice broke. "I'm so sorry, Poppy!"

Her grandfather patted her arm. "I'm okay. Okay, Marree. We prayed and God h-helped us."

"I know." She nodded, wiping her cheeks.

"Good Marree and Bree too!"

She sniffed. "Thanks, Poppy—I'm so glad you prayed!" She rubbed his hand, looking at the officer. "I hope he's all right. This was only his first outing from the nursing home. I never expected it could get crazy like this!"

"He'll be taken care of," the officer assured. "They're here."

"We need to call my mom to let her know what's happening."

"Sure—we'll do that."

"And he's going to need to eat soon. He hasn't had anything to eat or drink since lunch!"

"I'm okay," her grandfather said again. "I go like this—" He began to twitch his body, imitating the spasms.

Mari started. "Yes—like *that*! That's what he was doing!"

But then her grandfather stopped. "I fff—" He shook his head, struggling with the word. "Ffff—" Looking at Mari, he uttered another long moan, then grinned. "I fff—"

"Faked it?" she finished incredulously. "You *faked* all that?"

He nodded. "Yesss!"

"Oh, my word!" Mari flopped back onto the cushion with her hand to her face.

"Here's our paramedics," the officer said.

Chapter Thirty-One

"There you go! All fixed up! No stitches necessary!"

A paramedic had just finished tending to Mari's face when amidst the flurry of the police processing the crime scene and other paramedics assisting her grandfather onto a gurney, Mari heard one voice rise above the rest—the familiar voice she had been waiting for.

"No, this is *my* house!" Mac insisted from somewhere outside. "I need to get in there! I'm looking for my daughter! Is my daughter still here?"

Finally.

"It's Mac!" Mari told the officers, removing the ice pack from her knee to rise. "It's Mac Sinclair, Aubrey's father."

"Ma'am, please stay put—he'll be right in."

But Mari couldn't be stopped.

On her way she saw Mac greet Poppy as her grandfather was transported through the porch. Then he spied her and Aubrey waiting in the foyer and immediately knelt to crush his daughter to his chest.

"Are you okay, kiddo?" he asked.

In characteristic manner, Aubrey reverted to her previous hysteria, bawling with gusto on his neck until she had a need to talk, at which she sniffled, pushing away to wipe her eyes. "Dad, you're *choking* me! See—I was *right*! Mr. Eden *is* evil! Next time you should listen to me! He had a gun, and he pointed it at us! And he was mean to Grandpa Poppy!"

"You're safe now, little flower," he said. He rose, addressing Mari. "Are *you* all right?"

"Apart from my knee killing me, yes. It's been a—"

"I can't *believe* you were still here! What were you *doing*? I thought you'd left for Kingswood!"

His tone. "I—we went to look at the volcano."

"Right—and then you were *supposed* to go to Kingswood! My word, Marissa—do you see what might have happened here?" He blew out a breath, shaking his head.

Mari swallowed.

"You shoulda seen the police, Dad!" Aubrey declared. "They snuck in our house and arrested Mr. Eden! They put him in handcups!"

"Cuffs," Mari murmured. "Handcuffs."

Mac disregarded her. "They called saying you and Aubrey were in trouble. It took me forever to get here, and then the street was packed with squad cars and firetrucks and police tape everywhere! All I knew was that he was holding you hostage. I wasn't sure *what* I'd find! I'd didn't know if both of you would be alive or—" He stopped, looking away, his neck bright red. "Thank God it was over already!"

"Mac—"

"Did you give your statement?"

"No. I was—waiting for you."

He nodded. "Thanks. I'll take her out."

Aubrey's head swung up. "What? No, I want to stay with Mari."

"You can't." Mac turned to a nearby police officer. "I'd like to take her outside please."

But Aubrey had coiled her arms around Mari's waist. "*Please*, Dad! I want to stay!"

"You need to listen to your daddy," Mari said, unhooking her arms. "It won't take us long. Is Susan outside?" she asked Mac. "Take her to Susan."

"Why can't I stay?" the girl moaned as Mac led her out. "I want to stay! I want to be by Mari! No, Dad! Please! Please!"

Mari returned to the couch where the officer waited. "Almost ready," she said, her hands fidgeting nervously. She had not anticipated that kind of reaction from Mac.

When Mac returned, he gestured incredulously next door. "What the *heck* happened here? Did you see that? They're taking a *body* out of Eden's house! What's going on?"

"*What?*" Mari's jaw dropped as she stood to peer out the window. "Out of my—out of Roger Eden's house? I—I didn't know! Oh, I hope Aubrey doesn't see it!"

"It's covered, but *sheesh!*" He made his way to take a seat beside her, obviously shaken. "She's on the porch steps with Susan and another officer. They can't get her to budge from there 'cause she's *obsessed* with staying near you!"

And he was not happy about it, clearly. Mari felt that pit in her stomach.

"Well, that's understandable," the officer said sympathetically. "They've been through quite an ordeal together. She's going to need her."

"*Apparently!* Now, what happened? I want to know what happened!"

"That body next door!" Mari pointed over her shoulder with her thumb, her mind racing. "I bet he's our third guy, and I bet Roger Eden killed him too! It has to be the other man I saw—the one who was with the Whitmore murder victim before he died. I'll bet it's him! Oh, my word! Roger Eden really *is* evil. I had no idea! He could have—" Her hand popped over her mouth. She didn't even want to say it.

Mac jerked. "*Hello!* Would someone tell me what's going on here?"

"Yes, let's get started," the officer said, adjusting the notepad on his lap. "Let's start with the facts of what happened this afternoon, Miss Coleman."

Mari adjusted the ice pack on her knee, then as calmly and efficiently as she could, she shared how she had brought her grandfather to Mac's for an outing and how Roger Eden had helped them into the house to look at the volcano after Mac had called her the first time. Then she told how seeing the wounded dog led her to finding Ty West's makeshift camp.

She looked at Mac. "Ty's been *here* the whole time! He's been sleeping in a box beside your garage, living off the food I gave him from your fridge. That and a whole truckload of candy from Dixie's that he bought with money he found in your backyard!"

And that led to her telling of Ty appearing right then and him showing her the carry-on suitcase and the garbage bag under the tree. And then she told of listening to Mac's phone message—right as Roger Eden appeared for his dog.

"I about died, but Ty was a champ! He bolted out of there like lightning to get help! And then Mr. Eden shot his dog. Right there in front of me! And all the while Aubrey is in the house watching *Tom and Jerry* cartoons with Poppy."

Mac grunted, shaking his head.

"And where is the boy now?" the officer asked. He signaled for someone to collect the evidence in the backyard.

"I don't know. With his mother, I hope. Hey—my phone's back there too!" she called to the officer leaving the room. "Somewhere under that tree or in the bushes."

And then Mari finished by sharing what had happened inside the house.

Mac blew out his breath, shaking his head, and they sat together in silence.

The officer finished his notes, then shifted in his seat. "So here's what we know so far. Roger Eden's real name is August Borwich. As of this afternoon we've learned that he's connected to a string of armed robberies on the West Coast, including two gutsy bank heists that happened fairly recently. The money you found was a break in that case. And between his little hobby excursions, he disappeared to this perfect, sleepy Midwestern neighborhood living as a normal guy with a normal job."

Mac snorted. "Pest exterminator!"

"At this point the rest is speculation. We presume there was meant to be some kind of rendezvous with his accomplices last weekend that got interrupted by your kickball group."

"Interrupted by a *rainstorm*," Mari clarified. "Honestly, if it hadn't been for that downpour, that money probably would have gone unnoticed. But someone grabbed that backpack. My theory is that Roger Eden was ninety-eight percent sure it went to our house, but somewhere along the line, something caused him to doubt that. And that's when things turned toward Whitmore and Trey."

The officer nodded. "We're still trying to figure out how Trey West got tied into this."

Mac gave a cry, sitting back. "*I* gave him Trey's name. Roger was asking me why there were police looking around in the field, and I told him we thought a kid from Whitmore stole some stuff. He probed, and I told him. There was no reason not to!"

"Ah," the officer said, making note of it.

"And then these two other guys showed up," Mari went on. "On Monday after school I noticed two men in a metallic bluish teal car in front of Mr. Eden's house. One of them said hello to me. I didn't think anything of it until today when I saw the picture of the Whitmore murder victim again. Then it clicked and I remembered him. The same car was parked there again today with no one inside—which probably was driven there by our other guy, who very well may be the victim carried out of Eden's house just now! It makes me wonder if Roger Eden was hiding that money in the field *for* them or *from* them!"

The officer scribbled his notes. "We'll need a description of that vehicle. What time was that?"

"Right after school today. Roger Eden was out spraying weeds on his lawn. I mean the guy could have already been—" She shivered, trailing off.

"*If* it was him," Mac said.

Mari bit her lip, raising her brow. "Anyway, that was a substantial amount of money, and these two men probably showed up for a share of it—which took them over to Whitmore to rattle Trey's cage."

"Which was another break in the case," the officer stated, "since we now have a couple of eyewitnesses. It remains to be seen if August's gun is the murder weapon. The gun Ty West hauled off in his pillowcase belonged to Burne Batson, which is a completely different story. The two just happened to coincide."

"Unbelievable," Mac murmured, rubbing his forehead.

Mari looked at him. "And then Mr. Eden went over the camera footage again and determined that the money was in our, er—your house. He told me he never saw it leave, and he was convinced we had hidden the money to keep it for ourselves."

He eyed her. "And the supposed 'body' that Aubrey saw him burying in his yard—"

"—was his loot." She nodded. "And what I'd guess were his disguises. I don't really get why there's more cash back there than we found in the backpack—which was also a lot. Why that *and* the backpack? At least I hope that's all that's in his yard, and that there's not actually—you know—someone buried there!" She shuddered. "If it hadn't been for naughty Loki scratching under that fence, Ty wouldn't have seen it and dug it up. That guy was smooth. Everything was working for him."

"Yeah, 'til *you* showed up!" Mac remarked. "Roger Eden's perfect storm."

"So it appears," the officer agreed. "Pretty crazy!"

"Speaking of crazy—" Mari cut in. "It was pretty wild having the police descend on the wrong house! I was in here panicking for how to get your attention!"

Mac's head shot up. "They got the wrong house?"

The officer laughed. "Not exactly! It was fifty-fifty where Borwich would go. Converging on his house was partially a decoy, but in all actuality he could have been there. It was a risky decision, but we were hoping for enough of a distraction to get a team in here."

"Well, they were amazing! It worked, and we didn't hear a thing!" She turned to Mac. "I was in the middle of a plan to go for your handgun, but it was all over before I could get to it!" She set her ice pack aside. "Anyway, are we about finished? I don't really have anything more to share, and I'm concerned about Aubrey. She's going to have to process this, and I don't want her sitting out there alone!"

"This should do for now," the officer said, rising to shake her hand. "We'll be in touch. And if you think of anything else, let us know. Mac, same for you."

Mac dipped his head. "Thank you, officer."

As they moved toward the foyer, Mac clarified, "Aubrey's with Susan. She isn't alone."

"You know what I mean," Mari said. She paused by the door to face him. "She's *not* sleeping here tonight, Mac!"

"I already thought of that. I'll probably run up to my mom's."

She raised her chin in a nod, studying him.

"What happened to your cheek?" he asked. "And your lip?"

"Nothing. Just a double-whammy sort of day. I'll be all right."

"And your knee. Sorry. I can tell by your gait that you're in pain."

"It'll be okay. I'll just take something for it. And rest it."

He gave an amused grunt. "Right! Come on." He motioned for her to walk ahead.

Applause went up when Mari appeared at the top of the porch steps. She gazed out in amazement at her little Frost Street packed with emergency vehicles, some still flashing their lights. Ahead a modest crowd stood dutifully waiting for her on the boulevard behind a barrier of yellow police tape. She recognized Shannon and Colton right away, plus the DeSotos, Peter Watkins with baby Kenny, Pastor Keith from church, and JoAnne Strang with one of her daughters, all cheering for her safe exit from the house. At the bottom of the steps Aubrey promptly sprang up to resume her barnacle status, clinging tightly to Mari while a police officer helped Mrs. Gordon to her feet.

"Oh, hon! Thank God you're okay!" the older woman cried, embracing Mari. "I'm so *proud* of you! How on earth did you get through that without completely panicking?"

"Oh, there was panicking!" Mari confessed.

Mrs. Gordon laughed. "Well, we were all praying for you! Who would have ever known we had something like this going on in our little neighborhood?"

"Thank you. And yes—who would have thought it?"

At the curb Shannon rushed to hug her first, her face still blotchy from crying. "You scared the daylights out of us, Mari! I'm so glad you're okay! And *you*, little girl—way to be brave!" She patted Aubrey's shoulder, adding to Mari, "Mom jumped into the ambulance with Poppy. She said she'd see you at home."

The rest of the gang circled around, expressing similar sentiments and reiterating that they had all been praying for them. As Mari briefly relayed what happened, they listened, offering sympathy for what she and Aubrey had been through. Pastor Keith shook her hand, commending her for keeping her head. Even baby Kenny seemed delighted to see her, flapping his arms and lunging for her.

Peter chuckled, handing him over. "Hey, Kyla couldn't get away, but she wanted you to know she was praying for you. She's with her birth father."

"Tell her thanks," she said, laughing as the baby immediately reached back for his dad. "Tell her I'm praying for her too."

Then hearing another familiar voice, Mari turned to see Will winding his way around a squad car. "Mari Coleman!" he bellowed. "Way to freakin' solve a national crime case!"

"Hi, Will!" She shot a hasty glance around to note that Mac was still with Mrs. Gordon at the house.

Will gave Mari a quick hug, nodding to all. "Hi, everyone! I wouldn't be surprised if there were reward money involved in this. What'll you do with it?"

Mari lifted a shoulder. "Pay down my student loans?"

He huffed as everybody laughed. "You are *so* boring!" And then more quietly he asked, "Hey—you doing all right, Mars?"

"Yeah, we're okay." She smiled down at Aubrey, swinging her hand. "How'd you find out?"

Will jerked his head. "Mac. He was a little freaked out when he called, but then Dan called after and said you were okay. Sheesh—I *knew* you shoulda took the other job!"

She smiled. "Well, thanks for coming."

"Yeah." He motioned awkwardly toward the men. "So—I'm going over to talk to them."

"Okay."

Likewise, she made her way to greet Leah and JoyAnne. However, barely had they started their conversation when Mari stiffened, spying Tatum West over JoyAnne's shoulder. Tatum West—at the edge of the field across the street. She hardly recognized her without her Coffee Break uniform. The woman had just turned away, apparently leaving.

Mari laid a hand on JoyAnne's arm. "Hold on! I'll be right back—hopefully with someone for you to meet. Aubrey, I need you to chill with Leah and JoyAnne for a minute." She tapped her back, turning her toward her friends.

"Tatum!" she called, starting across the street. "Hey!"

Tatum twisted to look over her shoulder and paused.

"Hey!" Mari waved, hurrying to her. "Tatum—thanks for coming here! How can I ever thank you? If you hadn't called the police who knows what might have happened! You saved the day!"

Tatum simply stared, her eyes flicking momentarily to Mari's swollen lip.

"You might have even saved my life! Truly! And Aubrey's too—Ty's classmate. Thank you!"

"Well, you've ruined mine."

Mari's head snapped back. "What? Why?"

Tatum shrugged. "They'll do an investigation now and probably take Ty away from me. They've already arrested Trey."

"Well, maybe this will help turn things around for him," Mari said. "Maybe this is what he needs."

Tatum made an angry sound, leaning in to point her finger in Mari's face. "Listen here. I've always tried to do right by my boys. I work hard to give them the things they need, and then some do-gooder like you comes flying in like you own the world. You're all giddy that I saved your life, but you have no idea what it's like to have your kids' lives in danger every single day—either by something stupid that they might do or by the hands of another idiot. You've probably never spent a night in fear. No, you just live in your pretty condominiums and drive fancy cars without a care in the world. And then you throw out silly solutions—as if putting me and my son in some safe house is going to fix everything! You're naive, Mari Coleman! Completely clueless. Stop trying to rescue me and my kid and leave us the heck alone!"

Mari held her piece, studying her for a moment. Then, gesturing to the street, she asked, "Tatum, why did you come here?"

Tatum folded her arms.

"You must have had a reason. It's not super-convenient to walk across that field."

"I drove."

"Still, you came. I'd like to think it was more than curiosity that brought you to stand here in the street waiting for me to come out of that house. Why would you care what happened to me? Especially since I'm so rich and have such a fancy car, which is my dad's, by the way. But it appears you *did* care. You're right—I *don't* understand your life. I'm scared of your world, and I'd prefer to stay out of it. But you know nothing about *my* life either. You *think* you do, but you don't.

"It makes me sick to think of Ty being pulled from your home. I don't want that! But I'll remind you that it was *Ty's* decision to haul away that load of illegal drugs. Neither was I at fault for Trey's arrest. That was the result of *his* choices. And yet I find my heart going out to you, even though I can't relate to your world—just like you came here tonight for me. What is that, Tatum? Do we have to perfectly understand each other to simply care?

"I wouldn't presume to have a solution for you. If you think I have this ulterior plan for Ty or you, it's false. I don't have an agenda. I only hate to see you and your son hurting—that's all. So stop accusing me of trying to be a hero or something. I'm *not. I do* know of some people and resources that might be helpful to you—people a lot smarter than me—but you can take it or leave it. That's your choice. Meanwhile, thanks for caring to see how this came out."

They stood in silence.

Finally Tatum spoke. "I didn't come here for *you*. I came to find Ty."

The way she said it—Mari didn't think she meant it to be as insulting as it came out, but her words dug. She took a very patient breath. "Ty didn't stay with you?"

"He ran off," Tatum replied. "I assumed he came here." She sniffed. "You've been luring him away!"

Mari groaned. "Oh, come on, Tatum! It's not like we're best buddies! Ty's always been evasive with me. I have to chase him down to talk to him. I've been looking for him too, and this afternoon I found him by accident." She threw a quick glance toward the garage. "He's been camping out beside Mac Sinclair's garage, and he stumbled upon some important evidence related to what happened here at the Sinclairs' today. Come—I'll show you."

Mari led her across the street, slipping confidently under the police tape as though authorized to do so. Cutting through the yard to the back of the garage, she slowed, hearing a curious sound. She motioned for Tatum to be quiet, then slowly peeked around the corner. There he was—Ty, sitting cross-legged in the dirt beside the bloody dog carcass, crying. Seeing her, he turned away, immediately bringing his T-shirt up to wipe his face.

"Aww, Ty," Mari breathed, approaching. Crouching with her good knee, she dropped onto her bottom beside him. "I'm so sorry."

"It's dead. Somebody killed it," he said, dropping his head in another burst of tears.

Mari simply stroked the dog's side where the fur wasn't bloody, remaining silent until Ty finished his cry.

After a while he sniffed and looked around. "Where's Aubrey at? Is she okay?"

"With my friend. She's okay."

"Did they get the bad guy?"

"Yes." She looked at him, speaking gently, "You saved our lives, Ty. If you hadn't run for help like that, things could have been bad. I'm so glad you were here. Thank you."

He sniffed again, wiping his nose on his sleeve. His cheeks were streaked with dirt.

"Your mom is here. She came looking for you."

"I wanted to help the dog."

"I know. It's so sad. But your mom is worried. She cares about you."

He wiped his face on his sleeve again, then with a sigh of resignation, he pulled himself to his feet. When he finally noticed his mother behind the garage, he tensed, backing up a step as though he were in trouble.

"You need to come home now," Tatum said gruffly. She jerked her head toward Whitmore.

Without a word, Ty went along.

"Goodbye, Ty!" Mari called after him. "I won't be here tomorrow, and there's no school next week, so we won't be having kickball for a while."

He did not respond, but Tatum looked back with an acknowledging nod.

"Bye, Tatum," she added more softly.

And then she was left sitting beside the dead dog, stuck and unable to rise without killing her knee. She let out a long breath, sapped, body and soul.

It hit her then. Fragile and alone, she succumbed to the overwhelming ache in her chest and dropped her head, giving way to tears as the intensity of her day came crashing down. Glad to be out of earshot of anyone, she wept unrestrained into her shirt with deep sobs from within. So many distressing events had occurred that day—with Ty, Tatum, her grandfather, Aubrey—and she felt the pressing weight of each of them. But capping them off was the stab of Mac's glaring disappointment in her. What could she have done differently?

Then, having cried herself out, she caught her breath and quieted herself, resting her head on her arms, grateful for the emotional purge. That's when she heard the snap of a twig behind her. She twisted, spying Mac at the corner of the garage, standing where Tatum had been.

"Mac!" she squeaked awkwardly, hastily pulling herself together. "Uh—sorry. I didn't know you were there!" Oh, brother—how long had he been watching her?

He said nothing, approaching slowly to gaze down at Loki's lifeless body. Then he turned to survey Ty's camp tucked in the lilac bushes, his cardboard box tent, and the debris on the ground. With a quick wipe of his own eyes, he looked at her, shaking his head, unable to speak.

She sniffed. "He came back because of the dog. He'd been taking care of him. It's so sad." She pulled the neck of her shirt up to wipe her nose.

He nodded and looked away, resting his hands on his waist. After a long silence he asked, "Was that his mom?"

"Yes. Tatum West, my coworker from the Coffee Break."

"I saw you walk her back, and I followed." He paused. "I heard what you said to the boy. Well done, Marissa. You were super-kind."

"Thanks." She was too tired to say anything else. Physically and emotionally exhausted. And her bottom was damp.

"And Marissa," he said, indicating the scene around him. "Hey—I'm really sorry. I didn't know."

She shook her head, as if brushing it off. "It's okay. Um, you should probably go. Aubrey needs you. I'll be all right."

He nodded but didn't move.

"Here—" he said finally, offering her a hand. "You're going to need to get that looked at."

Gratefully she accepted his assistance, holding his arms until she had steadied herself. "My crutches are still in my back seat."

He nodded. "I'll get them. Do you need help walking?"

"No, I can manage. Thanks."

Mac hurried on ahead, but Mari followed more slowly, making her way carefully down the driveway back toward the waiting crew still on the boulevard. Mrs. Gordon had now joined Leah, JoyAnne, and Shannon, all of whom were trying to comfort Aubrey, who was visibly upset.

Mrs. Gordon pointed at her limping toward them. "See—? There she is! She didn't leave you!"

Aubrey's voice was accusatory. "Where *were* you? Where'd you go?"

Leah held up the tape for Mari to duck under.

"I was helping Ty's mom find Ty. I told you I'd be right back."

Aubrey was instantly pressed to her. "Ty? Why? Where was he?"

"Behind the garage."

"*Our* garage? Why?"

"He was here before. It was Ty who ran for help when we were in trouble. His mom called the police for us."

Aubrey's forehead puckered. "But why was he *here*?"

Mari slung her arm over the girl's shoulder. "We can talk about it sometime. Thanks for waiting, ladies."

"Oh, you poor thing!" Mrs. Gordon exclaimed. "You must be in a lot of pain! And your face is starting to bruise!"

Mari gave a painful smile. "I've had better days."

Mac arrived with her crutches, and she thanked him.

"Hey, little flower," he said, kneeling to address his daughter. "We need to pack for Grandma's. Let's go pick your clothes."

Aubrey threw Mari a pouty look, but Mari nudged her. "Go on, girl! Do you want him to choose without you? Who knows what he might pick?"

"Come." Mac held out his hand.

Grudgingly the girl followed, murmuring under her breath.

"We'll be staying there together!" he told her. "It'll be fun."

Mrs. Gordon sighed, watching them leave. "That girl was quite distressed when you disappeared."

"She's becoming an appendage," Mari confessed. "I'm feeling kind of bad about it."

But Susan waggled her head. "Oh, tut-tut! She needs you right now! You're a gift from God!"

Mari looked at her. "Thanks. It's a little mutual. I feel like I can't part from her quite yet. It was an intense couple of hours."

"Understandably so!"

"I'm trying to be careful. I heard what you said to me the other day— about not leading her on emotionally." She paused, debating a second, then went for it, asking, "So, um—do you know anything about Aubrey's mother, Elena?"

The older woman shook her head. "I don't. Only what Mac has told me. Last I talked to him he was very encouraged at how things were going with her. Very encouraged."

Mari lifted her chin in acknowledgment.

Pastor Keith butted in. "Hey, I've got to get going, Mari. I'm so glad you're okay, and I'll be praying for you."

"Same here," JoyAnne said, coming up to hug her. "I'm meeting up with Ariel at Jackie's. Susan's going to keep my little one."

"*Grandma* Susan," Mrs. Gordon added happily, smiling at the curly-haired little girl.

And so began the long goodbyes as one by one Mari's friends left.

"Can I take you home?" Leah asked. "I could drive your car and Danny could follow in ours."

"No, I'll take her," Shannon said. "Colt and I are going there anyway. He'll bring our car and meet us."

Mari didn't protest. She hugged both Leah and Dan before they left to walk down the block to their vehicle.

"Be right back," Shannon told Mari, following Colton to his car.

They had just departed when Mac and Aubrey returned, the latter toting a bright pink duffel bag.

"All set to go?" she asked Aubrey, who answered with a shrug.

Mac met her eyes. "You doing all right?"

"I'm all right. But I'm ready to call it a day."

"I bet you are! So, ah—Susan called me a minute ago with a suggestion." He shifted his feet a little awkwardly. "Feel free to decline."

"Decline—?"

"What would you think of having Aubrey overnight?"

Aubrey spun to look at him. "For real?"

"I know it might be the last thing you want to do, but—"

Mari shook her head. "Mac, she needs *you*. She's your daughter. I—I want to respect that, and I'm sorry things have gotten weird."

His brow rose in response. "I appreciate that—thanks. But tonight—I don't know—it might be best for her to be with you. She's—" He tipped his head with a silent appeal. "Unless you don't want her—"

"No—no, I'd *love* that!" Mari said hastily. "Honestly, I would. But are you sure?" At his sober response, Mari smiled down at the girl. "Well, we never did make it to my house this afternoon, did we, Aubrey? It would only seem right."

"Yes!" Aubrey threw her arms around her dad. "A slumber party!"

Mac nodded. "Just for tonight. I'll stay at Mom's or the DeSotos', then pick her up in the morning, if that's all right."

"Sounds great. Mac, tomorrow—" She eyed him. "You need to take the day off and stick to this girl like glue."

"I was going to insist the same of *you*!" he teased. "Don't worry—I'm planning on it. I'll stick to her like flour paste on newsprint! Also, Susan invited us to a barbeque tomorrow evening. She wants to have some family and friends over to support us and help us decompress. I thought it was nice of her."

"That is super-nice. I'd like that."

He nodded. "Okay. Can I give you a ride home?"

"Shannon is." Mari motioned down the street. "She's coming."

"Good." He paused, pursing his lips as he looked away for a moment. "Hey—I could never repay you for all you've done for us. I hope you know that, Marissa. I owe you so much."

Conscious of the sudden rush of heat to her cheeks, Mari answered lightly, "Thanks. Let's see if you still feel that way when she's in counseling someday."

He smiled, gesturing to Shannon's car. "Let's go."

Shannon and Colton altered their dinner plans to make tacos for a late supper at the condominium, doing their best to create a cheerful atmosphere for Aubrey to distract her from the trauma of the afternoon. As they were about to sit down, Mari's mother came home, reporting that Poppy had shown no adverse effects from his stressful day.

"They're keeping him overnight," she announced, sliding a tortilla onto her plate. "Lord willing, they'll send him back to the nursing home in the morning." She began filling her taco.

Everyone was relieved, and Aubrey asked if they could go see him.

"Maybe tomorrow," Mari suggested, also letting her mother know that Mac had put Poppy's walker in her car.

"Good to know. Thanks."

"What about school?" Aubrey asked.

"You get to skip out to spend the day with your dad," Mari declared.

Aubrey frowned. "But my volcano! It's not done, and I'm supposed to bring it tomorrow!"

"I think your teacher will cut you slack after what we've been through. You can take it Monday."

"There's no school on Monday!"

"Well, lucky you, huh? Don't worry, Aubrey! Your dad will work out your volcano issue."

And then after baths and braids and a board game in their pajamas, it was finally time for bed. Mari was more than ready. She read Aubrey a Bible story and then turned out the light. After a few minutes of fidgeting and giggling, Aubrey settled down and was solidly out.

Mari lay awake listening to her breathe. *Well, I've done it. I've created a major soul tie with Mac's daughter,* she mused. How was she going to navigate this?

Her phone chirped on the end table. It was Mac.

"Were you really going to try for my gun? You would have needed my PIN."

Mari put the phone on silent, texting back. "I was going to use Aubrey's date of birth and see where that took me."

She immediately received the flat-lipped icon.

She chuckled to herself. "Okay, I swear to secrecy, but you should probably pick a better PIN."

"Noted."

"Hey, A's pretty concerned about her volcano being late."

"I'll talk to her teacher when I call her out of school tomorrow. Thanks for the reminder. Is she still awake?"

"Out cold. Don't come too early. I'm hoping to sleep in."

"Good luck with that! A's an early riser. But noted. Text me when you're up."

Everything in her wanted to keep the conversation going. She paused, holding the phone, recalling Mrs. Gordon's report of how very encouraged Mac had been concerning Elena. "Okay. Good night," she replied simply and set her phone on the nightstand.

She was almost asleep when she remembered the coffee shop. Rolling over, she grabbed her phone to let her manager know that she was taking a personal day. He was still up, texting in return that Tatum had already requested a day off and had hinted that Mari would be too. It was a bit of a surprise to her, as it almost seemed like a kind gesture.

Chapter Thirty-Two

In the morning Mari and Aubrey had just started in on their fancy fruit parfaits in her mom's crystal stemware when Mac arrived at the condominium.

"Yogurt and granola?" Mari offered, but he declined.

"I was planning to have breakfast out," he remarked, eyeing their creations.

"I'm already eating, Dad!" exclaimed Aubrey, inserting a whopping spoonful of yogurt into her mouth.

"Slow down, girl!" Mari said. "Sorry, Mac. We were hungry."

"She can sip hot chocolate while I eat," Mac responded. "We'll probably stop in on your grandfather afterward."

"Yay!" Aubrey cheered, promptly shoveling in her next bite.

"Hey—slow down!" Mari said, shaking her head. "Excellent idea! Hopefully he'll be back home by the time you get there. And *she* seems to be doing just fine."

"Good. Thanks for having her."

When Aubrey was finished, Mari helped her collect her things and walked them to the door.

"See you tonight at Susan's?" Mac asked.

"Yes. See you tonight."

Mari shut the door and leaned against it. Mac already knew she was going, so his question about seeing her at the Gordons' sounded an awful lot as though he were saying he *wanted* to see her there. Oh, brother. Were they going to have to have an awkward talk? Mari wandered around the house thinking about it for a little while, then still exhausted from the previous day, went back to bed.

Later she skipped lunch to go visit her grandfather, although upon entering the facility she first made a beeline to the office to apologize for keeping him out so long the previous day. Of course, they understood it had been an emergency. She was relieved when they reported that other than being more fatigued than usual, he was acting like his normal self.

"Hello, Poppy!" she called when she saw him. He was sitting up in bed.

"Hello!" he returned cheerfully, immediately pointing out a cluster of three mylar balloons with colorful cartoony graphics on his bedside tray. "Mac and Bree came."

Mari dipped her head, amused that one of the balloons was congratulating him on his new baby boy. "Did they bring you those? Nice!" She could guess who picked them out.

"Yesss! Mac's girrl."

Oh, those twinkling eyes. She skipped to the next subject. "Poppy, about yesterday. I'm sorry to put you through that. That was not in my plan! I'm so glad you're okay."

Her grandfather pointed heavenward. "God's plan! I prrayed."

"Thank you. You also put our lives in danger by pretending to be sick! You scared me!"

"It's okay. I helped you. I care about you and the girrl. Mac's girrl."

Mari bit her lip. That's what she figured. He thought he had been helping—creating a diversion, maybe. At this point it didn't really matter. They had all survived. She simply smiled. "Wow, Poppy! You're speaking whole sentences!"

They both laughed. Mari found her visit unhurried and enjoyable, but at two o'clock she excused herself.

"Dad's coming home," she told him. "I'm picking him up from the airport for mom so she doesn't have to leave work early. He'll probably visit you tomorrow."

She kissed his head and was on her way.

Her car passed under the airport "arrivals" sign right as her dad texted that his plane had landed. As she waited at the passenger pickup curb for him to come out, she thought back to the day she had been stuck there waiting for Will to pick her up. Who could have guessed the crazy chain of events that would occur—all because her mother had sent Mac Sinclair to get her! She had been so perturbed at Will. In retrospect she was thankful that evening had unfolded as it had.

And there he was—her dad was coming out now! She waved, inching the car closer as he strode toward her. She always thought him so handsome.

"Mari! How's my girl?" he called, throwing his carry-on and briefcase into the back seat before getting in beside her. He leaned over to give her a peck on the cheek.

"Hi, Dad! How was your flight?" She checked her mirrors as she pulled out into traffic.

"Blessedly uneventful," he said, latching his seatbelt. "How are you? Mom says you've just had the adventure of your life."

She laughed. "That makes it sound like a *good* thing!" Despite the fact that he had already heard her mom's version of the story, she settled into sharing the backpack money saga with him on the drive home. Then having yakked most of the way, she asked him about his work, in turn hearing about his latest project and its complications as they trekked from the parking garage up to their condo. It was a pleasant visit, despite her mind frequently wandering to Mac and his daughter.

"Ah, it's great to be home!" he exclaimed, plopping onto his recliner after he had snapped open a Coke. "A guy can take only so many hotels!" He snatched the remote and turned on the television set. "What time does Mom get home?"

His hair seemed grayer at the corners. Mari snuggled onto the couch beside him, putting her feet up, glad they were alone. There was so much she wanted to talk to him about, though primarily about Mac. "Four-ish. She won't stop to see Poppy after work today."

He nodded, flipping through the channels.

"Dad, remember JoyAnne Strang from my high school days? We're friends now."

He frowned. "Wasn't she that troubled girl? Boy, she could sing! That girl had a voice!"

Mari had to pause a moment. "Um, yeah. That's her. It was kind of a big deal. We had a big talk, and things are good now."

"Yeah? Well, good for you. That's great." He let out the recliner footrest. "Hey, Mari—I set my glasses on the table over there. Would you mind getting them for me?"

Mari rose to fetch them.

"Thanks. How's your knee?" he asked. "Mom says you're not resting it like you should. You got to be careful, girl. We can't keep having surgeries."

"Yeah, I know. I'm trying to be careful."

"Well, good." He gave a wide yawn, motioning to the screen. "Looks like rain on Sunday."

"Does it?" She glanced at the TV. "We're going to the Gordons' for dinner tonight. You, me, and Mom. Mac Sinclair will be there too."

"Yeah. I've heard great reports about Poppy, thanks to him. Who would have thought one of those Sinclair kids would turn out to be a physical therapist?" He yawned again, switching channels. "Well, that'll be great. I haven't seen the Gordons in a while."

She was about to say more when he placed the remote on the end table. "I think I'll just take a little rest."

She smiled. "Okay. It's nice to have you home, Dad." She sat with him until she heard his breathing grow heavy, then went to her room.

Boy, that girl could sing!

JoyAnne *did* have a good voice. She couldn't argue with that. But it still stung to hear him say it. She stood glumly beside her dresser while the door to her old conflict with JoyAnne shouted to be reopened. No, she wasn't going there, Mari determined. Yikes! This concept of surrender wasn't easy!

Plus her dad. A swirl of confusing emotions regarding him stirred within. Granted, he had just gotten home; yet somehow she had expected something great between them—that he would get the gravity of what had happened in her life in the last few weeks and be excited about it and they would have a deeper connection or something. But he didn't get it. He didn't know. He didn't understand. She had to admit—she was disappointed.

She eyed herself in the mirror, her mind flashing back to her childhood and the various ways they had misunderstood each other. She couldn't really fault him. He wasn't perfect, but he was still a good dad. A great dad. Nevertheless, it was nice to know she had an *even better* dad. A Father who never grew tired and who cared about *all* the things on her heart, even the hidden matters. A Father who helped her in her weakness. She would be okay. She fanned out the tiny popup card from Mac, admiring the delicate art. Only two and a half hours until she would see him at the Gordons'. She sighed. Yes, she needed God's help.

When Mari and her folks arrived in the old neighborhood that evening, she saw that all the neighborhood police tape had disappeared except for that which was strung around Roger Eden's door and driveway. Exiting the vehicle, her dad shook his head in displeasure at their former house.

"Good—now maybe they'll get someone in there who'll lose that ugly fence! That should have been the *first* clue that Eden fellow was up to no good! It's a shame!"

Mari was glad he couldn't see how Mr. Eden and his dogs had dug up the yard beyond that fence. Recalling all the time and energy her dad had spent on their lawn in the past, she decided to keep that info to herself.

The aroma of grilled hamburgers hung heavy in the air, reminding Mari that she hadn't eaten since breakfast. As they made their way back to the Gordons' patio, Mari discovered that Mac and Aubrey were already there, as were the DeSotos, who had brought Howie and Hank Grant along to play with Aubrey. JoyAnne and Douglas were on their way.

"Hurrah! Here's our girl of the hour!" Susan cried when Mari creaked up on her crutches. She nested a large bowl of potato salad into an ice bed on their stainless-steel serving buffet and then wiped her hands on her apron. "How are you holding up, dear?"

"I'm doing fine," she returned. "Thanks for hosting this!"

"For she's a jolly good fellow!" Mac chimed from nearby, his eyes playfully threatening to start a chorus.

She shot him a warning glare. "Mac—no!"

Spotting her from across the yard, Aubrey flew to her side in typical fashion. However, as she was already deep in play, it wasn't long before she ran off to rejoin her friends in their makeshift fort in Susan's rock garden. But Mac lingered.

"I saw the balloons you picked for Poppy," she told him.

"That *I* picked, yes." He laughed. "Aubrey has taken to calling him 'Grandpa Poppy.' I suggested that we bring him a present, and she insisted he'd like the balloon with the little raccoon family."

"I thought it was sweet," she said. The subject reminded her of Mac's pocket gifts, and she looked away.

"He was in good spirits today. Thankfully he seems unphased by yesterday's excitement."

"Praise God for that! Did I tell you what he did last evening?" She relayed to him how her grandfather had faked the seizures, which caused Mac to throw back his head in laughter. "Well, it's funny *now*," Mari added, "but at the time it was so scary! It could have easily escalated things!"

Mac gave a good-natured shrug. "Glad it didn't! But he's a character, isn't he?"

Just being near him made her happy. She thought she ought to mosey away, but right then Mr. Gordon announced that the food was ready, and everybody gathered to eat.

Mac sat beside her, which made her glad. It was a small party, she told herself.

During dinner people started to inquire of her and Mac about what had happened next door with Roger Eden. And so began another telling of the whole event from start to finish, including Ty's role in it all. Eventually the subject changed as tangents veered here and there. Then Dan DeSoto threw out a silly remark, and the jokes began to fly.

As the evening wound on, Mari gravitated to talking with Leah and JoyAnne, while Douglas and Dan hung out as a pair, and Mac visited with her parents and the Gordons. At dusk the party moved inside, where it was warmer.

Settled in the living room, Mari asked JoyAnne to tell how she and Dougie had gotten together, and JoyAnne, of course, lit up, delighted to unfold all the details. Mari watched her as she talked, thinking back at how much God had changed her perspective on the girl. She was learning to genuinely appreciate her despite their contrasting personalities and upbringing. Plus, hearing her talk and laugh about normal things in her life revealed their many similarities. The biggest eye-opener, though, was seeing the beauty of humility in JoyAnne's life. Even her appearance seemed altered.

"You have a nice smile," Mari cut in.

"What? Oh—" JoyAnne halted in surprise. "I—thank you! It's one of my major insecurities, but I'm learning to accept myself. Anyway, as I was saying, when Douglas first proposed, I told him no. He's always been such a decent guy, and then there's *me* and the way I am. I was like, 'What are you thinking?' I felt like I didn't deserve him, and truthfully, I don't! But he persisted, and here we are! Only three more weeks until we're married!"

"I'm happy for you both," Mari said.

"Thank you."

"That's how I felt about Danny too" Leah offered. "I don't deserve him, but he loves me so much. Such a picture of God's grace in my life."

Later JoyAnne was beckoned by Susan to help prepare her dessert, and Leah volunteered to check on the children upstairs. As Mari was left alone on the couch, her eyes rested on the Gordons' front window, her thoughts reverting to the harrowing few hours she had had with the slippery Roger Eden. What a miracle that Ty had been there to run for help! On a whim, she stepped out to wait for her friends on Susan's porch, looking out toward Mac's and over the field.

Then grabbing her crutches from inside the door, she gently hopped down the steps and made her way past Roger Eden's empty house to the street, following it to the edge of the park where the little kickball field now blinked intermittently with fireflies. How ironic that not long ago she didn't even like children! Now she fondly pictured all the young people who had come to play with her after school—the little thirsty girl and the nosebleed girl, Connor Haddington, and the many others. She wondered what their lives were like in their homes. Each of those children was being shaped and formed by his or her parents and grandparents and teachers, some having a God frame of reference but others having barely any concept of God at all. Would her little kickball games make a difference in those lives? If she could roll back time, she would wield her influence sooner, she mused.

It was sad to think that those kickball days were over. She glanced wistfully at Mac's dark windows. Somehow letting go of her job watching Aubrey seemed a thousand times worse than breaking up with Will—and not only because of Mac. She wished she could have done so much more. More for Aubrey. More for the kickball kids. More for Ty West. Thank God that he had come to her with that pillowcase of drugs! Who knows what could have happened otherwise?

She hobbled over the dewy grass a little farther, glancing at the lights of Whitmore in the distance, thinking of all the times she had seen Ty trot across that field. What were he and his mother doing at this very moment? How was he processing what had happened to poor Loki? Could he talk to his mother about it? Could he tell his mom what it was like to sleep in a cardboard box and forage for his food? Did the two of them talk at all? Would Tatum punish him for running away? Of course, it was possible he wasn't even there; he may have been removed from their home.

So many unknowns, she thought gloomily. And Ty was only one of many children who lived in that neighborhood. She wished there were some way to help kids like Ty so that they didn't end up becoming kids like Trey. But what did that kind of help look like? Her throat grew tight. Someone needed to help those children.

But not only the children. Who was going to help the Tatums? Who was going to help those caught in cycles of abuse that had turned them so tough that they didn't want or need help? Who was going to help the Ariels who were floundering—or on their way to becoming Tatums if they slipped into their own cycles of dysfunction? Mari knew those apartments were overflowing with overwhelmed and hopeless women who needed God. They needed Jesus to love them and heal their wounded hearts. They needed forgiveness and salvation and a new way of life. Leaning on her crutches, she imagined the father in the prodigal son story, standing a far way off, watching for his wayward son to come home. And right now it was as though God were in her, standing, watching, praying, hurting, waiting.

Behind her the soft scrape of a foot on the pavement startled her. She whirled, peering into the shadows.

"It's just us," came Dan's voice. "Sorry—we didn't mean to scare you."

"I didn't hear you!" Mari took a breath, pulling herself back to the moment as the approaching DeSoto couple became visible under the streetlight.

"We came to check on you. I saw you leave, and you didn't come back."

"Yeah. I was just—" She trailed off, motioning to the kickball field and across to Whitmore.

They paused beside her.

"I was thinking about Ty living over there. No dad. Negative influences all around. It's just hard for kids like him.", She looked back at them. "It's kinda sad. I wish someone could offer some constructive change. You know, for kids who need it. For kids falling through the cracks."

Dan nodded. "Yeah. Me too."

"It's like a hamster wheel of dysfunction for some families, and the kids get caught in the middle. I wish there were a way to help turn things around. To break those cycles. But it's all so overwhelming. Someone would need a big plan and a *lot* of patience for that."

"Sure would," Leah said, gazing across the field, her face half illuminated by the streetlight.

Mari sighed. "I guess it's no different than anywhere else, but it's all so real now. Names and faces kinda do that, you know. All I can think about"—her voice caught—"all I can think about is Tatum working hard, struggling to raise her family—and then having to deal with this!" Hastily she brushed the corners of her eyes. "I'd love to reach her, but Tatum is—she's so hard and closed. Building trust with her seems impossible."

"But you've started," Leah said. "You're trying."

Mari opened her hand. "But that's a tiny thing. A drop in the bucket for the need. There are lots of Tatums and Tys out there. I just—I just want a magic wand to wave and make everything better!"

"Yeah, don't we all?" Leah murmured.

After a space of silence, Dan cleared his throat. "Have you ever considered that this 'someone' might be *you*?"

Mari snickered. "Right! What could *I* do?"

He didn't answer.

After a long while, she sniffed. "There are so many more kids over there. So many. A kickball club wouldn't be enough. I would want some kind of kids' Bible club with it or something like that. And maybe just once a week. But I could never do all that by myself."

"No, it's too much for one person," Dan agreed. "But what if you had help?"

"*I* could see helping with something like that!" Leah broke in. "I could do the Bible lessons. That would be super-fun!"

Mari looked at her. "We'd have to set some age categories. Like have the older kids play kickball while the younger kids do the lesson. Then switch. But still, we'd need more than the two of us."

"Three," Dan said. "I think you should talk to Pastor Keith about this. I bet there would be others who would love to jump in."

"Absolutely you should!" Leah echoed.

"Maybe *you* should talk to Pastor Keith," Mari said. "You're a coach. I don't feel qualified."

"I'd go with you," he offered. "But it's your passion that'll drive this."

"What if he nixes the idea?"

Dan laughed. "What if he *supports* you? What if you suddenly have a dozen helpers?"

"Do you really think it could work?"

Leah hooked her arm in Mari's. "Why not? I think it's a *great* idea!"

"I'm with her," Dan said. "We could offer free snacks—the kids would swarm to us!"

"They totally would," Mari agreed. "And know what else I'd do—? I'd get a bunch of coupons for free gallons of milk or something and print a parenting tip-of-the-day on the back. The kids could give them to their moms. We could even do the Mrs. Gordon thing and pick kids up for church." Mari let out a sigh. "That would be my dream."

"I like it!" Dan nodded, offering his approval. He glanced at his watch and smiled sheepishly. "And speaking of things I like—not to shut down a poignant moment or anything, but when we left, Susan was serving up her famous rhubarb crumble. I believe it's calling my name!"

Mari laughed. "Oh, I've had her rhubarb crumble—I understand the gravity here! Forget Whitmore! We'd better hurry!"

They all laughed. Mari turned on her crutches, and they all headed back.

The evening passed swiftly, and soon Mari and her parents were on their way home. Mari sat in the back seat trying not to think about—or read into—Mac walking her family to their car to say goodbye. Her folks didn't appear to notice anything unusual about it.

"Did you enjoy your evening, Nick?" her mom asked her dad.

"Yes, it was nice to get caught up," he answered. "And it's great that Mac Sinclair could buy his folks' place. Such a great neighborhood."

"Yes, he's keeping it up too. Mari says he redid the kitchen. The pictures look so nice."

"It's *super*-nice," Mari piped up from behind. "I'll show you the photos when we get home."

Her dad nodded. "Yeah, it's just too bad about him. He's such a bright guy, but he's in a tough spot."

Mari glanced at him in surprise. "What do you mean?"

"Oh, you know. He's kind of shot himself in the foot. Anyone he ends up with gets a package deal. He's got to shop for a wife *and* a mother, and she's kind of a handful, that girl."

Mari stared at the back of his head in disbelief. Everything within her wanted to blast him—to tell him he was narrow-minded and demeaning. As though single parents were some inferior class of people! Maybe God could give Mac *both*! But why bother saying it? That person wouldn't be her anyway, so what difference did it make to have a fuss? She folded her arms and sat back, feeling like a middle-schooler being carted home from some school activity. When had her dad gotten so *old*?

Mari was tired the next morning, having brooded on her father's comments well into the night. Nevertheless, she sucked it up, doing her best to share in Shannon and Colton's wedding excitement at their family breakfast at her father's favorite diner. Her dad didn't know Mac or Aubrey, she told herself. He didn't *know*.

Midmorning she left to go to her Bible study out on Leah DeSoto's deck. A lot had transpired since her attempted attendance a week ago—specifically with Ariel and JoyAnne and Kyla. Still, she was just as nervous, intimidated by the other attendees who were so much farther down the road spiritually than she was. But Kyla picked up on her vibes quickly, reminding her that it wasn't a contest.

"Everyone's here to grow," she said, her Bible pages flapping in the gentle breeze. "No one has 'arrived.'"

"Yes," chimed Leah, setting an empty mug onto the napkins. "The most important thing is Jesus—to know him and know his Word. *He's* the goal!"

Though incidentally spoken, the comments helped Mari let her guard down. There was no sense in pretending anything. Who did she have to impress?

Afterwards Mari and Kyla went out for lunch to fill the space of time before meeting with Candace and Quinn.

"We missed you at the Gordons' last night," Mari told her, seated across from her at their high-top table.

Kyla dumped a packet of sweetener into her iced tea. "Thanks. I was with my birth father. He's getting close. It could be this weekend." At Mari's concerned look, she raised a hand. "No, it's okay. I'll go back this afternoon. Truly, it's okay! I have total peace with being here. But I appreciate the support. Everybody's been wonderful." She lifted her sandwich, as if to take a bite, asking, "Have you ever heard my story of God healing my relationship with my birth father?"

As Mari shook her head, Kyla set her sandwich down, taking some time to relay the unfolding of past events and how God had helped her to forgive and release her birth father for abandoning her as a child.

"He's unhealthy in every way," she concluded. "Body and soul. But he's saved. Our relationship has been nothing but difficult, but I at least have a clear conscience before God that I have forgiven him and honored him to the best of my ability."

Mari had stopped eating during her story. "Wow—thanks," she said. "I needed to hear that!"

"Good!" Kyla picked up her sandwich. "Honoring your parents is one of God's top ten!"

Right then Mari straightened, as over Kyla's shoulder she spotted Candace entering the restaurant with her friend. "They're here!" she blurted in a hushed tone, lifting her chin to indicate the arrivals. "They're super early!"

"Relax," Kyla said, setting aside her sandwich once more. "We have good news for them—remember? Come on. Let's do this!"

Hastily Mari rose to hail Candace, waving for them to join her and Kyla at their table.

"Sorry we're early," Candace said. "We wanted to make sure we had the right place."

"No worries!" Kyla assured them cheerfully. "Would you like to order something before we get started?"

And then Mari watched as in such a disarming way Kyla skillfully led them down a path of getting to know one another before seamlessly transitioning into the study.

"Don't be nervous—we're not here to make you do anything," she said, handing around a half sheet of Bible verse references. "We're here to help you see what the Bible says, and today all we're going to talk about is the authority of God's Word. My phone number is on here, so if you think of any questions, text them to me during the week and we'll talk about them next time. So do either of you need a Bible?"

"We can share this one," Candace said, pulling the purple embossed Bible out of her tote bag.

Kyla let out a cry of surprise, then broke into a grin. "Hey—I recognize that Bible! Aww, I'm so honored that you have it! I think this is going to be a *rich* time together!" She smiled warmly at Candace.

It was a seemingly insignificant exchange, but from then on, as Kyla began walking them through the scripture list, Mari noticed a shift in Quinn, who now had adopted more of a defensive posture, becoming almost protective of Candace. Kyla apparently noticed too and simply turned her attention toward Quinn herself for the rest of their time together.

Afterward, alone in the parking lot, Mari asked Kyla how she thought the session went.

"I'm not sure," she answered. "I couldn't really tell. Let's pray for them—shall we?"

Then it was time for Kyla to return to her birth father, and Mari went home to spend the rest of the day with her dad.

In the morning Mari made a beeline to JoyAnne in the foyer before church, pulling her aside to talk near the bustling coffee bar, where Eagle Bluff regulars hurried to grab a last-minute coffee before the service.

"So, hey—I was thinking and praying over the weekend, and I thought I'd put out the offer to help you with Ariel. If you need it, that is. I thought since I already know her, I could spend some extra time with her. Maybe take her shopping for clothes. Or whatever you need."

But JoyAnne swung her head in defeat. "She left. She went back with her boyfriend."

"What?"

"Last night. When she got wind that Bats was gone, she took off home—well, to Cobra."

"No!" Mari's shoulders slumped.

JoyAnne nodded. "I know. The sad thing is that Bats will probably be released soon. So we'll see what happens. Unfortunately, she made it pretty clear that her boyfriend was not thrilled about having a baby. Neither is her mother."

Mari groaned. "What if we went over there—like took Dougie and Mac with us and maybe Dan? Maybe we could get her to come back."

"We've offered her every form of help we have, Mari. She knows our door is open. That's where she wants to be right now—with him."

"Yeah, but if her boyfriend is a loser—"

"He's not a loser in *her* eyes. It's okay, Mari. I told her I'd check in with her in a few days, and that we'll be ready for her if she changes her mind. She knows we're here for her. You can't control people."

"But what about her baby?"

"We're praying. And she saw the ultrasound. I guess I'm hopeful."

Mari let out a loud sigh. "What if someone talked to her boyfriend? Maybe Dan could try. Or Mac. Maybe we could talk to both of them together."

JoyAnne raised her brow. "I'm open to the possibility. Let's talk more, okay?"

Mari nodded. "Yes. And I'll pray too."

Since worship was already in progress when they entered the sanctuary, Mari followed JoyAnne along a side aisle, slipping in with her beside the Gordons. Will, she noticed, was sitting up front with Peter and Kyla Watkins.

Coincidentally, Mac also arrived late, taking his place beside Mr. Gordon on the opposite side of the row. In seconds, Aubrey was climbing across everyone's feet to get to Mari, squeezing in between her and JoyAnne. As Mari leaned back to acknowledge Mac at the other end of the row, he too leaned back, sheepishly flaying his hands as though his daughter were beyond his control. Straightening, Mari met Mrs. Gordon's gaze with an embarrassed smile, at which the older woman winked in return. Abruptly Mari turned toward the front. A wink from Susan Gordon? Goodness, what in the world was *that* supposed to mean? It made her want to laugh out loud! A *wink*?

Beside her, Aubrey let out a sudden gasp. She grabbed Mari's arm. "*Ty's here!* I seen him in the back!"

Mari blinked down at her in astonishment. "Um, *saw* him," she whispered, automatically twisting to peer behind Mrs. Gordon to the other side of the church. But her eyes bugged out in disbelief, for it was not Tatum West she spied there, but Candace and her partner, Quinn, sitting at the far end of the back row with a child. No way!

Immediately her phone chirped in her pocket. It was Shannon.

"OMG! You'd never guess who's here! Not in a million years! TATUM WEST and her boy! Don't look back or you'll embarrass her. Plus, guess who else? Candace is here too! Wow, Mari! What are you doing over there at the Break?" Her text was followed by two flames and applause hands.

Suddenly lightheaded, Mari gripped the padded chair in front of her. From that point of the service, she was unable to focus on any of the song lyrics, prayers, announcements, scriptures, or preaching. Every word spoken was sifted through a filter of how Tatum or Candace might perceive it. She knew that neither of them would likely hang around after the service, but she very much wanted to acknowledge their presence. She bit her lip, wondering who would bolt the quickest. Should she target Candace or head straight for Tatum?

"Can I go talk to Ty?" Aubrey whispered.

Mari nodded. "After church. Let's talk to him and his mom right away!"

So Tatum it was. Scarcely had Pastor Keith offered the "amen" to his final prayer when Mari rose to guide Aubrey out to the foyer, barely catching Tatum at the church doors.

"Hey!" she called, rushing over. "Hey—hello! I wanted to say hi to you."

Tatum straightened, tossing her head.

Keep it light, Mari told herself. "It's nice to see you. Thanks for coming. And you too, Ty. How are you?"

The boy offered a squirmy shrug.

Aubrey spoke up. "Thanks for running so fast to get help for us, Ty. Mari told me you saved us."

Ty mumbled something, looking downward.

"Did you finish your volcano yet?" Aubrey asked.

He shook his head.

"Yeah, me neither," she said. "It's still on my table at home." She looked up at Mari. "Can he come over and help me paint it?"

"I think that's a great idea!" Mari answered eagerly. "Let's ask your dad about it, okay? But you're at your grandma's this week—remember?"

Aubrey sighed. "Oh, yeah."

"We need to go," Tatum said briskly.

Mari gave a little wave. "Right. See you at work tomorrow." She let out a long breath, watching the two of them cross the parking lot. "Wow, good job, Aubrey! Put one here!" she told her, offering a fist bump. "That was extremely thoughtful to thank him for helping us. And to offer him to help on your volcano. Extremely thoughtful!"

A voice behind her asked, "Is this the little girl you watch?"

Mari turned to discover Candace and Quinn and their child. "Well, hello! What a surprise! Yes, this is Aubrey."

"Hi." Candace smiled happily, swiping a pink strand of hair around her ear. "We decided to try church this morning."

Keep it light. "Great! Thanks for coming."

"We might be back," Candace replied, throwing a quick glance up at Quinn, who gave a cordial nod. "But we're meeting friends for lunch, so we have to go." She waved, reaching for the door, and with a blast of fresh air the two left.

Mari smiled down at Aubrey, feeling both exhilarated and exhausted. "What a great teammate you are!"

The girl beamed. "I guess!"

Leah found them. "Hey, Mari! Real quick—want to do lunch with us?"

She had to decline. "Sorry. My dad's here. He's leaving tonight, so we'll spend the day as a family. Let's connect sometime this week."

"Yes, let's!" With a thumbs-up, she nodded and left.

Then Mac appeared for Aubrey. "Hey, wasn't that your coworker? Ty's mother?"

"Ty's mom, yes. Yes, it was. And another coworker came too. With her friend."

Mac's mouth curled into a proud grin. "Marissa Coleman, ambassador for Christ! Way to go!"

She brought her hand to her head. "I couldn't concentrate the whole service!"

He laughed, squeezing his daughter's shoulders. "Come on, little flower. We're going out for pizza!"

Aubrey gave a cheer. "But Mari can't come today," she told him. "Her dad's in town."

"Yep." Mari smiled. "See you, um—see you—" She wouldn't see them tomorrow.

"See you around," Mac said.

How can I go on like this? she asked herself, watching them leave.

Chapter Thirty-Three

After dropping her dad off at the airport Sunday night, Mari opted for the long way home, taking a few necessary moments in the car to think—which was akin to having a good cleansing cry, only this time without the cry. But as she meandered the city streets, her drive wasn't so cleansing, for her thoughts jostled and bounced everywhere, mostly telling herself what a loser she was and how everything was going wrong in her life. The idea of being single now was depressing. Was she going to be alone forever? Plus her dad. On the heels of all her talks with Dr. Grant, she had been so looking forward to connecting with him. But it hadn't happened. It was true. Her dad didn't really know her.

You can't go there, she told herself, realizing her alone time wasn't helping anything. What was the benefit of self-introspection when it was taking her down such a dark path? Done wandering, she returned to the highway, signaling to exit on Juniper, almost home. Then crossing the parking garage, she called herself up, adopting more of a Dr. Grant-like tone in her self-talk.

You're stronger than this, Coleman. Come on now! Your dad isn't required to know you. But God knows you.

I know, she reluctantly concurred, pushing the elevator button to her floor. The doors closed and the lift lurched to life.

Sometimes surrender is the only way to win, wisped Marilee Montayne's voice in her head.

"Okay, God. I surrender again," Mari said out loud to the ceiling. "I want *your* path for me, whatever it is. I'm going to follow you and do what's right, even if it's hard. But right now I'm so overtired I can't even think. You're going to have to take it from here."

The elevator glided to a halt at her floor. Wearily she let herself in to her condominium home and went straight to bed.

And then the new week began with a flurry as life moved on.

Mari's daily shifts at the Taiton Coffee Break were busy as usual, but to her surprise, subtle changes were taking place. First, though still plenty aloof and brusque, Mari noticed that Tatum West was markedly less hostile toward her. Her requests were now delivered in sentences—versus one-word commands. And the manager now invited Mari into his conversations with the woman, inquiring as to how her family was doing and asking her how the two of them could help her, at which Tatum had some honest concerns to report about Ty. Yet receiving their assistance for anything was still out of the question.

A second change was that it appeared Candace was becoming a Dr. Grant fan. At least once a day she offered to bus the dining rooms, stopping to visit with the professor before returning to the kitchen with her load of dirty dishes. Plus, the Saturday session with Mari and Kyla had piqued her curiosity about the Bible, and she was now asking Mari questions about what and how to read the Word. Still babying her knee, Mari sat on the stool while Candace worked around her, firing off her queries.

But not all the subtle changes were positive. To the extent that Candace had opened to matters of faith, *A-plus* Alyssa seemed to be picking up an attitude against the same. She now avoided Candace and snubbed Mari. To complicate matters, somewhere along the line, Mark had adopted the annoying obligation of passing on all of Alyssa's behind-their-back statements about their excessive religiousness. Sick of hearing the critical secondhand digs, Mari blasted him in a weak moment, urging him to stop listening to gossip. She assumed the manager would hear a twisted version of the scolding, but she didn't care. She was so done with Mark's indiscriminate mouth.

Dr. Grant, too, was now embroiled in a faculty drama with those who wanted him out of the Coffee Break altogether. Mari thought he seemed remarkably peaceful about his dilemma.

"Oh, it'll all blow over eventually," the professor said, offering Mari his mug to add to her crate of dirty dishes. "I'm just praying and working hard so that I'm still here when it does!"

Their routine conversations had become a highlight in her day, as were her daily chats with her grandfather when her Taiton shifts were through. And since she did not have a childcare job to run off to anymore, her visits with Poppy were unrushed, although she did feel that lonely ache whenever she headed home from Riverview. She would much rather have a jaunt to Frost to see Aubrey and her noisy throng of friends.

And Mac.

Thankfully, he did check in with her now and then, updating her on the "body count" next door—his facetious, albeit morbid way of tallying the police department's latest finds in his former neighbor's backyard, as observed from the heights of Aubrey's old room. It turned out that Roger Eden had quite a savings buried in various boxes and bags back there. But mostly Mac asked about her knee and how she was doing in her recovery from the Ty West and Roger Eden drama. Mari welcomed his texts, but it sometimes felt as if they only exaggerated the distance between them.

As one week spilled into another, Mari's evenings were now spent helping Shannon with wedding projects or connecting with Leah or JoyAnne—enough activity to keep herself occupied and distracted from all her daydreaming about what might be happening on Frost Street.

On the last day of the month—a Thursday evening—she met Dan and Leah DeSoto at the church to confer with Pastor Keith about her fledgling idea of a Whitmore kids' club. To her relief, he was stoked about the prospect of starting an outreach in the Whitmore neighborhood. He recommended the three of them form a team and create a plan for implementing Mari's vision and meet back with him soon.

It was later at home that evening when Mari realized she didn't want to return to Boston in the fall. The idea of finishing her degree at Taiton instead gave her great peace and joy. Every facet of the change seemed logical, and she would have a natural opportunity to collect the rest of her college belongings when she and her family attended her cousin Missy's wedding in July.

Truly, there was so much to stay for—Tatum, Ty, Candace, the Whitmore endeavor, her new friends. And Ariel too, maybe, if she turned a corner. She crossed her fingers on that. Even JoyAnne had declared to her that Mari was an asset to Sunlight without even working there. Mari was in awe of the goodness of God. How amazing that God would so abruptly bring her home from Boston—bitter, confused, and alone—and transform her into a gatherer of the lonely and hurting! He was making her a tool with which to do his work.

Yet part of the decision to stay was difficult too, for she was forced to acknowledge her struggle to release Mac. *Dang it,* she chided herself. *He's working on restoring his marriage! Are you going to honor God in this or not?* A change was required. Yet another surrender. But it was so hard.

Getting ready for bed that night, she paused by the dresser to wiggle the tab on the stormy sea card Mac had given her, moving it from calm waters to tempest. She sighed. Was Mac an idol? Had she created a soul tie with him? Was that why she couldn't let him go? Was she putting him before God? Before she could talk herself out of it, she purposefully gathered up every one of Mac's notes and cards and slipped them into the waste basket beside her dresser.

And then she felt sick. It was as though the little papers cried out to her for rescue.

No, she told herself, setting a firm boundary.

In desperation she donned her pajamas and escaped to Shannon's room to crawl into bed with her. Delighted at the surprise, her sister slid over, and the two of them talked and giggled together like little schoolgirls for a long while. But when they quieted down to sleep, Mari opened up.

"Shannon, I need to tell you something. I have a *terrible* crush on Mac Sinclair."

Shannon snorted. "Who wouldn't? He's a great guy. But I thought you said he was married."

"*Was.* Yeah, I know. Still, I do."

"Well, he's a little old for you, but at least you have good taste."

Mari remained silent, reminded of the time she had confessed the same to Shannon about Peter Watkins. *Get over it,* she had said back then. She couldn't handle hearing those words again. For the millionth time, she reminded herself of JoyAnne's word picture of God's vast storehouse of dog bones. Yes, God knew her and had good in store for her. He wasn't stingy. He had no shortages in his kingdom. She could trust that if he had someone for her, he would lead her in that direction. To someone who was right for *her*. She simply needed to cooperate and follow.

I really only want Mac, she told him honestly, nestling into her pillow. *So you're going to have to help me with that!*

And then as the night passed, April came to an end, and a new month began. And although she had had hopeful expectations for the first of May, the day turned out to be the worst.

It was Friday, and Tatum didn't show up for work. Both Mari and John, the manager, knew her calling in sick was a cover, but what could they do about it? Furthermore, the second Mari clocked out, Candace announced that her partner no longer wanted her to meet with Mari and Kyla. She handed back the Bible in a plastic bag.

"What do *you* want to do, Candace?" Mari asked, her car keys dangling as she held the bag.

Candace wouldn't look at her. "What *I* want isn't really an option right now."

Mari raised her brow. "Do you think that's healthy?"

"I don't have much of a choice."

"Yes, you do! You have more of a choice than you realize!"

"No, things could get bad. I think I should just leave things alone." Nervously she swooped her hair behind her ear.

Mari boldly placed the Bible back into Candace's hands. "You tell Quinn that you decided to keep the Bible. Then tell her she doesn't have to come on Saturdays, but *you* haven't decided yet what *you're* going to do. Kyla and I will be there, and we hope to see you. But it's *your* choice. Either way, I'll be your friend. And I mean that."

Candace took a deep breath, nodding. "Okay. I *do* want to come. It's just—hard."

Mari's head bobbed. "I get it. But being controlled by someone is hard too. You need to think about where each of those hard paths will take you."

Also that Friday Poppy fell at the nursing home. It happened in the morning on his way to breakfast, and he was already back from the hospital by the time Mari arrived there after her Coffee Break shift. Miraculously he hadn't broken any bones, but the incident became another red flag factor in determining whether he was able to return to his assisted living status or not.

"I walk too fast," Poppy cheerfully explained to Mari from his bed that afternoon.

Her mother found the accident upsetting.

"I worry they're pushing him too hard," she commented as she stopped home to change her clothes before heading over to Riverview to see him. As she snatched up her purse to leave, she paused to say goodbye to Mari. "I'm having dinner with some friends after seeing Poppy, so have a wonderful time tonight, sweetheart!"

Mari snickered, gesturing to the television. "Oh, yes, Mom. I'm planning on having a *wonderful* evening!"

Her mother kissed the air. "You're a beautiful girl, Mari!" Leaving, she crossed paths with Shannon, who hustled in for the same purpose—to change clothes before Colton picked her up for a date. When she was ready, she came to hang out with Mari while she waited.

"How's Poppy?" she asked, picking at a fingernail.

"He's okay. Bruised is all. Mom's headed there now."

Shannon nodded, then looked over, eyeing her. "Want me to fix your hair?"

Mari shot her a look. "Tonight? Why?"

"Just for fun. Be right back." Shannon made a quick jaunt to her bedroom, returning with a handful of hair clips and ties. "Okay, I'm going to do this twisty sort of updo thing. I need the practice for a wedding party I'm doing next Friday."

Mari scooted forward in the chair. "Have at it!"

Shannon's fingers worked nimbly, but Colton arrived before she finished. He joined them, watching in fascination from his perch on the arm of the couch.

"There. Done," she said, tapping Mari's shoulders. "Go look and tell me what you think."

Rising, Mari peered at her hair in a nearby mirror, admiring her sister's fancy work. "Nice! I like it!" In the reflection she spied Shannon and Colt exchange glances, and she curiously turned. "What?"

But Shannon merely shrugged. "You look nice!" She nudged Colton. "Let's go."

Mari studied her fancy hair for another minute, then moved to gaze out the window to where a line of vendors had set up that afternoon for the Arts Festival that weekend on Taiton Green. Perhaps she would go explore tomorrow afternoon after her Bible study. Maybe with her mom, if she wasn't busy. Or with Shannon, if she wasn't doing something with Colton. She sighed, turning back to un-pause her show on the television.

Barely had she gotten comfortable when there was a knock at the door.

Oh, Shannon, she mused, padding down the hall to let her in.

"Let me guess—you forgot your keys again," she said, opening the door.

But there stood Mac, dressed up in jeans and a nice shirt. She gaped at him in surprise.

He smiled. "Hi. Shannon let me in."

She frowned in confusion. "Shannon? What are you doing here, Mac? Is everything okay? Where's Aubrey?"

"Aubrey's fine. She's with her grandma. And I think you already know why I'm here." He gestured. "May I come in?"

He smelled good too. She pulled the door wide, her heart slamming in her chest. Here it came. The talk. Would she keep her convictions?

"Um, h-how's it going with Aubrey at your mom's?" she burbled, suddenly self-conscious of her lemon-print pajama pants and bare feet.

He paused inside the door in the broad hall. "Exactly as I expected! High drama and endless bellyaching that she isn't at home with *you*."

"Well, I've missed her too." She closed the door and stood looking at him. He had come to talk to her. She could hardly believe it.

"How's your knee?"

"Good, actually. I've been super-careful, and it's finally settled down."

"Glad to hear it." He let out a long breath, glancing down the hall and back at her. "Well, I came with two questions for you."

Oh, brother. She squirmed, crazy nervous. "Um, okay."

He tugged his thumbs at the corners of his pockets, as though nervous himself. "I think it's safe to say we've got a little chemistry going on here between us. I figured it was time to talk."

Her face was warm. "Right."

He smiled. "I wasn't expecting this, you know. I wasn't looking for anyone. I had laid all that relationship business down long ago, but then here you came, blasting into our lives, and I—well, I'll just get to the point: Am I too old for you? I understand ten years *is* quite a spread, and if it's too much of a gap—" He shrugged, trailing off.

"Technically, it's only nine years and eight months."

His chin rose. "Ah, right—but who's counting, huh? Is that your answer? I can't ask my second question until I know."

His eyes. "I've, um—never thought of you as too old."

"Good." He nodded, his mouth curling into a smile. "Then, question number two: Would you like to go on a date with me?"

Just say yes.

No, you're going to ask your questions!

Mari straightened, folding her arms. "Well, it depends. I also have two questions for *you*."

Following suit, Mac folded his. "Fire away!"

"Okay. First, what's the story with Aubrey's mother? I want full disclosure. It goes against my conscience to—to, um—date someone who's working on restoring his marriage."

His brow shot up. "My marriage?"

"Well, your former marriage. This is Aubrey's *mother*. I think Aubrey deserves at least an effort in that regard, don't you? I don't want to get in the way of that. It would be *wrong* to get in the way of that. My conscience won't let me."

Mac raised his left hand, flaying his fingers. "I'm not married. I have

449

never been married."

"What?"

"Where did you get that idea?"

"Well, you—"

He cocked his head.

"You, um—I read—" She plastered her hand over her face. "Okay, true confessions—I looked in your journal. You had written that you were praying for the restoration of your marriage. I saw it."

He made a sound, dropping his arms. "Yeah, of *her* marriage—Elena's! Her dad—Aubrey's biological grandfather—asked me to pray for them. For her and her husband. She's gone through a year of treatment and is finally making some progress. Any future relationship with Aubrey is contingent on her getting sober."

Now her cheeks were burning.

"So—you were in my journal."

"No—I only saw that part. So, um—yes, I was. Sorry."

"Digging through my trash too, apparently, since a card I threw away somehow ended up in my Bible."

Mari smiled impishly. "It was a really nice card!"

"Yeah, I thought so too. But I couldn't finish it 'cause you were dating someone else!"

She closed her eyes, letting out a long breath.

"But that's when I knew I had a chance," he added.

She shook her head. "I'm sorry, Mac. It all happened so fast, like a whirlwind. I suddenly realized that Will didn't hold a candle to you, and it just—it took a while to navigate it all."

He nodded, smiling. Those eyes. Those eyes and the way he was looking at her. "And I apologize too for butting in like I did. That was wrong and irresponsible of me. I admit I was smitten on that second day you watched my daughter, and I couldn't stop thinking about you. But I had to make myself knock it off. I'm very grateful to be standing here."

She humbly agreed. "Same. And me too."

They looked at each other.

"So—you have another question?" he asked.

She nodded. "Yeah—what *took* you so long, Mac? I've been so miserable! Why'd you wait so long to come and talk to me?"

He chuckled. "Oh, come on—it was a matter of honor! I thought I'd give poor William Wallace a little dignity before swooping in on his girl. I didn't find out you broke up until a few days after the fact, and hey—he's a

450

nice kid. He deserved a little time to heal."

"Yeah, a week or two." She smiled.

He grinned. "Twelve days since I found out about it. It was long for me too. But out of respect I *did* talk to him, so he knows what I'm up to with you."

"I should have broken up with him when he forgot me at the airport."

He shrugged. "If you had, you wouldn't have spent the night at Riverview, and you might not have started watching Aubrey. We might not be here tonight."

"You're right."

Then they both laughed. He spread his hands, and she threw her arms around his waist.

"Oh, Mac," she murmured into his chest.

"Don't worry about Elena," he said, holding her against him. "I'll tell you everything—I promise."

Eventually she moved, and he loosened his arms. "In all actuality, Mac, *Will* broke up with *me*. He told me I needed to mature spiritually, and he's completely right. So I'm warning you—and you already know it—I have some growing to do."

"Oh, I *did* hear about that!"

Mari leaned away. "For real? He told you that? Sheesh, what else did he tell you?"

"He cautioned me that you're not a fan of The Wok."

"Oh, brother! Well, that *is* true!"

He let her go. "I'll keep that in mind. So answer my question, Marissa Coleman. Do you want to go out with me? I'd like to take you on a date—lots of dates, starting with the Arts Festival tonight on Taiton Green. Can I take you there? I'd like to introduce you to my coworker—the one who makes the cards. Dan and Leah are going. I thought we could meet up with them."

"I would *love* that, Mac!"

Pleased, he dipped his head. "Good."

"And Aubrey? Oh, yeah—never mind. She's with your mom—whom I'm looking forward to connecting with one of these days, by the way."

"Great. Yes, they're having an overnight. Plus, I don't exactly want her along. Look—can I be clear on something? I'm thrilled that you love my daughter, but I want you to know that I'm not shopping for a mother for Aubrey. I mean—it's a factor, but this isn't about her."

She nodded. "And likewise."

"Okay, good. Your father seemed a little concerned about that. I'm not looking to be rescued from anything."

"My father?"

"Yeah. I called him today to make sure he was okay with this. Since I'm so much older than you."

Mari blinked in surprise. "My *dad* knew you were coming here? Wait—then my mom—"

"Yeah, she knew it too. And Shannon. I called her this afternoon to see if she would let—"

"—let you in the building," she finished for him. "Okay, that explains a lot! I was wondering why she had a sudden need to do my hair!"

"Which looks great, I might add. You look very nice." He smiled, nodding his approval.

She snatched a handful of lemon-print fabric. "These are my *pajamas*, Mac. And right now, I'm going to change!"

He whistled in relief. "I was hoping I wouldn't have to suggest that! Would you like me to wait here, or are you going to invite me in past your foyer?"

She waved him in. "I won't be long—I promise! Go check out the Green through the window—you'll see the whole Arts Fair setup! I can hardly wait!"

In her room Mari threw a fresh pair of jeans on the bed and snatched a blouse from her closet. But in the middle of getting dressed, she paused to retrieve Mac's little notes and cards from her trash, breathing a prayer of thanks to God as she laid them out on her dresser. Indeed, sometimes surrender was the only way to win.

Mac rose when she joined him in the living room. "There we go—that's better! So—with or without crutches?"

"Are you kidding? Without!"

"All right. But hey, first—" He stepped close, taking both her hands. "Just being honest here, Mari. I've made enough mistakes in my past to know I can't go back there. I want God to be first with us, okay? I told your dad that I have every intention of honoring Christ and you in this relationship, and I meant it. I need to know that you feel the same way."

"Thank you, Mac." She squeezed his hands. "Completely."

"Good. And then I have one more question for you."

"You and all your questions! Well, I have one too!"

"Do you?" His forehead puckered. "Would it by chance have anything to do with wanting your old job back?"

452

Chapter Thirty-Three

"How did you know?"

"Well, I think that just answered my question! I know one little girl who's going to be thrilled!"

She held up her fingers. "*Two* girls!"

"Mari, the whole neighborhood will be glad to have you back!"

She smiled, feeling giddy. "I'm so glad! Speaking of the neighborhood, I wonder what Mrs. Gordon will think of this—of us dating."

He motioned toward the door. "Susan? My guess is she'll be delighted. She's only dropped a thousand hints to me about how wonderful you are and how great you are with Aubrey!"

Mari spun her head. "She has?" She threw a hand to her chest. "I'm so relieved! She's my trump card of approval. Thanks for telling me that, Mac!"

Then, as they were riding down the elevator, Mari let forth a laugh, shaking her head in amazement. "Mac—look at us! Isn't this crazy?"

He smiled. "Yeah—who would have ever thought I'd ask little Mari Coleman on a date?"

"Who would have thought I'd *want* to go on a date with that rascal, Mac Sinclair?"

Mac drew back. "Hey, now! Speaking of rascals—I'll have you know that Will Wallace wasn't the only reason it took me twelve days to come here. I've had some concerns about you—some honest concerns that needed a little time."

"About *me*?"

"Yes. I just needed time to confirm that something wasn't going to be an issue."

She waggled her head. "What are you talking about, Mac? What are your concerns?"

He shrugged. "I just wanted to make sure—" He paused, his eyes twinkling.

"*What?*"

"Well, I needed to know you could stay out of the police station for a week. At minimum!" He sliced the air for emphasis.

She batted him. "Mac Sinclair!"

He howled out a laugh.

"Any other concerns?"

He still wore that amused look. "Okay. Well, since you asked—it's not a 'concern,' but there *is* something I need to get off my chest."

She tossed her head. "And what's that?"

He set a hand at his waist, pausing for effect. "Remember that kale you found in my refrigerator?"

"On my first day?"

"Yes." He grinned. "My mom stocked my fridge. I would *never* buy kale. I don't have the slightest idea what it even looks like."

She stared in feigned shock. "Mac Sinclair! You don't like kale? I am *so* disappointed!"

"I hope this isn't a deal-breaker."

"Well, that's a pretty big confession! I don't know—I'm going to have to think about this now!" She sighed dramatically, shaking her head.

"For the record—I didn't say I was a kale *hater*. More like kale *ignorant* is all."

"Oh. Well, that's different. Better, but I'll still have to think about it." She smiled up at him.

He caught her hand and kissed it. "All right, Marissa Coleman. You do that. You take your merry old time to think about it."

But she had already made up her mind. She had made up her mind about a lot of things—about loving and obeying God, about letting him use her to serve others, about loving Mac and Aubrey. She squeezed his hand, hugging his arm.

He winked, motioning as the elevator opened. "After you."

About the Author

The daughter of a cattle rancher, Joan Crombie grew up in a small town on the prairies of South Dakota. In 1985 she graduated from St. Olaf College with a B.A. in English Education. She and her husband Steven Crombie have raised five children—one daughter and four sons. Currently they reside in beautiful southern Minnesota where they pastor a church.

Joan infuses her writing with wisdom gained from ministry and raising a family. She has always liked fiction where an ordinary girl unwittingly steps into a mystery, and in her stories, she seeks to couple that with helping her character identify lies she may have believed about God and combat those lies with biblical truth. Having experienced firsthand the freedom of a healed heart, her passion is to help women grow deeper in the love of God and knowledge of him as their very personal and caring Father.

Her hobbies include thrift shopping, reading, traveling, visiting historical museums, and spending time with her many delightful grandchildren.

To contact the author or to learn more about following God or about some of the concepts in this book, visit www.joancrombie.org.